Maybe Someday With You

Give a girl the right shoes and she can conquer the world.
Marilyn Monroe

Also by Norah Pritchard

NORTHFIELD SERIES

The Other Side of Forever

Maybe Someday With You

If You Were Mine - Coming Soon

Be Your Everything - Coming Soon

COOKBOOK

Dinnertime: Fast and Fresh Family Meals for Every Night of the Week

Maybe Someday With You

A Northfield Novel

Norah Pritchard

W/L
WILLOWCREST LANE

~

First edition: June 2024

Editor: Evident Ink

Proofreader: Red Adept Editing

Cover design: Wildheart Graphics

Photographer: Madison Maltby

To my sisters, Melanie and Jennifer. You two set the bar high for all the best things in life. I'm so thankful to call you not only family but my best friends.

Chapter One

THE HEAT WAS GETTING to her.

"This one's for you, Amber," Jake said with a cute grin on his baby face. The adorable blond regular's arms strained his Northfield Fire Department T-shirt when he held out the shot glass she had just poured him.

Amber Hart's wild streak, the one her family had been warning her about for years, butted against her good sense and came out victorious, and she tossed the shot back with a flourish.

She didn't drink often, but the unseasonably warm June heat was making her edgy tonight. Oh, and stress too. Yeah, she had plenty of that.

The too-sweet butterscotch schnapps hit the back of her throat hard, and she sputtered. Everyone in Northfield knew she made killer drinks, but she didn't drink often enough to take the shot without grimacing. She just hoped her boss didn't see her.

"Stop drinking my liquor, woman."

Busted. Killian Kennedy had the face of a dark angel, so beautiful it could make you weep, but right now he looked more annoyed than anything as he stared pointedly at her through the pass-through window. Oops.

"Sorry, boss. I didn't want Jake to drink alone," she said cheekily. Killian was no stranger to her impulsive decisions, but he loved her anyway.

"Jake," Killian yelled back.

"Yes, sir?" Jake ducked his head to see Killian.

"Give any more shots to my bartender, and you're cut off."

"You got it, sir." Jake winked. He was adorable, really, but oh-so-young. She was inching a little too close to thirty to think about dating the rookie or anyone else, really. She couldn't remember the last man she'd gone out with. She dismissed that depressing thought quickly.

"Your scallops are burning, Killian," she said, knowing that would get Killian to leave the bartending to her. The man took great pride in his food. Good thing his shift was ending soon, and he was leaving her in charge.

She turned back toward the sea of uniforms crowding the bar. The pub was the unofficial hangout of the off-duty Northfield Fire and Police Departments. The men and a few women all ribbed her like a little sister and tipped her generously for putting up with their nonsense. She knew most of their families, too, at least the ones who were from Northfield. Perks of working at a small-town bar in your hometown.

"Cute outfit, Am," said Allie. Her sister sat next to her husband, Davis, on the other side of the bar, poking her straw around the lemon-drop martini Amber had made for her.

Amber did a little spin behind the bar to show off the sequins on her new Jean Paul Gaultier skirt, which she'd bought last year on Poshmark for a steal. "Thanks. Want to borrow it?"

Allie snuggled into Davis's side. "Should I borrow Amber's skirt?" Amber made a mental note to get water for her sister.

Allie was a lightweight, and she rarely got out after having the twins.

Savannah and Tessa were almost three and the apples of Allie and Davis's eyes. If ever there was a more perfect family to be born into, it was Allie and Davis's. They were crazy about each other, for one, and their little blended family of Allie's son and Davis's kids from their previous marriages doted on the little girls' every whim.

Davis leaned in and whispered something in Allie's ear that made her turn bright red. Allie and Davis had been married four years now, and they still acted like newlyweds. It was kind of cute, but Amber would never admit it.

"Get a room, you two," Ford said, scooting onto the barstool. "Hey, Amber." Ford Clairmont flashed his all-American grin at her, and Amber wondered again if she was broken. Ford was handsome, successful, and wealthy, and all she wanted to do was ask him to rub the tight knot between her shoulders. What a waste.

"Hey, Ford." She expertly tossed a coaster in front of him with a flick of her wrist. "I think they're trying to make more babies."

Allie's head whipped around. "Take that back, Amber Hart, or you're going to do an overnight at our house. Davis, did you hear that?"

Davis raised his head from nuzzling Allie's neck and grinned wolfishly. "I wouldn't mind making more babies."

"Are they for real?" Amber asked.

"I know. It's disgusting." Ford smiled. "Kind of makes you want to settle down and make some cute babies, though."

"Not for me." Amber shuddered. She loved her nephews and nieces more than anything, but kids were an automatic no for anyone she dated, no matter how sexy their dad was.

Kids, puppies, plants. No, thank you. She didn't trust herself to keep any of them alive.

"Good. Don't. I need all the free babysitters I can get," Allie said.

"It's busy tonight," Ford said, checking out the packed bar.

"Yep." Amber deftly slid a stack of tips off the bar from a group of college boys and stuffed them in her pocket. Aside from her boys in uniform, they were her second favorite customers. Young and fun, but they didn't have much money.

But the tips in her pocket were a reassuring weight, and the night was young still. Plenty of hours left to make money. The tightness that had a permanent hold on her shoulders lately drew into a familiar spring.

"Everything okay?" Allie asked, studying her with sharp hazel eyes. As the oldest of the four Hart sisters, Allie didn't miss much. Since having the twins, Allie was busier than ever, but she and Amber were still close. "You don't usually work Friday nights," Allie said.

"I picked up some extra shifts," Amber said breezily.

Allie's eyes narrowed. "Why? Aren't you still working for Mrs. Pearson? Did you get fired already?"

"Hey, rude," Amber said. "I didn't get fired. That ship sailed to Florida." Her latest gig as a personal assistant had been great while it lasted. It was mostly keeping track of Mrs. Pearson's appointments, filling up her pill containers, and driving her places, but she liked the lady. They had some good times together, and Amber had been sad to see her move down south. Working for her had been one of her favorite jobs to date. And, yes, she'd had plenty of them.

"I don't 'get fired,' anyway. I prefer to leave in a blaze of glory." That sounded much better than the truth: her track record of holding down jobs sucked. It was so well known that the number of jobs she'd had over the years was a family joke.

Waitressing, office work, that one time she started a dog-walking business—she had worked them all, but none of them panned out for one reason or another.

But she wasn't ready for that much introspection on a Friday night.

Allie sighed. "Right. Well, whatever comes next, let's hope you decide to stick with it. I just want to see you happy."

Amber saluted. "Got it, boss." She had been picking up shifts at the pub for the extra cash, but she really needed another job, one with benefits, preferably. Her car was on the fritz, and the window AC unit had stopped working right before the heat wave. Sleeping in her apartment had not been fun this week. "Know anyone hiring, Ford?"

"Actually," Ford said, swirling his drink in his glass, "Theo's assistant eloped. Left him without any warning."

"Really?" Allie looked excited. "You could totally do that job, Amber."

"Yep." Ford nodded. "The sooner the better. Knowing my brother, he hasn't left the office since she eloped. You want me to put in a good word for you?"

Amber snorted. "Can you imagine?" she said. She laughed again just thinking about working for the mayor. Theo Clairmont was No Fun with capital letters. "That would be a disaster."

No one else was laughing.

"Why not?" Allie frowned at her. "You're organized and smart. You have plenty of experience, and you need a steady job with benefits. What's the issue?"

How to say this delicately? "Theo Clairmont has a massive stick up his ass." Or not, but she wasn't known for her tact anyway.

"Ouch," Allie said. "What's the mayor ever done to you?"

Amber ignored that.

Ford grinned. "True. To be fair, he's got a town to run, but I'm definitely the fun brother. I'd hire you in a second, but my secretary scares me. I can't ever fire her. I think she'd poison me."

"Just think about it, Amber. It's a good job," Allie said.

"Will do. Hey, you never showed me the girls' dance costumes," Amber said. Showing off the girls never failed to distract her sister. The phone came out, and she was done talking about Theo Clairmont. Everyone in Northfield loved the mayor. Except her.

He was polite to her, sure. Theo Clairmont's manners were impeccable. But that was it. He certainly didn't bother to display any of the easy charm that Northfield was so in love with.

From the first time she'd met him, when she was a starry-eyed, stupid teenager in a bad spot, her wild streak had surfaced every time she saw the mayor. He was just so proper that she couldn't resist poking him to see how far she could push before he lost some of that polish.

For years, she had watched him command every room he stepped into with a natural confidence that irked her to no end. Men respected him and sought him out, and women of all ages sat up and took notice when the mayor arrived. In turn, the mayor was charming and patient, earning him countless awards and accolades during his years in office. But when it came to her, Theo Clairmont was noticeably cooler.

It was a feeling Amber was wholly unfamiliar with. She knew a thing or two about charm. You couldn't work as many service jobs as she had without learning how to wield a smile and flirt like a connoisseur. It was kind of what she was known for and what made her so good at bartending.

She enjoyed talking to people and learning about them, and yes, fixing them up too. She looked around proudly. There were a few couples in the pub right now that she'd had a hand in matchmaking. She was friendly, dammit.

Yet Theo Claremont looked right through her as if she didn't exist.

It hadn't always been that way, but Amber quickly dismissed the thought. She didn't want to ruin her good mood.

Later, after Allie and Davis left, the pub swelled with the Friday crowd, and the pace picked up. Amber flitted around, mixing drinks, and pouring wine and beer.

For most of her life, she had heard she was too much. Too flirtatious, too outrageous, too much for most people to handle, so she had started to embrace it rather than make herself smaller to fit someone else's idea of how she should behave.

Once, when she was in middle school, she'd stayed home sick and binge-watched a Marilyn Monroe movie marathon. She'd studied Marilyn's mannerisms and her effect on men the way some people studied textbooks, fascinated by the power one little blond woman held.

Some women, like her mother, Annette, exuded a natural authority, and others, like her sisters, had a calm, confident way about them.

Amber had Marilyn. Now, there was a woman who knew how to use what she had to make an impression. Well, minus the disastrous results toward the end of her life, but Amber didn't focus on those. She channeled her inner bombshell when she needed an extra boost of confidence.

"What can I get you, boys?" Amber asked, leaning over the bar a smidge, knowing her tight white tank top dipped enticingly into her deep cleavage.

She was a firm believer in making an outfit her own, which was why she had cropped and shredded the boring white T-shirt Killian made them wear into a tank top, leaving a playful fringe that swung teasingly between her stomach and the waist-band of her sparkly skirt.

She leaned down farther, watching the men's reactions with amusement. Not too much. The pub was a family establish-ment, after all. She just liked to tap dance on the line between outrageous and respectable.

"Can you do that thing with the cherry stem, Amber?" Ethan, another fire department rookie, asked hopefully, pushing his way closer to the bar.

Men. So predictable. She grinned.

"Now, why would you want me to do that, Ethan?" She winked and popped a maraschino cherry from the garnish tray into her mouth, eating the fruit and leaving behind the stem.

"Ow-ow-ow." Catcalls pierced the air as Amber worked the cherry stem with her tongue and looked at the court of eager faces crowded around her section of the bar. A mix of apprecia-tion and lust looked back at her, just how she liked it.

She pursed her red-lipsticked lips and wiggled her tongue around, finally thrusting out the perfectly tied cherry stem to her audience.

She crooked her finger, gestured Ethan closer, and curled her fingers around his scruffy jaw and drew him toward her lips.

His face turned eagerly, just in time to swipe the air as Amber snatched the twenty-dollar bill from his other hand and shouted around the stem, "Pay up, boys!"

The pub doors opened again, and Amber looked over auto-matically, her tongue still offered in triumph.

And met the cool blue eyes of Mayor Theo Clairmont.

He stood just inside the doorway with a tall, slender brunette on his arm, easily commanding the attention of the room he had just stepped into as people noticed his arrival.

The mayor's dark hair swooped back from his forehead neatly, revealing a chiseled, smooth-shaven jaw and devastatingly handsome face. Even from behind the bar, she could see how his perfectly fitted, no doubt obscenely expensive suit molded to the tall lines of his body.

Icy blue eyes held hers, and an unexpected shiver shot down her spine.

He didn't look at her with interest. It wasn't outright disdain. Theo Clairmont looked at her with a calm sort of assessment that left her feeling oddly, inexplicably, exposed. She was instantly annoyed.

Men like Mayor Theo Clairmont were born into privilege and power: wealthy, handsome, with a clear path laid out for them. They conducted their lives on golf courses and in boardrooms, spaces where she had never been invited or welcomed, unless she was taking notes or serving refreshments.

They had no concept of the struggle and sacrifice it took to survive in this world, while she worked two jobs just to make ends meet. She had worked for people like the Clairmonts her entire life—pouring their drinks, taking their orders, catering to their every whim behind the scenes.

Pure stubbornness made her hold his gaze until the crowd surged to greet him, and, like a shock of icy cold water, she jerked back to reality.

"Can you do it again? Take all my money," Ethan groaned. He slapped a crumpled pile of dollar bills on the bar toward her.

The warmth of the pub intensified as Theo, phone pressed to his ear, led his date through the crowd toward a table of people, looking every inch the confident, charismatic picture of success, while she picked the cherry stem from her mouth and eyed the damp dollar bills on the bar.

She was really, really tired of being the one behind the scenes.

∾

Theo Clairmont was not amused. His eyes burned from lack of sleep, and the music in the pub was reverberating in his skull while he waited on hold.

His assistant, Kelsey, had managed his life efficiently until last week when she eloped. Who eloped anymore? Why she didn't just go down the hall from their office and have the judge marry her, he'd never understand. Now, he was left with a mountain of loose ends on top of his regular workload.

Ah, hell. With the grueling week of work he'd just had, he should have just canceled tonight and gone home to bed instead of coming out for a drink with his campaign staff.

"Welcome to the pub." Amber Hart tossed four coasters onto the table. Theo glanced up for a brief second—long enough to notice her new hair, cotton candy pink mixed with blond curls. Outrageous, as usual.

She was looking directly at him, a faint smirk playing on her lips. "We've got ice cold beer on tap, or a selection of New York's finest Finger Lakes wines. What'll it be?"

"Chardonnay, and make sure the glass doesn't have spots on it." Neal Barclay said, his longtime chief of staff. Neal looked around, frowning. Theo knew that look. Neal had inspected the interior of the pub and found it lacking. Theo didn't care. He liked it here. There was an unpretentious charm to the dark interior that was a welcome change from the formal events he usually attended.

"You got it. No spots. Spotless. Free of spots," Amber said. She popped her hip out, making her long, feathered earrings dance around her face. Theo turned back to his phone call.

"No," he said into the phone. "That won't work. It was supposed to be for the twenty-first. Yes, I realize this is short notice. Who? Beckerman booked it? Damn it. No, not you. I meant—"

"Theo, did you hear me?" His date, Addison, tugged on his sleeve. "I think we should order something really special."

Theo covered the mouthpiece on his phone. "I'm sorry. I've got to take care of this."

"Do you remember what today is?" she added with a coy smile.

Theo looked at her blankly. "Friday?"

Addison pouted. "It's my birthday month, Theo. You said you were going to take me out somewhere nice, and instead you took me to this shitty little bar."

Birthday month? Theo held back a groan. "Right. Just give me a minute to—"

The woman slid off the chair and stood over the table. "This is so boring. I'm going to meet my friends. Call me if you want to join me later." She blew him a kiss and waltzed out of the pub.

"Well, that was awkward," Amber said brightly, leaning over to take back the extra coaster.

Theo raised an eyebrow at her obvious enjoyment of the situation.

She smirked. "I'll get you a beer, Mr. Mayor. You look like you could use it. Be right back with those."

"Really, Theo? You forgot her birthday?" Charlotte, his director of communications asked, disapproval written all over her face.

"Yeah." Theo sighed. "In my defense, I met her last week." Still, he felt like an asshole. He knew agreeing to take Addison out was a bad idea. She was funny, and—okay, he wasn't going to deny it—she had legs for days. He was a leg guy, through and through, but he knew it was a bad idea the first time they went out. He worked far too much to give a relationship the time and attention it deserved.

Neal frowned at him. "Stunts like that"—he nodded toward

Addison, who had stopped to talk to a table of off-duty officers—"do not go over well with your voters. Your approval rating is already down thirty-three percent, and Beckerman's has doubled. I know you don't want to hear this, but these numbers tell us you've got to make some serious changes to your image to have any chance of being reelected in November."

"What's wrong with Theo's image?" Ford, his youngest brother, slid into a chair. "Did you suddenly start mugging old ladies?" He tossed a handful of complimentary peanuts into his mouth.

"Theo, Neal's right," Charlotte said quietly, putting a hand on Theo's arm. "The polls are consistently favoring Beckerman. He's painting himself as a family man in his ad campaign, and voters are eating it up. They see him as more stable and reliable."

Theo knew Charlotte was right, but it didn't take the sting out of her words.

"Beckerman's a prick," Ford said. "I played golf with him once, and he was bragging about shagging the waitress while his wife was pregnant."

"It doesn't matter who he shags as long as he looks like a family man," Neal said bluntly. "It's all about optics."

Theo winced. While Neal was incredibly successful at getting Theo's father reelected for multiple terms, they didn't see eye to eye on everything. Theo usually kept the peace because he respected Neal, but sometimes things came out of his mouth that made him wonder how similar they were at all.

"His family image is resonating with voters," Charlotte said.

"What do you want me to do? Adopt a golden retriever and start baking apple pies?" Theo asked sarcastically.

"That'd be better than the gossip about who you're dating

this month all over the town's Facebook page. People want to see their mayor settled down," Neal said.

That damn Facebook page would be the death of him. Whoever ran it had too much time on their hands, and Theo was their favorite subject. He dated, yes. But Theo wasn't an indiscreet lover. He didn't flaunt his dates or talk about them at all. In fact, he tried his best to avoid the spotlight as much as possible when it involved his personal life.

His last relationship was over a year ago with a local reporter, Pippa Shelton, before they decided their demanding careers left little time for a relationship, and he had dated only casually since.

But lately, he had been thinking about the future. Now that he was thirty-five, the thought of meeting a woman and starting a family had crossed his mind more often than not. It would certainly make his grandmother happy.

His record leading Northfield spoke for itself, despite what his constituents thought of his personal life. He poured his heart and soul into protecting Northfield's charm and sustainability, only to be reduced to his dating history.

The Clairmonts had been shaping Northfield for generations. Theo's father held the title of mayor for twenty-eight years before he retired and Theo was elected in his place. The following year, in a shocking accident that had shaken the entire town, his parents' privately chartered plane went down not long after takeoff, and no one survived. The pain of losing his parents was still deep and raw.

It was why Philip Beckerman's campaign was so distasteful. Beckerman, with his car-salesman talks and grandiose plans, represented everything Theo opposed. His latest proposal to pave over the village green—a space the Clairmonts had protected for generations—was a clue to his short-sighted, profit-driven mindset.

Theo couldn't stand the guy. Beckerman's vision for Northfield threatened to undo everything Theo and his family had worked for hard for all these years. Losing the election in November wasn't an option.

"We need something to replace the speculation. Something that shows you've turned a new leaf." Charlotte said.

"He was just named Rochester's most eligible bachelor," Ford laughed. "That would be a one-eighty."

"My personal life is not on the ballot," Theo said tightly.

Charlotte, always the voice of reason, nodded. "It shouldn't have anything to do with whether or not you can lead the town, Theo, but that's not how politics work. It's all about perception. Right now, you're seen as the fun mayor, not the family mayor. Four years ago, that got you elected, but now voters want to see you settling down. They want to see that you're committed to the needs of the families here. We need to shift the narrative fast."

Ford sat forward. "If you need to cut some of your girl-friends loose, I can help with that. Take one for the team and all."

"Why are you here again?" Theo glared at his younger brother.

"To provide brotherly support," Ford said with a wounded look. "And my date is meeting me here later," he added.

"Son, you can play with anyone you want, but you need someone steady by your side, someone who knows how to play the politics game, leading up to this election and after." Neal looked him in the eye. "Do you want to be reelected or not?"

Theo scrubbed a hand over his face. He did want to be reelected more than he could put into words. Aside from a brief rebellion in college, he'd always known he wanted to follow in his father's footsteps. He loved his job, loved making Northfield a better place and planning for the future. His father used to tell

Theo that leading a town took a servant's heart, and Theo never forgot it.

He'd gone to college for political science and then gone on to law school, all the while preparing to run when his father retired. When that day came, Theo won by a landslide. He'd spent the last four years working his ass off to make this place he loved better for everyone, and he couldn't help the resentment that his job was in jeopardy because of his sex life.

"It's not just the dating, Theo," Neal said. "It's who you're dating. These women are not exactly cut out for a life in politics. You need to settle down with someone who's wife material. Find yourself a nice woman who's ready to have your babies. Someone who... who... knits?" Neal looked around the pub as if a magical knitting woman were waiting in the wings before his eyes homed in on Charlotte. "Someone like Charlotte."

"Me?" Charlotte asked, a hand to her chest. "I'd never marry Theo, and besides, what makes you think I knit?"

She sounded inexplicably hurt, Theo noticed.

Theo glanced at her in equal horror. "I'm not marrying you. I'm not marrying anyone."

Neal leaned forward and Theo recognized the look. Theo respected Neal's experience, but he was out of his mind. He wasn't marrying anyone for his job, especially not Charlotte. She was like his sister. He glanced at Charlotte and was relieved to see the look of horror still on her face.

"I meant more like finding a nice woman to date steadily for a while," Charlotte hurried to add.

"Amber," someone near the pool table yelled, and Theo's gaze drifted to the bar to look for her. She wasn't hard to find.

In all the years he'd known her, he had been aware of her as soon as he stepped into the same room. Her laughter rose above the music and the noise, vibrant and dazzling, attracting people to her like magnets.

She was weaving her way in and out of the crowd of off-duty firefighters and police officers, passing out drinks and pocketing money, teasing and bantering with each of them. Amber's energy practically sparkled in the dim lights of the bar, but he turned back to the table.

"Look at her," Charlotte said. "She's beautiful." Theo glanced sharply at Charlotte's wistful tone, but she was staring at Amber.

For a split second, Theo let himself drink her in. Even when he met her as an eighteen-year-old girl, Amber Hart was the kind of woman who demanded attention. He just didn't make a habit of giving it to her.

She was bent over the pool table, in her little sparkly skirt that made his eyeballs throb, taking a practice shot while Northfield's finest shouted encouragement and envisioned themselves behind her, no doubt. Her pink hair and lush body made her impossible to ignore.

It always surprised him how strong the bolt of lust was when he let himself look at her. He'd always gone for tall, cool brunettes—refined women who were as motivated and driven as he was. Not someone who dressed like a six-year-old with a Bedazzler had gotten a hold of their clothes. Yet he reacted with a primitive awareness that took him by surprise whenever they were in the vicinity of one another.

She was striking, with her heart-shaped face and big hazel eyes that seemed perpetually amused. Of course, he was a man and had noticed those generous curves too.

He dated women who were... "Predictable" wasn't the right word. From her wild hair to her too-short, too-tight clothing, there was nothing predictable in the package in front of him.

That didn't stop him from admiring the way her tight skirt moved over the curves of her ass as she walked away. Her tanned legs were on perfect display, and as he watched along with the rest of the bar, she leaned over to shimmy even farther over the pool table for a shot. Theo had the distinct impression she knew exactly what she was doing, and she was enjoying every minute.

"We could use someone with connections like hers," Neal said idly. "Do you think it's true she's slept with most of those guys?"

Ford's normally easygoing expression turned hard. "Watch yourself. Amber's a friend."

"Are you really suggesting I date the local bartender for the sake of politics?" Theo said icily. "Do you hear yourself?"

"I was suggesting you hire her, not date her. I know she's looking for a job," Ford said. "She has some experience as a personal assistant, and I told her I'd put in a good word for her."

"You can't hire her." Neal scowled. "But you could get to know her and use some of her connections. If anything else happens, well, I've heard she's a good time." He smirked.

Theo was momentarily stunned into silence. That was low, even for Neal.

"I won't allow you to do that," Ford said firmly. "She doesn't deserve to be used. That's not you, either, Theo."

"I agree," said Theo, relieved. Jesus. Since when did town politics get so cutthroat? "Grant's a police officer," Theo said, referring to their middle brother. "How much better connected can we get?"

"Grant's a detective in Boston. He doesn't have any connections here. Not like her." Neal jerked his head toward Amber, who let out a peal of laughter just then. She was talking to the captain of the Northfield Fire Department and a group of veteran firefighters. Theo had been in his fair share of town hall meetings with the captain. Cap was an influential man to have in his corner. Cap appeared to be fully in Amber's. She leaned up and kissed his cheek.

"Most of these guys have some kind of connection to her entire family," Neal observed, practically rubbing his hands together in glee. "Look at her. She's even got Cap eating out of her hands."

Ford shrugged. "Amber's a good person who could use a steady job with benefits. She's a little wild, but she's got great energy. Hiring her might get that stick out of your ass." He grinned.

Theo tapped his fingers impatiently on the table. "I can't work with someone like that. Can you imagine her in an office setting?"

"Hiring her is a terrible idea." Neal scowled. "She's clearly not office material."

Theo found Amber again in the crowded bar with another group of people. She radiated vibrant energy that drew people to her just to be near all that light.

Theo glanced at Ford. "You don't think this is a good idea, right?"

"Actually, I do," Ford said, smiling. "Amber's smart, good with people, and she's bound to have some fresh ideas. You could use someone like her managing your life. I'd consider it a personal favor if you hired her. I think she'd be good for you."

"What if you just talk to her and see if she's even interested?" Charlotte, ever the voice of reason, suggested. "You don't have to decide now. Besides, she might say no, anyway. She's not exactly struggling in her current job."

"One she's not very good at," Theo said, glancing irritably at the empty table. "I'll go get our drinks."

Chapter Two

"I'T'S A HOT ONE TONIGHT," Captain Peter Buttaglia, otherwise known simply as Cap by everyone in Northfield, said, looking around at the packed bar. Amber could almost see him counting heads for the fire code.

"I don't mind. It makes people thirsty, which makes me more money." Amber slid another stack of ones off the bar.

"Everything okay, honey?" Cap asked. He studied her with sharp blue eyes. She let her smile spread from merely sexy into dazzling territory. "That doesn't work on me, Miss," Cap growled.

Amber toned it down to a softer, more genuine smile.

"You've been working too much lately," he said gruffly.

"Me, work too hard? Never. Everything is perfect, Cap." Aunt Sophia and Cap had dated for a few years now. He was a regular, welcome fixture at their Sunday family dinners, with his keen observations about everything from local politics to what grew best in his gardens.

Cap snorted. "Keep telling yourself that."

Sometimes he could see a little too much.

Amber pointed her finger at his beer. "That's your last one

for the night or I'm going to call Aunt Sophia to come and get you on her way home from Bingo."

Captain studied her shrewdly before allowing himself to be distracted. Faux horror filled his face at his girlfriend's name. "Let a guy live a little, would ya?" Aunt Sophia inspired that look from many people with her bossy ways, but Amber knew the captain was smitten all the same.

"See you at Sunday dinner." She reached up to kiss his grizzled cheek.

"Amber, phone's for you," Miguel, her line cook and general pain in the ass, bellowed through the pass-through window. The slam of a stainless-steel prep bowl let her know what he thought about phone calls during the middle of a Friday rush hour.

"Tell them I'm working," Amber bellowed right back.

"You think I didn't tell them that?" More pots and pans banged. With Killian gone for the night now, Amber was supposed to take any important calls. She headed toward the kitchen.

"Northfield Pub," she said impatiently into the phone.

"Is this Amber Hart? This is Dana with Agency Debt Collections." The perky voice threw her for a second.

Shit. Shit. Shit. "Ye—*no*. She doesn't work here," Amber blurted, and she slammed the phone back on the wall.

Miguel shook a sauté pan of mushrooms, looking at her over the steam knowingly. "When you don't answer your phone, they get sneaky."

She stared at the phone, biting her thumbnail. "It was the wrong number."

"Yeah." He snorted. "Better take the next one. They won't stop."

"Shh," she hissed, looking around. Her family were regulars at the Pub, along with everyone else in Northfield. If they found out she was being hounded by a debt collection agency, they would... well, they would want to help. She pushed the horrifying thought aside.

"There won't be a next time. It wasn't for me," she said.

It was fine. Everything was fine.

She had hours left to make enough tips to cover her rent and put a little down on the loan she owed. She had been in some tight spots with money before, and she always got out of them. *But they had never called her at work before*, an unhelpful voice whispered.

The first beats of her favorite song thrummed through the air when she stepped back behind the bar, and the ball of stress and anxiety that had kept her wound so tightly quivered.

"Nope." Cap grabbed her arm as she walked by. "Remember what happened last time."

But it was too late.

The spring pulled taut. One last effort before it snapped, but it wasn't a match for Def Leppard. Come on. Eighties hair metal got her every time. Karaoke was her kryptonite, and everyone knew this was her favorite song. Her boys were already calling her name to get on the bar.

A little voice of reason tugged at her, but she pushed it away. Blame it on the heat, or the phone call, or just plain bad decision-making, but Amber allowed herself to be lifted onto the bar and then up to standing.

A mic appeared in one of her hands and a bottle of vodka in another, and Amber looked over to the band. Eden, the lead singer, winked and began singing in her sexy voice about being hot and sticky sweet.

Amber forgot about the stack of bills waiting for her at home. She forgot about car repairs. She forgot about the credit card that was maxed, and she let the music wash over her while she sang. She poured shots into open, willing mouths as she shimmied back and forth across the bar and let herself forget everything.

Until her foot slipped on a puddle. She let out a whoop and slid straight down on her bottom on the bar, the ice-cold vodka spilling over her chest. She lay there laughing, only to stop when two bossy hands clamped onto her shoulders and pulled her up to sitting.

A soft thud against a hard chest, and suddenly she was looking directly into Theo Clairmont's unreadable blue eyes.

This close, she realized his eyes were not merely blue. They reminded her of deep water, lighter on the surface and darker the deeper you went. A tendril of something liquid hot slid through her body, and she realized she wanted something from him. Something other than disinterest or, worse, amusement.

Raising her own eyebrows in a challenge, she tipped the mic until it rested on his lips. "Sing," she said breathlessly.

Theo batted the mic away impatiently, and she was suddenly aware of her legs spread wide on either side of his torso, his body strong and firm and hot between her thighs. His expensive cologne filled her senses while an awareness throbbed through her, leaving an empty ache low in her stomach.

It was the closest she had been to having a man between her legs for as long as she could remember. Theo shrugged off his suit jacket and jerked it around her shoulders.

"I'm hot," she said, trying to shrug off the jacket.

"You're wet." Theo's cool eyes slid down her body and stopped. Amber followed his eyes down at the wide strip of fabric clinging to her skin, making the lacy pale pink bra she wore under almost transparent. Her nipples perked up right on cue, and a delicate shiver skimmed over her at the suggestive words.

The mayor's icy disapproval wavered for a moment. It felt like a small victory, but she savored it.

Impulsively, she grabbed the nearest drink on the bar and tossed it at his chest. "Now we match," she said. Her heart beat hard enough that she was sure he could hear it. Whether in fear or defiance, or maybe excitement, Amber held his eyes while a dark splotch spread over his chest, molding it to the hard plane of muscle there.

Theo's hands tightened on the lapels until she was barely on the bar, leaning precariously on his chest. The mayor seemed to be familiar with both the gym and the golf course.

His body was a large, solid rock, and for the briefest moment, she allowed herself to rest flush against him. They paused like that for a long, electrified second while the music and the dancing faded around them.

"What the fuck is going on here?"

Eden's voice cut off on a jarring note, and the speaker gave feedback in a piercing screech. And then there was silence.

Killian was back. Amber's eyes widened in panic and she looked at Theo instinctively—for what, she didn't know. There wasn't anything life had thrown at her she couldn't handle on her own. As soon as she realized what she was doing, she jerked her eyes away and leaned back.

Killian stood with his arms crossed over his chest, a look she'd never seen on his face.

She swallowed hard and tried a dazzling smile. "Hey, boss," she said. "I'm making you so much money right now."

"Get off my bar and meet me in my office," Killian snapped. "Last call," he shouted on his way back.

She closed her eyes briefly. This was so not good. Her ears were still ringing from the last time he chewed her out for dancing on the bar. It was unfair, really. It was all in good fun, and the patrons loved it. Killian could be such a hardass.

When she opened her eyes, Theo was studying her. His gaze was cool again, enough so that she shivered.

She shrugged off the luxurious silk jacket that probably cost more than her rent.

"Keep it," he said in that ridiculous, deep voice of his. Since when were small-town mayors allowed to talk like that? All husky and intimate. A delicate shiver skimmed over her, which, of course, made her even mouthier. "You're not decent."

She leaned in closer until her lips brushed his ear and murmured, "The fun ones never are."

She hopped off the bar and didn't look back.

AMBER STOOD in the doorway of Killian's office. The faint scent of cigars lingered, reminding her of the many heart-to-hearts they'd had in this room. She braced herself, knowing she'd pushed Killian's limits more tonight than at any other time. "Look, I know you said—"

"Close the door, Amber," Killian said quietly. He had never looked at her like that.

She swallowed hard.

"Do you want to tell me why you're dancing on my bar again?"

She tried to deflect with her usual charm. "Well, you see, we were down in sales coming into the last hour, so it was actually a smart business decision. You know you make twice as much later on in sales when we do karaoke. I was really looking out for your bottom line."

"Stop." Killian ran his hands through his hair, looking frustrated. "Don't pile that bullshit on me. This isn't about sales. Do you want to get us closed down? Would you like to jeopardize my liquor license? For fuck's sake, the fire marshal was leaving when I walked in. You know he wouldn't hesitate to slap a fine on me or worse. Is that what you want?"

"It's not that serious," she started, but Killian cut her off.

"What you don't understand is that life really is that serious."

Ouch. That one hurt. She'd heard that her entire life, most especially from her mother: to get serious. As the tapping of Killian's pencil lent an uncharacteristically tense air to the room, remorse filled her.

The pub was a special place for her. It had been her soft landing when she needed a place to come back to. No matter which job or idea didn't work out the way she thought it would, Killian always had a spot for her behind the bar. He was more than a boss or her friend; he was the mentor she'd never asked for but desperately needed.

"Okay," she said meekly. "I'm sorry."

Killian sighed, his expression softening. "I know you're trying to find your way, Amber, but I can't keep overlooking these things. This place, these people, they rely on us."

The room felt smaller, the weight of his words pressing down on her. "You're right. I didn't think about the others," she admitted, the reality of her actions hitting her. "It won't happen again." The resignation on his face alarmed her.

"It won't happen again because I'm letting you go."

"What? You can't mean that." She stared at him in disbelief. "I need this job. You don't understand. I have to pay—" she stopped abruptly. No way was she going to get into her money troubles with her boss, friend or not. Those were locked up tight, and she planned to keep them that way.

She tried one more time with her best smile. "Killian, please. I'm begging you. You know me. I'm a hard worker, and I always show up. Please give me another chance."

"I'm sorry, love." He shook his head. "I need you to understand that this is my livelihood. There are people who depend on me, and if this place is closed down, it affects more than just you having fun."

"But... what will I do?" She flinched even as she said it, furious it had come out at all, but the reality of the situation was making her dizzy.

Working at the pub was the one constant in her life. All the dreams she'd had over the years had slipped through her fingers. Even college hadn't worked out like she wanted it to. She had quit early, once more disappointing her family of smart, successful women and their expectations of her.

All her life it had felt like she was in limbo while the world moved forward. Sure, she had her body, which she used skillfully. She wasn't ashamed of using what she had because she knew she was smart too. She had charm; she loved to make people laugh, and she had street smarts. Maybe not the kind of smarts that showed up on a school transcript, but she wasn't without skills.

Suddenly, her list felt horrifyingly inadequate, and she wondered how much longer she could keep up the pretense of holding it all together.

Working behind the bar was the one familiar anchor in the chaos that was her life. It was all too much in that moment, and, to her horror, tears welled in her eyes. She blinked furiously to make them go away. She never cried. Never. She wouldn't start now.

Killian came to the front of his desk. Dimly, she felt him reach for her hands. His blue eyes, usually filled with teasing good humor, were somber. "Start by thinking about what you want. You have so much potential. You're smart. You're a hard worker. Take some time to figure that out. If you need any help, financial or otherwise, you know I'm here," he added gruffly.

It was the concern in his voice that finally shook her out of her stupor.

She jerked to her feet. "I don't need help." She let out a brittle laugh. "You know me. I always land on my feet."

Killian nodded. "I know you do," he said thoughtfully. "Maybe you need to figure out why you keep falling."

And that was her cue to leave. If there was one thing she didn't waste time on, it was thinking about her inadequacies. She tugged her hands away from his.

She paused at the door. "I'm truly sorry. I would never want to put your business in jeopardy."

She snuck through the back door, thankful that no one was there to see her walk of shame. Johnny was leaning against his motorcycle when she stepped outside, one motorcycle boot crossed over another, his arms straining the sleeves of the old Northfield Fire Department T-shirt he wore. A wave of affection stole over her at the sight of him, and she waved. Ever since they met, Johnny had been looking out for her.

They grew up together in Cedarwood Village, the low-income housing track on the outer edge of Northfield. When you grew up outside of the wealthy Northfield bubble, you stuck to others like you. It made it a lot less awkward when your friends wanted to come over and hang out.

One day over the summer, she had been walking around their complex, bored and looking for something to do, when a pack of boys she knew from school started chasing her, and not in a tag-you're-it sort of way. Jeff Lloyd, an arrogant kid with a mean streak, was the leader.

Amber was like any other middle school girl, with teeth too big for her face and gangly arms and legs, but her chest made her stand out. She had developed earlier than anyone else in middle school, much to her embarrassment.

She knew Jeff had started a rumor that she had let him touch her boobs last school year, and the boys chasing her had wandered down from the village, bored and looking to try their own luck with her.

It was the first time Amber could remember being truly afraid.

She took off running as fast as she could, but Jeff grabbed her from behind. He had her wrapped up tight and was taunting her when Johnny came out of his mom's apartment, fists flying.

At fifteen, Johnny had shown the promise of the imposing man he was now. Jeff had known he was in trouble as soon as he saw him. He'd dropped Amber on her butt by then, but Johnny charged, sucker-punched Jeff, and followed him to the ground. The other boys ran away, but Johnny wouldn't let Jeff go until he'd apologized. Red in the face, snot running down his nose, Jeff had promised never to bother her again.

Johnny had been her protector ever since. A little more than that for a brief time, but they had quickly realized they were too similar to be anything other than friends.

She sighed. "You heard, huh?"

A flash of white teeth showed in his tanned face. "Causing trouble again, short stuff?"

"Don't call me that," she said automatically.

"What did you do now?" he asked, and a little frisson of irritation sparked. Why did everyone assume it was her who did something?

She poked his broad chest, but just as suddenly, the spark sputtered and died. "Karaoke on the bar." Her shoulders slumped. "I can't believe Killian fired me."

The corners of Johnny's mouth pulled down. "I'm sorry, babe. After that last time Killian reamed you out, I didn't think you were gonna do it again." He held out his arms, and Amber leaned into his broad chest with a sigh.

"Why do I keep messing up?" she asked, her voice muffled in his shirt.

"I don't know." Johnny threaded his fingers through the hair at the back of her neck and rubbed. She sighed in relief. Everything hurt, probably from her fall on the bar, and her tank top was sticky with vodka. She leaned back.

"Thanks for waiting for me."

"You got it. Do you want to come back to my place for a drink?" he asked.

For a second, she considered it, but she shook her head. "No, I have a terrible headache. I'm going to head home and take a bath."

"Whose is this?" he asked, fingering the suit coat she still wore around her shoulders.

"You wouldn't believe me if I told you."

Johnny studied her then leaned forward and kissed her softly on the forehead. "Do you need anything before I head out?" he asked.

The thing about Johnny was that he understood her too well. They had the same guarded approach to life and relationships because of their upbringing, and they both would rather hightail it out of town than feel vulnerable. But when the rubber hit the road, they were there for each other.

"No, I'm good. Thanks. Go find some cute girl to pick up who doesn't smell like a liquor cabinet."

"That's the plan." He smirked, already putting on his helmet.

"Thanks again for waiting." She leaned in for a hug. Before she could step back, Johnny caught her jaw, tilted her head up, and looked into her eyes.

He was handsome in that bad-boy way mothers warned their daughters about, but when you grew up with someone, you saw them through all stages of their life. Amber had seen

Johnny grow from the adolescent boy with a chip on his shoulder to the man she knew today, a brave firefighter who would put his life at risk in a heartbeat to help. She had seen it all, and she loved him as if he were family.

"Take some Advil and call me in the morning. We'll go out for a big greasy breakfast." He opened her door and closed it behind her with a flourish.

Amber started her car and was waving as he pulled out of the parking lot when her car sputtered and died.

She closed her eyes, leaned against the steering wheel, and let out a scream of pure, elemental frustration. Groaning at the way her back creaked at her, she got out and stood in front of the engine, willing it to start. It was times like these she wished she had had a dad to teach her about cars. As it was, she didn't know the first thing about engines.

Frustration bubbled over. She let loose with a hard kick to the front bumper with her Converse and promptly started swearing. "Ow, ow, shit, ow, fuck!"

She hopped around on one foot, swearing like a sailor. Finally, feeling marginally better from her tantrum, she straightened.

And screamed again because Theo Clairmont was leaning nonchalantly on his car, watching her.

"Car trouble?" he asked with his eyebrow raised.

"Did your Ivy League education teach you to state the obvious?" she asked nastily.

"I guess you don't need my help, then," he said evenly, turning to leave.

"Wait." She closed her eyes and attempted to gather her composure. It was amazing how she could manage to charm an entire bar full of men, yet this one could reduce her to feeling like a child throwing a tantrum.

An unwelcome memory of another late night with him

coming to her rescue came to mind, and she instantly dismissed it. She'd come a long way from needing anyone's help, especially from someone like Theo Clairmont.

And yet... Amber looked back toward the pub and chewed her lip. If she went back in, she'd have to ask Killian for a ride. She considered calling Johnny, but she knew he wouldn't be able to hear her over the engine of his motorcycle. Besides, he was probably on his way to another bar to pick up a lady friend. She could walk the few blocks home, but her body was already screaming at her.

"Wait," she called out. He didn't, even though she knew he heard her. Asshole. "Wait," she called again, hopping over. Her toes better not be broken.

"Can you give me a ride? Please."

Theo turned back around without a word and led her around the Mercedes. He brushed her hand aside when she went to get the door and held it himself.

She settled into the buttery leather seats, every overworked muscle in her body lovingly cupped in luxury. It was a beautiful car. It put her little ice-skate-looking car to shame. She couldn't hold back a deep sigh as she settled in.

"Oh, this is fancy, Mr. Mayor. Too bad you're not driving your date hom—" Her words were cut off as he closed the door briskly. She smirked.

Theo slid his long legs under the steering wheel and started the car. She idly watched the streetlights cast his face in interesting shadows, giving the moment a dream-like quality. In what other reality was she sitting in the mayor's car, getting a ride home?

The combination of blessedly cool air-conditioning, adrenaline dump, and worry from the last few days caught up with her suddenly, and she sank deeper into the leather with a grateful sigh.

"Where to?"

She gave him the address of the historic Phoenix Hotel, which had been renovated into apartments, a few blocks away. "Thanks," she said quietly, all joking aside.

His crisp white shirt glowed in the dark car except for a round splotch of amber. A twinge of shame pricked her conscience. Did she really throw a drink at the mayor? Not for the first time, Amber wondered why she did the things she did.

Theo glanced over at her. "Playing the damsel in distress doesn't suit you."

Amber stiffened. "Really? Because playing the arrogant, rich white guy suits you perfectly," she shot back, her pride stung and shame gone.

The car hummed in silence before Theo spoke again. "Your boyfriend needs a lesson in manners. He should've stuck around and let you go first out of the parking lot."

Amber rolled her head toward him, all of her irritation coming back in a rush. "Johnny has more chivalry in his pinky finger than you ever will."

Before she could lay into him further, he turned into her parking lot and got out. Amber was already trying to get out of the car when he offered his hand. She brushed it aside. "I don't need any help." She glared up at his face before stomping up the steps of the three-story brick building.

She sensed Theo behind her and sped up until she reached the entrance. Of course he would walk her to the door. Theo was the epitome of a rule follower, but there was no way she would let him see her apartment.

The Phoenix was nice enough, but she knew where Theo lived, where he had grown up. The Clairmonts came from old money, and the mayor's current house sat on one of the ritziest streets in Northfield.

There was no way she was going to let him in to judge her

apartment or, worse, her life. He'd have to get in line for that. "Stop following me. I said I'm fine. Go home. I'm not sleeping with you," she tossed at him just for the shock value.

Theo's eyes widened the tiniest bit, and she wanted to high-five herself for getting a reaction. At least she wasn't a ghost now.

"I'm walking you to your door. I realize you're not used to this type of behavior, but that's what gentlemen do." He reached for her key, covering her hand with his big, warm palm before unlocking the door and pushing it open.

She slipped past him before he could see inside and closed it until she was peering out behind a crack. Theo stood just outside her doorway, tall, remote, and powerful in the dim hallway light.

Even without light, she knew his eyes were back to a cool, assessing blue. A shiver made its way up her spine. Her best defense was always a strong offense.

"Thanks for the ride, Mr. Mayor. I'd invite you in for a drink, but I don't have any warm milk."

"I'd rather not take a chance of it being thrown on me." He looked pointedly down at the amber stain on his white shirt and turned to leave.

"I'm sure you have more exciting things to do, anyway, like organize your sock drawer," she said to his back, faintly ashamed of the utterly limp trash talk. She could do so much better when she had her wits about her.

"More like alphabetizing my books," Theo called back. It was terrible timing because he had already started down the stairs, his steps solid and confident, taking the last word with him.

Yeah, she would never, ever work for that asshole.

Chapter Three

As the mayor of a small town, Theo was used to dealing with people from all walks of life. He prided himself on being logical and reasoned, no matter what the people of Northfield threw at him.

When Mrs. Slaughter shouted obscenities about his "bullshit liberal progressive agenda" during town hall meetings, it didn't rattle him at all. Leanne Forrester liked to send around petitions to change the street names to Marvel superheroes every few months. Even the town gossip about his dating life didn't bother him much.

Northfield had quirky people just like any other town, but he took it all in stride and dealt with everything his job threw at him in the only way he knew how: with order and structure, and he loved every minute of it.

Hell, even the publicity that came along with being the mayor of a small town was a small tradeoff for the satisfaction he felt in serving Northfield.

But Amber Hart tested his patience. She always had. The sight of her splayed out on the bar, laughing, her wet shirt clinging to the round curves of her breasts in that pink lace bra, played on repeat in his head. She had thrown a drink on him, for Chrissakes.

Part of him wanted to laugh it off, to chalk it up to another crazy Amber antic, but another, deeper part of him couldn't shake off the concern. From the first time he saw her, he'd felt like he was in the eye of a hurricane, and yet he couldn't help the surge of protectiveness he had always felt for her.

He hoped like hell that no one saw the drink-throwing incident because it was exactly the kind of thing that would blow up on the town's Facebook page. Events like that could tank his chance at reelection and make either one of them the subject of town gossip.

Logically, he knew he should distance himself from her before he was dragged into her whirlwind, but here he was, sitting in her parking lot to make sure she got inside safely.

Theo thought about the intimate moment he had witnessed between Amber and her boyfriend, John Rossi, or Johnny, as the Northfield Fire Department knew him. Theo was familiar with Johnny and most of the fire department from community outreach events and various fundraisers they attended, although he hadn't been aware Amber was dating him. It shouldn't matter. Just like Neal's comment about her sleeping around shouldn't have stirred an undercurrent of irritation in him.

Yet for all the outrageous behavior she had shown that evening, Theo couldn't shake the image of Amber standing alone in the parking lot. She was a petite woman to begin with, but she had seemed even smaller standing alone in the empty space.

When she had closed her eyes, utter exhaustion had washed over her and arrested him. It had happened so quickly, her delicate features dazzling enough to a man, had softened until she looked lost for a moment. Tired and lost like that night all those years ago. His phone rang, snapping him out of his thoughts.

"Theo, your grandma's having a rough night." Lucille, the night nurse, greeted him. Since Georgina Clairmont's breast cancer diagnosis, Theo had hired her to stay with his grandmother at night, first as a nurse when the chemo made her sick and now as a companion.

Theo's heart sank. "Is she still awake?" After his parents' passing, Theo's grandmother had never fully recovered. The grief of losing her son and daughter-in-law had ravaged her. A breast cancer diagnosis last year had further sidelined her. Theo and his three siblings spent as much time as they could with her, and Lucille took over when they couldn't be there.

"Yes, she's playing the piano right now."

Theo knew what that meant. Georgina, or Georgie, as they called her, since she detested being called something so mundane as Grandma, was a renowned concert pianist, but now she only played when she couldn't sleep. She and Theo's grandfather had traveled the world for her performances. Even after having children, his grandparents had shared their love of music and traveled often as an extended family. By the time Theo was eight, he had visited most of the continents. Theo liked to think that experiencing so many diverse cultures shaped his passion for public service. One couldn't see the world and not feel empathy and compassion for the human experience.

"I'll be right over." On impulse, he stopped at a diner, picking up Georgie's favorite treat—a strawberry milkshake—before heading to his childhood home. Georgie had never played favorites, but Theo had always had a special bond with her, which was why she always called him first. She was funny and still sharp as a tack, but being sick over the last year had worn her down, and he was worried.

The elegant house sat just outside suburban Northfield. A large iron gate opened automatically as he drove up. He parked next to the fountain and took the steps up into the foyer of the home he had grown up in. He remembered how he used to play hide-and-seek with his brothers and sister in the rooms and how their laughter had filled the house.

Lucille met him in the living room with a teal bathrobe wound around her stout body, orange curlers in her wiry hair, and a stubborn look on her face. "She'll be mad I called you, but I don't care. That woman needs to rest."

Theo wrapped her up in a tight hug. "I'm glad you did." He handed her a bag. "Here, I got you something."

Lucille peeked in and then grinned. "Oh, you amazing boy." She pinched his cheek. "You know chocolate pie is my favorite."

Lucille was the only person in the world who called his thirty-five-year-old self a boy, but Theo didn't mind. He left her happily eating in the kitchen and followed the sound of the piano.

Georgie Clairmont sat on a bench in front of a baby grand. She was tiny sitting there in her bathrobe, hunched over the keys. Her head, covered in a soft knit beanie that the nurses at the cancer center handed out, was turned away from him. He sat next to her on the bench.

"Lucille called you." It wasn't a question.

"She's worried about you. You need to rest, Georgie."

She finished the notes, letting the music linger until a comfortable silence settled around them.

He handed her the milkshake. "Strawberry. I had them spike it so you could sleep."

A smile crept onto her lined face. "Where's yours? You don't sleep either," she said.

"I don't need it like you do. Besides, I had a drink at the pub with Neal and Charlotte before coming here."

"Neal." A flicker of distaste shadowed her face. "He's working you too hard, just like he did your father." She sniffed. "Do I smell wine?"

"It's a long story."

"Charlotte was there? How is she?"

"She's good. Working hard on the campaign."

"I always hoped you and Charlotte would end up together." Almost absently, her fingers danced over the keys.

"Charlotte's as much a sister as Lieren is," Theo said. It was true; Theo, Grant, and Ford had grown up with Charlotte and teased her like they had teased Lieren, their baby sister. Charlotte was a good friend and a hard worker in the office, but that was all.

"I know." She sighed. "I used to love going out for drinks with your grandfather. I'd order a Manhattan and feel so fancy."

"I'll take you out." Theo grinned. "You can watch pink-haired bartenders throw drinks at me."

Georgie stopped playing and smiled broadly. "Is that what happened tonight? How delightful. Did you deserve it?"

"Of course not," Theo said. "I was the perfect gentleman. And your definition of 'delightful' and mine are very different." Theo nudged the milkshake toward her. "Drink."

Georgie dutifully sipped, one hand dancing lightly over the keys again. "Perfect gentlemen can be perfectly boring, my dear. You never did learn to play piano, did you?"

"Why would I when I could listen to you?"

Georgie leaned her head on his arm. "Because it's fun. Because taking a risk can open up worlds you can't imagine. Sometimes I wish..." she trailed off. "I worry about you, Theodore. You're always so wrapped up in your work, just like your father and your grandfather were. You don't take any time to enjoy life. Your father always said he would when he retired, and he didn't get the chance," she said quietly. "I worry we burdened you with their legacy."

Theo winced at his full name, his father's name. Georgie was the only person he allowed to call him that because he knew what it meant to her. The pain of losing his parents was a constant reminder to him to continue to give everything he had to Northfield.

Theo held her hand gently. The skin was paper-thin. "Georgie, I'm where I want to be. The work I do—it's important to me. I don't need anything else. I'm happy."

"Life is about the chances we take." She set the milkshake down. "I just don't want you to get to be my age and regret not taking any."

"I know you worry, and I appreciate that." Theo squeezed her blue-veined hand gently before grinning. "My only regret is that I won't have any of your wild stories to tell my grandkids one day."

"You could." Her eyes lit up with memories. "We did have good times. I wish you'd find someone and fall in love like your grandfather and I did. Now he's gone, and what do I have left that matters except for all of our beautiful memories? What if you wake up one day and look back on your life, and you don't have that because you gave your best years to your job?"

"Now that's the booze talking. Let's get you to bed before you start campaigning for more great-grandkids," Theo teased. He helped her up, noticing how frail her bones felt.

"I want a whole houseful of them, but you won't stop working long enough to give me any." Georgie stopped and gave him a hard stare. "There's more to life than work, Theodore."

"I'm content, Georgie, but I'd be even better if you would get some rest." He stood and held out his arm. "Let's get you upstairs."

Later, in his home office, Theo replayed Georgie's words while he worked. Since he'd grown up in a family with a strong political legacy, the weight on his shoulders had felt immense at times. The dedication and commitment displayed by his family had instilled in him a sense of duty from a young age, and when his parents died, that responsibility had become more important than ever.

Theo worked hard to make Northfield the kind of place where people wanted to settle down. It wasn't easy work, but he considered it his life's work, and he wanted a shot at four more years. Beckerman had snuck up on him in the polls, but Theo was up for a challenge to his office.

And yet, Georgie's words hung over him as he worked late into the night. He knew he worked too much. For the first time, however, he felt a bone-deep exhaustion as he looked at the stacks of paperwork and mail that had piled up since Kelsey left. He should be sleeping, but lately sleep had been elusive. When he tried, his mind refused to shut off, cycling through tasks and upcoming decisions until he finally gave up and went downstairs to work.

When Ford had brought up Amber's name as a replacement for Kelsey, Theo hadn't really considered it, but now, looking around at the stacks of paperwork on his desk, he wondered if he was making a mistake by not offering the job to her.

Life is about the chances we take.

Solving problems with logic and reason was second nature to him. This one seemed deceptively simple. He needed an assistant. Amber needed a job. It was a gamble, but his grandmother's words repeated in his head. Why not just try it?

Lord knew he needed the help. Why not see if Amber Hart was up for the job?

Chapter Four

"So, you got shit-canned, huh? Nice work." Valentine Monroe, Amber's neighbor, smirked and threw herself onto the couch.

The girl's pitch-black hair hung in limp strands over her face, and her black clothing stood out like a death knell in Amber's colorful apartment. It was early Saturday morning and already sweltering hot with no AC. One more thing she couldn't afford to fix.

"Get out," Amber said mildly. "You're not helping." She sat cross-legged on the floor, surrounded by fabrics and patterns, her fingers deftly picking the stitching out of a swatch of fabric.

Throughout her apartment, various bins and baskets overflowed with scraps of fabrics, jackets, and a shoe collection that made her tingle in her loveliest places.

All of her clothing was thrifted or purchased at deep discount from boutiques. Clothing was the one thing in her life she knew with absolute certainty she was good at. Buying it, designing it, choosing the exact right shade to flatter people—she knew her stuff.

She'd had a fascination with fashion since she was little. How what you wore made a statement about you and how you could change that impression on a whim. It was a creative escape she had held onto from the first time her aunt Rosa brought her a little secondhand Singer sewing machine into their apartment.

She stroked the silky Versace print in her lap. It looked like Frankenstein's monster now with the cuts, but she had an idea to turn it into a cute scarf dress that crisscrossed over her chest and tied at the waist.

"I'm almost eighteen. I can take your spot. Think Killian would hire me?" Valentine asked. Val, her little sister, Holly, and their mom, Sandy, had moved into the apartment next door to Amber's last year.

Amber had met them during one of her volunteer shifts at the Maple Street Center, a temporary shelter for domestic violence survivors. She collected secondhand clothing throughout the year, gave them a wash, and usually added something pretty, before donating them to the women and kids there.

Amber had connected with Sandy and the girls on their first night at the shelter and eventually helped get them their apartment, although she had told no one else that. Sandy was a proud woman, and she was trying her best to make a living and raise the girls.

Amber helped them out as much as she could. It made things tight financially, but she had made it work for almost a year now. Her little setback at work wouldn't change that.

"Nope. We've been over this. Where's Holly?" Amber leaned her head back against the couch and heard the telltale crackle of cellophane. Her stack of overdue bills. When she got home last night, in a fit of temper, she had stuffed them under her couch cushion. Out of sight, out of mind and all that.

With the sun coming in and the scent of bacon wafting up from the downstairs apartment, Amber could almost close her eyes and forget that she had no money and no job. What she would have was $200 in the bank after she paid her rent. As for the loan, she wasn't going to think about where that would come from.

"Why do you care? You're not my family," Valentine sneered. Well, she tried. Her heavy black eyeliner hid some of her glare.

"But I've always wanted a sweet sister just like you," Amber shot back. "We could do each other's hair and stay up all night and talk about each other's crushes."

"You're so weird. And you're way too old to be my sister." Val's nose wrinkled in disgust.

Amber knew there was a cute smattering of freckles hidden under the gobs of makeup on Val's face, but they never saw the light of day. One day, Val would turn into a lovely young woman. Today was not that day.

Dealing with teen angst took her most impressive charm skills, and she wasn't usually successful. Sarcasm tended to work better with Val, anyway.

"Seriously, where's Holly?"

"I left her next to a white van in the parking lot."

Amber glared at her. "Not funny."

Val rolled her eyes. "Relax. She's at Allie's for breakfast. You know your sister's a way better cook than you, right?"

"Thanks, Elvira. So, tell me again about this kid in your AP English class. What's his name?"

Despite the dyed-black hair that Val kept artfully arranged to hide her face, a rosy flush colored her cheeks. "Dylan. He asked me to the Midsummer Night Ball, but I'm not gonna go," she said nonchalantly. "That dance is so lame. Everyone gets drunk and acts stupid."

True, if Amber's own night was any indication. Because the school was so small, Northfield hosted a ball every summer for the entire high school. It was a special night that the town went all out for. The girls got their hair and makeup professionally done and wore designer dresses, while the boys wore tuxedos and rented limos. Amber would never have been able to afford to go, but her date had paid for her ticket, and she made her own dress. No one had been able to tell it wasn't designer.

Unfortunately, it had ended up ripped, and she had walked home, regretting her choices that night.

"I could buy your ticket, if you wanted to go," she said carefully. "And you could wear one of my dresses. I've got more than I know what to do with."

"He already bought the tickets. He works for his dad at some technology company. But maybe I could borrow a dress? If I decide to go, that is." She scowled. "I don't even know if I like him like that. He's so nerdy."

"Ah," Amber said thoughtfully. "Not cool enough."

"Ew. Rude. He's totally nice, and he's so thoughtful..." Val tossed a pillow at Amber. "You did that on purpose."

Amber caught it and propped it behind her back. "Duh. So why don't you want to go out with him?"

"It's weird. He's, like, so nice that I'm scared I'll ruin it." Val picked at her black nail polish. Despite the heat, she wore an oversized hoodie that she had pulled up to her chin like a cocoon as she sat huddled on the couch. "I can be kinda mean." She looked up and glared at Amber. "Don't you dare laugh."

"I wouldn't dare," Amber said solemnly. Val was kind of scary, but Amber knew how much she loved Holly and Sandy. The kid had been through a lot in her seventeen years. She hoped Dylan could recognize that and be patient.

"Whatever. I don't even care."

Ah. The refrain of every teenager. Amber hid a smile while Val got up and opened the fridge.

"Don't you have any real food here?"

"Ramen," Amber said. She let Val escape, recognizing that

behavior too. It was eerie watching Val sometimes. Amber saw so much of herself in Val's stubborn independence.

"I'm still gonna talk to Killian about a job." Val threw herself onto the couch again.

"Your only job is to graduate from high school next month and get into college. And who's going to watch Holly at night, huh?" Amber asked. "Your mom works, and I'll have another job soon." *Hopefully*. "We've talked about this before, Val."

"If I got a job, I could help you guys out." Val's voice dipped, all traces of snark gone. "I know you've been helping my mom out with money. Let me help too."

"You let us worry about that," Amber repeated firmly. "Did you sign up for the summer SAT test yet? What about filling out those college applications I left for you? It's not too late. Colleges save room for late applications."

Val picked at her sleeve. "No. I told you; I don't even know if I want to go to college, and all those applications cost money to send in."

"I told you I'd take care of those. See, I'm making it rain here." She grinned and grabbed a pile of tips from the night before on the coffee table and let them drift down over them, hoping Val would let it go. Amber would get four more jobs if she had to, but she didn't want Val worrying about money.

When the three of them had moved in last year, she'd quickly taken the girls under her wing. Holly was a sweet little angel. Her sister was more like Satan, but Amber had a soft spot for her. Val had a lot of potential, and Amber wasn't going to let her waste it like she had.

"Fine, treat me like a child, but we're not done talking about this," Val said, disgust clearly on her face. "I don't need a college degree to wait tables. It's not like you ever got one."

Amber didn't even flinch. Val could be ruthless, but Amber had been around longer. It took a lot more than mentioning her failed college experience to shake her up. "Oh, I used the rest of your milk," Val called on her way out. "And good luck today. It's hot as balls in your apartment."

Teenagers were fun.

Despite Val's best efforts, Amber knew exactly what was behind her prickly attitude because she had been in that same place plenty of times. Truthfully, she still was.

As soon as she met the three of them, she recognized her own family. Sandy was a good mom, but like Annette, she worked nights, and the girls were on their own enough to get into trouble without someone to watch out for them.

Val was a smart girl, and if she didn't have someone to push her, she was going to end up working a steady stream of odd jobs to pay her rent instead of going to college. Soon the years would pass, and she'd be sitting in a stuffy apartment, jobless and broke at nearly thirty years old, trying to figure out why she felt like she was moving in reverse while everyone else sped by.

Well. That was too depressing to contemplate. Amber half-heartedly picked a few more stitches out before getting up to stretch her back and check the fridge. She peered at the sad-looking assortment of half-empty condiments and an unidentifiable takeout container Johnny had left in her fridge when the doorbell rang.

Expecting Johnny, Amber swung the door open wide and stepped back. "I was just wondering what you left in my fridge —" she said and then stopped short.

Theo stood in her doorway, wearing a pair of silver aviators and a crisp white button-down with slacks, looking every bit as untouchable and remote as last night.

She swung the door closed.

"A morning person, I see," he said, stopping the door with a polished loafer.

"It's way too early to put up with you." She wedged her bare foot against the bottom of the door and sent up a prayer that he couldn't see too much of her shabby apartment.

Theo grinned and tucked the sunglasses in the collar of his shirt. Two undone buttons revealed the strong, tanned column of his neck. His hair, perfectly swept back in place, revealed the sharp contours of his cheekbones and proud nose. A face that probably hadn't seen many closed doors.

"Hello, Amber. May I come in?"

"No," she said, attempting to close the door in his annoying face again. No one needed to look that perfect on a weekend. It wasn't natural. He had probably slept like a baby in a perfectly air-conditioned bedroom. The thought further soured her mood.

Theo's gaze swept over her, assessing. "Nice outfit."

Amber glanced down at her cutoffs and tangerine bikini top with the oversized gold buckle holding the two skimpy triangles together. The top was a touch too small over the girls, but she wasn't naked. Besides, this was her apartment.

"This is a vintage de la Renta." She had stalked the eBay listing forever to win it for a steal at the last possible second. "My AC is broken," she muttered. "What do you want, Mr. Mayor?"

He sighed. Deeply. "Call me Theo. May I come in?"

"Still no."

He looked at her strangely. "I'd like to talk to you."

"About what?"

"I have a proposition for you."

Amber's eyes narrowed as a flashback of other well-suited businessmen with shady offers came to mind. She couldn't help the flicker of disappointment that the mayor was a mere mortal, after all. Somehow, his cool manners and elegant facade had fooled her. "If you're here for some kind of 'special services,' you've got the wrong idea."

A flush crept up his neck. "That's not what I meant," he said stiffly. "I would like to offer you a job."

"Doing what?" Suspicion laced her tone, and she crossed her arms.

"My assistant unexpectedly eloped last week. I need someone to fill her position, and you were highly recommended."

Ah. Now it made sense. "Ford put you up to this?"

Theo nodded once. "Ford suggested that you might be interested."

She thought about it for less than a second. Did she need the cash enough to be at the beck and call of those icy blue eyes all day? "Yeah, no thanks." She started to close the door only to find Theo's foot still wedged at the bottom.

"May I ask why? You are looking for a job after last night's... misfortune. Right?"

Amber narrowed her eyes. "This might come as a shock to you, Mr. Mayor, but not everyone jumps to do your bidding or wants to. I'm not interested in working for you. You've done your duty to Ford. Now you can leave."

"You don't even know what the job entails," Theo said.

"Let me guess, fetching your coffee? Please. I have better things to do than be your glorified maid. The answer's no." Had she served coffee and taken dry cleaning for employers in the past? Absolutely. But the thought of working for the mayor chafed in a way that made her tone sharp.

The scales were already alarmingly tipped in his favor and had been for a long time. Something in his knowing eyes made her feel like he could see all the way inside her, where she didn't even want to look herself. Besides, the last thing he needed was yet another woman at his beck and call. She wasn't that desperate.

"Excuse me," Theo said, looking utterly bored. "I thought

you might be interested, but I can see I was wrong. Good luck on your future endeavors."

Good luck, indeed. She stood in the doorway until the slam of the heavy outside door jarred her, and she jumped.

How ridiculous to find herself staring after a man when she'd spent her entire life making sure she was the one who left first.

Chapter Five

"ARE YOU LOSING WEIGHT?" Lily asked, looking her over critically.

"Yeah, your boobs look smaller," Allie said enviously. The blond cherub in her arms giggled. Sisters. They could be brutal, but Amber loved hers.

Allie, the eldest, and Lily and Evie, the twins, were the youngest, with Amber smack dab in the middle. Out of the four of them, only Allie and Amber had double Ds. A blessing to some but a curse to others who knew about the back pain and unwanted attention they sometimes garnered.

"Boobs," the toddler said loudly. "Boobs!"

It was the grand opening for Lily's new wellness studio, and the entire Hart family had shown up to celebrate Lily's business venture. Amber had spent the week since being fired helping Lily put the finishing touches on the studio, and it looked fantastic.

The location was perfect, right on Main Street, next to Morning Glory Bakery. The perfect place for drawing people and then getting them to stay to work off the divine chocolate croissants from next door with dance and yoga classes. Amber's stomach growled. Her sweet tooth had been sorely deprived this week.

Amber adjusted the slightly too-loose Versace scarf dress that had fit her perfectly the week before when she measured and cut it. A week-long diet of ramen noodles and bananas would do that to you. The diet of someone with a mountain of overdue bills.

She had spent a hot, sleepless week working on the studio's opening during the day and job searching in the evenings when it was too hot to sleep. At the moment, she was feeling the effects of little sleep and too much stress.

It was fine. Everything was *fine*. So what if she had stopped getting her mail because she didn't want to see any more overdue bills? Who cared if she hit the ignore button on her phone once a day for the unknown number she suspected was perky Dana from the debt collections agency? And she didn't even want to think of what she'd have to sell to come up with the money for Val's college applications. Amber had been in tighter situations before and come out on top.

But she was really tired of bananas.

Allie pressed a kiss to her daughter's blond curls. Amber adored all her nieces and nephews, of course, but Savannah had a special place in her heart. Something about the mischievous twinkle in her eyes and how fiercely she protected her sister, Tessa, who was gentler, like her mother.

Savannah also looked like a ragamuffin all the time. Her curly blond hair refused to be tamed, and her purple princess dress had dirt streaks on it. Amber gently held her chin and wiped a smudge of frosting off her round cheek. "Savvie, tell your daddy you want another sissy or brother, okay?"

"'Kay," Savvie said, happily wedging another bite of pastry in her mouth.

"Tell Auntie Amber you want a cousin next," Allie said, giving her sister the eye.

"Sorry, kid," Amber laughed. "I can't even keep a house-plant alive."

Allie shifted the little girl higher on her hip and pinned her with a stare. "Speaking of staying alive, how's the job search going?"

"No one is hiring right now. All the college kids came back for the summer and took the serving jobs. I emailed my resume to a temp agency, but I haven't heard back. I'm so screwed," Amber said.

"Skooed."

"No, baby, that's a rude word," Allie murmured. "Maybe this will be good for you, Am," she said.

"Did you miss the part where I said I was fired? What's so good about that?" Amber winced. "Fired" was such a harsh word. She liked to think it was simply a break. An indefinite one. Surely Killian would call her and offer her job back. Who was taking her double shifts? She was the best bartender he had, besides Simone, who never sang karaoke on the bar. Fine, maybe Simone had an edge. Still, Amber was a huge part of the pub. Everyone knew that. Didn't Killian miss her?

"Maybe this could be a good thing," Allie said gently. "You've been working yourself ragged taking on all these odd jobs. Maybe you take this chance and go back to school or find something with benefits that makes you happy."

Amber let out a bitter laugh. "Happy? Every time I get close to happy, I mess it up. It's like I'm programmed to self-destruct." And then, because that truth cut so sharply to the bone, she deflected. "I still think you should get a stripper pole in here, Lily. That's way more fun than yoga."

"I don't know how to use one," Lily said, adjusting one side of the wide gold ribbon that hung between the door frames. Evie stood on the other side, fluffing the tie.

Evie and Lily were so identical that even their family members sometimes couldn't tell them apart. Luckily, Evie regularly wore a kickass collection of glasses to complement her outfits. Amber wasn't even sure if she needed them, but Evie worked as the librarian at the Northfield Library, and it helped lend her some gravitas, she said. Today's choice was a bold, tortoiseshell cat-eye.

In a little while, the mayor and a local news crew would be here to cut the ribbon and officially open the doors of Pure Bliss Wellness Studio.

At the thought of seeing Theo again, tension coursed through her. Working for him would be a disaster on both their ends, but there was a small part of her that regretted turning him down so quickly. Maybe it was the part of her that was growling—her stomach didn't always agree with her impulsiveness.

"I could teach you how to pole dance," Amber said. "I used to clean this lady's house who had one in her basement. She thought it was a laundry hanging pole. We looked up tutorials and learned how to use it." Amber flexed her arm. "Incredible workout."

"I don't think the mayor would appreciate a stripper pole on Main Street," Evie, ever the most pragmatic sister, chimed in.

Amber snorted. "He wouldn't know what to do with a stripper if one sat right on his lap. Besides, I'm thinking about starting up my dog-walking business again."

Allie's eyebrows shot up. "The one you almost got arrested over?"

"I was *rescuing* that dog," Amber said defensively. "Mrs. Bovenzi would roll over in her grave if she knew her loser son was mistreating Puddin' like that." She'd had a few choice words for the dumbass who left the pampered little dog outside all winter long, forcing Sheriff Rush Callahan to step in intervene between them. No biggie.

"You know you could have your old job back with Mom if you wanted it," Allie said carefully. "She always says your designs for her clients were the most creative she had ever seen."

"Creative." Amber snorted. "Her clients only wanted designs that looked like a doctor's waiting room. They hated my ideas."

Amber's relationship with her mother, Annette, was complex. Annette was the epitome of self-made success, while Amber was... not.

For years, Annette juggled work and school and the demands of starting her own business, leaving the girls with their aunts or eventually on their own when Allie and Amber were older. It had been hard on them all, but they made it, and it paid off. Annette's design firm was wildly successful, and she had a reputation as a savvy businesswoman now.

When Amber dropped out of college, Annette had offered her a job at her design firm. Decorating other people's homes quickly bored her, despite it being a good job. Annette's wealthy clientele didn't appreciate her colorful designs, anyway.

Amber had quit to save Annette from letting her go. She would rather not eat for a year than accept her mother's charity job, but it still chafed that she was the only one in her family of women who couldn't seem to get her life together.

"You're as proud as she is. Too proud. She would help you in a heartbeat. She loves you, Amber. All she wants is for you to find what makes you happy."

Amber smiled brightly. "I don't need any help."

"What about selling your clothing?" Allie asked. "I did some research on how to get started. You could ask some boutiques to take your designs on consignment."

"Sell my clothes?" she asked, shocked to her core. She had been collecting her wardrobe for years, searching out vintage finds online and browsing boutiques for those one-of-a-kind-pieces that felt like winning the lottery when she finally found them.

"No," Allie said calmly. "Sell the ones you design and make."

"That's just a hobby." Amber let out a laugh. "Nobody makes money in the real world selling clothes."

"You could." The conviction in Allie's voice was humbling. "You have so much talent with your designs and the way you create. I want to see you use it."

"That's hysterical. Those are just for fun." Amber said firmly. Talking about her designs always made her feel self-conscious. Her designs were the one good thing that she hadn't messed up in her life. All the odd jobs, all the business ideas, the plans—they had all fallen through. She refused to let the one thing she was actually passionate about out into the world only to see it fail like all of her other ideas. "Besides, I have a job offer I'm considering." Shoot. She hadn't meant to tell anyone about that, but as usual, her mouth moved faster than her brain.

"Really? Where?" Evie asked.

"At the mayor's office," Amber said with a confidence she didn't feel.

"Did Ford put in a good word for you with the mayor?" Allie asked.

"To do what?" Lily asked.

Amber looked around and gestured for Lily and Evie to come closer. "The mayor likes happy endings in his office." She stage-whispered it, watching Evie and Lily's eyes widen with shock. "Two hundred for each one." She nodded seriously. "I'm considering it."

"That dirty bast—" Evie sputtered while Lily stood frozen, her wide eyes wide with shock.

Amber bent double, laughing so hard her empty stomach protested. "You guys, your faces," she howled.

"Not funny, Amber. I was ready to go out there and tear him to shreds when he got here." Lily whispered furiously, two spots of bright red on her cheeks.

"I love you two," Amber said. She finally straightened up and wiped her eyes. "No, he needs an assistant, but I'd never work for such a tight-ass."

"The mayor does have a tight ass," Evie said, adjusting her glasses and admiring it from the window.

Amber peeked out, and sure enough, Northfield's golden boy had arrived for the ribbon cutting.

Dressed in his usual tailored suit despite the heat, with a pair of aviators tucked into his crisp white collar, the mayor looked like a *GQ* ad come to life out there with mere hot, sticky mortals. Judging from the crowd of women surrounding him, she wasn't the only one to think so. He was taller and broader than most of the surrounding people, and as she watched him talk, his white teeth flashed in a warm smile that few could resist. She liked to think she was immune.

"Is Tucker coming?" Amber asked.

"He's really busy and traveling for work a lot, so I don't think so," Lily said, avoiding Amber's eyes.

Amber caught Evie's eye skeptically, but they held their tongues for once. Lily had enough going on today.

Tucker, Lily's boyfriend, was notorious for not showing up. Amber privately thought Lily could do a whole lot better, but he seemed to make her happy.

"We're ready," Annette said, coming from the kitchen in an ultra-chic navy sheath dress, complete with a toddler on her hip. Tessa, her hair in a neat pink bow, pointed at the double strand of wickedly expensive South Sea pearls wound around Annette's neck. "You want to wear Mimi's pearls, sweet girl?"

Annette whipped them off as if they were plastic and handed them to the little girl, while Amber watched in amusement. Annette might have had to give up many of the softer moments with her girls in order to provide for her family, but she was making up for lost time with her grandkids. She would never be a stereotypical grandma, but there wasn't a doubt in anyone's mind that she loved her family.

"I expected a call this week." Annette's soft smile faded, and she fixed Amber with a stare.

"Been busy, Mom," Amber said. "Places to go, people to see."

"No job yet?" Annette asked.

"I'm taking my time. There's no rush," Amber said with more bravado than she felt. Annette had a way of looking right past her flippant responses that always made Amber feel like she was a teenager lying about her grades again.

"We'll talk at Sunday dinner," Annette said, and Amber held in a sigh. She was not looking forward to Sunday dinner for once. All the aunts and extended family would be there to hear about her latest failure. You would think she was used to being the black sheep in her family, but it was getting old.

"Come on, let's go find Daddy. He's building the balloon arch for Aunt Lily." Allie headed back toward the mini kitchen in the back, where the aunts were yelling at each other about how to set up the refreshments. Ah. Family.

Lily didn't look like she was listening. "I don't think he's going to make it." She peered nervously out the front windows at Main Street.

Amber tugged her away and wrapped an arm around her. "The studio looks beautiful, Lils. We're all so proud of you."

"Thank you. I couldn't have done it without all of you," Lily said, adjusting her ballerina bun. Lily and Evie were the only two in the family with their dad's fair skin and clear green eyes, while the rest of the Hart women took after Annette's Italian side. At least, that was what Amber assumed. Annette never talked about their dad, and Amber didn't blame her.

"I think those bracelets you made to hand out are going to be a big hit," Evie said, examining one of the colorful beaded bracelets. Each one had the studio's name and colors.

"Come on," Amber said, threading her arm through Lily's. "Let's open your new studio."

In the surge of family and friends through the door, Amber lost Lily in the crowd. She let herself fall back and watched as Lily took her place at the top of the steps. Pride and admiration mixed with a bit of sadness swelled in her until she had to swallow hard around the knot.

Seeing Lily make her dreams come true put her own life in stark contrast. Her future had always been less defined. Aimless. Murky, even, especially when compared to all the ultra-successful, driven women in her family. She couldn't help but wonder if that would ever change.

SHE SNUCK under the ribbon just as Mrs. Dubois, the mayor's secretary, handed Theo the oversized scissors. It was standing room only at the top of the steep stairs, with everyone crowded around to get their first peek inside the studio. Someone jostled her for a better view, and Amber found herself wedged in between Theo and the building.

Despite the warm day, Theo's customary suit still looked fresh while everyone else, including her, was battling with the humidity. Her dress didn't have much fabric to it, but what there was stuck to her limply. Not so for the mayor. Even his short, dark hair was tamed into submission, as if even Mother Nature didn't dare touch him. The mayor emanated a confidence that relied on more than her own flimsy bravado. She idly admired the back of his tanned neck and the outline of his muscular arms in his suit and wondered what it must feel like to have everything under control.

As if she said it aloud, Theo turned toward her, causing her to lean back farther or be squished by his bulk. She winced when the rough brick building cut into her bare back.

"Excuse me," Theo murmured, surprise on his face when he saw it was her. A large, warm hand settled on her waist and drew her gently away from the wall, and a jolt went through her at the heat. She rather thought his hands would be cold, considering the cool, controlled demeanor he projected.

She was close enough to catch the subtle, expensive scent of his cologne. Theo studied her for a brief second, his gaze dipping to her deep cleavage on display, down to her feet in red cowboy boots, and back up without expression.

Once again, it felt like he had taken her measure and found her wanting. Irritation and an undeniable spark of something else flared through her hotly.

"Us peons are just happy to bask in your shadow, Mr. Mayor," she retorted. To her surprise, the corners of Theo's generous mouth curved, revealing a set of dimples that completely transformed him.

Theo Clairmont had *dimples*.

Wicked, oh-so-appealing dimples.

It really was a shame that he was such a dud because the mayor did hot, melty things to her insides, and he had since she'd been a rebellious teenager and he a twenty-five-year-old man.

Amber was no stranger to men. She had dated enough to recognize that deep, hot pool of desire that swelled whenever she got close to Theo. She recognized attraction for what it was, a simple chemical reaction. She was smart enough to know that Theo Clairmont was just that: red-hot lust, the kind that made her shift slightly just to feel the silky slide of fabric on her body and the answering response deep in her body. She didn't even like the man. He made her feel strangely exposed and altogether not like herself.

And yet... she couldn't help but wonder what he was like in bed.

She'd bet money he was coolly polite. *May I please fuck you now?*

She pictured him, icy and restrained, even in the throes of passion. Probably wouldn't dream of anything so impolite as bending a woman over a desk and fucking her senseless. The kind of sex that made you see stars.

The mayor struck her more as the roses-and-candlelight type, who liked things neatly arranged on a pristine bed. Boring and vanilla. She made it a habit to steer clear of that type. Those men usually craved the aftermath: the soft, intimate whispers under the sheets afterward, maybe a bite to eat, and getting to know each other.

Her tastes leaned more toward the thrill of the moment, the dizzying, electrifying excitement, rather than the unveiling after. She didn't stick around for that.

While Theo did his official mayor thing, Amber stood behind him and idly surveyed the crowd. All the usuals were there. Other business owners, including her mother, whose studio was also on Main Street, and two of her aunts, who owned a florist shop close by, along with curious locals and some reporters having a slow news day, all crowded onto the steps to see the sainted mayor.

She recalled a recent news story that had Theo trailing behind another candidate, but looking at him now, she couldn't imagine why. He certainly looked the part, and she knew from listening in on conversations at the pub that the fire and police departments respected him. Even Cap, who didn't play political favorites, had a grudging respect for the mayor's work ethic.

Her stomach growled quietly, and just as she thought no one heard, Theo turned his head imperceptibly to meet her gaze. This close, she could see that the tiny laugh lines next to his blue eyes were paler, as if he spent a lot of time in the sun. That haughty eyebrow skyrocketed. She *hated* that eyebrow.

So she yawned. Loudly. "Oops. Excuse me."

Someone laughed in the crowd. Theo didn't miss a beat in his speech, but his eyebrow stayed down, so she figured they were even on her mental scoreboard.

Amber felt a little guilty admitting it, but the town politics had never interested her very much before. Every November, she did her duty and voted for Theo and his father before him, although she would never, ever admit that to him. When Amber was little, Annette took her and her sisters on a trip to the Mount Hope Cemetery in Rochester every year. They visited Susan B. Anthony's grave and placed their "I voted" stickers on her tombstone to show support for the pioneer. It was a little macabre, sure, but Annette treated them all to breakfast after at a greasy-spoon diner with the best chocolate-chip pancakes on earth.

Mmm. Chocolate. She could almost taste the little morsels melting in her mouth. Tomorrow was Sunday dinner at Annette's with the entire family. Despite being sick to death of ramen, she would probably have to make up some excuse not to go. She really couldn't stand talking about another failure on her résumé with her family giving her pitying looks. *Poor Amber, she lost another job.* Well-meaning, but she was so very tired of hearing it. She was so very tired of *living* it.

It was enough to sink her into a deep depression, so she

looked around at the crowd instead and caught sight of Savannah toddling like a drunken sailor toward the edge of the stairs. Someone's frantic whisper, "Savvie, no, come back," warned her, but the little girl let out a mischievous giggle, took another step, and tumbled in slow motion headfirst down the stairs. Amber's heart leaped to her throat while she watched, frozen in horror, and too far away to stop her.

Theo's arm shot out and gripped Savannah's chubby little ankle just as she went ass over teakettle in her princess dress.

The crowd gasped then cheered, and Amber heard the telltale clicks of cameras and phones in the audience. Theo, still gingerly holding a now-laughing Savannah, bent to put her down. He turned back to the mic as if nothing had happened.

Amber looked around in disbelief. Where was his team? This was the perfect PR moment, and Theo was just going to waste it? One would think he got his position on good looks alone because it definitely wasn't his marketing skills, she thought in disgust. No one wanted to hear about the history of the building when there was drama to see.

Before thinking too much about it, she jumped into action, sweeping down to lift Savannah back up. "Hi, Savvie. Want to smile big for the camera?" she whispered, pointing at the news camera. Savvie's eyes lit up. Her favorite thing in the world was stealing everyone's phones and taking selfies whenever she could, like the little diva she was.

"Take her and smile," Amber whispered, gently placing Savanna into Theo's arms again. Very muscly arms, she couldn't help but notice.

The little imp looked up at the man holding her and patted his cheek. "S'mile," she demanded, and Theo did what any self-respecting man would do—he smiled, dimples and all.

Oh, yeah. *That* was the look that would win him the election.

Impulsively, she reached up and messed up his hair. Not a lot, just a few pieces that curled over his forehead and made him look appealing tousled. Approachable. Less *GQ*, more hot guy next door. Yummy.

"Mr. Mayor, over here!" *Click.*

"Smile over here, Mayor!" *Click. Click.*

"Did you see him save that baby?" *Click.*

Amber sat back and watched smugly. She did have a knack for putting people in their best light.

"That was clever," Lily murmured from beside her.

Amber shrugged. "It's good publicity for your studio too." But something had shifted in the instant she had decided to orchestrate the moment. It felt good. She had known exactly what to do. Maybe working for the mayor wasn't quite as crazy of an idea as she thought. Maybe he needed her and didn't know it?

Besides, Sunday dinner was looming, and the thought of facing her family without a plan made her queasy.

The next half hour of mingling and celebrating flew by. Every time Amber spotted Theo, people surrounded him, vying for his attention. She watched for her opportunity for a while, noticing that Theo took his time listening to every single person who waited to talk to him.

Eventually, she gave up and busied herself cleaning up and networking with moms and kids looking for dance classes. Amber made sure they all left with a brochure and a bracelet, which turned out to be a huge hit with the kids.

She looked again for Theo, but seeing him engaged with a young family, Amber grabbed a brownie and snuck away to Lily's office to wolf it down in peace. Double chocolate with a chocolate ganache frosting, her favorite. She was leaning on the desk, licking the last bit off her fingers , when someone knocked.

"Door's open," she called.

Theo walked in, looking just as pristine as when the event started. She self-consciously smoothed back her flyaway hairs. When she realized what she was doing, she quickly crossed her legs, draped herself across the desk, and purred, "You found me. Take me, I'm yours, big boy."

"I came to say thank you," he said stiffly.

Amber straightened up. "Relax, Mr. Mayor," she grumbled, rubbing her ribs where Lily's stapler had jammed into her. "I'm just messing with you."

"I think you missed your calling," he said, strolling into the office with his hands in his pockets and eyeing the desk.

"As what? A slutty secretary?" She snorted. "Been there, done that."

Theo looked at her strangely. "I was thinking more along the lines of the boss."

Oh. "Nah, too many rules to follow."

Theo walked closer. "You have something right..." He pointed at her chin.

"What? Here?" Amber swiped at her face self-consciously. Seriously, why did this man always make her feel so awkward? She dug deep for Marilyn. "Why don't you show me?" she purred, blinking up at him.

Theo held her chin in his hand, much as she had Savannah's earlier, and inspected her mouth closely. He was so close she could have leaned forward and brushed against his chest. His fingers were firm on her chin. She inhaled deeply. Leather and sandalwood and man. It was surprisingly earthy and entirely delicious. Amber's breath stuttered. "Chocolate," he said.

Amber jerked her chin away. "I was eating a brownie," she muttered. "You know, chocolate and caffeine? How normal people get through the day."

Theo let go of her chin and stepped back, and she could breathe normally again. "I wanted to thank you for earlier."

"You're welcome. It was too good of an opportunity to pass up." She shrugged, pleased in spite of herself. "You really do need help. That was a perfect PR moment, and you almost blew it."

"The job is still open." He raised an eyebrow. "Would you like it?"

She didn't even hesitate. "Yes, but I have conditions."

Theo nodded. "I assumed you would. Name them."

"I want my first two weeks' pay on my first day." That would cover Val's college applications, the SAT test, and anything else she would need as well as Amber's late bills, and she could put some money down for the collection agency.

"What? Why? That's absurd. We're a government office. I can't just pay you up front."

"So you can't change your mind and fire me before then."

"Fine." The twitching of his eyelid fascinated Amber. The cool, calm, and collected mayor did get hot and bothered, just not by the usual means. "Anything else?"

"Yes." She thought. "I want a... a bonus if you're reelected." Amber's tone was firm, but she was shaking inside. Now she was just poking the bear. "A thousand dollars."

"Done."

Amber's jaw dropped. "D-done? You agree to pay me a grand in November?"

He smiled slightly, no dimples in sight. "I would have offered you more. Next time, start higher." He stepped back and straightened his immaculate tie. "Are we done?"

She narrowed her eyes. "One more thing: I don't cook, so don't get any ideas."

Theo paused on his way to the door. "I very much doubt you have anything I would want to eat. Is there anything else?"

Amber smiled slowly. "This is going to be so much fun."

Theo sighed. "That's exactly what I'm afraid of."

Chapter Six

On Monday morning, Amber rang the doorbell of Theo's house and tried not to fidget. Theo had asked her to meet him at his house at eight o'clock sharp because he had an early meeting and wasn't going straight to the office.

She checked her watch impatiently. She was only a few minutes late, but she was prepared to explain that it was her car's fault.

Johnny had managed to get her started again, but Betty, as she affectionately called her car, had done that sickly sputter thing again this morning when she started her. She wasn't that old, but she had been a lemon since the day Amber bought her. Amber was sure she needed something in her engine replaced.

She lifted her hand to knock on the door again.

"You're late."

She jumped and turned around to look at the man who had snuck up behind her. And continued to look. Theo stood before her, bare chested and panting slightly. It figured the mayor was a runner. One of her least favorite things to do. What was the point of running if no one was chasing you? She could, however, appreciate the sight in front of her. From the neck down, perhaps, to avoid the scowl on his face.

The early-morning humid air must be to blame for the sudden breathy catch in her throat. The mayor was more... undressed than she had ever seen him before. His hair was damp and curled messily down over his forehead. He was shirtless and *oh, my*. She stopped there for a long moment to appreciate the sight.

Fine, dark hair covered his broad chest, tempting her fingers to touch. His waist was narrow, his stomach tight with muscle, leading down to a furrow of dark hair that disappeared into shorts that slung low from his hips. Long, powerful thighs, tight with muscle, stood slightly spread in front of her. His lack of a suit exposed a raw masculinity that made him seem larger and rougher than she was used to. *Gimme*.

"Are you done?" he asked with that one arrogant eyebrow arched, crashing her back down to reality.

Nice to look at, maybe, but still the same arrogant, entitled man.

"Look who's decided to grace me with his presence. And here I thought I was the late one," she said.

"My day starts at nine. Yours starts at eight. It's eight fifteen."

"Sorry, boss," she said unapologetically. "Betty was being fussy." She nodded toward her car in the driveway. It wasn't lost on her how out of place her trusty little red Mazda was in Theo's driveway. Theo's home was more of a residence.

The tall Victorian, with gables, trim, and elegant windows, seemed like it was from another time. Yeah, he would never see the inside of her apartment with her secondhand furniture. That they were from different worlds had never been so apparent.

Amber wasn't usually self-conscious about her upbringing

in Cedarwood Village, but standing in front of Theo's house gave her a long-forgotten twinge of discomfort. She lifted her chin and raised her own eyebrow in a haughty impression to even them up.

Theo gave her an unreadable look and reached around her to open the door. She followed him into the foyer. Her heels had seemed like a good idea this morning. She always forgot that they were more for sitting pretty than for following cranky men around rambling old Victorian houses.

The fast clicks echoed on the shiny wood floors all the way to the back of the house, where French doors let out to a stone patio that held a hot tub under a pergola. A quick impression of neat rooms filled with tasteful furniture—simple, expensive, and not a thing out of place. What else had she expected? "Nice place you got here, Mr. Mayor. Do you work from home often? 'Cause I could get used to this," Amber said.

"Some days. This is my home office." He led her into a room closed off by glass French doors and handed her a stack of mail. "Start with this. Open everything and sort it into piles. I'm going to shower. I'll be down shortly. Take messages if anyone calls."

"Got it, boss. Need any help washing your back, give me a shout." She smiled up at him innocently.

"Inappropriate," he called back, and Amber grinned. This was going to be fun. Lord knew she had had worse jobs in the past.

She looked around the office space. It was more of a library with a desk, all done in dark wood and elegant gray with an oversized desk by the window. She settled herself in the leather chair and got comfortable.

Okay, mail. She could totally do this. She had plenty of experience in an office setting, although it wasn't her favorite place to work. She much preferred jobs where she could use her creativity, but beggars couldn't be choosers.

Unfortunately, sorting Theo's mail took her only a few minutes. He had several boring events coming up, which she put aside, and bills that she sorted by due date. She looked for any juicy subscriptions to porn, but from what she could tell, Theo's social life consisted of golf tee times, boring town budget meetings, and a long-running breakfast date with his grandma.

With the mail sorted, she wandered over to look at the framed pictures on the wall. In many of the photos, Theo was with his father or what she assumed was his grandfather from the resemblance. Both men were tall and dark and aristocratic in their three-piece suits. In every one, Theo had a serious look on his face.

She poked around the desk for a few minutes. Not a thing out of place. She shifted the stack of papers on his desk an inch to the right, just to be perverse.

"If you're done snooping, you can follow me." Theo appeared, buttoned and tied to perfection again in a charcoal suit and tie. He led her to a modern chef's kitchen that could fit her entire apartment.

"Sit there." He pointed at the massive marble island with barstools.

She headed toward the counter instead, just to be contrary, but the bonus check floated in front of her eyes, and she took a sharp right toward the island instead to try to wiggle up onto the stool. Her pencil skirt was mighty tight around her knees.

Theo paused in the middle of taking out a blender. "That doesn't look very..." He waved vaguely toward her. "Comfortable," he finally said.

"Comfort's overrated." Amber smoothed her hand over the slim white column of her skirt. She had paired it with a red off-the-shoulder blouse for a Marilyn office vibe. "I thought you'd appreciate the effort," she said. Unlike her, Theo kept his eyes above her neck. Of course he did.

"You'll break your neck in those heels," Theo said finally.

Amber smiled. "These old things? They're practically slippers," she lied, knowing full well the four-inch black patent leather heels with the darling ankle strap were anything but comfortable.

She eyed a package of kale as Theo started adding ingredients to the blender. "Don't tell me you're one of those people who drinks green juice?"

He looked down pointedly at the assortment of kale, green apples, and celery on the counter. "Would you like one?" he asked politely.

She hopped off the stool to look suspiciously at the various bags and jars on the counter. Her stomach rumbled, reminding her that she hadn't eaten yet.

"Not only are you late, you didn't eat? Don't you know breakfast is the most important meal of the day?"

"No, thanks." She dug around in her hobo bag for the package she had tossed in there a few weeks ago. "Here," she said. "I've got muffins."

Theo's lip curled. "You're eating that for breakfast?"

Amber took a bite of the mini muffin and moaned. Spongy, cakey deliciousness. Maybe a little stale, but these things never went bad. That was the beauty of them. "Muffins?" she said around a mouthful. "You know. The breakfast food?"

"You mean those preservative-packed chemical shit storms? No, thanks. I'd rather eat something that doesn't have a shelf life longer than my car."

"Oh, lighten up. This is the breakfast of champions." She grinned and waved the half-eaten muffin under his nose.

"Thank you, no." He turned around and started to make his concoction.

Amber hiked herself onto the counter next to him.

"Do you mind?" he asked.

"I like to watch," she said, flaking off a blue spot from her muffin before she popped the rest in her mouth. She really hoped it was a blueberry and not mold. "So, what's on the agenda?"

"I have an interview at ten with *CityScape* magazine," he said, pouring a thick, gelatinous mass of green slime into a glass.

The sight of his tanned forearm flexing distracted her. His shirtsleeves were rolled back, exposing the gold-tipped hair and heavy gold watch on his wrist. A hint of heat flared. *Down, girl.*

"And a Zoom call before that."

"I'd probably be a grouch if I started my day like that too," she said.

"This is me on a good day," he said dryly. "There's still time to quit."

"I'm not a quitter, Mr. Mayor." She slid off the counter and beamed up at him. "Your life is going to be so organized you won't even recognize it."

"That's what I'm afraid of." He sighed and held out a set of keys. "Meet me in the garage."

"I get to drive?" she asked hopefully. No way was she going to get that lucky. Betty was cute and mostly reliable and all but boring as hell to drive.

"Consider it a necessity. I need to take a call, and I'd rather not break the law."

"And we both know you're a rule follower, aren't you?" She made grabby hands. "Give 'em to Mama."

She made sure to put some extra oomph in her step on her way to the garage. She rather liked the sound of her heels making noise in the silent house.

～

～

His workday hadn't even started, and he was already regretting hiring her. Ford owed him big-time. He did not have time to be distracted by the bit of fluff trying to wiggle her butt into the car and hiking her skirt up her smooth, tanned thighs.

When he first saw her at his door this morning, he had stopped in his tracks and stared at her while she had her back turned, knocking on his door. She was... outrageous. All her curves encased in that tight white skirt and red top designed to draw attention to her bare shoulders. Some kind of knot caught up her cotton-candy hair with pieces tumbling around her face. He had the strangest desire to see if the pink strands were as soft as they looked. And then there were the silly, strappy heels. Theo was gone for a gorgeous pair of legs in high heels. He knew hiring her was a terrible idea.

"Get in, loser! We've got places to go," she yelled and then slammed the door closed.

He opened the door. And held out his hand for the keys.

"Kidding, boss, kidding. It's from *Mean Girls*. You know?" She blinked up at him, all innocent and sweet, but he knew better.

He crossed his arms and glared.

She hiked her chin and glared right back.

"Okay, okay. I get it," she finally said, seeming to weigh her options. "You're not a movie-quote guy. I'm sorry."

Theo wasn't fooled for a second. This woman was the most impulsive, reckless woman he had ever met, and it wasn't a compliment. He was going to be late for two meetings if he didn't give over the keys, which he did reluctantly.

She turned to him. "It's a really funny movie where—"

"Just drive," he snapped. The less they talked, the easier it would be to fire her. Theo had no doubt that was going to happen. There was no way she could handle all that the job entailed, but at least he could tell Ford he tried with a clear conscience.

"So, where to, boss man?"

"My name is Theo. Not Mr. Mayor. Not Boss or Boss Man," he gritted out. "Just Theo." He could have sworn he heard her mutter "boss hole," but he let it go. "We're meeting a reporter at the Red Lounge for an interview at nine thirty." He was already setting up his laptop for the first call of the day. "I have to take an important call right now. I programmed the address into the navigation system already. Just get us there on time, please." He put in his earbuds and straightened his tie. The governor of New York was an old friend of his father's. He had scheduled a video call to talk about Theo's future after the election.

With another distracting wiggle, she hiked her skirt up to mid-thigh to drive, and Theo's concentration went out the window. The rhythmic play of muscles as she sped up drew his eyes back to that smooth expanse until he was furious with himself. Since when did a fantastic pair of legs distract him from his work?

Through sheer force of will, Theo dragged his eyes away in time to assure the governor that he would win the election and join him in the city to strategize his next political move. The governor had a few choice things to say about the latest polls. Theo did his best to assure him he would do everything in his power to change that in the coming weeks.

"Sounded intense." She glanced over at him curiously when he disconnected. "This Beckerman guy's creeping up on you in the polls, huh?"

"A healthy democracy thrives on diversity," Theo said stiffly.

"Sounds thrilling," she said, sounding anything but thrilled. "Do you ever do anything just for fun, or is it all work and no play with you?" She hit the button to roll down the window and held out her hand in the oncoming wind. "Do you feel that?" she shouted over the wind. "Isn't it wild?"

"Slow down," he snapped. "The speed limit's forty-five." They were on a stretch of road leading toward the outskirts of town, heading into downtown Rochester. Theo knew from experience there was a small hill that could make a car catch air if you were going too fast. "You're going to get us pulled over."

"No, it's not. It's sixty-five," Amber laughed. "I know this road like the back of my hand." She looked over at him, her hair whipping wildly around, her full lips curving, and her skirt inching higher until Theo caught a glimpse of blue panties. She looked so alive in that moment that Theo found himself staring.

The hill was just ahead, and the low purr of the engine let him know she was speeding up. "Dammit! Slow down." The Mercedes took the hill lightly, catching air for a long, weightless moment that flipped his stomach and reminded him of roller coasters he had ridden as a child, until the car hit the ground hard enough to jar his teeth.

He shot forward and instinctively reached over to grip her thigh, hard, steadying her. The muscles jerked, and she turned to look at him, exhilaration and laughter bubbling from her. Theo's breath caught at the look there. His hand still gripped her thigh.

"Wasn't that fun?" she asked, grinning at him until flashing lights in the rearview mirror cut her off.

"Fuck." Theo swore, pulling back his hand as if he'd touched fire.

"Relax. It's fine. You're gonna pop a blood vessel if you keep it up."

"Relax?" He bit out. "Did you miss the conversation I just had with the governor of New York about not making any waves before the election?" But she wasn't listening. She was waving at the officer. He'd give it until tonight before this was all over social media.

"Hi, Ben," she called. "I'm so sorry," she said, sweeter than any other time Theo had heard her. She pushed her hair out of her eyes and bit her plump bottom lip.

Ben, who looked all of twenty years old, grinned down at her appreciatively.

Unreal. Theo's mood soured even more.

"Hi, Amber." The officer whistled. "Sweet car. This yours?"

"I wish," she purred. "This is my friend's car, but he let me drive it. I got a little carried away. Sorry about that."

Theo leaned around her, and the stupid grin on Ben's face faded. "I'm sorry about that, Officer," Theo started, but Ben wasn't paying attention.

"Yeah, it's fine," he nodded at Theo and leaned his elbows on the window to talk to Amber. "You know how you told me not to keep calling Delaney?" he asked Amber. "You said chicks like it when we give them some space to miss us? Well, I took your advice, and it worked! She called me this morning, and we're going out later this week." He beamed at her. Theo tapped his finger impatiently. No one noticed.

"What a lucky girl she is!" Amber said. She patted his cheek. "You make sure to bring her flowers."

"I will. Thanks a lot, Amber. Hey, we miss you over at the pub, you know. A bunch of the guys told Killian he was a dick for firing you. Everyone knows karaoke is your thing."

Amber sighed. "I miss you boys too. But I have a new job with the mayor." She leaned back, and for the first time, recognition showed on the kid's face.

"No shit. Hey, you sign my paycheck," he said. "Cool. Thanks for approving that raise. Okay, well, don't go so fast next time. It's not safe." He leaned in and whispered something in Amber's ear that Theo didn't catch. "See ya, Mr. Mayor." He tapped twice on the hood of the car and loped back to his cruiser.

Amber opened her mouth, but Theo cut her off. "Don't say a word."

And she didn't. All the way up until she parked the car in front of the restaurant. "My lord, we have arrived," she said with a flourish of her hand. A grin teased the corner of her mouth.

Theo's patience snapped. "You think this is a joke? This is amusing to you? This is my career at stake. I know that means nothing to you, but this is important to me." He took a deep breath. "Look, just... try to take this job seriously, please." He got out of the car and slammed the door. And for once in his life, he didn't help a woman out of the car.

Inside, the lounge was quiet. Small groups of guests in suits sat around the lobby area, talking quietly. Servers milled around, getting ready for the lunch rush, polishing silverware, while a bartender wiped down the bar.

The calm was soothing after the wild ride getting there. Sitting on the black leather couch in the middle of the lobby was his second meeting of the day, Pippa Shelton. He took a deep breath and smiled.

"I'm sorry I'm late," he said, leaning in to kiss the cheek she lifted. "We ran into some traffic," he murmured.

"It seems I'm destined to wait for you, Theo," she said, just as intimately, smiling into his eyes. Theo knew that smile. He'd tasted it and felt it whispered against his skin in the early morning light. He returned it, only to stiffen when he heard the telltale sound of Amber's heels coming in behind him.

Amber knew how to make an entrance. She had none of the reserve most people did when walking into an open space. No demure looks or half smiles while she looked for a familiar face. Amber walked into the lounge as if the sharp *tap-tap* of her heels didn't echo off the walls and draw every eye toward her.

Amber spotted them and headed over. "Hi, I'm Amber, the mayor's assistant. Can I get either of you anything?" she asked as if she hadn't just been reamed out.

"No, thank you," Theo said curtly. "We're going to do the interview here. Why don't you come back in half an hour?"

"Actually, I'll take a seltzer," Pippa said. She smiled up at Theo and shifted closer until her expensive perfume wafted around them.

"You got it," Amber said brightly. "Be right back."

This interview for *CityScape* magazine was an important one. He knew Pippa was interviewing Beckerman, too, and he needed to be on his game.

Pippa sat and patted the cushion next to her. "So, Mr. Mayor, you've had a little competition this go-round, haven't you? Beckerman's support base is growing. Why do you think that is?" she asked slyly, when Theo took a seat. She was one of the most skilled reporters the city had. Theo wasn't surprised she went straight for the jugular. In fact, he enjoyed her sharp mind as much as he had enjoyed her soft mouth before their jobs got in the way and things naturally ended.

"I think that's a sign of a healthy democracy, to have a range of voices and ideas presented for our town's diverse needs, and I welcome the debate that this election brings," Theo answered easily. They went back and forth until a familiar laugh pealed through the quiet lobby. Loud, uninhibited. Undeniably charming despite its complete disregard for anyone else's peace of mind.

It took effort, but he kept his gaze focused on Pippa's face and tried to remember the last question. "I respect Mr. Beckerman's commitment to serving Northfield, just as I'm committed to fostering a town that thrives on inclusivity and innovation, and I look forward to continuing to engage with all members of our community." It was his usual response to the media, fortunately, because his attention was diverted.

From the corner of his eye, he watched Amber lean over the bar and adjust the bartender's collar, and from the look on his face, he was thoroughly enjoying her attention. The bartender was tall and lanky, with curly blond hair, and a good deal younger than Theo was. Amber laughed again, and Theo realized she had yet to do that with him. She had laughed *at* him plenty, but that sound, that light, joyful sound, was one she had been keeping to herself. He frowned.

"Theo?" Pippa's voice brought him back to the present. "Did you hear my question?"

"Excuse me. I'm distracted this morning." Theo tried his best to get back on track. "What were you saying?"

"I wonder why." Pippa mused, looking toward the bar. Amber was in the center of an audience now, apparently telling a story that had the waitstaff enthralled. Probably about how she had almost landed him a ticket earlier, he thought sourly. "Looks like I'm not getting my drink after all."

"Sorry about that," Theo apologized. "It's her first day on the job."

"Hmm," Pippa hummed thoughtfully. "Well, I should go. Hopefully, we'll catch up soon," she said. "I've missed you."

"Yes, see you," Theo said, already heading toward the bar.

"Are you ready to go?" he asked with icy formality.

Amber turned, her lashes a dark fan against the smooth, silky skin of her cheeks, creating a striking contrast. Her pink hair stood out like a blaze of color in the middle of all the gray and chrome in the restaurant. No wonder she drew an audience. She was like a live wire, and, God help him, he was drawn to her, too, he thought, not without some ruefulness.

While he watched, her smooth, bare throat drew his attention. In the delicate hollow there, her pulse fluttered fast and furious, belying the mischievous look she was giving him.

"It's been fun, boys," she said, shimmying off the barstool in her tight skirt and teetering in her heels. He reached out to steady her and gripped her arm. It was like an electric shock to his system, touching that smooth, tender skin on the inside of her elbow with his thumb, and they both froze.

She looked up at him, that little chin pointing up in defiance, and held his eyes while a teasing smile tugged her full mouth.

Theo dropped her arm. "If you're done playing, we have to get to work." He gestured for her to go first.

She blew a kiss to the bartender. "Bye, Anthony. See you soon." Her heels clicked on the floor, every bit as captivating as her entrance.

"Another boyfriend?" Theo asked when they got outside.

"Nah, I never date men who are prettier than me. Too much competition." She started for the driver's side, but Theo held the passenger door open pointedly.

"If I promise to drive like a grandma, can I drive?"

"Not a chance. Get in."

She sighed and slid in. "Fine. But I'm choosing the music. How do you feel about eighties hair bands?"

Chapter Seven

THE RIDE back to Northfield was subdued. Amber tried to talk to Theo, but he switched on talk radio and turned it up. She got the message.

Who knew what crawled up his butt again? She had apologized for speeding, and they didn't even get a ticket. She had gone to the bar to get their drinks and run into her old friend Anthony. They had chatted for a bit, but she would have brought them their drinks, eventually.

If that had ruined his day, then the mayor was strung more tightly than she thought. Maybe he was mad she interrupted the reporter and him? There had definitely been an underlying current between them. She almost asked, but she didn't want to get her head bitten off again.

She sat back and enjoyed the scenery instead. Northfield was known for its charming original architecture and quaint old-world feel. The mayor's office sat nestled between the town hall and the community library on Main Street in a charming little red brick building draped in ivy. The post office was just down the sidewalk, along with cute little boutiques where Amber liked to window shop. At the end of the main drag was the village green, where the town held the Harvest Festival every fall and Candlelight Night in the winter.

On a Monday morning, the sidewalks were just starting to fill up with shop owners out sweeping and watering their flowers. Amber waved at some familiar faces.

If she wasn't so irritated at Theo, she could grudgingly admit that he did a marvelous job making sure Northfield was a welcoming place to live. Where she grew up, in Cedarwood Village's dilapidated tenements, the housing didn't quite fit the aesthetic of the rest of the town, but Amber could appreciate the appeal just the same.

Her family had come a long way since those early days in Cedarwood, and Amber had just as many good memories growing up on the edge of all this charm as she did bad ones. Like Johnny. She never would have met him if she hadn't lived in Cedarwood. She made a mental note to call him. He still didn't know about her new job.

Theo, apparently over his snit, was back to being a gentleman because he came around to open her door when they arrived in the parking lot. Mrs. Dubois, who Amber recognized from the ribbon-cutting ceremony, was seated behind a desk like a sentinel.

"Good morning, Mr. Mayor," she said. Her gray hair was neatly sprayed into place, the sides and top slicked back as if she dared a piece to escape and break ranks. Amber guessed not many dared break anything around Diane Dubois.

Mrs. Dubois's fond gaze slid to Amber, trailing behind Theo. Amber sized her up immediately as the gatekeeper to the office.

"Good morning, Diane," Theo greeted her, setting a white paper bag with the Morning Glory Bakery logo on it down on her desk. Diane's gaze rested on Amber, doubt written all over her face at what she saw. Amber knew when her measure had been taken and she'd been found lacking. There wasn't one instance, other than with Theo, of course, when she couldn't use her considerable charm to win people over, and she made up her mind then and there that she was going to win over Diane Dubois.

"A chocolate croissant?" Diane's eyes lit up, and she looked up at Theo adoringly.

"Never miss a Monday," Theo said. The dimple made an appearance so quickly Amber thought she missed it. "Diane Dubois, meet Amber Hart, my new assistant," Theo said, introducing them.

"I think I'll like working here if we get treats on Mondays," Amber said, eyeing the bag hungrily.

"Too much sugar will kill you," Diane said dourly.

"But what a way to go," Amber said. "I'm all ears if you have any tips or advice for taking care of the mayor. How does he like his coffee?" she asked cheerfully. *Black, like his mood.*

Diane stiffened. "I take care of that for the mayor."

"I can get my own coffee, Diane. I've been telling you that for years," Theo said, but the fondness took any sting out of his words. "Come on back. I'll show you around."

The office was an interesting mix of old and new. Large six-paned windows let in plenty of light, casting a soft glow on the exposed wood beams that vaulted the high ceilings. Vintage rugs covered newly refinished wood floors leading to a hallway of offices. "This is Todd Myers, community outreach," he rapped on the open door.

A man in retro black glasses and a blue bowtie looked up from a computer.

"Todd, Amber Hart, my new assistant."

Todd took his glasses off and stood up to shake her hand. "We've heard so much about you."

"All good, I hope."

"Not all. That would be boring." He grinned. "We'll talk later, I'm sure," Todd said as Theo led her away to the next door with a gold plate that read Charlotte Thornton. Amber knew of her, although they hadn't met formally.

The Thorntons and the Clairmonts were two of the oldest families that had settled Northfield and were practically royalty. Just in the five-minute drive to work this morning, Amber had driven by at least four buildings with their last names engraved on them. Theo knocked lightly.

"Come in." Charlotte sat behind a desk with two computer monitors. Amber assessed her expertly. Her suit was too large and a sad beige that seemed to absorb the light in the room rather than reflect it. With all the colors in the world, Amber had never understood why someone would wear that one. "Hello again, Amber."

"Nice to see you again. Hope you enjoyed your wine."

"Charlotte, I meant to ask you about the dinner this Saturday," Theo said. While they talked, Amber played one of her favorite games. The makeover one.

Charlotte's boring blouse became a vintage Gucci floral in hot pink that she'd had her eye on forever on eBay. Amber squinted, trying to see Charlotte's hair color. Oh, yes. She'd take down that severe bun and give it some body, maybe a few highlights to put warmth into her face. And those pearl earrings were tasteful but boring. Amber was just getting warmed up when Theo cleared his throat.

"Did you get that?" Theo said, looking up with a frown. Amber jumped, guilty.

"Yep, got it all. Dinner party, Friday," she said brightly.

Theo's scowl let her know she'd been caught daydreaming, but he didn't say anything. "This," he said, pointing at the last office on the left, "is Neal Barclay's, chief of staff. He's not in right now; you'll meet him later at the Monday morning meeting."

And finally, at the end of the hall on the opposite side, Theo stopped. "This is my office." He took out a key and unlocked the door.

Amber followed him inside and inspected the room. Theo's desk was a huge mahogany monstrosity that sat in front of a large window. Various college and law school degrees hung in frames on the wall behind his desk. Photos of Theo's father and grandfather with various dignitaries lined the wall. She would bet money they had been in those exact spots for decades. In fact, everything in the room looked like a tribute to the Clairmont family legacy.

The one bright spot was the fireplace at the opposite end of the room. There was a long, comfortable-looking brown leather couch that sat in front of it, giving the room a touch of coziness and the alluring scent of leather.

Theo narrowed his eyes. "I see that look in your eyes. I'm going to tell you this once: don't touch anything in this office. I know where everything is, and I like it that way."

"Okay, Mr. Mayor," she said meekly, already wondering what the surface of his desk would look like if it were cleared off. And that box of files next to his desk must make it hard for him to find things. He really did need a pillow for that couch to warm it up. Everything was so old and boring-looking. Her creative juices kicked in, but Theo had already left when she turned around.

"And here's your office." He led the way out and turned into the office next to his. "You can do whatever you want here, but don't touch my office."

"Got it, boss," she said, saluting him.

"Call me Theo," he snapped on his way out.

She kept her mouth closed. It was a silly thing not to call

him Theo, but it evened out the ever-present scoreboard, and she wasn't going to lose.

Besides, it never failed to get a reaction, and she'd take that over indifference any day.

The door closed with a snap behind Theo, and she was alone in her office. She walked over to the chair and spun it around once, twice, three times. *Not bad for an office job.*

In the past, she had worked in everything from cubicles to coffee shops, and as far as offices went, this one wasn't bad at all. It needed a serious update, though. The mayor's office should reflect the current inhabitant, not the one in office three decades ago. She leaned back in the chair and put her feet up on the desk, admiring the way the little rhinestone buckles gleamed.

All she had to do was work hard and really stick it out for six months. She was a hard worker; she knew that, no matter what anyone else said. Sometimes she was a little impulsive but not this time. She was going to be the best assistant Theo had ever had. But first, she needed to know what the job entailed.

She puttered around the office, mostly changing her email signature to different fonts and colors until she was bored out of her mind, and she headed out to get the lay of the office, so to speak. She started with Todd. He looked like he knew all the good stuff about what went on in the mayor's office.

An hour later, Amber was sitting on the edge of Todd's desk, leaning over his arm to read the latest gossip on the North-field Facebook page when there was a brisk knock on the door.

"Come in," Todd said.

"We're ready for the meeting," Theo said after a pause. He leaned in the doorway, taking in the scene with one quick glance. Amber took the same opportunity to study him.

He was deceptively casual, with his hands in the pockets of his trousers, his maroon tie perfectly knotted, his tall body relaxed and confident without artifice in a way she was suddenly, inexplicably, envious of. He was in his element while she felt, alarmingly, out of hers.

And he was glaring at her again. Whatever. She flipped her hair and slid off the desk, making sure to flash some thigh to even things up a bit. She didn't miss the darkening of Theo's eyes as she did either. *Point for me.* "Thanks for showing me the ropes, Todd," she purred. She paused in the doorway and looked up into Theo's unreadable eyes. "I'm all yours, Mr. Mayor," she said lightly.

Theo's eyes slid to her throat, of all places, then back up to her eyes so slowly it felt like he was dragging his big hands over her body. "Follow me," he said coolly.

Amber followed him down the hall, admiring his shape from behind. The man could wear a suit with the best of them. She fanned herself.

The conference room was at the end of the hall, where Neal and Charlotte sat on either side. Theo sat down at the head of the table, and Amber took a seat next to Todd and pulled out her notebook. She thought it was a nice touch, the notebook and the pen she had behind her ear. Very diligent.

"Neal, this is Amber Hart, my personal assistant," Theo introduced.

"Pleasure to meet you," Neal said, looking her over. He lingered a little too long staring at her breasts. Amber summed him up immediately. Mid-sixties, slick suit, even slicker combed-over hair.

He was the epitome of a certain kind of man creeping into his later years with a hard-on for proving he was still a ladies' man, all the while holding women in disregard. She had encountered men like him plenty of times before. He glanced at Theo, taking his seat at the table, and lowered his voice. "You look familiar. Have we met before?"

"I'm sure I'd remember if we had." She tugged her hand back from his damp grip.

"I believe it was at the pub. Weren't you giving a show on the bar?" Neal said blandly enough, but Amber caught a subtext that made her eyes narrow.

"All right, Charlotte, give us a rundown of the finances," Theo directed. He slipped on a pair of black-framed glasses.

Oh, my. The Clark Kent look *really* worked for the mayor.

He looked up and caught her staring. His lips curved in that sexy little knowing half smile, and a dimple started to show.

Amber panicked and pointed at her chin. *You have something right...*

He frowned and wiped at the nonexistent speck on his jaw. *Here?*

She shook her head. *Other side.*

He wiped the left side and looked at her suspiciously.

She nodded, beaming, and went back to pretending to take notes. The pages were filled with her newest design idea. She had found a bolt of gauzy white fabric at Goodwill for a steal and was drawing sketches of dress ideas while Charlotte strung together numbers so fast that Amber stopped listening. Idly, she noticed that Theo, Neal, and Todd gave Charlotte one hundred percent of their attention. Even Neal was taking notes, and she got the impression he didn't listen to many people.

She studied Charlotte curiously. Lord knew the woman didn't command a room with her clothing. A small-boned woman with sharp, dark eyes and thick glasses that did nothing for her green eyes, Charlotte seemed to want to blend into the conference room with her matching, boring tan suit. Her neckline didn't show even a bit of cleavage. Nonetheless, there was something compelling about her that Amber tried to name until she got bored and looked for a distraction.

From where she sat, she could see out the window to Main Street, where a little dog was trying to hide itself behind a large planter filled with begonias outside the bank. She looked again. Was that Puddin'? She peeked back at the conference table, where everyone was still engrossed in Charlotte's boring report. No one would notice if she crept off to the window and took a look.

She got up and tiptoed over so that her heels wouldn't make noise and looked out the window. There was a familiar tail poking out, but she couldn't make out whether it was Puddin' from where she was.

"Are we boring you, Miss Hart?" came a lazy drawl from behind her.

"No, not at all, just checking the weather," she said, taking her seat again. *That loser son of Mrs. Bovenzi probably kicked her out again.* She made a note in the margin of her otherwise still-empty notebook to check behind the planter later.

"All right, Todd, what events do we have coming up?" Theo asked, looking over a sheaf of papers.

Todd adjusted his gingham bowtie. "We have the Finger Lakes for a Cause Charity Dinner event on Saturday night. I have you down as a plus-one with Addison LeVine. Is that still the case?"

Amber looked up interestedly.

Theo was already shaking his head. "No. It's just me."

"The plates were pricey," Todd said. "Is there anyone else you could bring?"

"Theo, this would be an excellent opportunity for Amber to meet your supporters. She'll be working closely with them in the coming months as the campaign events gear up," Charlotte said.

"Actually, Pippa Shelton would be a better choice," Neal interjected. "We could leverage her media coverage and influence with the younger demographic of women we need."

"Amber," Theo said abruptly, "you're free on Saturday." He pinned her with those blue eyes.

It was more of a statement than a question, and she bristled. She wasn't free. She had plans. She always had fun, exciting plans on Saturday nights, especially now that she didn't work at the pub. It was her regular bath date with her electronic boyfriend. "I'm bus—" she started.

"Good. It's settled," Theo said briskly.

"I have the perfect dress to wear," Amber said. "I just got found this cute vintage Pucci—"

"No!" Theo almost shouted it. "God, no. Just... just take this and buy something with a lot of... fabric."

Amber opened her mouth to protest, but Theo reached into his back pocket and pulled out a black card. Amber's mouth snapped shut.

"Here. You'll need something to wear. It's a black-and-white theme. You and Charlotte can take a half day and go shopping for something appropriate."

She really wanted to tell him where to stick that shiny, beautiful card, but also... shiny, beautiful card in her hot little hands for a day of shopping? *Please*. She wasn't a fool. She made grabby hands, and Theo slid the card over. This time, he didn't hide his smile.

"You're going to bring her?" Neal said, clearly trying to mask his shock. "Are you serious?"

Theo looked over. "Is there a problem?"

"Look," Neal said, "the Finger Lakes dinner is a black-tie event. It's all about optics and perceptions at this stage of the election campaign, and Amber's not exactly..." Theo's brows drew together, and Neal hurried to add, "The typical guest. We need to be on our game, and no offense"—he nodded curtly toward Amber—"but you're relatively risky."

Amber grinned. "If you're worried I'll start dancing on the bar again, I only do that when the dollar bills come out."

"Yes, I've heard that," Neal murmured.

"Enough," Theo barked. He leaned forward and pinned Amber with steel blue. "There are people there that I'll need you to talk with and make connections. Is that something you can handle?" He raised an eyebrow. It was a challenge if she ever saw one.

"Of course I can." She jerked the card away and tucked it down her bra, safe and sound. "I can talk to anyone."

"Theo, your campaign can't afford unpredictability right now," Neal warned.

"Relax, Neal, I've got this in the bag." Amber winked at him, and Neal's expression darkened. She shrugged. Not her monkeys, not her circus. If Theo wanted her there and handed over his credit card, who was she to argue? "Come on, Charlotte," she said. "Let's go shopping."

"Lord save us," Theo muttered.

AMBER MET Charlotte at Mrs. DuBois's desk. "Sure we can't tempt you into coming shopping with us, Diane?" Amber asked playfully. "I've got a black card, and I know how to use it."

"I should hope you use it liberally." Mrs. Dubois eyed Amber's skintight pencil skirt and top. "Your workwear looks like... you're gasping for air."

Amber winked and pointed toward her head. "Us blondes don't need much," she said, twirling one long, pink-tipped end.

Mrs. Dubois's lip quivered before she ironed it flat with her top lip and buried her nose back in the stack of files.

Almost gotcha. She'd have the woman laughing by the end of the week.

Charlotte and Amber walked down to one of the upscale stores that lined the Erie Canal. There were a few hidden gems down there that Amber visited, but the store Charlotte dragged her into wasn't one of them. No consignment clothing in this place. The racks were filled with designer names and matching price tags.

Amber looked over, noticing how Charlotte's eyes lingered on some of the more daring dresses on the mannequins. Amber pointed at a black sheath dress. "This would look great on you. It's... less beige."

Charlotte laughed self-consciously. "I only have this one personality, I'm afraid." She plucked at her suit coat. "Boring beige."

Amber turned toward her. "Did you ever play dress-up as a kid? What were your favorite outfits?"

"Not really," Charlotte said. "I mostly just studied. I went to school and studied. I was a wallflower for most of school. The only boys that would talk to me were Theo, Grant, and Ford, and that's only because they were practically family," she said ruefully. "I guess I just never really bloomed."

"How do you feel about that?" Amber asked carefully. She wasn't trying to force a metamorphosis on the woman, but trying something new couldn't hurt. Amber thought back to all of her looks over the years. Maybe she was an extreme case, but she changed her looks more often than she changed her socks.

"I suppose you could say that I have always followed the path that was in front of me. It's comfortable that way." She glanced at Amber with a little smile. "Boring too."

Amber fingered the lace hem of a black slip dress. "Yeah, I get that. And the flip side is that I've tried on so many that I'm not sure which version I started with."

"I envy you," Charlotte said. "You're not afraid to take risks."

Amber let out an indelicate snort. "Oh, I'm afraid all right. This"—she pointed at her Marilyn outfit—"makes me feel a lot braver than I really am." She held up the black dress. "Sure you don't want to try this on?"

"Don't you think that looks a little..." Charlotte hesitated, and Amber knew that only good manners stopped Charlotte from finishing the sentence.

"...slutty? Trashy? Sexy as hell?" Amber prompted her. She held up the black slip dress thoughtfully. "Yeah, it could be a little shorter." She looked over at Charlotte, who paled. "You could totally pull this dress off, though."

"I don't think it's quite the look I'm going for," Charlotte said diplomatically.

Amber shrugged. "It's just a look. Think about how you want to feel, then pick what to wear."

"I want to feel..." Charlotte looked embarrassed.

"Tell me. I'll make it happen."

"It would be fun to feel sexy for a night, I think," she said hesitantly. "No one ever looks at me that way."

"Hold my beer," Amber said then laughed at Charlotte's expression. "We're going to make a little sexpot out of you yet."

"Oh, no. That's not what I want," Charlotte said quickly. "I have a little black dress I bought in college that will work. Still fits perfectly."

Amber winced. She'd bet money that Charlotte's dress was a shapeless box of a dress. "How about something like this?" She held up another black gown. It was classic with a twist. When she turned it over, a low plunge in the back turned the dress from stately to subtly sexy. It was perfect.

"I suppose that would work," Charlotte said doubtfully.

"It's perfect. Demure with a hint of sexiness that will make you feel like a million bucks."

"I guess it can't hurt to try it." Charlotte held out a dress. "I think something like this would look beautiful on you," Charlotte suggested, bringing out a demure white dress from the rack. It was elegant, with a high neck and long, filmy sleeves—and so very boring.

"Hate it," Amber said immediately, dismissing it. Yet, as she glanced at Charlotte's hopeful expression, she hesitated. "Maybe if we shortened it?"

"I know it might not be quite what you're used to, but this event is formal," Charlotte explained. "With Theo in a tux and you in this, you two would be striking together."

The reaction to that interesting choice of words she filed away to examine later.

Amber studied it a while longer until a new shape came together. Yes, that was exactly how she wanted to feel. "Okay, I'll take it." She grabbed it off the rack. Charlotte let out her breath and smiled.

"Come on," Amber said after they checked out. "Let's spend Theo's money on something fun." She grabbed Charlotte's arm, and they headed up the cobblestone sidewalk until Amber took a sharp left into the chic French lingerie store.

"Here? I don't think..." Charlotte stammered.

"Don't think," Amber said firmly. "The boss said get whatever we need."

Naughty, shimmery bits and pieces of satin and lace draped over mirrors and dressers in the soft light. She dragged Charlotte over to a wall of bustiers. "Look at this white one," she said, fingering the delicate whalebone and lace. The front demi cups were daring, revealing just enough to tantalize, yet the white gave it a touch of innocence.

"I wouldn't even know how to put that on," Charlotte said.

Amber studied it. She opened the bag with the dress she had just purchased and finally nodded.

Charlotte grew nervous. "What are you thinking?"

"I'll take this one," Amber said firmly, pulling the white bustier down from the shelf, "and this too." She grabbed a matching set of thong and garters. "OK, your turn. What stands out to you?"

Charlotte immediately shook her head. "JC Penney is more my style."

"Yeah, that's not gonna work," Amber said. "This is a fancy event, right?"

"Yes, but nobody's going to see my underwear," Charlotte said.

"If they're lucky, they might." Amber raised her eyebrows and wiggled them. "Come on, anything you want. What would make you feel your sexiest, most beautiful self?"

Charlotte looked around the store, and an expression of intense longing flashed so quickly Amber wasn't sure she caught it. She followed Charlotte's eyes to a set of pastel pink bra and panties. It was sheer, so sheer that it did less to cover her than to frame a lady's softest parts. There was delicate green lace embroidery edging the cups of the bra and the matching panties. It was insanely sexy while also demure. Amber nodded in approval. Definitely Charlotte's vibe.

"We'll take one of those," Amber said to the saleswoman. She looked Charlotte over critically. "In a small, and I'll take the white one in medium."

"I really don't think Theo—"

"I really don't think about Theo either. Come on, let's go." And she marched them up to the cash register and pulled out the shiny black card.

"That was really fun," Charlotte said on the sidewalk. "Thank you for going shopping with me."

"We're not done yet," Amber said. The black awning of her friend Lucy Merchant's beauty salon was visible in the distance.

She grabbed Charlotte's hand and headed that way. "We have one more stop."

The Pretty Parlor was quiet when they walked in. A woman with a clipboard had her back to them.

"Hey, Lucy," Amber called. Lucy Merchant, Amber and Allie's childhood friend and neighbor from Cedarwood, turned around with a smile.

"Hi, what are you doing here?" Lucy asked. "Time for a touch-up?" She looked over Amber's pink ombre.

"No, not for me this time. This is my friend, Charlotte."

"How do you do?" Charlotte greeted Lucy politely.

"Charlotte needs a makeover," Amber announced.

"Oh, no, I don't need a makeover. I like my hair. I haven't cut it in ages," Charlotte protested.

"I know. We're gonna fix that," Amber soothed. "Just a little change. Do you trust me?"

Charlotte hesitated. "I think so. But no pink," she rushed to add.

"No pink. I promise. Remember, we're just trying on something new," Amber said. She met Charlotte's wide eyes in the mirror, and they weren't talking about hair.

"Well, okay, but if I'm going to do this, then I want you to try something new too."

"What?" Amber asked, skeptically. "I've tried everything."

"What if you skipped the pink this time and let your natural color come through? I think that would look beautiful on you."

Amber looked herself over critically in the mirror. She remembered the day she had Lucy color her hair pink. Mrs. Pearson had just let her know that she was moving, and Amber wouldn't have a job.

Instead of picking up the classifieds, Amber had gone out looking for something to distract her. She was going to miss that old lady. The sadness welling inside her had needed an outlet bigger than she could come up with, so she ended up in Lucy's chair with pink highlights.

And she loved them. But she knew them for what they were: a distraction. She was really good at coming up with distractions.

She fingered the curls thoughtfully. "I suppose that's a fair trade," Amber said. "Lucy, what do you think?"

"Sure. I've always wanted to see your hair a little shorter," Lucy said. "Maybe up to your shoulders. It would show off your pretty face," Lucy said. "Something a little more sleek. A little more 'I am woman, hear me roar.' What do you think?"

Amber looked in the mirror and wondered what Marilyn would do.

She shrugged. "It can't hurt to try something new."

Chapter Eight

"Good morning, Diane," Theo nodded to Diane on the way in the next morning.

Diane looked up from the envelope she was putting postage on and fixed him with her usual stern look, but Theo wasn't fooled. Diane was one of the few people who couldn't be charmed, bought, or cajoled out of her opinion of you, and Theo counted himself lucky that she was on his side. He kept her in a steady supply of chocolate croissants and flowers on her birthday to make sure of it.

Theo knew she was an intimidating woman. Hell, she scared him sometimes, too, but in all the years he'd known Diane, he had never known her to be cruel. She just didn't suffer fools.

"Good morning, Mr. Mayor," Diane said formally. Her wiry hair was pulled back tight in the same bun she had worn since the nineteen eighties, when he met her. She wore no makeup, and her idea of office wear was a rotation of utilitarian suits, navy and black for winter, gray and tan for the rest of the year. Come to think of it, Theo hadn't ever seen Diane in anything else, even at the Christmas parties he hosted every year.

"You're looking lovely this morning," Theo said, taking the stack of mail she held out. "Tan is your color."

"And you're looking tired," she said tartly, "or I'd say the same." She looked at him severely. "Still not sleeping?"

"I'll sleep when I'm dead," Theo said with a wink. It had been after two when he finally put his computer away and fell asleep, but that was usual these days. "Is everyone here?" he asked casually, as if he hadn't already checked for Amber's car in the parking lot when he pulled in.

Diane pursed her lips tightly. "Your assistant called to say she was going to be late."

"Was there a reason?"

"She said..." Diane looked down at the phone notes she meticulously kept. "Betty is being a stubborn bitch, and she would be there as soon as she could get her lazy butt moving."

Theo's jaw went slack for a second. Inappropriate laughter threatened before he stifled it. "Thank you, Diane," he said gravely. "Perhaps we can direct her toward the mechanic's shop when she arrives."

Theo strode down the hallway, nodding to Todd and Charlotte on his way to his office. Amber's office door was open, and he took a quick peek inside. She had left her notebook on the desk and a pen with a fuzzy purple tassel on top.

He shook his head and made his way to his office. He had a mountain of work to catch up on today. After yesterday, he had been so distracted by his assistant that he didn't accomplish even half of what he usually did, and he wasn't happy about it. He had spent a sleepless night thinking about all the reasons she wasn't a good fit for the office. Time management, for one. He checked his watch again. Nine fifteen. Where the hell was she?

When she was in the office yesterday, she didn't know the first thing about office etiquette. She spent most of the morning talking to Todd. He frowned, remembering her draped over

Todd's desk like some kind of vintage pin-up girl, all softly rounded curves that he had a hard time tearing his eyes away from.

When she'd stopped in the doorway in front of him, he'd caught another glimpse of her pulse beating furiously in her throat. How absurd that with all those luscious curves, it was that little unguarded flutter he couldn't stop thinking about.

She was a distraction.

One that he didn't have time for. With the election coming up, he couldn't afford to take his focus off the goal. That was partially why he had sent her and Charlotte out for the rest of the day. That, and he knew if Amber chose a dress from her own closet for the Finger Lakes dinner, he might have an actual heart attack.

Did the woman ever dress for comfort? The image of her in those black heels with the tiny strap around her ankle made him sweat. As soon as he caught a glimpse, he wanted to feel them digging into his back. On his shoulders. Draped over his desk.

See? Distracting.

"Why are you glaring at a blank screen?" Ford asked, leaning on the doorway.

"I'm thinking," Theo said shortly. Ford's law office was next door to the town hall, and they frequently stopped into each other's offices. Theo was usually glad to catch up with his brother.

"Listen, I have to run to an early deposition, but I wanted to check on Amber. How's she doing?" Ford asked.

Theo ticked off his fingers. "She's late for the second day in a row. She doesn't know how to work in an office. She dresses like a Victoria's Secret model. That's not distracting at all," he said wryly. He held up a fourth finger, but Ford was laughing.

"That good, huh?" Ford smirked. "That is one hell of a woman."

A thought occurred to Theo that made him stiffen. "Did you and she ever..."

"No," Ford shook his head. "But not for lack of trying on my part," he said. "She's allergic to kids." Ford's son, Landon, lived with him full-time after his ex-wife bailed with some big-shot producer she'd met when Landon was a baby.

"Doesn't she have plenty of nieces and nephews?" Theo knew of Davis Henderson from several development meetings. He'd heard he married Amber's sister, Allie Hart, a few years back, and Theo saw both of them around town with their menagerie of kids.

"Yeah," Ford shrugged. "But having a kid is different from living with one. It's a hard pass for some people."

Just then, Amber peeked her head around the doorway.

Red. It was the first coherent word that made its way into his brain. Then, *heels.* Then, *holy Mother of God.* The woman was going to kill him. Red heels, fitted white blouse, tight black pencil skirt. She looked like a fifties pin-up model. He pinched the bridge of his nose hard.

"Hi, sorry I'm late. Did you get my message?" she asked breathlessly. Her blouse, snuggly cupping her generous breasts, heaved, and those full, smooth slopes gripped Theo until he forcibly shook his head. *Jesus.*

Then he noticed something else. "No more pink hair?"

She fingered her darker hair and shrugged. "New job, new hair."

"Hi, Amber," Ford greeted her. "Theo said things are going well for you here."

"He did?" Amber shot Theo an uncertain glance, and Theo winced for an entirely different reason. It was that same quicksilver look on her face from that night in the parking lot. A little uncertain, a little lost. Wholly different from her usual boldness. A protective instinct hit him out of the blue, and he stood up.

"Ford, I'll see you later this week," he said curtly.

Ford blinked. "Have I just been dismissed?" He grinned at Amber, whose dazzling smile was back. "See you around, Amber. Don't let this guy work you too hard." Ford gave him a knowing look that Theo ignored as he closed the door firmly behind him.

"Come in and take a seat," Theo said more formally than he intended. He adjusted his tie and took a seat behind his desk. He breathed more easily with the monstrous desk between them.

Amber sat down, tucking one leg over the other, and whipped out a pencil from behind her ear. "I'm at your service, boss."

Theo passed over a paper on the desk without a word.

"What's this?" Amber asked.

"This is a list of your job duties. If there's anything you don't know how to do, let Diane know."

Amber tapped the pencil on the sharp white tips of her bottom teeth. "Sort your mail, pick up your dry cleaning, make travel arrangements. I think I can handle it," she said dryly. "Is there anything else?" she asked with a hopeful note.

"No, that's everything."

She continued as if he hadn't spoken. "Because I've been thinking about your campaign, and I have some new ideas about how to get your numbers up. Northfield's population is turning over. They want to know the mayor—"

Theo cut her off firmly. "No. That's not in your job description."

She shrugged. "I guess I'll just take messages, then."

Theo looked pointedly at his watch. "Yes, that's the idea."

"Are you sure there isn't anything else I can do?" she prodded.

Theo leaned back in his chair. "No," he said evenly. "There's nothing else that I want."

She looked like she wanted to say more, but she stood instead. "Door open or closed?" she asked.

"Closed," Theo said firmly.

For the rest of the morning, Theo worked just as hard at keeping his thoughts from straying to the woman in the office next door as he did on the speech he was writing.

Three times he was interrupted.

"Come in," he said the first time.

She opened the door and read from a paper. "Mr. Wivell called. He wants your opinion on building squirrel bridges on Main Street to increase safe passage." Her lips quivered when she met his eyes.

He cleared his throat and tried for professional interest. "Please tell him I will take that under consideration."

"On it." She nodded smartly and spun on her red heels. His collar felt too tight, and he was suddenly too warm. Theo cursed the heat outside and took off his suit jacket.

The second time she knocked, he looked up and the feeling of anticipation surprised him. Kelsey would never have interrupted him this many times. He wouldn't have allowed it. He took off his glasses. "Yes?" he asked, already anticipating her heart-shaped face in the doorway.

"Message from a—" Amber paused, her brow furrowed in mock seriousness. "Mrs. Slaughter. She wants to know what— wait, let me make sure I get this right." She cleared her throat. "'What woke bullshit' is on your agenda for the next state of the town address?" She looked up innocently, and Theo caught the mischievous look in her eyes. "What shall I tell her, sir?"

"Please tell her," he said just as solemnly, "that the agenda includes mandatory yoga for all council members, to improve flexibility in decision-making."

"Understood, Mr. Mayor." Amber's lips curved delightedly.

"And Amber?" Theo added as she turned to leave. "Hold all future messages, please."

Amber nodded. "Got it, boss. Priorities only."

An hour later, she came back with a Post-it note and put it on his desk silently.

R.E. Annual Pirate Day. A formal request for "Talk Like a Pirate Day." Do you accept? Yay or Nay.

Theo stared at the note for a full ten seconds.

Amber held out a purple pen.

Theo took it and checked *"nay"* with a heavy hand.

Disappointment made her lips pouty. He had a brief, wicked hot thought of taking that full bottom lip between his teeth. He waited until she turned around to leave. "Amber," he called.

"Yes, sir?" She turned with an eyebrow raised.

The air in his office seemed to disappear, and Theo had a sudden image of those red heels digging into his back again.

"No more interruptions."

"I wouldn't dream of it." She closed the door with a little snap.

And Theo was alone in his blessedly quiet office again.

Which was no fun at all.

At noon, Amber cracked open her Diet Coke and fished a package of Red Hots out of her purse. She had typed a report, made a golf reservation, and thought up inappropriate Post-it note messages to write to Theo for the last hour since he kicked her out of his office.

She snickered, remembering Theo's reaction to her interruptions. Every time she knocked, she was half-convinced Theo would lose his patience with her, maybe even fire her, but she couldn't seem to stop herself.

It was that wild feeling that had gotten her in trouble her entire life, but with Theo, she couldn't seem to stop herself. If she were honest, she didn't want to. It was like earning a congressional medal when she got him to loosen up. That yoga joke had been pretty good, actually, not that she would tell him that.

Theo needed more fun in his life, as far as she was concerned. Now that she had her hands on his schedule, she could confirm that he did very little aside from work. No wonder he looked tired.

Idly, she popped a few pieces of cinnamon candy into her mouth and pulled up Phillip Beckerman's website. His event schedule for the summer was full of her favorite Northfield events: the carnival, Fourth of July fireworks at Canandaigua Lake, the arts festival on Main Street—the guy was everywhere this summer.

She pulled up Theo's calendar and compared, made some notes with her favorite pen, which she took time to admire. She was just finishing up when Theo appeared in her doorway.

"I'll be back in an hour," Theo said, rolling down his shirt-sleeves over tanned, muscular forearms that she eyed with interest. His classic gold watch gleamed at her, drawing attention to the forearm porn in front of her.

If she were in charge of his campaign, she'd make sure to grab some shots of Theo just like that. He had the casual, confident grace of a man who was a born leader. Not for the first time, she wondered how Beckerman was topping him in the polls.

"Got it. I'll just be here, making sure things run like a well-oiled machine." She slid the Post-it notes under her notebook and blinked up at him.

Theo eyed her suspiciously before staring at something else. Amber followed his gaze to the Twinkie wrapper on her desk.

"Is that your lunch?" he asked, distaste written all over his handsome face.

"Yep. Want some?" she said, already breaking the Twinkie in half. She licked the sticky white cream with relish.

"Good God, no. Do you have something else to eat?"

"Yeah," she said. "I brought Red Hots." She dug in her bag and waved the box of candy at him. "Want one?" she asked with a mouth full of Twinkie. "They're my favorite."

He sighed. "Come with me. I'll buy you lunch."

Free lunch? Amber popped up. "I'll just grab my purse."

Aside from Mrs. Dubois eating what smelled like egg salad, the office was quiet for the lunch hour. Outside, all up and down Main Street, election signs painted the sidewalk in bold promises.

ELECT PHILLIP BECKERMAN - A NEW VISION FOR NORTHFIELD
ELECT JANE GILDERSLEEVE - KEEP OUR TOWN GREEN
ELECT MAYOR THEO CLAIRMONT - HONORING TRADITION, LEADING WITH INTEGRITY

Theo pointed down the street toward the Northfield Pub. "Do you want to eat there?" he asked. "Or there?" He pointed at a cozy little diner in the opposite direction.

Amber hesitated. In a town as small as Northfield, there was no way she could avoid running into Killian, but she was still feeling too raw for that encounter. It wasn't even so much him firing her, which she could finally admit had happened. It was what he said after that was still stuck in her gut.

Maybe you need to figure out why you keep falling.

Yeah, no thanks.

"I don't feel like eating bar food. Let's go there." She pointed at the diner.

Theo looked at her knowingly, but she turned and walked ahead. She didn't have to think about anything at all on such a beautiful day. She waved at Mrs. Kittleburger, who was watering the petunias in front of the town hall. Every shop they passed, someone called out "hello" to Theo, and he stopped to chat. He knew each person by name and inquired about their families or their businesses with genuine interest while Amber hung back and watched him do his thing. It was yet another strongly disconcerting moment for her—to not be the one in the spotlight—but for once in her life, she was content to watch someone else take the stage.

At the diner, Theo held the door. Once she and Theo were inside, the room came to a standstill before people came over to greet him, including the waitress, Eden. Amber knew her from singing at the pub and considered her a friend, or at least an acquaintance. She wasn't the friendliest person around, and she kept to herself mostly, but she was polite, and Amber had always liked her.

"Nice to see you again, Eden," Theo said.

"Hi, Mr. Mayor. Always glad to see you. Would you like your regular booth?" Eden asked. She wore her long, dark hair in a high ponytail, and her cat-eye liner was perfectly drawn.

Eden had worked at the diner, serving breakfast and lunch, for years, but everyone in Northfield knew her best for how she sang at night. She was a regular on stage at all the local bars for a reason. Her voice was a masterpiece of emotion that made everyone wonder why she didn't leave town to pursue a singing career. With a voice like hers, she could have sung anywhere in the world. Instead, she worked at the Maple and

Main Street Diner during the day and tore hearts out one by one at night.

"Yes, please," Theo said.

Eden led them back to a booth along the wall of windows that looked out over Main Street. The smell of burgers and fries made Amber's stomach growl. Aside from half a Twinkie and some Red Hots, she hadn't eaten anything yet today. She was still trying to catch up on bills, and grocery money was tighter than usual.

"Unsweet tea, like usual?" Eden asked, and Amber glanced up with interest. Eden was one of the few people who didn't seem to have fallen under the charming mayor's spell. She knew she liked this woman. Eden didn't look impressed with either one of them. She looked rather tired and distracted, actually.

"Yes, please," Theo said. He looked at Amber. "What would you like to drink?"

"Diet Coke," she said, daring him to say anything. He didn't.

Eden snapped her book closed and left the table.

Amber glanced at the menu and then settled back more comfortably in the red leather booth. "So, what's it like to have an entire town at your beck and call?"

Theo fixed her with that look, the one that was partway between exasperated and amused. "If I had everyone at my beck and call, you wouldn't have been in my office with those messages this morning."

"Those were important messages from your constituents, sir," she said, bringing one hand lightly to her chest. "I was only doing my job." She trailed one finger down the deep valley of her V-neck blouse and watched Theo's reaction. His eyes didn't waver from hers. She dropped her hand. "Do you ever get tired of that?" she asked abruptly.

"Of what?"

"Being the go-to person for everything. The one everyone expects to solve their problems."

"No, I don't," he said, looking genuinely surprised. "I love my job. I've never wanted to do anything different. It can get heavy at times, but it's what drives me," he said simply.

"I've always wondered what it must be like to be the responsible one. I've never had that, thankfully." She laughed lightly. "I don't think anyone would come to me for life advice. Dating advice, I've got that covered. For example, I could have told you it was a bad move to ignore your date—"

"You seem to have done well for yourself since that night," Theo interrupted quietly.

Her eyes flew to him and stayed. She knew which night he was talking about, and nope, they were not doing this. Somehow, in the ten-plus years since, they had never spoken of the night he had found her on the side of the road in a torn ball gown, and she planned to keep it that way.

"I'm sure you're joking," she smiled, dazzlingly bright. "Everyone has heard about all the careers I've had. It's a running joke around here how often I find a new one."

For a moment, she thought he would press the issue, but he just nodded. An understanding of sorts, a silent acknowledgment of her boundaries, and she let her breath out slowly. "Tell me about your last job," he asked instead.

"The pub? I've worked there on and off since I graduated from high school." A little twinge of sadness caught her off guard. She really did miss that place. "I read a little something about you on the town's Facebook page, Rochester's Most Eligible Bachelor." She smiled teasingly, on more familiar ground. "I guess your date that night didn't get the memo about what a stud you are, huh?"

"Before the pub. Where did you work before then?" he asked.

She suddenly remembered the college degrees on the wall behind his desk. He must have been a fierce attorney. She was struggling not to squirm under those cool blue eyes, and yet another thought occurred to her.

He wanted to know her.

She could sense it in the seriousness of his gaze and the utter focus he gave her across the table. It was not empty small talk or biding his time. He wanted to know *her*, not the version of herself she gave to everyone else. It was thrilling. It was terrifying.

She covered up her sudden breathlessness with a nonchalant shrug. "A few places," she said, looking around for Eden. "I'm starving. Are you ready to order?"

He pressed, "Where did you work?"

"Here and there," she deflected, sitting back with a huff. "The usual haunts of the highly ambitious—a brief stint in owning a dog-walking business, some interior decorating at my mom's firm, a little pole dancing to keep things interesting. You know, the usual." She crossed her arms in irritation. "What's with the ninth degree?"

He raised one eyebrow. Impulsively, she leaned over and forcibly pushed it back down. His skin was warm to the touch, and she hesitated there with her finger on his brow. "This eyebrow of yours makes me want to commit homicide," she said quickly, leaning back and withdrawing her hand.

Eden set down iced tea and Diet Coke in front of them. "Are you ready to order?" she asked, not looking very interested either way.

"We are," Theo said. He looked at Amber.

"Cheeseburger, medium well, extra pickles, and crispy sweet potato fries, please," she ordered.

Theo handed his menu to Eden. "I'll have the summer berry kale salad, please," he requested politely.

Amber pretended to gag. "Kale? Seriously, kale? Who actually eats that?"

"Every time I've seen you, you're eating something out of a package," he said dryly.

She tried for a laugh. "I'm cheap and easy. What can I say?"

Theo shook his head slowly. "No," he said simply. "You're not." His eyes held hers. She was painfully, thankfully, aware that whatever might have heard about her, he knew the truth. She wasn't ashamed or embarrassed by what some people assumed about her. She even encouraged it when it suited her purpose. She had a knack for self-preservation, and she wasn't afraid to use everything at her disposal.

But it was a heady feeling to be seen.

"Did you go to college after high school?"

"Yeah, but I dropped out. Just wasn't for me." She shrugged.

"What did you do after that?"

Amber sighed loudly. "Can we talk about something else?"

"Why?"

"Oh, I don't know, because I'd rather not dwell on my failures in front of a man whom the town thinks walks on water." she said sharply. "Why do you want to know?"

Theo looked genuinely surprised. "I'm curious how someone as resourceful as you didn't have a Plan B," he said.

Amber scoffed. "Don't you know? I have a magic ability to screw up every opportunity that comes my way," she said, and she hated the hint of bitterness that tinged her voice. How ironic that her tolerance for what people said about her sex life was vast compared to what was said about her character. One she knew wasn't true. The other was her greatest fear.

Theo didn't flinch at her tone. "If you don't like that version of yourself, change it."

And that was her cue. The last thing she needed was a pep talk from Theo Clairmont. She leaned her elbows on the table and rested her breasts on them, giving him a pretty view. "Are you saying you don't like this version of me, Mr. Mayor?" she purred with her usual wide-eyed look of utter fascination. It never failed to elicit at least a double take.

Theo's eyes dropped, and rather than replying with a familiar leer, he looked disappointed. "I've been meaning to ask you about that advance check," he said instead of answering. "What did you need that money for?"

"I had some things I needed to buy. Makeup, hair things, a new dress." She batted her eyes.

"And your air-conditioning," he probed. "Was that something you needed to get fixed?"

Amber thought about her still-broken air-conditioning. "No."

"Is it your car? You mentioned that's why you were late this morning. Did you get that taken care of?" he pressed.

Eden slid two plates in front of them, and Amber jammed a fry into her mouth to avoid further questions.

"Here," Theo said, offering her a bite of his kale salad. "Try this."

"Thank you, no," she said firmly. "I'd rather not eat bird food. What's with the twenty questions?"

"I'm curious why you're so broke if you've been working all this time," Theo said, not unkindly, but she bristled nonetheless. She bet he wondered. Men like Theo Clairmont had no idea what life was like for the other half, and she didn't feel inclined to tell him. Let him think she was a flighty mess who couldn't balance her checkbook for love or money. She didn't owe him anything.

Amber looked back at him boldly. "You and everybody else, but it's none of your business. Let's just say I have champagne tastes on a beer budget," she said, yawning. "I'm ready for a nap. You've got me working too hard."

"Ah. Distraction again. Fine." He sat back and looked her over coolly. "I'd have thought that extra hour of sleep this morning would have helped with that."

She ignored that. "How about this?" she said as an idea came to her. "Let's play truth or dare. We each get a turn, and you can choose to tell the truth, or you can take a dare."

"Are we in middle school?" Theo asked.

"Come on, it'll be fun, and I know you need more of that in your life. I've seen your schedule," Amber cajoled.

Theo looked at her pointedly. "You go first."

Amber sat up excitedly. "Dare, of course," she said, challengingly.

Without hesitation, Theo scooped up a huge bite of kale salad on the end of his fork and held it out to her. "Try this," he dared.

Amber immediately balked. "Never mind. You don't play fair. I'll die if I eat that."

"You'll die if you don't," Theo smirked. "Where's your honor? You said you wanted to play this game."

"Fine." She opened her mouth, and Theo slid the fork between her teeth. They locked eyes for a moment before Theo pulled his arm back. Amber made a show of swallowing and pretended not to gag.

"That's disgusting. I'll probably get salmonella from the lettuce," she said.

Theo laughed. "You'll probably add five years to your life because of those micronutrients."

"Okay, now it's your turn," she said. "Truth or dare?" She raised her eyebrows in a challenge.

Theo sat back and stretched his arm over the back of the booth, the very picture of an amused, confident alpha male. He was so going to regret this. "Truth."

She smirked. "Since you're so interested in what I eat, what's your secret guilty-pleasure food?"

His eyes hooded as he considered, and he leaned in closer. "You want to know my guilty pleasure?" he asked huskily. The noise in the diner seemed to fade away until it was just the two of them.

She nodded, staring at those beautiful, sensual lips. "Oh, yes."

"Peaches," he said slowly. "Warm, ripe peaches baked with a scoop of cold vanilla ice cream on top."

"Yes, please," she whispered.

Theo cocked an eyebrow, and she blinked.

"Check, please, I meant," she said into Theo's laughing blue eyes. She grinned back.

He looked down at her burger, which she had demolished. "Are you ready to go?" he asked, a decorous, respectable mayor once again.

"Chocolate milkshake to go?" she asked hopefully.

Theo looked at his watch. "I have a meeting. Next time, Red Hot."

Red Hot. She kind of loved that. She let her hips sway extra-sassily on the way to the door and hoped he was appreciating the view.

Theo opened the door, and his hand made its way to her back to usher her out first. The touch sent a shiver through her body. She couldn't help but think of all the other places on her body she wanted to feel his hands.

Chapter Nine

At seven o'clock on Friday night, Theo pulled into the Phoenix's parking lot. He made his way up the stairs of the red brick building to Amber's apartment and rang the doorbell.

"Be right there!" Amber yelled. A minute later, the door opened a crack, and Amber peered out.

"Are you hiding a dead body in there?" Theo asked, frowning. He tried to look around her, but she closed the door even more to block his view.

"Only the last dinner date I had. He was annoying. Let's hope you're more entertaining," she said brightly. "I'll get my purse. Wait here." She closed the door and locked it, and Theo was even more intrigued. What didn't she want him to see in there? He pictured sinister things that could be discovered and plastered all over the news while he waited. By the time she opened the door, he was scowling fiercely, anticipation and dread racing through him.

Then the door opened, and Amber slipped out, closed it, and stood framed in the doorway. His scowl dropped and he stared. She was at once the most innocent-looking temptress he'd ever seen. He took in her white dress with a glance, nearly groaned out loud, and vowed to keep his comments to himself.

"What the hell are you wearing?" he said. He knew it was the wrong thing to say. Growing up with a strong, independent mother, grandmother, and sister had taught him that, but it came out all the same. He couldn't help it. He had never seen a dress that looked like... like... *that*. And he had been to countless avant-garde black-tie affairs.

She had on some sort of tight white corset-looking thing that cinched her waist so that it was impossibly small, thrusting her full breasts up, with her round hips flaring below. His mouth went dry. An inch-wide strip of tanned stomach showed between the edge of the corset and the skirt, a filmy, see-through fabric that touched the floor. It appeared she had a short white skirt underneath that saved it from being completely see-through. A small drop pearl on a silver chain around her delicate throat was her only jewelry.

"Do you like it? I made it myself." She held the skirt out, showing her white satin heels with bows on the ankles.

Ah, hell. "You made it?" he barked. "What the hell did you buy with my credit card, then?"

Amber twirled, letting the skirt flow and settle around her, looking completely unaffected while he felt the need to sit down. "I bought the white dress that goes under it, silly. And then I tore off the top and sewed on the skirt."

"I can see your underwear in that." He waved at the see-through skirt, through which he could not, in fact, see her underwear. But it was close.

"How do you know I'm wearing any?" she said with a smartass grin.

He fixed her with a look. "I can see them."

"What color are they?"

"Blue," he guessed. "And what"—he waved at the corset-looking thing without looking—"is that? A bra?" he asked.

She burst into laughter. "It's a bustier."

"A bustier," he repeated gravely. *What the hell was that?* He pinched the bridge of his nose. "Okay, okay, all right. Are you ready to go?" He was a grown-ass man, and he could keep his urges under control, and if anybody else had a problem with it, he would help keep their urges under control too. He held out his arm to hand her into the car.

"Who are these bigwigs I'm going to meet tonight?" she asked as they drove.

"You're going to meet the larger donors tonight and the police and fire department heads, although I assume you know them already?" He saw her nod. "Mr. and Mrs. Sterling are the hosts. They own the winery and the Grand River Hotel. They've been supporters of my family since my grandfather's time in office."

"All right, got it. Charm him. Chat up his wife."

"You don't have to charm anyone. Just be yourself."

She snorted. "That is myself. I'm charming. Relax, boss. This is going to be fun." She punched a button on his dashboard, and loud music filled the car.

"Would you mind?" He turned it back to talk radio.

"Yes, I mind. We have to get in the mood."

"Get in the mood?" He raised his eyebrows.

"I've never been to a fancy dinner like this, and I haven't eaten all day to save room. Plus, I spent a lot of time sewing this dress." She held up her fingers and wiggled them. "I've got pinpricks all over."

"You really made the dress?"

"Of course, I made the dress."

He looked at her with new appreciation. "Nice work," he said gruffly.

"You like it?"

He paused, considering. It was outrageous, bordering on scandalous, and vastly different from anything they would see tonight. And, yes, he liked it. He loved it, actually. It was the epitome of Amber. "Yes, I like it," he said simply and smiled at her.

She grinned brightly enough to light up the car. "Thanks."

Theo felt himself staring, an unexpected warmth surging through him.

Lights glowed softly as Theo pulled into the driveway of a beautifully restored mansion on Canandaigua Lake. He tossed the keys to the valet and went around to help Amber out of the car, strangely excited to walk in with her on his arm.

Generally, he disliked these events, although he attended them regularly. They came with the position, fundraising and networking, getting to know the most powerful and influential people in the city, but he tolerated them more than anything.

Theo held out his arm to Amber, leading her in. Elegant couples in pure black and white filled the ballroom, creating a stunning picture as they stood in the entry. As eyes turned toward them curiously, Theo felt a slight tremor in Amber's fingers that made him glance down. He was so used to the attention and the media that he sometimes forgot how overwhelming it could be. A fierce, protective urge took him by surprise, and he closed his hand over hers and squeezed gently. Her little stubborn chin came up, and the crowd swallowed them.

"Hello, Amber, Theo," Charlotte said a while later.

Theo looked down and did a double take.

"Charlotte?" he asked, as if he didn't know his childhood friend. Because he didn't. The woman standing in front of him with Neal at her side wasn't the shy, retiring woman he had grown up with. Charlotte had undergone her own transformation. Her black silk dress hugged her body like a second skin, and her hair fell softly around her face. Had he ever seen her wear her hair down like that? He stared in surprise while her face flushed prettily. "You look..." Words failed him.

"She looks stunning," Amber said firmly. She looped her arm through Charlotte's and gave them a wave. "We're going to get a drink."

"I was going to say lovely," Theo said thoughtfully as they walked away. The back of Charlotte's dress was another surprise. It was cut down to a deep V in the back, exposing miles of her bare skin. He blinked. It was true. She did look lovely. Charlotte had always possessed a soft, fuzzy, cozy attractiveness, but tonight it appeared as though all the blurry edges had sharpened, and she had come into clear focus. The effect was profound. Theo grinned, inordinately pleased that his friend had tried something new.

"Who knew she was hiding that body under those grandma suits?" Neal said under his breath.

"Take it easy, Neal. Isn't she the same age as your daughters?" Theo asked. Neal had two daughters with his ex-wife, both only a few years younger than Charlotte.

"Ah, but she's not my daughter," Neal said. "At least she's got a dress on. Your new assistant is wearing lingerie," he snickered.

"She made it herself," Theo said shortly. He was in no mood for Neal. He searched the crowd for honey-colored hair.

"I know it was a terrible idea to bring her," Neal was saying. "She looks like a stripper in that, and now she's got Charlotte looking like one too."

Cold fury filled Theo, and his fist clenched around the champagne glass in his hand, almost tightly enough to shatter it. "Keep your observations to yourself. They're not welcome," he said icily.

Neal looked up, surprise on his face. "I'm not saying

anything that anybody else here isn't thinking, and you know it. She's got a reputation for sleeping with most of the Northfield police and fire departments, and now it looks like you're next. I told you that first night she was a disaster waiting to happen. It's your career that's at stake, Theo, not hers. Women like her are a dime a dozen." He tossed back his glass of dark amber liquid. "Don't kill the messenger," he said stiffly before walking away.

Almost immediately, another couple took Neal's place, and Theo found himself in a steady crowd of people while fury ate at his insides.

Neal had been a close family friend since Theo could remember. There wasn't a time when he had visited his father in the mayor's office and Neal hadn't been there. Family dinners, even some vacations, were all entwined with memories of Neal Barclay and his then wife and daughters.

But over the years, Neal had changed. His divorce and then Theo's father's and mother's deaths had hardened him to a point that Theo didn't recognize him anymore.

His gaze was drawn to Amber throughout the night, watching how she interacted with people easily. She was charming, always the center in a group of people, always smiling and laughing in genuine delight. Men and women alike were drawn to her. She was a mix of genuine warmth and wicked humor that was hard to resist. Lord knew he was failing.

He thought about their lunch earlier in the week and how she had refused to talk about her life before working for him. Was it embarrassment? He knew she hadn't finished college, but what had she done after, and why was she so evasive?

It irritated him that he wanted to know. She was his assistant, and he had never been overly involved with Kelsey. Yet, he couldn't stop himself from wondering what her life had been like in the years since he first met her.

She had been so small in the back seat of Grant's patrol car, her gown torn and tears streaking her cheeks with a look on her face that dared anyone to feel sorry for her. He had admired her courage then, just as he did now, and he remembered thinking that the world was going to feel the impact of all that determination one day.

She was the same woman now, yet the layers she'd wrapped herself in intrigued him. She was smart and a hard worker, yet she showed up late to work. She was witty and funny and fearless, and yet her work history was abysmal. She was a contradiction he couldn't figure out. He wasn't even sure if he wanted to, he thought irritably.

A while later, Theo looked up from the couple he was talking to when he heard her voice. Amber was holding court, unsurprisingly, on the balcony. Johnny stood next to her, dressed in a tux, grinning down at her. His hand rested familiarly on the small of her back. Theo put his drink down and headed toward her.

"I was hoping you'd be here," Pippa said, stopping him with a hand on his elbow. She was elegant and lovely in a strapless black ball gown, her dark hair glossy against the silk.

"You're looking well tonight," he said, trying to hide his impatience. His eyes went back to the balcony, but Amber wasn't there anymore. Theo's gaze scanned the crowd for a scrap of a white dress.

Where had she gone? And with whom?

"You look handsome yourself," she said. "I was hoping you would call me this week."

Theo looked at her blankly. "It was a busy week. Excuse me," he said. "There's something I have to take care of."

He was just going to make sure she was okay, as he would any friend or employee.

He followed a long hallway and stuck his head in the first

room, a salon; it was empty. The next room was an empty sitting room. The third door down the hallway was mostly closed. Behind it, he heard a familiar peal of laughter, and his stomach clenched. He knew that laughter; his ears had been tuned into it all night.

"Open your mouth wider." A man's low, husky voice.

Theo stiffened.

Amber's smoky laughter followed. "I can't take any more."

"You can take it. Open your mouth."

She moaned. "The juices make it too slippery."

Theo's eyes nearly crossed with rage. He jerked the door open and stared.

Amber sat on the couch in front of a wall of books, her head tilted back, with Johnny in front of her. His back was to the door, one hand on his hips, the other near Amber's cheek.

Theo's heart thudded to a complete stop and dropped to his feet.

"What the fuck is going on here?" he demanded.

Amber peeked around Johnny, who turned more slowly. He seemed to assess the situation with a knowing smirk on his lips. Both of them were fully clothed.

Amber looked up, teasing laughter in her golden eyes. "Come in, Theo. Oysters on the half shell. Want to try?" she asked. "I've never had one before." She took a sip of champagne and sighed. "I could get used to this life."

"No, thank you," Theo said stiffly. His heart was still thundering in his ears. "Are you ready to go, Amber?"

She took another delicate sip of champagne and stood. "Have you met John Rossi?" she asked politely.

Theo nodded at Johnny, who grinned knowingly at Theo.

"I guess we're *blowing* this popcorn joint," she said cheerfully. She hugged Johnny goodbye. "Wait, before we leave, we didn't get to see the lake," she said as they left the room. "Come with me." She took his hand and tugged him through the French doors leading to a balcony overlooking the lake.

Suddenly, she bent over laughing, holding her stomach.

"What are you laughing about?" he asked irritably, even though he knew.

"Oh, boss," she wheezed. "You should have seen your face."

Theo walked away to look out over the lake. "What did you expect me to think?"

"You thought I was giving him a blow—" She broke off into peals of laughter again.

Theo didn't feel amused. In fact, he was still battling the rage swelling in his chest. He looked around at the people watching them curiously and cursed softly. He was angry with himself for feeling anything at all when he walked into that room. He should have felt the same way he would have if it were Charlotte he had interrupted, instead of this still-simmering anger at another man he didn't even know. It wasn't like him to be jealous or suspicious, and yet here he was.

"I can't wait to tell that story," she finally said, wiping her eyes.

"I think that's one story you want to keep to yourself," he said stiffly.

"Why is that?" A wary look replaced her amusement.

Theo didn't like where this was going, but he was almost helpless not to say it. "I'm sure you know why."

The laughter in her eyes was gone now. "I've been labeled a lot of things, but 'concerned about opinions' isn't one of them. Especially yours," she finally said. For once, she wasn't laughing. Her shoulders were straight, her chin high. She turned her back to him and looked out over the lake.

"It doesn't matter what I think or what anyone else does," he said to her back. "It matters what you think. Does it bother you?"

She was silent, still looking at the water.

"Is he your boyfriend?" he asked abruptly.

"Wouldn't you like to know?" She turned slightly until he could see her, a familiar, dazzling smile on her face.

"Yes," he said simply.

She studied him, a teasing grin tilting her pink lips up. "Race you to the beach," she finally said before picking up her skirt and running lightly down the stairs.

Theo watched her white skirt float down the steps and take the lighted path down to the lake. He wasn't going to follow her. He was going to go back inside and network with the people who supported him and trusted him with the next four years. He owed it to them and to his family to do the right thing.

"Fuck," Theo muttered, right before he took the stairs two at a time.

~

"You came." Amber stood at the end of the lantern-lit pathway, watching the lake when Theo joined her. She tipped her head and let her hair tease her bare back, enjoying the caress of the wind and the heat radiating from Theo's body. She knew he was watching her, could feel his tension, and it excited her, a tangible reminder of the heat that seemed to simmer between them.

Theo was the most uptight, straitlaced, responsible man she knew, and none of those were flattering. There was no good reason on earth why she continued to tease him as she did when she needed to keep this job, and yet she couldn't seem to stop herself.

"Yes," he said, a low rumble in the quiet. The lights of the lake house and the dim noise of the party felt far away from where they were, even though it couldn't be more than a few dozen feet.

"I didn't think you would." She turned her head to find him watching her. His eyes were darker than before, and his hair tousled from the wind so close to the lake. His cool reserve was firmly in place again after the fire in his eyes when he had walked into the study to find her with Johnny. Theo's judgment had cut deeper than she expected.

Hurt. Attraction. It was a dangerous combination. One made her rebellious, and the other made her risky.

"I came to see you after that night too," he said, and dammit if the sincerity in his voice didn't cut right through the facade they'd built over the years. She knew exactly what night he meant. How could she forget the night she had first met Theo Clairmont?

"I know," she said after a while. She lifted her chin. "I didn't want to see you."

When Grant and Theo Clairmont had pulled up in a Northfield police cruiser that night ten years ago, Amber knew immediately who they were, and she'd wanted to melt into the road rather than see them.

Everyone in town knew the Clairmont family, if not for their history of philanthropy, then for the regular media attention their dad garnered as the mayor.

Even back then, Theo had been larger than life, handsome and broad-shouldered, tanned from weekends at his family's lake house. He'd told her later as they drove her home that he was on summer break from college.

He had seemed to her to be from a different planet than her, sitting in the back of a cruiser, still slightly drunk, wearing a gown that was ripped down the side. Certainly, Theo Clairmont appeared more sophisticated and well-mannered than any of the guys she was used to in Cedarwood Village, and it made her even more uncomfortably aware of the contrast in their worlds.

The night had begun innocently enough. She'd spent days sewing her dress because she couldn't afford to buy one, but it had turned out beautifully. After her date, Owen Masterson, a handsome kid from a good family, picked her up, they had danced until she was reeling, feeling all the effects of a full-blown teenage crush. When Owen suggested they get out of there early to party privately, she didn't hesitate.

They were drinking in an empty parking lot when Owen suggested she go down on him. Queasy from the alcohol, she had refused, and Owen got angry, calling her a tease. Nausea and hurt had settled like lead in her stomach, and when she got out of the car, he tried to pull her back, ripping her dress when she resisted.

Owen had begged her to get back in, and when she told him to go to hell, he squealed out of the parking lot, leaving her to walk home, where Theo and Grant found her.

It was one thing to be burned by a high school crush, but it was a life-altering experience to get into the back of a police car and feel the weight of sympathy and maybe a little pity from two men who had their lives together.

Not that Theo had made her feel that way. Theo had tried to make her comfortable on the ride to her house, but Amber was too raw and exposed. She had fallen back on her old defenses, cracking inappropriate jokes and— it was mortifying to remember—but she had even hit on Grant, who had been quiet and professional as he declined her request to show her what he could do with his cuffs.

At one point, Grant had taken her aside and asked her gently if she wanted to be taken to the hospital. She had turned red knowing what he thought had happened and told him flippantly he should have seen the other guy, but the damage to her pride was done.

Theo had found out where she lived and come to check on her the next day. She remembered the shock when Allie told her the mayor's handsome eldest son was standing on their shabby front step.

She imagined him taking in the differences in their lives up close, and she couldn't take any more embarrassment. Instead, she'd hidden where he couldn't see her and asked Allie to send him away.

When she went to school on Monday, the aftermath was merciless. Owen's retaliation was to insinuate to everyone that he broke it off with her because she was too slutty and hit on his friends.

Her natural flirty ways and teasing were twisted until she had picked up a reputation that stuck around right on through adulthood. Eventually, she had learned to lean into them and control them that way rather than fight a losing battle.

She bent down, took off each high heel, and set them on the edge of the path before walking toward the beach. The soft sand still held onto the heat of the day, and the lake sparkled under the moonlight. They were alone as far, as she could see, although anyone on the lake house balcony could look out and see them down by the water.

"Let me guess. Neal's afraid I'm going to cause a scandal, and you're going to lose the election because of me. That's what this is really about, isn't it?" She laughed, low and seductive. "Don't you know I'm a liability, Mr. Mayor? I've slept my way around the ranks of Northfield's bravest, and now I've got my sights set on you."

She turned abruptly and tailed one finger across the perfect bow tie of his tuxedo. "Just imagine the depraved things I'd want from a good, upstanding pillar of the community like you."

He frowned and leaned back until her finger dropped.

"Don't do that," he said.

"Do what?" She turned fully now, her defenses firmly back in place.

Suddenly, he reached out and curled his large, warm hand around her neck.

Amber stiffened, feeling the heat and strength in those long fingers. His thumb rested lightly at the base of her throat and stroked there. She held her breath, feeling her pulse beating frantically against his thumb.

"Don't pretend. This gives you away every time," he murmured. His eyes were heavy-lidded while he studied her as if he were choosing which part of her body to taste first. Her breathing stuttered, and impossibly, the tiny pulse beat faster. "This little flutter won't let you hide your emotions." He stroked it once, twice, up and down, watching it beat faster while the breeze whipped her skirt against his legs, and she stared up at him in the dark.

"I don't care what anyone thinks about me," she finally said. "Especially you. You've wanted to think the worst of me since I saw you at the pub. Come on, I could practically see you holding up red flags."

"That's not fair. I offered you a job, didn't I?" The warm summer night suddenly felt cold.

"And you're waiting for the minute I screw up so you can say 'I told you so' and fire me."

Theo looked at her for a long minute. The urge to hide her eyes made her want to squirm. He always made her feel like he could see right through every facade she tried on and she was suddenly, unbearably, exposed. "Do you want people to take you seriously?"

How did he manage to pierce through all her nonsense when no one else could? She didn't know, but she realized she was going to cry if she didn't stop the flood of emotions. And she would never, ever let Theo Clairmont see her cry. "Truth or dare?" she asked suddenly.

For a moment, she wasn't sure if he would let her distract him, but he dropped his hand. She wanted to grab it and hold it to her. She wanted his hands all over her body, the heat keeping away the chill she felt inside.

He put his hands in his pockets and shrugged. "Truth, of course."

"Truth again. How predictable, Mr. Mayor."

Theo's eyes dropped to her mouth and lingered. "You keep assuming things about me," he murmured. "Why is that?"

She held his eyes, her breath coming in fast little pants, and wondered suddenly if he was going to kiss her. She wanted to feel those firm lips against hers. She wanted to taste him and see what burned under his cool exterior. "You don't strike me as the kind of man to give in to an impulse," she said huskily.

"Don't underestimate me, Amber," he said, holding her eyes steadily. "I'm not always a gentleman."

She held his eyes in challenge. "Prove me wrong, then. Pick dare."

For a moment, she thought he would. His eyes narrowed and his nostrils flared, and between her and Theo simmered heat so thick she could feel it pulsing between her thighs and in the tightening of her nipples.

His eyes were a deep, heated blue. Theo glanced behind him at the party in the distance and when he met her eyes, they had cooled again.

"Truth."

She let out her breath. "I saw you talking to that reporter, Pippa Shelton."

Theo looked at her. "Is that a question? I'll answer yours if you answer mine. What's Johnny to you?"

"That's not the game." She made a pouting face. "Truth or dare. That's our game. Which one do you want?"

"Truth," he said again, firmly.

"Tell me," she said, leaning in, "what is the most scandalous place you fantasize about having sex?"

Theo's eyes flared, and before an evasive answer could spring from his lips, she crossed her arms and looked at him challengingly.

For a long minute, she didn't think he would answer. "My desk," he said abruptly. "After hours in my office, against it, bent over it, or on your knees under it." He raised a haughty eyebrow, but she couldn't even protest.

"*Your* knees," he'd said.

Yes, that was exactly how she wanted him. Seated at his desk, professional and reserved, until she dropped to her knees in front of him.

She closed her eyes, imagining the look on his face as she slid her hands up his muscular thighs to unbutton and untie the clothing that made him a respectable leader in the community, revealing inch by inch the beautiful man beneath.

She would take her time stroking him, feeling the thick length of him harden under her teasing hands before finally tasting him with her mouth. He would be a gentleman even then, she knew, carefully holding her head as if she were fragile while she took him apart at the seams.

She would sit back and slip her dress over her head, revealing the garters she'd worn just for him with the high heels she'd caught him staring at and give him something to look at as she took him deep into her throat. Liquid hot need pulsed in her, and she nearly moaned.

"Your turn. Truth or dare?" She opened her eyes to see him with his hands on his hips, waiting.

Amber laughed to cover her desire. "Dare, of course, and I

don't believe you," she said confidently. "What could a lights-off, bedroom-only kind of guy like you dare me to do?"

"Give me your panties," he ordered.

Amber's mouth dropped open, and the air between them instantly throbbed again with intensity. His words from earlier in the night echoed between them.

I can see your panties.

How do you know I'm wearing any?

She backed up a step and grinned, wickedly delighted by this new naughty side of him. She lifted the filmy white skirt slowly to the shadowy tops of her thighs while Theo watched her, hunger on his face.

One inch. Two. Three inches of silky-smooth thigh bared to the night sky.

She looked up and caught his gaze. A wicked smile on her full lips, she slid the dress up that last inch to show him what was under it. Theo let out his breath in a sharp, gratifying hiss.

Smooth, beautifully bare skin, pale against the tan lines from her bikini. Amber in all her confident, naked glory.

"I told you I wasn't wearing any," she said cheekily.

She dropped her dress and ran back toward the balcony, her laughter trailing behind her.

Chapter Ten

"DOWNWARD DOG, ladies. Ground yourself in the vibrations of the earth," Lily said in a soothing voice that carried over the thirty women in the village green with their heads down on yoga mats and legging-clad bottoms in the air.

Amber's muscles tensed as she held the position, and her stomach growled, a reminder of the hectic morning. She had woken up late after the previous night at the lake with Theo and didn't even grab a dreaded banana on her way out the door.

But today was Lily's first Saturday yoga class on the village green, and she had promised to be there, even if she was regretting her life choices right now.

"Old people are so weird," Val said. She had given up the pose and sat on the mat, eyeing the women around her.

Amber almost smiled. Val was a grounding force all right, but Amber had poked and prodded her out of bed and made her come. "Just do it for Lily," Amber grunted.

"And now let your body flow into warrior," Lily said. Her soothing voice blended into the quiet morning. It was all very peaceful, really.

"You should totally dye your hair purple ombre next. It's so boring without the pink," Val said. "Now you look like every other tool that works in an office."

Maybe "peaceful" wasn't the right word.

"Thanks. I'll take that into consideration." Amber huffed as she flowed into a warrior. "Are you taking hair suggestions? Because I have a few," she said.

"Not from the geriatric crowd," Val said, smirking. She squinted. "Hey, isn't that your new boss?"

Sure enough, Theo was running along Main Street, tanned muscles glistening in the early morning sun. As he rounded the bend toward the green space where their mats were, he caught sight of Amber.

He grinned, his charming white teeth and dimples on display.

She felt that smile like a shot of tequila, straight down to her toes, leaving a burn in its wake so powerful she almost fanned herself.

She stared too. Theo's gray T-shirt clung damply to his broad chest and his powerful thighs. He looked hot and sweaty and thoroughly male. She would never have guessed her least favorite activity could be quite so... riveting. The look on his face when he'd stood next to her at the lake crossed her mind. For a moment, she had thought he was going to kiss her, as crazy as that would be.

Because it was crazy.

This was the best job she'd had in a long time, and she would not mess it up by sleeping with the boss. How trite would that be? Even so, a small part of her had hoped his impressive control would snap. He had shocked her in the best possible way with his dare to take her panties off, and true to form, her wild streak had come out in full force. She still couldn't believe she'd flashed him. Freshly waxed and everything. She stopped breathing, remembering the look of hunger on his face.

And lost her balance, tumbling over, and nearly knocking Val over with her. "Ow, you're heavy." Val pushed Amber back to her mat. Amber glanced back, but Theo's back was to them now. She flopped over on her back and held in a groan. Would she never not make a fool of herself in front of the man?

"Shh," Jessica Thompson hissed sharply. She stood in a perfect warrior position, glaring. "Some of us are trying to find our inner glow."

"Inner glow?" Val asked, snapping her gum. "You'll have better luck finding Narnia with that attitude, lady."

"Ladies, let's free our minds to accept the peace and stillness of the morning," Lily said, her voice floating nearer.

Amber felt a foot nudge her ribs. She looked up guiltily at her sister. *Sorry*, she mouthed.

Lily rolled her eyes and made her way up and down the aisle of mats.

Amber forced herself to forget about the mayor's naughty dare and pay attention to the last bit of class.

But it was hard.

After class, Amber and Val sat on one of the benches scattered around the green and waited for Lily to pack up. When she joined them a few minutes later, Lily took out her inhaler, took two puffs, and held them in.

"Are your lungs tight?" Amber asked, worried.

While Evie was the youngest, Lily was the sister they all looked out for most. She and Evie were born prematurely, with underdeveloped lungs, but while Evie's had strengthened as she grew, Lily's had given her problems all her life.

Dancing, her true love, was a double-edged sword for Lily. The physical activity helped her stay fit and made her lungs strong, but it could just as quickly make it harder to breathe during an asthma attack. She was never far from her inhaler.

Lily shrugged and exhaled the medicine. Her hair was swept back into a low ponytail, and her creamy skin was makeup-free. A few freckles scattered over her nose, making her look younger than her twenty-six years. "No more than usual in this heat. It makes it harder to breathe." She inhaled the medicine, held it, and blew it out again. "I saw the mayor run by."

Amber avoided her sister's eyes and rolled up her mat. "Hmm. Did you?"

Lily looked at her curiously. "You still work for him, don't you?"

"Of course I do," Amber said. "It's only been a week. What? Did you think I blew it already?"

Lily squinted in the sun and shielded her eyes. "No," she hedged.

Amber poked her in the ribs. "Yes, you did. Admit it."

Lily hesitated. "Not that you blew it. It's just that office jobs don't typically last for you."

"Not anymore," Val said, joining them. "She's drinking the Kool-Aid like the rest of the office rats now. Did you see her corporate hair?"

Lily looked behind Amber's head at her ponytail. "No more pink?"

Amber glared at Val, but Val just shrugged. "It was time for a change," Amber said. "You could use one too." She tugged on the dyed-black strands arranged that hid Val's eyes. "Want me to take you to see Lucy?"

"No," Val said scornfully. "I'm not a sellout. I'm never going to change who I am."

Lily looked back and forth between them. "Change happens whether we like it or not. If you're not changing, you're not living."

"Not me," Val said with the unshakable confidence of a seventeen-year-old. "I'm out. Gotta go pick up Holly and then look for Narnia."

"Remind me again that teenagers turn into less feral adults at some point," Amber said, watching Val's oversized back cargo shorts and grungy band T-shirt get swallowed up by a sea of women in spandex.

"She's a hard nut to crack." Lily nudged her elbow into Amber's side. "Reminds me of someone else I knew at that tender age."

"Who, me?" Amber shuddered. "Please. I never got into grunge."

"No, but you had a chip on your shoulder a mile wide." She met Amber's eyes. "You're very good to that family."

Amber hugged the mat to her and shrugged self-consciously. "They're good people that ran into some bad luck."

Lily stared at her hard. "Is that why you're so broke?"

"What? I'm not—" Amber started, but Lily held up her hand.

"You don't have to tell me anything, but I got a call from a debt collections agency about an overdue bill." Concern showed in Lily's eyes. "I know you've been helping them out financially for a while now. Is that why you took the job at the mayor's office?"

Amber started to deflect, but she shrugged instead. "I just hate to see them struggle like we did, you know? Holly reminds me of you and Evie, and Val's too young to worry about food and money. Sandy's working as hard as she can, but money's tight. I help out when I can, that's all."

Lily's eyes softened. "I won't ruin your reputation by telling anyone what a softie you are. How can I help?"

"You can't," Amber said firmly. "Theo's paying me the big

bucks, and I'm getting caught up now on bills. Besides, you just opened the studio. You need to focus on that."

"You're still taking care of me like I'm Holly's age," Lily said with a touch of frustration.

"And I always will." Amber changed the subject. "How's it going with you and Tucker? Did he ever show up for the grand opening?"

Lily looked down and picked at a peeling paint chip on the bench. "No. He came up the next day."

"He missed your big day?"

Lily stood up and hefted the portable speaker over her shoulder. "It's fine. He doesn't understand my passion for dance anyway. He's too practical for that."

Lily and Tucker, high school sweethearts—football quarterback and homecoming queen—had always been the perfect couple. Tucker had played football for Northfield High School and took the team to states twice, winning them the championship. He had an offer from a Division II school, but the momentum petered out for him after high school, and Tucker never got it back. The team let him go eventually because he couldn't match the talent at that level. Now, Tucker sold life insurance and reminisced about his glory days to anyone who would listen. He was a slick-talking charmer who gave Amber hives whenever he was around.

"I'm sorry, Lily," Amber said finally. "I wish he had been there to see you. You deserve that."

Lily smiled and shrugged. "Hey, I saw you and Theo Clairmont were... interestingly aware of each other when he ran by."

"You know me. I couldn't not ogle the good mayor. You know you did too."

"Yeah." Lily grinned. "I totally did. Who knew all those stuffy suits were hiding that body?" She nudged Amber's ribs. "It looked like a little more than that, though."

"Eh, it's nothing."

"Since when do you get all red talking about hot men? You're always so guarded. It's kind of nice to see you affected."

"I'm not affected," Amber said, ignoring the "guarded" part. "It's just an attraction." She shrugged. "It happens."

"I'm just saying that it looked like some interesting chemistry." Lily sighed. "Sometimes, I wish I could be more like you. Strong, independent. Badass."

"Me?" Amber laughed. "Badass? Add in 'broke' and 'one impulsive decision away from being fired daily,' and you'd be more accurate. God, don't let Mom hear you say that. She'd never forgive me for influencing you." She looked at her sister with new concern. "Are you that unhappy with Tucker?"

"I don't know," Lily said quietly. "I've been in love with him for so long, I don't even know what my life would look like without him."

Love, Amber thought, didn't look like leaving your partner alone during milestones. But what did she know? She had never been in love before. Lust was much more her lane.

Lust had boundaries and, more importantly, an expiration date. Romantic love had always made her uncomfortable. Familial love? She had that down. She adored her family, as loud and opinionated as they were. Platonic love? Yep, she had plenty of experience with that. Johnny came to mind. They had tried romantic love briefly, but she quickly realized that type of love wasn't for her. It was too vast. Too consuming.

Lust was her comfort zone. Just maybe not with her boss, as regrettable as that was.

"We're all here to support you if you want to find out," Amber said gently.

Lily looked over the park and cleared her throat. "How silly that I'm afraid I don't know how to be alone."

Amber reached over and grabbed Lily's hand. "Listen, I

only know how to be alone, so there has to be a comfortable middle ground somewhere. I'll let you know if I find it."

They both laughed.

"Yeah, Allie found that with Davis. Too bad we can't clone him. Sister wives? Would that be too weird?"

"Way too weird," Amber said firmly. "And way too many kids."

Chapter Eleven

"The Hope Gala is on the twenty-seventh. You're giving the keynote speech there, and then there's the Historical Society lecture lunch series, where you'll be introducing the history of the early settlers to western New York."

Amber rested her chin on her hand and gazed out the window as the sound of Neal's voice droned on. Monday morning meetings were such a snooze fest. She had started the day on the right foot, even getting to the office at eight on the dot for once. When Theo got in a while later, she had his schedule printed and ready for him and had pulled the meeting notes he'd requested. She'd restrained herself and only left him one little Post-it note with a Twinkie on his desk.

Re: kale: in case of overdose, eat Twinkie immediately. Repeat as necessary.

She hadn't heard any wrappers opening, but he also hadn't yelled at her yet this morning. Things were going well.

She peeked out the window and saw a familiar tail disappear behind the planter in front of the bank again. She had walked to the village twice over the weekend to look for Puddin', but the little dog was nowhere to be found. Amber left food and water just in case she came back. The poor dog must be hungry.

"You haven't attended a Rotary Club meeting since the winter, Theo, and they're starting to complain. Are you taking notes?" Neal asked sharply.

Amber jumped and looked away from the window. "Yup, got it," she said, taking another note.

Check calendar for more boring events.

She really was trying to pay attention, but Neal's idea for community-building events seemed to be geared for the nursing-home crowd. She recrossed her legs and idly admired the strap on her newest Poshmark find, black patent leather T-strap Mary Jane heels she'd paired with adorable black cigarette pants and a fitted white blouse from Yves Saint Laurent, the coveted 1966 Rive Gauche collection.

Years ago, she had been browsing all her favorite vintage boutiques when she stopped dead in her tracks outside the shop's window. She had begged the owner to put it on layaway for her and had scrimped and saved to buy it. Yet another instance of ramen and bananas coming in clutch, but every time she wore the blouse, she felt like a movie star. Totally worth it.

"There's a municipal bond investment seminar at the end of the month at the community center. You can present the bene-fits and potential returns of investing in that," Neal said. Theo nodded, adjusting his glasses while taking his own notes.

Straight and narrow Mayor Theo Clairmont was firmly back in place this morning. His perfectly pressed navy suit and light-blue tie were a stark contrast to the hot and sweaty man she had locked eyes with on Saturday morning.

Or flashed on Friday.

Her cheeks heated thinking about that, and she quickly looked out the window again as Neal picked up steam. He seemed bent upon making Theo the most boring, pretentious mayor in the world. No wonder Beckerman was rising in the polls. Anything other than a municipality meeting had to be a better way to connect with the community.

But what did she know? She was just there to take notes. She looked out the window for Puddin' again.

"Are we boring you, Ms. Hart?" Theo asked with one eyebrow raised.

Ignore. Ignore it. Think about the bonus check, she said to herself, but the eyebrow did it, just like every time.

"Funny you brought up the word 'boring.' I have some ideas," she said brightly. "I was looking at Beckerman's events calendar for the summer, and he has much more family-friendly activities lined up. Maybe you could add some fun events to your calendar."

Charlotte nodded encouragingly. "That's a good point." Amber smiled at her gratefully, and Charlotte gave her a subtle wink.

Neal snorted. "Family-friendly activities? What is this, a carnival? We're running a serious campaign here, not a circus."

Theo sat back and crossed his arms. "Go on. I'm listening."

Amber felt the same excitement building that she felt whenever a design came to her, and she flipped open her notebook to review her notes from the week before. "It's about being visible in the community, showing people that you're interested in the same things they are. You used to play baseball, right? What if you threw out the first pitch at a Northfield Little League game? It's a great photo op, and—"

Neal cut her off with a wave of his hand. "Why would he want to?" Neal asked sharply. "That's not where the money is."

Amber looked him in the eye. "That's where the majority of the younger voters are, and they care about what's happening in the community too."

"The people that run the community have the money, and they're at the municipality meetings," Neal shot back.

"I think it's worth a conversation about changing up our approach," Todd said carefully in the tense silence. "We could plan for you to have a good mix of traditional events and more casual community-based events on your summer schedule."

"Casual? Our campaign strategy is to turn the mayor into a weekend baseball dad? This is politics, not a popularity contest at the PTA meeting," Neal said.

"Your polling numbers are suggesting it's a popularity contest that you're losing," Amber snapped. She looked at Theo directly. "This isn't your father's campaign anymore. Even your election signs need a modern twist: 'honoring tradition, leading with integrity' is great, but the younger generation of voters want to be seen and heard about things that matter to their generation, not their parents' and grandparents' generation."

"That photo with my niece was all over social media. People need to see an accessible side of the mayor instead of seeing you hobnobbing with rich, old guys on the golf course." Amber knew she'd offended Theo as soon as she said it, but it was too late. Theo's eyes went cool, and his jaw tightened, but it was true. Neal was out of touch if he thought Theo could win an election with the same old strategy they had used for Theo's grandpa's time in office, for crying out loud.

"Why are you even in this meeting?" Neal said. "Shouldn't you be getting us coffee?"

No, he did not just say that.

Theo saved Amber from a response that most likely would have resulted in her being fired.

"Neal," Theo barked. "Uncalled for."

"I apologize," Neal said, looking anything but sorry. "We're not running a campaign on whimsy and feel-good moments. We need serious strategies for serious voters. Not... whatever this is."

He waved his hand vaguely at Amber. The message was clear as a bell.

Her face blazed, and she bit down on her lip hard in order to not tell Neal where he could put that coffee. So what if he didn't like her ideas? She was mediocre at most things, but she knew people. She *knew* Theo's campaign needed new life breathed into it or he was going to lose.

"Thank you for your input, Amber," Theo said, tight-lipped and stiff, in the tense silence. "Neal is right. We need to concentrate on our key demographic. These distractions aren't going to win an election. Let's move on to discussing the budget."

For the rest of the meeting, Amber tried not to take it personally that Theo had essentially sided with Creepy Neal. She knew the pressure he was under and that new ideas were a risk.

She knew all that, but it still stung to be dismissed.

"He's not going to be happy about this," Todd murmured, leaning over Amber's desk to look at her computer on Friday morning. "He despises social media."

Amber grinned. "Who doesn't have social profiles in this day and age? It's a missed opportunity." She clicked on the last tab and voilà—Mayor Theo Clairmont had his own accounts across all the major social channels.

Northfield had its own social accounts for the town, of course, but Theo needed his own profiles to work for him. It was basic public relations, and now her boss had one too. With an updated slogan.

Theo Clairmont

**Serving historic Northfield, NY. A New Chapter for
Northfield.
Reach out, share your vision, and let's make it
happen together.
#MayorClairmont #NorthfieldNY
#NorthfieldForward**

She was quite proud of her little project. Since the disastrous meeting on Monday, she had spent the week being the perfect personal assistant despite Theo giving her suspicious looks every day as if he were waiting for her to get herself fired.

Oh, she still left him cheeky Post-its, and she couldn't stop herself from sneaking in to organize his files and tidy up his desk, but she had been lying low for the most part.

Until this morning when she had been scrolling her socials and saw Philip Beckerman's post. It was a photo of him and his kids and a big, goofy white poodle right before he threw the first pitch at a Northfield Little League baseball game. The post had almost three thousand likes, and it hadn't even been twenty-four hours.

That was *her* idea.

Granted, it wasn't something that hadn't been done by hundreds of mayors of small towns before, but she knew what a great event that would have been for the mayor to do. Plus, Theo would have enjoyed it, she knew. The man needed some fun in his life.

Instead, he was going to boring historical lunches that Neal had set up. What a waste.

So, on a whim, she decided to bring Theo into the twenty-first century.

"I hear the boss now. Well, it's been nice knowing you." Todd winked and ducked out of the doorway just as Theo greeted Diane on his way in. He'd had a breakfast speaking engagement at a local university earlier, and she hadn't seen him yet today.

"Coward," she called after him. "Good morning, boss," she chirped when Theo stopped in her office doorway.

He held up two yellow Post-its. "Lily Hart requests a permit for goat yoga on the village green?" One eyebrow rose in skepticism.

"It's all the rage," she said innocently.

"Squirrel bridges and goat yoga. How very forward-thinking of our town."

She handed him another Post-it note and watched as he read it. Pippa Shelton had called earlier to let Theo know that she heard he would be at the theater tonight for the annual Clairmont scholarship announcement and ask if Theo would like to share her family's box seats. It was a smart move. Not quite asking him out but paving the way to spend the evening together.

She didn't quite like the way that made her feel, which was beyond silly. "Theater date, huh? You are a wild one. Hope this one has a better ending than the last date you went on," she teased.

"It's not a date," Theo said curtly. His phone buzzed, and he looked down. "'Congrats on joining the dark side,'" he read. "'Can't wait to see all the boring shit you post.'"

He looked up at Amber with a question in his eyes, and she wilted a tiny bit. She hadn't quite expected Theo to find out this soon.

"What's Ford talking about?" he asked.

For a minute, Theo looked dark and menacing, looming in the doorway, and her belly did that slow, sinuous tug that reminded her that she wouldn't mind seeing the mayor looming over her bed exactly like that, all darkly handsome and stern. Who knew she had a kink for tall, dark, and angry?

"Mm," she murmured, still caught up in her fantasy. She'd make him unbutton his proper white collar and tug his tie loose. Maybe he would use it to bind her hands to her bedpost...

"Amber!"

Her fantasy fell apart.

"What?" she said irritably. How long had it been since she'd had a good fantasy? And, of course, the man himself was ruining it.

"What is my brother talking about? I don't have any social media, right? Right?"

"Well," she hedged, "you did, technically. The town has handles, but it's a huge oversight that you don't have your own, so I fixed it." She smiled brilliantly.

Theo scowled.

Dammit. Would Marilyn never work on this man?

"Delete them," he snapped. "I don't even know how to use a hashtag, much less post things that the public can see and comment on."

"Todd agrees with me," she said to his back.

"I did not," Todd yelled from down the hall. "I told her you'd be mad."

Amber got up and hurried into Theo's office, where he was searching for something.

"I promise I'll handle the accounts. You won't have to use a single hashtag or post anything," she soothed. "It's going to make a big difference, you know. Beckerman's all over social media at these community events. This is a prime opportunity."

Theo sat down abruptly in his chair and pushed his hand through his hair, leaving it disheveled, the way she liked it. *Settle down, girl. Angry sex isn't an option. Although...* She forced herself to stop that train of thought. There would be no sex with her boss. Period. Full stop. Unless he took that tie off and...

Theo pinched the bridge of his nose and closed his eyes. "I just had the longest two hours of my life listening to Mrs. Nielson passionately detail the significance of every brick in the old town hall. Please just... delete them."

He sounded so tired that Amber took pity on him. He really did work too hard. He was always the last one to leave at night, and she knew he worked at home too. He needed something other than work in his life.

"I'll take care of it," she said. Right after he was reelected, she added silently. "I'm going to lunch. Need anything while I'm out?"

"No, thank you," he said. He shuffled the few papers left on his desk, frowning. "Have you seen the budget proposal file? I could have sworn I left it right here."

She walked around him to the file cabinet. "I filed them for you." She set it in front of him with a flourish.

Theo's brows snapped together. "I told you not to touch anything on my desk," he growled.

Geez. His angry voice really did it for her. She shook off a shiver and widened her eyes innocently. "I just did a little filing," she soothed. "Heading to lunch. Gotta run," she called back and practically ran past Diane, who was having tuna today.

Diane's lips twitched, and Amber took a precious moment to wink at her. "That's his 'I love you' voice, right?"

"Amber!" he barked, and she pushed the door open to the humid summer air and blessed silence.

Someone was cranky.

As hot as it was, she'd rather find a nice, cool bench in the shade to eat her Twinkie and drink her Diet Coke without Theo's judgy eyes on her nutritional choices.

She headed down Main Street and stopped to chat with Mrs. Nally at the bookstore about the romance book display in the windows and complimented her lovely purple sun visor. Amber pointed at her own short purple sundress. "Twins!"

Farther down Main Street, Sheriff Rush Callahan was writing a ticket for a car parked in a handicap spot when she walked by the diner. She made sure to give him an extra dazzling smile and was met with a curt nod. That was a specimen of a man. The uniform, the badge, the muscles. It all worked for Sheriff Callahan. He had the whole broody, mysterious vibe going for him.

She found a nice spot under a maple tree to eat and took her lunch out of her bag when a pitiful mewing sound stopped her in her tracks. "Puddin'?" she said cautiously. "Come here, girl."

A small face with deceptively pitiful eyes poked her head around the planter in front of the Northfield National Bank.

"Puddin', it is you. Come here, baby. What are you doing out here?"

Puddin' had seen better days. When she lived with Mrs. Bovenzi, Puddin' had been a plump little thing, all dolled up with bows and a rhinestone collar. The old girl looked like she'd fallen on some hard times now.

Amber picked up the dog. She was skinny now and a little smelly, too, but Puddin' was an actress, if nothing else. She laid her head on Amber's shoulder and looked up at her with big, sad eyes.

"Where's your owner, Puddin'?" she soothed, patting the dog's back gingerly. She knew full well where Mrs. Bovenzi's son was, probably home drinking like usual. She had tangled with the distasteful man once already, but how could she let Puddin' go back to him?

Puddin' made a pitiful noise, between a mewl and a howl, and it was a done deal. She was such a sucker for an underdog. "All right, fine. You can come with me, but you have to be on your best behavior. I mean it. I'm already on thin ice at work. Theo will fire me for sure if he finds you."

She carefully set Puddin' in her oversized bag and made her way awkwardly back to the office. Fortunately, Diane wasn't at her desk, and Amber all but ran to her office and closed the door.

She set Puddin' on the floor. "You can't make any noise. Just lie down and sleep." Puddin' looked up at her and slowly blinked. "I know, I know. I'm gonna take care of you. I'm not gonna send you back to the bad man, but there's another bad man next door." She paused. "Well, he's not quite as bad, but he signs my paychecks, and I really need to keep it that way."

Amber dropped to her knees and spread her cashmere sweater—a vintage find she had searched for months for—in the corner behind her desk, where no one could easily see her. "Don't you dare pee on this."

Puddin' was fully trained, but Mrs. Bovenzi liked to say she was temperamental. She did whatever she wanted, when she wanted, in other words. "I saved up for a month for this sweater. You better tell me if you have to go out."

"Amber, have you seen—?"

Amber sat up guilty, hoping Theo hadn't gotten an eyeful of her ass in the short dress, and tried to look casual. "Seen what?" Shit. That hadn't lasted long. She sucked at subterfuge.

"What is that?" he said carefully.

"That's Puddin'."

"What," he asked very carefully, "the hell kind of name is Pudding?"

A muscle in his jaw began to tick, and Amber figured sheer bravado was her best bet. She was ninety percent sure she was getting fired today anyway, but she wasn't going out without a fight.

"Puddin'," she corrected. "No, it's not my dog. I can't have dogs where I live, but Puddin' is your new strategy for winning the election."

"Tell me you did not get me a dog?" he asked coldly.

"Everyone knows a dog increases your likability by a million."

Theo's eyes narrowed. "You just made that up."

"Maybe not a million, but it's a lot." She scrambled to her feet and found her phone. "See? Beckerman's already caught on." She held out the phone to the picture of Beckerman and his dog. "Puddin' is going to be your campaign buddy. Who doesn't love this face? She loves people."

Right on cue, Puddin's doggy lips trembled in a smile, and she let out a little pouty yip. The dog belonged in Hollywood. Amber picked her up and stepped closer to Theo. In her heels, she was almost level with his collar.

"You've got to be kidding me," Theo said. He sniffed. "What's that smell?"

"She's been mistreated. I used to walk her for Mrs. Bovenzi, but when she died, her son took her. He's drunk and he forgets to feed her. She's in bad shape."

"Then you take her home." Theo crossed his arms, and Puddin' took the opportunity to lean over and rest her head on his chest.

"No, can't do that," she said. "No pets allowed."

"Then take it to the pound."

"Can't do that either. Did you know I worked there one summer?"

His eyes narrowed. "Let me guess, you were fired from there too."

She shrugged. "I organized a picket line outside. They weren't very understanding."

She tipped her head back to look up into his eyes, and for once, she didn't have to channel anyone. "Please take her? It's just temporary until I can arrange for something else. I promise I'll take care of everything. I'll set up a crate at your house, and I'll go buy her food right now. Just give it a few weeks and see if there's any difference in your poll numbers. Please?"

Theo studied her eyes for a long moment before seeming to decide. "Fine. But it's temporary," he added when she squealed.

"Thank you," she said, and she would have kissed him in gratitude except for the voices down the hall.

"Good choice, Theo," Charlotte yelled.

"Sucker," Todd added.

Amber grinned happily up into Theo's eyes. "You won't regret this."

"I already do." He turned to leave.

"Wait. Did you need something from me?" she asked, remembering when he first came to her door.

He turned around, and she was surprised by the sudden flush of color on his cheeks. "I left something for you on your desk," he said gruffly, and went back to his office.

Amber looked over. Sitting on her desk was a tall, thick, delicious-looking chocolate milkshake with a Post-it stuck to it.

In Theo's bold black handwriting, he had written:

#Imsorry #nottoooldtohashtag #teamgoatsandsquirrels

She swallowed hard, suddenly in danger of melting faster than the milkshake.

Chapter Twelve

"Tell me again how you managed to get Theo to adopt this mutt?" Ford asked later that afternoon. He had stopped by to talk to Theo and had been shocked into speechlessness at the sight of all the employees in Theo's office admiring a dog.

"It's temporary," Theo said. "Is she going to pee on my rug?" he asked Amber.

"Of course not. She's perfectly potty trained," Amber said reassuringly. Theo watched broodingly as Amber leaned over to pet the dog that he was now fostering. He almost couldn't believe how she had made it happen. Actually, he could believe it, especially as she smiled at the dirty-looking dog lying on her back, accepting belly rubs on the expensive oriental rug in his office. He was almost ashamed of how easy it had been for her to convince him.

Theo had always prided himself on his ability to maintain professional boundaries, to make decisions based on logic rather than emotion, yet here he was, talked into fostering a dog he didn't want and adding yet more chaos to his formerly orderly life.

He was uncomfortably aware that she not only had considerable persuasive skills but that her passion, her energy, her irreverent mouth all had a hold on him. And it wasn't just him.

Charlotte, Todd, and even Diane sat around the room, taking turns admiring the smelly animal. He wasn't a monster; his office was not a horrible place by any means, but Amber's presence over the last two weeks had changed things here. There was a relaxed camaraderie that she brought to any situation with her warmth.

"Will you keep her here during the day, Theo?" Charlotte asked. She was sitting on the floor next to Amber, her feet crossed at the ankles, wearing a simple, classic red dress that gave her features a glow he wasn't used to seeing. Hell, had he ever seen Charlotte wearing anything that bold?

Now that he thought about it, Charlotte had undergone more subtle changes since the night of the Finger Lakes Dinner. It wasn't anything drastic that he could pinpoint, but as Charlotte sat on the floor, laughing with Amber, it seemed as if more than just her clothing had changed, and he had a feeling Amber had a hand in that too. What was happening to his office?

"I'll take care of her. You won't even notice she's here," Amber answered, dangling a squeaky toy in front of the dog. Puddin' batted it away and nosed Ford's hand to keep petting. "I already ran out and grabbed her food. I'm going to leave at five o'clock, and I'll meet you at your house and show you everything you need to know."

"Tell me again where you found her?" Ford asked.

Amber looked down, and Theo knew it was not good news.

"Did you do anything illegal?" Theo asked with dread.

"No," she said, and when she looked up, he recognized the smile. That smile always came before trouble with her.

He groaned. "Did you steal this dog?" Theo asked.

"I didn't steal her. I *rescued* her," Amber said indignantly.

"She was on the sidewalk in front of the bank, and she doesn't have any tags."

Theo narrowed his eyes. "Do you know who she belongs to?"

She bit her lip. "Maybe. I'm not sure."

He could practically see the wheels in her head turning, and his temper flared again. "Am I going to have an irate dog owner knocking on my door, telling me I stole his dog?" Theo asked.

"That's my cue to leave," Ford said cheerfully. "I don't want to hear anything that might make it hard for me to defend either of you in court." He gave Puddin' one last scratch and got to his feet.

"I'm leaving too. I have a date," Todd said.

Diane and Charlotte followed and closed the office door behind them. Theo looked at Amber. She was on her hands and knees, reaching for the toy. Her skirt slid up the backs of her thighs and stopped just short of revealing whether or not she made a habit of not wearing any panties. A heavy, hot weight settled in his groin, making him uncomfortably aware of how long it had been since he'd had sex. Too long.

And the solution to that problem was not crawling around his office on her hands and knees, despite what his cock was screaming at him. Theo had never crossed a line with a woman in his employ, and he was irritated by the thought crossing his mind as often as it had with his new assistant. He stood up abruptly.

"I'll get it." Anything was better than getting a hard-on in his office.

Images of Amber, soft and wet and bare, spread out for him like a buffet on his desk seared his brain. He crouched down awkwardly and looked under the couch for the toy. And came face to face with a hot, stinky tongue. Puddin' panted doggie breath in his face. Theo grimaced.

"See? She likes you," Amber said. She looked delighted, on her knees in front of him now.

"Oh no, don't eat that," she said. She leaned down again and reached for the toy Puddin' was trying to swallow. Her skirt slipped farther up the back of her thighs. She was pretty and lush in that ruffly little dress that made him want to slip his hands up her smooth, silky thighs and around to the soft, bare cleft he'd only had a glimpse of. He suddenly, painfully, wanted a lot more than a glimpse.

"She smells. I'll give her a bath tonight at your house. She just needs a little love and attention, don't you, girl?" she cooed. Puddin' sighed deeply and put her head on Theo's shoe. "She knows a soft touch."

"This is pathetic," he said. "We need a golden retriever, at least. She's pitiful-looking."

Puddin' let out a moan, and Amber covered her little floppy ears. "Don't say that; you'll hurt her feelings. She's perfect."

"Perfect for the pound," he muttered.

"Thank you," Amber said, looking up at him. Her hazel eyes were more green than gold with her purple dress on and softer than he'd ever seen before. A faint, spicy hint of cinnamon lingered around her, distracting him. "I'm so grateful she doesn't have to go back to that awful home. I promise you won't even notice she's here." She looked down. "Look how she's scratching her chin. Isn't she so cute?"

He glanced at the dog. She probably had fleas. "If she's so cute, why don't you keep her?"

"No can do. I don't do animals, plants, or kids," she said, avoiding his eyes.

"Why?" he asked.

She laughed; the sound tinged with disbelief. "Can you even imagine? I can barely take care of myself." A shadow of something flickered across her expression, prompting Theo to bend down to look at her face.

"Why do you say that?"

She hesitated so long he didn't think she would answer. "Because I ruin relationships just as consistently as I do careers," she said quietly. She lifted her chin. "I've learned it's easier to not even try."

They were so close he could feel the heat of her body. Her hair was up today, with pieces loose around her face, and he was close enough to see the light dusting of freckles across the bridge of her nose.

He stared, wondering how the brazen, sexy woman in front of him could show him her bare pussy one minute and then look as shy and vulnerable as she did now. She challenged everything he thought he knew about himself, his perceptions, and his priorities, and yet he was drawn to her. It was a sobering thought.

A sharp rap on the door turned both of their heads. Johnny stood in his doorway, taking in the scene without expression. Theo knew exactly how it looked: he and Amber alone in his office, on the floor, so close their bodies were almost touching.

Theo stood up and helped Amber to her feet and wondered yet again at the relationship between Amber and John Rossi. He was reasonably sure they were just friends because Amber herself had told him she didn't do relationships, but why wouldn't she answer him when he asked?

"Hey, Johnny." Amber got to her feet, showing a flash of thigh, and hugged him. Irritation and something sharper pierced Theo as Johnny wrapped his arms around her and kissed her cheek.

Johnny held out a set of car keys on his finger to Amber. "Here's your keys, babe. I had a rookie follow me over and park it."

Babe. Theo gritted his teeth at the casual intimacy.

"Thanks. I owe you one," Amber said.

"What's wrong with your car?" Theo asked.

"Nothing. Betty's fixed now," she said lightly.

"It was your carburetor this time," Johnny said. "But your transmission is shot too."

"Oh no." Her brow furrowed. "How much do I owe you?"

"I got it. You can pick up breakfast the next time we go out."

Jealousy, thick and stabbing, shot through Theo.

Johnny met his eyes and gave him a slow grin. "Our girl has a sweet tooth. Did you know that? Chocolate-chip pancakes are her favorite."

Theo ignored that. "I would've given you a ride," Theo said to Amber.

"Don't need one, boss."

Boss. He was so fucking sick of that word.

"All right, I've got a night shift to get ready for," Johnny said. "Still on for Friday?"

"Sounds good." Amber scooped up Puddin'. "I'm leaving too. We'll walk you out."

"Thanks, babe." Johnny leaned down and kissed Amber's cheek, holding Theo's gaze as he did so. "Later, Mr. Mayor."

Theo nodded and grimly wondered about his odds of being reelected with an assault record.

~

"You shouldn't have done that," Amber said once they left Theo's office.

"What? I can't kiss my friend on the cheek?" He grinned knowingly, that same grin that meant trouble wasn't far behind. Johnny liked to push the boundaries even more than she did.

Amber tugged his burly arm down the hall. His Northfield

Fire Department uniform shirt barely fit over his arms, he was so big, but he let her pull him along. "You didn't do it for my sake."

"I know." Johnny smirked. "Relax, babe. Can't make it too easy on the guy."

"He's my boss. I'm not trying to be easy. And you're complicating things."

They were whispering as she led Johnny out of the building, but he stopped abruptly in front of Charlotte's office.

"Hey," he said, crossing his arms over his broad chest. Amber rolled her eyes. She had been watching Johnny charm women with that smile since they were kids. There was no way Miss Prim and Proper Charlotte would look twice at a guy like Johnny.

"Sorry, we're just leav—" Amber stopped because Charlotte was staring. She was sitting at her computer, glasses on, with a pencil paused in midair, staring boldly at Johnny, who started right back.

"Er. Do you know each other?" Amber looked back and forth in the awkward silence. Charlotte's red sheath dress fit perfectly, and her hair was soft around her face rather than her usual severe bun. She looked calm and confident and lovelier than ever.

Slowly, Johnny straightened up off the doorframe and walked toward her.

"Charlotte Thornton, this is my friend, John Rossi," Amber said.

Charlotte held out her hand. Johnny held onto it, and they stared at each other without blinking.

They stared at each other for so long that Amber got uncomfortable. "Should I wait outside?"

"Oh, sorry." Color flooded Charlotte's cheeks, but she didn't take her hand back.

"Why don't you come out when you're... er, done?" Amber said, backing out of the office. What in the world just happened?

She walked past Diane, who was eating burnt popcorn. She was just opening the car door when Johnny came out.

"Sorry about that." He shook his head like he was clearing it.

She eyed him. "What was that all about?"

"We, uh, met at that Finger Lakes dinner."

Well, well, well. Go on, Charlotte, you little minx.

"Be careful with her, Johnny. She's a sweetheart." Johnny had as much luck as she did at relationships and for the same reasons. They both bolted as soon as that awful feeling of vulnerability reared its ugly head.

The difference between them was that he had a lot more women in his wake than she had men, and yet he was never called a slut. The irony wasn't lost on her.

He grinned that bad-boy smile and got on his bike. "See you."

Later that evening, Amber let herself into Theo's house with the spare key he had given her. She had joked that he was moving pretty fast for a new relationship, but he hadn't cracked a smile. She let it slide, considering he had agreed to let Puddin' stay with him for a while.

"You'll be much more comfortable here," she chattered to the dog as she put away the food and treats and various dog things Theo would need. "He's got a thing for rabbit food, so don't expect any good scraps."

Puddin' stopped sniffing around the kitchen and stared with a rather disgruntled expression on her face.

"I know. It's a fault of his, but I'll bring you something good when he's not here."

The dog lifted her nose disdainfully, and Amber laughed. That was the Puddin' she remembered. She knew a soft touch and could lay it on thickly when she needed to, but Amber always pictured Puddin' as practical more than anything else. She did what she had to do to survive. Amber understood that sentiment perfectly.

"Don't go far," she called out as Puddin' meandered out of the kitchen.

Amber puttered around the kitchen for a while, looking in the fridge for something to eat and finding washed produce in glass containers and more types of lettuce than she could identify. He didn't even have a single pint of ice cream in his freezer, the psychopath.

She set up Puddin's new crate in the living room and decided she needed something soft that smelled like Theo so she could bond with him. "I told him you sleep in a crate, so pretend like you do," she said.

"Come on, let's go take a bath." She figured Theo would feel happier with a good-smelling dog, since he didn't want one at all.

There were four doors at the top of the stairs. The first one turned out to be to Theo's room. The interior smelled like him, dark and sexy, masculine, and she had the sudden urge to lie down on his bed and envelop herself in his scent.

Instead, she headed to the bathroom. The en suite bathroom was just as tidy. No cap off the toothpaste or little dark hairs in the sink for her boss.

"Come on, Puddin', hop in." She gave the dog a boost into the tub and got to work with the special shampoo she'd picked up. The more she scrubbed, the more Puddin' perked up, and the wetter Amber got.

By the time they were finished, Puddin' looked ready for a nap, and Amber needed a change of clothes. She stopped at Theo's dresser to look for two T-shirts: one for Puddin's crate and one for her. The first drawer held neat rows of folded socks, and she smiled, remembering how she had teased him that first night about going home to organize his sock drawer.

The next drawer was his folded T-shirts. She grabbed a soft gray Columbia Law school T-shirt and hesitated only a second before taking off her soaked dress and bra. If Theo came home, he wouldn't mind her borrowing an old college shirt while her dress dried, and his T-shirt was almost longer than her dress anyway, hitting her at mid-thigh.

"All right, let's get you something to eat." She picked Puddin' up and wrapped her in a towel, and Puddin' snuggled close, getting her wet all over again, but she gave the dog a kiss on her little head anyway. "You're safe now," she whispered.

"Amber," Theo's deep voice came from downstairs.

Amber looked into Puddin's velvety-brown eyes and tried for stern. "This is your chance for a second first impression. Make it a good one." She set her down, and Puddin' disappeared.

She heard the second Puddin' found her man and paused at the top of the steps to watch.

"You're all wet. No, stop. Okay," Theo said, bending over to scratch the dog's head gingerly. Puddin' flopped over onto her back and spread her legs wide in blatant invitation, her tongue lolling out of the side of her mouth. "This is moving quite fast for me, Puddin'," Theo murmured, and Amber laughed out loud.

Theo looked up, a smile on his face, and froze, his eyes fixed on her chest. She looked down to see the T-shirt clinging damply to her breasts where she was holding Puddin'. Her nipples, clearly outlined, stiffened into points at the look on his face. She swallowed hard.

"I gave Puddin' a bath and got a little wet. Hope you don't mind that I borrowed your shirt."

"Would you like to borrow pants?" he asked tightly.

She looked down skeptically. "Why? Do you have a pair that would fit me?"

"Probably not," he said. "But put them on anyway."

"Why? Is it bothering you?" she teased. She held out one leg from the step and pointed her polished toes. "This old T-shirt covers almost as much as my dress."

"Amber," he said tautly, "right now, I'm not your boss, I'm not your friend, I'm not the mayor. I'm a man, and you need to put something on."

"What if I don't want to?" she asked, taking another step down. She expected him to take a step back, but he didn't.

Instead, his large, warm palm circled her neck. His fingers slid into her hair and tugged her head back, his thumb settling in the hollow of her neck. He stroked his thumb lightly against the pulse there. Her breath was coming in faster pants now, her body hot and aching in all the places she wanted his hands.

"This is a terrible idea," he murmured. His hands were rougher than she expected and warm on her neck as he stroked the indent at the base of her throat. She closed her eyes and swallowed hard, imagining all the other places he would take his time stroking. She opened them to find his, dark and intense, looking at her.

"Those are my favorite kind," she whispered back and felt the response in his body. She wanted him like she wanted her next sugar fix, and just as she knew too much sugar made her sick, she still wanted every last bite of him.

Slowly, watching her eyes until the last second, he dipped his head and replaced his thumb with the soft, hot press of his mouth, a kiss where her heartbeat fluttered. She tilted her head back to give him access to the underside of her jaw and closed her eyes at the feel of his lips playing over her throat. "Mmm," she moaned. She was rewarded with the stroke of his tongue.

Puddin's indignant howl pierced the air.

Amber looked down and laughed shakily. "Sorry, girl. Are we ignoring you?" Puddin' laid her head on Theo's shin and glared balefully up at her. She looked up to laugh with Theo only to find his face serious.

"Stop looking at me like that. Nothing happened," she said.

"I'm your boss, Amber." Theo said tightly. "We just came very close to crossing a line."

"I know," she mused playfully, despite the flutter of anxiety in her stomach. "I've had a lot of really dirty fantasies around that dynamic." She laughed genuinely when she saw Theo's face. She would never get tired of teasing him. "Relax, boss. It was consensual and fun." She wiggled her eyebrows exaggeratedly to hide her unease. "Want to hit first base before your date?"

Theo scowled. "It's not a date."

"I don't care if it is," she said, and even to her ears, she sounded like a liar.

"Amber," he said quietly, watching her with those cool blue eyes that pierced right through her, "I'm not dating anyone."

"Oh," she said, the significance not lost on her. With the heat of playful lust cooling, unease took its place. She was never good in the aftermath of desire. The intimacy of it had every instinct in her screaming to back away, at least, or to leave in a blaze of glory. She settled for backing up. "I better let you get ready. I already fed Puddin', and her crate is all made up." Flippant. Cheerful. Evasive.

"Thank you," he said, more formal than a man who had just had a half-naked woman ready to wrap around his body should be. He looked at her in that way of his that made her want to pull her T-shirt over her face for some measure of protection. Only it wasn't her body that was in danger.

"Okay if I borrow your shirt?" she asked. Down two more steps, far enough that she couldn't see the knowing look in his eyes.

Chapter Thirteen

AMBER CALLED Val as soon as she got home. "I've got a carton of Rocky Road and Red Hots." It was time for the big guns. It was almost embarrassing how turned on she still was from that brief, electrified moment with Theo on the stairs tonight. The man had only touched her neck, of all places, and she was still shivery and tingling, her nipples hard points that she wanted to rub against him.

Desire wasn't new to her. She had a healthy sexual appetite and no shame when it came to indulging in it, although finding the right man proved harder. Living in a small town meant that she had to be judicious with whom she slept because if it went south, she'd most likely be serving him beers at the pub. Well, she would have before she was fired.

Over the years, she'd had casual hookups, mostly with men from surrounding towns looking for something casual and fun, but inevitably things got deeper than she was comfortable with, and she always, always bailed.

Relationships were not her thing. She had accepted that a long time ago, but it had left some ornery men in her wake who hadn't always been as understanding. All the more reason to keep things casual, but even so, it had been a long time, and she had pent-up desire lighting up her body until she felt like it would take only one tiny fuse to set her off.

That was why she had to stay firmly on the professional side with her boss. It wouldn't do at all to have to face Theo at their Monday morning meetings after doing all the dirty, debauched things she wanted to do to him.

It just wasn't smart to sleep with your boss. Even she knew that, and she wasn't known for making great life choices. But the attraction was hard to ignore, and it was even harder to cover up her response to him walking around in his immaculate suit and tie, looking like a present she could unwrap and savor.

She needed a distraction.

"Be right there," Val said, and twenty seconds later, she padded across the hall in her bare feet.

Moments later, Amber and Val were nestled on Amber's couch, eating ice cream and candy on a Friday night, a box fan humming on the coffee table in front of them. In other words, pure bliss.

"No Holly tonight?" Amber asked.

"Nah," Val said, dumping a handful of candy in her palm. "My mom's got the night off. They're having a *Twilight* marathon." She looked over. "Stop eating all the marshmallows."

"Make me," Amber mumbled with her mouth full. "You didn't want to join them?" It was rare that Sandy had a night off from her serving job.

Val snorted. "*Twilight*? Please. Bella's an emotional wreck who can't live without a man. I told my mom not to let Holly watch it, but no one listens to me."

Amber dug around in the carton for another marshmallow and handed it to Val. "Speaking of messy romance, how's it going with Dylan? Did you decide about the ball?"

"I said I'd go with him," Val mumbled around a mouthful of candy.

"You're going to the ball with him?" Amber tried very hard not to show her glee. "This is perfect!" Briefly, she thought back to her own ball, but she pushed the thought away. Val wasn't going to have a repeat of that. She'd make sure of it.

"Really? Was your ball that memorable?"

"God, no. But now I get to live vicariously through you."

"Hmm," Val said skeptically. "Like that show *Dance Moms*?"

"No," Amber laughed. "I promise not to be that weird. Besides, you're way smarter than I was at seventeen. I was stupid and vulnerable at the same time, but I learned my lesson. Now I just stick to stupid." She crossed her eyes until Val cracked a reluctant smile.

Val flopped back down onto the couch. "I don't have anything to wear."

Amber clapped her hands together and looked up at the ceiling. "I was made for this moment."

"Nothing weird."

"I'm offended. I don't wear weird things. Come with me, child." She held out her hand and dragged Val to her bedroom, where she opened her closet with a flourish. "You've come to the right person."

"You're so totally weird."

An hour later, the contents of Amber's closet were strewn around her room, and Val was admiring herself in a black dress in front of the mirror. Amber had tried for some color, but Val shot everything down until Amber pulled out a black vintage 1950s dress with a white Peter Pan collar. The bodice was slim fitting, flaring out to a knee length A-line skirt with a slim black belt around the waist.

"This feels very me," Val said, turning in front of the mirror.

"It really does," Amber said. She tried to rein in her excitement, but the dress—a little bit funky, a little bit classic—was made for Val. Amber could guarantee no one else would have the same dress on. She had convinced Val to pull her hair back away from her face and was reminded again how lovely Val was when she wasn't giving off her don't-look-at-me-or-I'll-kill-you vibe. A surge of pride and protectiveness took Amber by surprise.

"You're welcome to borrow it."

"Maybe I will," Val said casually, but Amber noticed how, when she took it off, she hung it carefully over her arm. Val paused at the door of the apartment. "Thanks," she said casually.

"You're welcome," Amber said just as nonchalantly. A huge grin broke over her face when the door closed behind Val. Well, that was a successful night. She could never go back to her own disaster of a ball, but maybe she could help Val make some happier memories.

When she got into bed later, she reflectively checked her phone on the nightstand. No messages. She had only let herself check a few times during the night, because every time she thought about Theo sharing a box seat with Pippa at the theater, she felt a surge of jealousy that didn't make sense. Theo could date anyone he wanted, of course. Successful, leggy brunettes who had actual careers were his type, and she knew it well after seeing him with a new one on his arm frequently over the years.

And still, she tortured herself by checking the time again. It was still early enough that the two of them probably went out for a drink at some fancy cocktail bar. She thought about Theo's warm hand helping Pippa into the car and walking her up to her apartment like the gentleman he was. Pippa's AC probably wasn't broken, and she wouldn't be embarrassed to invite him up. Her life was calm and orderly, and Amber would bet she'd never been fired for dancing on a bar.

Jealousy, longing, and pent-up desire battled inside her until she finally forced herself to pick up her new romance novel. Fictional boyfriends were so much better. Mostly. There was just that one way they didn't quite measure up. Ugh. Just as she was falling asleep, the phone buzzed.

THEO

Did you hijack my T-shirt for the dog's crate?

AMBER

Depends. Was it your favorite, or can the dog and I have a tug-of-war with it?

THEO

Expendable.

AMBER

Then yes. :) Dogs like to have their humans' scent nearby… unless you want Puddin' to sleep with you?

THEO

Not a chance in hell.

AMBER

Why not? Pippa doesn't like sharing the bed?

THEO

Pippa's not here.

AMBER

Good. You need your sleep.

THEO

I never sleep.

AMBER

Why not?

THEO

I don't know. I just haven't been able to for a
while now.

AMBER

Puddin' would make an excellent bed
companion.

THEO

Feel free to reclaim her.

She fell asleep with a smile on her face.

AMBER RAISED her hand to knock on Allie and Davis's front door, but it swung open before she made contact.

"Hey, Aunt Amber. Come on in," Sammy said, leading her into the foyer. "We're hanging out in the living room until dinner's ready."

She followed him, noticing how much taller Sammy had grown in recent years. He was almost as tall as she was, reaching that stage of adolescence of long, gangly limbs that would one day grow into a tall, handsome, kind young man. Last year he had stopped playing baseball and taken up guitar instead. It turned out the kid was a natural and was rarely without his pick and guitar now.

Geez. What was wrong with her today? She was never this sentimental. She swallowed the lump in her throat and pasted on a smile. Sunday dinner was no time to get teary. The aunts were all here, not to mention her mother. They were like sharks, searching out a hint of emotion and going for the kill.

Soon, Amber would be sharing about that almost-kiss she had shared with her boss and the confusing mix of emotions that had been swirling in her ever since.

But she didn't want to think about Theo today. It was the weekend, and she already thought about him entirely too much during the week.

A cacophony of noise from the kitchen and living room greeted her, and Amber thought back briefly to how much life could change. When Allie was married to her first husband and living in New York City, she had lived in a luxury penthouse that felt like a silent, modern chrome museum whenever Amber came to visit.

The house Amber walked into now shared nothing in common with that place. The Henderson home was warm and welcoming to all, including the people they had picked up along the way. Amber walked past the toys, stepping over Walter, their golden retriever, who was sleeping in the middle of it all, as usual. She waved to Val and Holly.

She had dragged them along to Sunday dinners about a year ago. The Hart family had embraced the sisters and taken them under their wing immediately, despite Val's death glares. The aunts could handle teenage angst and more.

"Hey, guys," Amber said to the living room full of people. Claire, Davis's daughter from his first marriage, had Savvie sitting on the couch with her feet on the coffee table and was painting her toenails. Ben and Sammy were sitting next to Holly on the couch, with Xbox controllers in their hands. Every time Sammy looked at Holly, redness flooded his cheeks, and Holly giggled.

"Pretty colors, Savvie. Did you pick those?"

"Wainbow," Savvie said happily, wiggling her tiny foot.

"I see that. Very nice." Amber leaned down to kiss Claire's head. She gave Ben an affectionate noogie and smiled at Val.

"Hey Amber," Davis said from the chair by the fireplace. He held Tessa in his lap, her sleeping body nestled against his broad chest.

A wave of warmth and maybe even a little longing washed over her at the sight. Sometimes, in her more honest moments, Amber could admit that being a mother would be a dream come true. Allie and Davis did parenthood so seamlessly that she wondered sometimes what it would be like to have a little one look at her with unconditional love and trust.

Life wouldn't be so lonely, for one. For someone who kept herself surrounded by people, in her more intuitive moments, she knew she was lonely. She had her family and Val, and Sandy, and Holly, and her regulars at the pub, of course, but that wasn't quite the same as having a family of her own.

And then she remembered her track record with anything that mattered. The idea was beautiful, but the reality was that she would probably mess up motherhood like everything else in her life.

"Hey," she said to Davis. She took a seat on the couch next to him. "A little late for a nap, isn't it?"

Davis gently stroked Tessa's silky curls away from her face. "She's been tired today."

"Poor baby," Amber said. "Want me to hold her for you?" She was itching to hold the sweet little bundle of Tessa. It wasn't often the twins were still long enough to cuddle.

Davis grinned crookedly, his warm brown eyes crinkling, and she was reminded that her sister had married a stone-cold stud.

"Coward," he said mildly.

Who was annoying. Amber crossed her arms. "What? No. I'm just being selfless." She peeked behind her to see if anyone in the kitchen had heard them. "And be quiet," she hissed. "You'll wake the baby."

"You're probably off the hook. They're all distracted by Val's news."

"*Good*," Amber said with feeling. She looked at Val on the other end of the couch. "What news?"

"They found out about Dylan asking me to the Midsummer Night ball." Val rolled her eyes. "Aunt Giulia wants to do the flowers, and Aunt Sophia wants Cap to have a talk with Dylan before we leave."

"Maybe you could bring him to Sunday dinner," Amber said.

"That's a good idea." Davis nodded. "We'd all like to meet him."

"Never. Not gonna happen," Val said, looking through the kitchen doorway just as Sophia and Giulia were fighting over a wooden spoon. Sauce splattered on their aprons, and the two women bent over laughing.

"Oh, I don't know. I think it's pretty special, what we have here," Amber said.

Val crossed her arms and looked disgusted as she and Amber watched, but a minute later, she looked over at Amber and said, "Yeah, maybe."

"This is good timing," Amber said. "So, they don't care about my new job?"

"Amber, you made it. I heard you were fired again." Aunt Sophia peeked around the corner and fixed her with the eyes. The ones that could make grown men squirm.

"That's old news, Auntie. Amber's got a new job now," Lily said from behind her. She was drying her hands on a dish towel.

"Well, don't go messing this one up too," huffed Aunt Sophia. "Come into the kitchen so we can see you."

"Good luck," Davis murmured. Amber stuck her tongue out and followed the women into the kitchen like she was lining up for a firing squad. Same difference.

"I don't know why you don't work at our floral shop, honey. I can't think of anything better than arranging flowers. We know plenty of men we could introduce you to while you're there," Aunt Giulia was saying from the stove.

Yep. No, thanks.

"Thank you, Aunt Giulia," Amber said. "I'm all set, though. My job at the mayor's office is going well." She hoped she hadn't messed that up with that sizzling hot encounter on Theo's stairs.

"I talked to Cap, by the way. He told us all about the night you were fired. Really, Amber, you know the pub is a family establishment," Sophia chided.

"What's it like working for the mayor?" Aunt Rosa asked, and Amber threw her a grateful look. Aunt Rosa was a sweetheart. She winked and grated more Parmesan cheese into the salad.

"I schedule a lot of meetings for him. Other than that, not a whole lot. I'm trying to get him to visit some more fun places to connect with a younger crowd." Amber settled herself on a stool by the island.

"Oh, yeah? The carnival is coming up. Everybody's there. You could put the mayor in the dunk tank. I bet that would be a huge hit," Allie said from the sink. "Is it hot in here?" She waved a dish towel in front of her face.

The idea wasn't without some merit. She envisioned people throwing things at him and getting him dunked. Theo, bare-chested in a water tank, would earn some definite votes. Now she was just feeling horny. She could admit it.

"Or what about the outdoor movie night up at the school? Everybody goes to that," Allie said.

"I'll try my best. It's not like I haven't been mentioning it to him."

An hour later, they were all crowded around Allie's over-sized farm table, stuffed to the brim with meatballs and spaghetti. Amber sat back in her chair and looked around at her family.

"Here, have some more," Rosa said, giving Davis another helping.

"I don't know if I could eat another bite—okay, thank you," he said, accepting the plate but not eating.

Allie smiled at him affectionately. Amber noticed her full plate.

"Why aren't you eating? Are you pregnant again?"

"Oh God, no," Allie blanched. "I just haven't been feeling very well today."

Davis rubbed her back. "Tessa seems a little off too."

"Tell us more about your job with the mayor, Amber," Aunt Sophia said from the other end of the table, eyeing her. "I hope you're not dressing like that at the office."

"Like what?" Amber knew her family loved her. Being surrounded by so many smart, sarcastic, and clever women had buoyed her spirits and comforted her throughout her entire life, even if they were a little overzealous sometimes.

"Like that. Your boobs are hanging out, and your skirt's too short. What is that anyway that you're wearing?"

Amber held out the skimpy sundress. "But it has pockets. See?"

While they chatted around the table, Amber studied her mother. As the youngest of her sisters, Annette was the most solemn. She sat at the head of the table, listening and observing the dynamics with a sharp eye. It was hard not to draw parallels between their lives.

When their father left, Annette had transformed her pain into a silent, stoic force that drove her to go back to school and change her life on her own terms. It was hard to believe they were even related if you just looked at how they handled adversity.

But one thing she had in common with her mother was her relationship with men. As far as Amber knew, Annette had never had another serious relationship after their father. Like her mother, men were simply something she enjoyed and kept at a safe distance.

"Amber," Annette said quietly. Everyone at the table, even the little ones, looked up. "Congratulations on your new job."

"Thanks, Mom." How was it that her mother could still make her squirm? "I'll try not to mess this one up."

Annette sipped her pinot. "Keep that in mind and see that you don't underestimate yourself."

Chapter Fourteen

On Monday morning, Theo pulled into the parking lot of his office and swore softly. The sight of Amber's empty parking spot, missing her little untrustworthy car, shot a ripple of unease through him, unsettling him even more than he cared to admit.

As he walked up the steps and into the office, lack of sleep and a near-constant hard-on from Friday night contributed to his frustration. It wasn't just Amber's absence that unsettled him; it was the reason behind it. Theo had crossed a line by touching her, and the complete deviation from the man he knew himself to be had left him shaken.

Theo had always prided himself on his control. He was a professional, and he certainly didn't allow his feelings to cross over into his professional life. Yet all those barriers had crumbled when he'd seen Amber standing on his stairs in his T-shirt, smiling at him with those teasing eyes.

He had reached out to her almost before he knew what he was doing. It was beyond reckless, something he had never been before, but then again, he'd never known another woman who affected him like Amber.

"Where is she?" he said to Diane, setting down the bag with her chocolate croissant on her desk.

Diane looked him in the eye. "I'm sure she has a good reason. Just give her a little while to show up."

Theo did a double take. In all the years that Diane had worked for him, he had never seen his stickler of a secretary defend an employee who was late.

"You know her car is acting up," Todd said as he walked by the office.

"Remember, Theo, she might stop at the bakery. She loves to bring in donuts for us," Charlotte said when he paused in her doorway.

When Theo got to Neal's office, Neal looked up with a smirk. "I hate to say I told you so, but I knew she couldn't handle this kind of job. It's been almost a month. When are you going to realize she needs to go?"

"Things come up," Theo barked. It wasn't like Amber not to show up. Late, yes. She had a habit of that, but she always showed up. Worry ate at him.

"It's something new with her every day. Did you know she broke the coffeepot yesterday and she mixed up the meeting times for you? She's a pretty girl, Theo, but she's not the right fit for this job, and she's going to cost you if you keep her around."

Anger, fierce and protective, sparked in Theo, surprising him with its intensity. "Mistakes can be corrected, Neal," Theo said with an edge of steel in his voice. "I think we can all agree Amber's brought creativity and energy to this office, which has been missing."

Neal's face pinched. "I understand that you think she's... different, Theo, but these distractions add up, and we can't afford that this close to the election."

The unspoken challenge made Theo's jaw clench, and he locked eyes with the man he had thought of as another father figure. "I appreciate the concern, but let me be clear: Amber's potential outweighs her mistakes, and I intend to give her a chance to prove that."

Neal opened his mouth then seemed to think better of it. "Understood," he said stiffly.

Theo headed to his office to call her. No answer. Anger and worry gnawed at him until he gave up pretending that he could do any work today without finding out where Amber was. He threw on his suit jacket, grabbed his keys, and headed out.

"Don't yell at her, Theo," Charlotte said as he walked by.

"Maybe bring her a milkshake," Todd suggested.

When he reached Diane, she silently handed him a Twinkie package. "Give her this."

Unbelievable.

For once, Theo drove to the Phoenix above the speed limit, and he took the stairs to Amber's apartment two at a time. He knocked on the door and waited, his heart pounding with a mix of anxiety and something else. He knocked again. "Amber?" he called, his mind creating images of things that could have happened to her.

The door across the hall swung open, revealing a woman in a white button-down shirt and black slacks, a half apron tied around her waist. She looked to be only in her mid-forties, but there was a weariness etched into her features that made her seem older.

"Can I help you?"she asked. "Oh, hi, Mayor Clairmont. You don't want to go in there," she said once she noticed where he was standing.

"What? Why?" Dread filled him.

"Amber's sick. I checked on her this morning, but I have to go to work now. My new manager is a real prick about calling out before a shift." She turned back to her door and locked it.

"She's sick? What's wrong?" he asked.

"They all are. My girls are sick. Everybody's sick. They had a Sunday dinner at her sister and brother-in-law's house, and somebody shared a flu bug," she said tiredly.

Theo winced. "Stomach flu?" He could handle a lot of things in life, but the stomach flu made him blanch. "Does she need anything?"

"She'll be okay," she said. "I'll try to come home on my break if it's slow and check on her again. Doesn't she work for you?"

"Yes, she's my assistant. I can handle it," he said decisively. "Can you let me in, please?" Theo knew his position as mayor made him more trustworthy than most people, but he held his breath while he waited for her answer. He didn't want to have to make a scene by calling the building's super, but he would in an instant to make sure Amber was okay.

The woman sighed. "All right. I have a key. I'll let you in. I don't really get a lunch anyhow, and I can't take any more time off or they'll cut my hours."

She unlocked the door, and Theo stepped inside. His first impression was of a chaos of color. There were fabrics and ribbons, even a feather boa on a mannequin in the corner, but Theo's attention quickly shifted down a hallway.

"Sandy, don't come in here. I don't want you to get sick," Amber said from somewhere in the back. She sounded weak and thready.

He quickly walked to the door of a bedroom and paused. Amber was lying in between the bed and the door, curled up on her side in the fetal position. His heart stopped. He bent down and put a hand against her forehead. It was hot and dry to the touch.

"Amber, what's wrong?"

She opened her eyes, and it took her a moment to focus on him. "You're not Sandy," she said.

"Is he a friend of yours?" Sandy asked from the doorway. Sandy stood in the doorway with her arms crossed, ready to toss him out if Amber said the word.

"He's my boss," Amber said then squeezed her eyes shut and groaned. "Are the girls okay?"

"They're better than you are. Their grandma is coming over to take care of them. I have to go to work, but I'll check in with you later," Sandy said. "Just rest and I'll bring you some soup when I get off."

Amber's already pale face blanched at the word "soup," and she lifted a hand weakly to wave goodbye. Theo gently pushed her hair back from her eyes.

"Go away. Let me die in peace," she moaned.

Theo ignored that. "Why are you on the floor? Are you hurt?" He quickly inspected her for blood or obvious injuries and sighed in relief when he found none.

"So hot," she said. Her eyes squeezed tightly shut, her lashes forming dark fans against her too-pale face.

"Okay. Up you go." Theo brought a hand under her back and one hand under her knees, lifted her into his arms, and set her gently on the bed. It was a twin from the looks of it, and he sat down gingerly on the side to avoid breaking it with his weight. Amber curled her knees up and started shaking.

"Have you had any medicine?" he asked.

"Just wanna sleep."

Absently, he noticed that her green sleep shorts and tank top had tiny frogs on them, and her hair was a wild mass piled on top of her head. She looked younger, softer, in her frog jammies without her usual short skirts and tight tops, and for a second, his chest felt strangely tight at seeing this side of her.

Amber was so rarely anything other than brash and full of life. She opened her eyes, and lucidity was there for a second. "Don't look at me," she mumbled.

"Don't be ridiculous." He tucked her fuchsia and orange quilt up around her bare shoulders. "Stay right there. I'll be back."

Amber nodded and closed her eyes again.

In the kitchen, Theo opened the fridge for water. Aside from a few sad-looking, half-empty condiments and takeout boxes, there was nothing there. Her cupboards had an assortment of Pop-Tarts, Twinkies, and chocolate that had him shaking his head.

He poured a glass of water from the sink, scrounged around the cabinets to look for a fever reducer, and, finding none, went back to the bedroom. She was shivering now, back in the fetal position. Her chattering teeth echoed in the small room.

He pulled the blanket up where she had come untucked. "Here, drink some of this. How long have you been sick?"

"I'm cold," she said, closing her eyes.

Theo took his jacket off, rolled up his sleeves, and piled another blanket on her. Then he went looking for a washcloth in the bathroom. He found a truly scary number of lotions, soaps, and unidentifiable makeup stuff on the counters, along with a stack of washcloths in a basket.

Once, when Ford's son Landon was in kindergarten, he caught the stomach flu. It was right after Ford's wife left them, and Ford was in the middle of an important trial, so there was no one to take care of the kid. Georgie was going through chemo treatment and couldn't be around anyone who was sick, so it was Theo who took care of Landon. It was a trial by fire, but they had made it though, and he felt reasonably sure he could handle this.

Theo grabbed a washcloth, wet it and wrung it out, and brought it back into Amber's room. When he laid the washcloth on Amber's forehead, her eyes opened.

"Go away, you'll get sick," she said, but it was almost unintelligible with her teeth chattering.

"Hush. I'm taking care of you." Theo checked her forehead again. It was burning hot to the touch.

"You always do," he thought he heard her murmur, and he paused, remembering another night many years ago. But then her face scrunched up, and she looked ready to cry. "What's wrong?" he asked, smoothing her hair back from her pale face.

"Am I wearing my frog pajamas?" she asked. She looked so pitiful he tried hard not to laugh.

"Yes, I believe so," he said solemnly.

"I don't want you to see me like this," she whispered and promptly closed her eyes.

"Don't be ridiculous. You're beautiful," he said as he dialed Ford's number. "Ford, I'm at Amber's. She's sick. Can you bring me some things?" He listed off the things that had helped make Landon more comfortable, added a grocery order and a change of clothes, and got off the phone.

Amber was sleeping now, but her body still shook uncontrollably. The bed shook with her. Despite her chills, the room was almost unbearably hot. He checked the window AC unit—broken—and swore softly.

He sat back down and glanced around the room curiously. Her bedroom was tiny compared to his, with mismatched furniture and a lamp draped in a red scarf in the corner that gave the room an amber glow. Her entire apartment would fit into his living room.

There was a bookcase stacked with well-loved romance novels. It shouldn't have surprised him, but it did. So his prickly assistant was a romantic at heart.

Her nightstand held various pots and jars of what he assumed were lotions as well as a photo of Amber and her sisters and mom in dresses. They were all beautiful, all grinning at the camera, bold and confident, with their arms wrapped around one another. One sister, Allie, he thought, held a bouquet. On Amber's nightstand was a paperback book lying face down with a half-naked brooding man holding a woman on the cover. Theo smiled.

Amber shivered again, and Theo did a quick search in her closet, but there were no more blankets. He hesitated only a second, knowing this would blur the lines even further between them, before taking off his tie and dress shoes and getting into bed with her.

He gathered her shaking body into his, wrapped his arms around her securely, and settled in for a long night.

Chapter Fifteen

WHEN AMBER WOKE up the next morning, she didn't know where she was. She opened her eyes in stages, cautiously checking to see if the stabbing pain from the last twenty-four hours would appear again, but all she felt was groggy and so hollow her stomach protested.

She kept her eyes closed, trying to think of the last time she had actual food. Gradually, she became aware that she wasn't on her bed, although a quick peek through her lashes confirmed she was in her bedroom.

No, instead of her comfortable bed, she was sprawled out on something hard and very hot to the touch. A hand was tangled in her hair, cupping her neck lightly, and long, hairy legs tangled between hers at the bottom of the bed. Her hand tickled where it lay under the bottom edge of a pair of shorts. Men's running shorts.

She lifted her head in confusion and saw something she hadn't seen in her bed in a very long time. A man. Her head was resting on Theo's thickly muscled, hairy thigh. Even more confusing, there was a tiny black tattoo on his upper thigh. She blinked. A microphone?

She moved back to her pillow and studied the man beside her. Theo's face was even more handsome and almost boyish at rest. His usually smooth-shaven cheeks were bristly, and his dark hair had escaped its style to curl softly over his forehead.

He breathed deeply and easily while she watched. His lips were parted slightly, and... her breath caught as she registered this new detail: his chest was bare. She closed her eyes and breathed in his warm, masculine scent. She wanted to enjoy the moment a little longer. Who knew when it would happen again?

"Amber," he rumbled, or at least that was what it felt like so close to his chest. A hand came up and rested against her forehead, familiar and intimate. His body relaxed at what he felt. "No fever," he murmured.

She lifted her head to find him watching her. "Hey," she finally said, feeling uncharacteristically shy.

"Your fever broke." His hand still rested on her face. She didn't move away from the touch.

"Yeah. You stayed." She frowned. "You shouldn't have. You're going to get sick."

He closed his eyes and lowered his head back down to the pillow. "I never get sick."

She closed her eyes again and drifted for a while until her body reminded her of a pressing need. "I have to use the bathroom," she finally said, reluctantly dragging herself away from all that heat.

She gasped when she saw herself in the bathroom mirror. Her hair was a rats' nest, and her face was swollen and puffy. She sent up a brief thanks that Theo had come after the worst of the puking had happened, but it was still bad. Very bad. Only a shower would fix this. She brushed her teeth twice while the water heated and then took the longest, hottest shower until she felt like a human again, all the while thinking that Theo Clairmont had slept in her bed.

And she had been sick. *What a waste.*

"Here's a towel," Theo said, and she jumped guiltily in the shower. He couldn't see anything with her opaque shower curtain, but it was still disconcerting to stand so close while she was naked. "How do you feel?"

She considered it for a moment. "Like I could eat a horse, but if I don't sit down soon, I might fall over." It was the truth. The adrenaline of waking up on Theo had worn off, and she was starting to shake. She turned off the water.

The shower curtain rustled, and Theo's arm appeared with a towel, which she took gratefully.

"What day is it?" She wrapped it around her and drew back the shower curtain to find him leaning against her vanity. His chest was indeed bare, and his hair looked like he'd run his fingers through it all night long. He looked rumpled and adorable as he held out his hand to help her step out of the tub.

"Tuesday. I can't believe I fell asleep. I never do that," Theo said, frowning.

She used a washcloth to wipe the steam from the mirror and rummaged around in the vanity for a comb. "You've said that before. Why don't you sleep?"

He watched her comb her hair in silence for a while. It should have been uncomfortable sharing these intimate moments with someone she wasn't in a relationship with, but it wasn't. "It's always been hard for me to shut my mind off," he finally said. "Mind if I use your shower?"

"It's all yours. There's a fresh toothbrush in the drawer." She dried off and put on a fresh set of pajamas, pulled her wet hair into a bun, and found her glasses. Her eyes ached too much for contacts.

By the time Theo stepped out of the bathroom in a cloud of

steam, she was back in bed. The shower had taken it out of her. Not so much that she couldn't appreciate Theo's naked chest. He put a pair of trousers back on, but his chest was still bare and distracting, even in her weak state. *Down, girl.*

He frowned when he saw her in bed again and came to sit at her hip. "How do you feel?" he asked, testing her forehead again. It was a casual, natural gesture that clued her in to how close they had been over the last twenty-four hours.

"Oh, no," she groaned, remembering. "Allie and the kids and my family. I hope they're not sick too."

"I talked to your mom and Allie. They're doing about as well as you are."

Amber's eyes popped open. "You talked to my mom?"

Theo shrugged, his eyes dark and unreadable. "She called your phone several times, and I answered. She said the whole family had the bug. I told her I'd stay with you."

Amber smiled crookedly. "You have no idea how much you're going to regret that. My mom will tell my aunts, and they'll be knocking on your door soon to meet you."

"That demographic in particular likes me," Theo said dryly. "Glasses, huh?" Theo added, nodding toward them.

A flicker of self-consciousness crossed her mind, but she was too tired for pretense. "Even Marilyn Monroe had to take her heels off sometimes," she said quietly.

Theo studied her with an intensity that made her heart pick up. "I like this version of you," he finally said, and warmth spread through her. It wasn't often she didn't have a single artifice to bolster her, but sitting on her messy bed with no makeup, no easy smile, and an unsexy pair of pajamas, these ones with puppies on them, was surprisingly comfortable. Maybe she was still feverish.

"I had groceries delivered," he said. "You rest and I'll bring you some food."

Heavenly. She closed her eyes and listened to the unfamiliar sounds of pots and pans in the kitchen. It wasn't that she didn't enjoy cooking. Her family were all excellent cooks, and she knew many recipes by heart, but it wasn't very fun to cook for one person. She'd rather spend her time sewing her designs. She closed her eyes and drifted off to the sound of Theo making himself at home.

A WHILE LATER, she woke up to Theo setting a plate on her lap and something green and mucky-looking in a glass on her nightstand. She scooted over and patted the bed. "Come sit." The only other surface in her bedroom was the floor.

Theo sat down with his own plate and leaned next to her against the head of the bed. They ate in companionable silence for a few minutes. Amber was ravenously hungry. Her stomach seemed to be back to normal even if her body wasn't. She finished the last bite of buttered toast and sighed happily. "Thank you."

"Here," Theo said, handing her the green juice. "Drink this."

"What? No. Gross. I thought that was for you."

He sighed. "It's just vegetables and fruit. I made it sweeter than usual. Just try it. You need the vitamins and minerals."

She eyed the glass suspiciously, but the guy had spent the night taking care of her. It was the least she could do. She took a tiny sip. "Oh. It is sweet."

Theo grinned. "I added carrots and apples."

"But I don't own a blender," she said.

"I had Ford buy one and bring it over along with some other things."

"Oh. Well," she said. "That was actually really nice of both of you."

"We're nice guys." Theo leaned back against the headboard and closed his eyes.

Amber settled back and did the same. "Did he bring you those running shorts?"

One eye popped open. "Yes."

"They're pretty short."

The other eye opened, along with a raised eyebrow. "Just ask. I know you saw it. You hung onto my leg like a koala bear all night."

She sat up, willing to let go of the koala bear comment for something better. "You have a tattoo?" She was dying to know about it. It was small enough and in a spot that meant he clearly didn't want anyone to see it. Naturally, she wanted every detail. "Of a microphone?"

He sighed. "Yes, it was a brief moment of rebellion when I was in college."

She gasped. "Tell me everything."

"It was stupid," he muttered. "During spring break, my buddies and I decided to hit this little beach bar. Things got... out of hand," he finished dryly.

"This is going to be epic," Amber said happily. "What happened?"

A sheepish grin spread over his face. "The details are fuzzy, but the gist of it is we made complete fools of ourselves singing karaoke on the beach." A red tint appeared on his cheeks while she watched, fascinated at this other side of him. "I woke up with a permanent reminder inked on my leg of being young and stupid, and my dad had to fly down to bail me and my friends out for being drunk and disorderly." He turned his head to look at her. "That's how I ended up in Grant's squad car that night. It was part of my punishment."

Oh. Even the casual mention of that made her uncomfortable. Not so much for what happened but for how Theo had seen her. It had been a blow to her pride she still felt to this day.

"Did it work?"

"It made me seriously think about if I wanted to follow in my dad's footsteps. He was always respected in our community and known for his integrity and leadership, and there I was, risking all of that over something stupid. So, yeah, it worked. It shifted my perspective about the job I had wanted since I was a kid. I didn't see it as something I had to do anymore. It was something I wanted to do, to honor him. I try to do that every day now that he's gone."

"I think your parents would be so proud of you."

He rolled his head and smiled at her. He looked so sincere and, yes, tired, lying there next to her in her bed. She could see it in the tiny lines next to his eyes and the pinch of his mouth, and she suddenly wanted to tuck him into her bed and make him rest with her. Who was taking care of him while he took care of an entire town? Theo was the kind of guy who loved his family, showed up every day to listen and work for the people, stayed with her while she was sick... Who took care of him?

Her chest was doing that flutter thing that only happened when she was around him, a confusing mix of fear and exhilaration that made her feel dizzy. Time to change the subject.

"Tell me the truth. Did you snoop through my stuff?"

Theo started to answer her, but she held up her hand. "I'm not ashamed to admit I snooped in your house that first day."

He opened his eyes and rolled his head toward her with that eyebrow of his quirked in amusement. "Find anything?"

"Just your subscription to *Mommy Milkers Monthly*." She wrinkled her nose when he laughed. "Seriously. Aside from your adorable standing lunch date with your grandma, you do nothing besides work." She turned to smile at him, expecting him to laugh, but he was looking at her without a smile.

"I found these," he said, reaching down to the side of the bed. He pulled up the sack of bills, the cellophane loud in the silent bedroom.

Amber's heart thudded to a stop. "Those are private." Shame flooded her, seeing the tangible example of her many failures in Theo's capable hands, and her anger kicked in full force. "You have no business looking through my private things," she snapped.

Theo's expression didn't change. "Your neighbor came over to check on you too."

"Sandy? I remember that."

"No," Theo said quietly. "Valentine Monroe. We had a long talk about how you've been helping her mom and sister get by for the last year. She asked me if I had any job openings."

Amber's eyes flashed. "Don't you dare hire her. Val's graduating soon. She needs to focus on her future, not financial worries."

Theo just looked at her, and she suddenly felt very, very exposed. "Is that where all your money's been going? Why did you let me think you were irresponsible?"

She sighed and closed her eyes again. "I'm tired."

"Why didn't you tell me?"

"Because it's none of your business. I'm taking care of it."

"That's why you needed an advance on your paycheck." He wasn't asking her, but she nodded anyway.

"And your car? It's still not fixed? And the AC unit?" He nodded to the window. "Your empty fridge."

She kept her eyes closed and just nodded. "Yes," she said simply. "I'm catching up now, but yes." Finally saying it out loud was a relief. Like it wasn't some hush-hush thing she had worried about over the last year. She would always look after

Val, Holly, and Sandy, but it felt good to acknowledge the weight of it with someone else. "She's just a kid. I want her to go to college in the fall and make sure she does something with her life. I don't want her to have to worry about money or have to work and leave Holly alone. Anything could happen to either of them. I've just been helping out when I can. You're more than generous with my salary, and things are a lot better now. Truthfully, I forgot I had stuffed those in the couch."

Theo was looking at her thoughtfully. It made her nervous to think of all the layers he was so good at seeing through. "Why give up on your own dreams in the process?"

She sighed. "It's a pattern for me. As soon as I get close to success, I sabotage myself. School, jobs, anything important to me, I find a way to derail it."

"Why is that?" he prodded quietly.

"I don't know. It's certainly not genetic. My family is full of go-getters. I'm the only one who can't keep my life on track." She tried hard not to let the old hurt and frustration seep into her voice, but it came out anyway.

"So you spend your money and time making sure Val doesn't make the same mistakes." Theo murmured, studying her bare face. "What would you do differently if you had the chance?" he asked abruptly.

She didn't even have to think about it. "I'd chase what I love and not worry so much about failing."

"And what is it you love?"

He was oddly intent as he studied her face, which was the only reason she didn't say something flippant. Admitting her biggest dream out loud to some world was something she hadn't done before. The vulnerability of it made her slightly queasy. "I'd open a clothing boutique... and sell my designs there." She was suddenly, unbearably, self-conscious with her dream hanging in the air.

Theo was silent. And then he nodded. "I have no doubt you'd be a success at anything you are fully committed to."

The air seemed to have left the room. She was lightheaded for a minute, absorbing those words like a diver sucking in precious air, until she mentally shook herself back to reality. She reacted the way she always did, with a deflection. "Anyway, that was fun baring my soul, Mr. Golden Boy. It's your turn. Time for truth or dare." She raised her eyebrow at him in challenge.

Theo's eyes narrowed. "I'm in your bed. I think it's time you called me Theo."

Amber winked. "Don't count on it. What's it going to be? Truth or dare?"

"Truth," he said immediately.

"Why do you listen to Neal when you know I'm right about your campaign?"

Theo was quiet for a moment. "It's complicated," he said finally. "When my dad died, Neal represented a bridge to my father's legacy, and the expectations and relationships that came with him settled on me." Theo shrugged. "Navigating that has been a challenge since my father died. Everything I do, I do because I love this town."

"I get it, the link Neal represents to you, but can't you see you won't have a chance at another term if you won't change your approach? You have this amazing vision, and you work hard to make it happen every day, but you have to take a risk and trust me on this. Northfield loves you, but I think seeing you in a different light is key to your next four years."

Theo rubbed his eyes tiredly. "Georgie would agree with you. My grandmother," he explained at her questioning look. "We call her Georgie. She's been on me for the last year to let Neal go and have more fun and take risks. I get so caught up in working that I let Neal steer this part of the ship. As you know," he said, eyeing her, "I'm not great at the PR stuff."

"Maybe it's time to let Northfield see a new side of you." Amber grinned. "I think I'd like Georgie. Lucky for you, I've been told I'm a fun time. We're good for each other, huh?" She nudged her shoulder against his.

"We are." He smiled, dimples and all, and her heart turned over with an audible creak. All the years of dust and rust from disuse seemed to shatter at that smile. It made her lightheaded but not scared, which was a wonder in itself. "Your turn. Truth or dare?" he asked.

"Dare, of course, but can I take a rain check?" She snuggled down into her pillow, suddenly exhausted. Too much introspection did that to a person.

"Do you promise to do whatever I come up with?" Theo drew the quilt over her shoulders and tucked her in securely. His hand lingered on her hair and smoothed the strands away from her face.

She closed her eyes. "Please, boss. There's nothing you could dare me to do that I'm scared of."

She drifted off to the sound of Theo's quiet laughter.

Chapter Sixteen

"I want you to train with me to run a 5K race."

"What?" Amber said. Her fuzzy pen clattered to her desk, and she knew her mouth was hanging open. Theo leaned nonchalantly against her office door and dropped a bomb on her.

"That's my dare." He strolled into her office and sat on the edge of her desk, nudging her package of Twinkies into the garbage. Puddin' looked up in disgust. This was her prime napping time. "Oops. Sorry," he said unapologetically.

Amber narrowed her eyes. "That was my lunch." She moved her can of Diet Coke to safety.

"I'll take you out to lunch," Theo said. "The Dash for a Difference 5K is next month. The dare is for you to run it with me." He leaned down to pet Puddin' on the head. She immediately rolled over onto her back, eyes still closed. Theo grinned and scratched her belly. "You promised."

"I did not," she said, aghast at the thought. "I don't run."

Theo crossed his arms smugly, and she admired the strong curves of his shoulders where his shirt stretched taut. She wished he would put his suit jacket on. She'd get a lot more work done around the office if she wasn't lusting after her boss, especially now that the imprint of his body lying flush against hers was still singed in her mind, and oh, God, what a body it was. She let her eyes drift to his legs, remembering how she had her face nuzzled against the tanned, powerful muscles of his thigh.

Was it smart to want her boss so much she felt lightheaded at the faintest hint of his cologne? Definitely not. Their talk yesterday had given her a new admiration for Theo's dedication to working hard at something that truly mattered to him. This wasn't just a job he had inherited; it was a calling to make a real difference in people's lives.

It put her own less than stellar life choices front and center. She was used to that, but seeing Theo pour himself into his work had kindled the tiniest flicker, a yearning to find something similar in herself.

The more she got to know Theo, the more indelibly he was marked in her brain... and other parts of her body. Other, lower, hotter parts that were humming along with him so near her.

An image of that long, hard body over her instead of under, crowding her and absorbing her at the same time... She shifted back in her chair and fanned herself with her notebook. Theo smiled, a slow, knowing curve of his wide, sensual lips.

"That's my dare. You said you weren't scared of anything I could come up with, and this is what I'm choosing," he said calmly.

He was in full mayor mode, reasonable and patient as he listed the reasons he thought he could torture her. As always, it made the little streak of wildness she kept mostly contained pulse to life.

"That's not fair," she said indignantly. "I was sick. You took advantage of me."

"You gave me your word. That's how truth or dare works." He raised his voice. "Right, Charlotte?"

"I'm afraid that's how the game works," Charlotte called back. "Don't die, Amber."

"Traitor," Amber shouted down the hall.

She'd have to play dirty now. She sat back in her swivel chair and slowly crossed her legs, making sure a good amount of her smooth thigh showed in the slit of her royal blue wrap dress.

It was another piece she had designed years ago for a temp job at an office downtown. The job hadn't lasted—the manager had wandering hands whenever she brought him his daily coffee, but the dress was a win. The silk draped over her breasts and hips like it was made for her body, making her feel sexy and demure at the same time. But the real stars of her outfit today were her hot pink high heels with the sexy straps at the ankles and the tiny poofs of pink faux feathers at the toes.

She looked up under her lashes at Theo to see him staring intently at her legs. The heels were a ridiculous showgirl kind of sexy, and she had worn them deliberately. She had a sneaking suspicion Mr. Buttoned-Up Mayor had a thing for high heels. She wasn't above using them to her advantage. "Some people aren't meant to run, boss," she said, trailing a finger down from her knee to her ankle. "These legs are more sashay than sprint. Blame it on the short muscle fibers. It's a thing."

Theo blinked slowly as if coming out of a trance before shooting her a knowing look. "Uh-huh. Find your sneakers. I'll be at your house tomorrow at six thirty a.m.," he said. "Be ready."

"I won't be," she snapped, miffed that the heels hadn't closed the deal. The phone on her desk rang. She picked it up while staring Theo in the eyes. "You've reached Sal's Birdland," she said, daring him with a look to say anything. She listened for a minute. "Yes, I still work here, Mr. Kemper," she sighed.

"Sorry about that. I'll put you through." She pressed the button to send the call to Theo's office phone.

"Sal's Birdland?" Theo raised a brow.

She shrugged. "I like to keep 'em guessing." Theo turned away, and she thought of something. "Did you send me a new AC unit?" she asked suspiciously. The box had shown up at her door first thing this morning with no note. Her landlord wasn't responsible for the window units, and she didn't have the extra cash yet to spring for fixing it. As soon as she saw it, she had a feeling Theo was responsible. Her pride stung, but mostly she was grateful not to have to sleep in a sauna.

Theo raised a brow as if the question was preposterous and strode out of her office.

At four o'clock, she got her notepad and pen ready for the final meeting of the day. The agenda she had typed up earlier said they were discussing the Hope Gala. The annual event at the Grand River Hotel, another property owned by the Sterling family, was Theo's largest annual fundraising effort that benefited the Maple Street Center for Domestic Violence, where Theo, Amber had just learned, sat on the board. Of all of Theo's meetings, this was one she had a personal interest in.

"Thank you for coming, Edward, Cade," Theo greeted them warmly.

Edward Sterling was tall and broad, and his loud, booming laugh fit his personality perfectly. His debonair blue gingham suit was fabulously flamboyant and faintly vintage. Amber half expected him to pull out a straw hat and twirl a cane like in the movies. She was smitten instantly.

"Neal, Theo, always good to see you," Edward boomed. He shook Neal's hand politely but pulled Theo in for a hug, which Theo returned.

"And you, Miss Hart." Edward turned, looking her up and

down with a practiced eye. "Beautiful dress. It's an Elie Saab, isn't it?"

"No, I made it, but thanks," she said and laughed when Edward grabbed her hands and held them wide to admire her dress. She knew they were kindred spirits.

"You are just fabulous, my dear. My wife would pay good money to wear that." He turned to the tall man behind him. "This is my son, Cade. Theo, I believe you and Cade went to Columbia together. Cade's in town helping me get some things in order and keeping me on task."

"It's good to see you again, Cade," Theo greeted the tall man next before leading Edward into the conference room, leaving her alone with Edward's son.

It was safe to say Cade didn't share his father's boisterous personality. The tall, strikingly handsome man's suit was just as expensive and professionally tailored, but Cade Sterling was the picture of cool reserve. When she finally made it to his eyes, Cade was smiling faintly at her. His eyes were a shade of green she had never seen before, light and piercing.

"Cade Sterling," he murmured, holding out his hand. "We haven't had the pleasure of meeting yet."

"That's a surprise. Amber's *very* well known around North-field." Neal's voice dripped with insinuation. "Shall we?" He said it so quickly that by the time Amber absorbed the hit, Neal had turned into the conference room.

Embarrassment and anger stained her cheeks bright red when she caught Cade's gaze. He was frowning after Neal, but Amber knew the game. While she couldn't control the heat warming her face, she could control her outward reaction, and the best way to deal with men like Neal Barclay was never to let them see a weakness.

"After you," she said, gesturing grandly toward the conference room. She held her smile firmly in place and lifted her chin high.

Cade seemed to understand and let it go. "Ladies first."

For the next half hour, Amber took notes and fumed silently. Neal had never made it a secret how he felt about her, but to have him insinuate in front of a stranger that she was the town slut had triggered a different fury. The injustice of it, the unfairness, stung deeply.

"The Hope Gala is our biggest fundraiser of the year, as you know," Neal was saying. "The Grand River Hotel lends itself perfectly to a sit-down dinner with our usual art and antique auction. It was always quite successful for Theo's father," he added a touch smugly.

Amber bit the inside of her cheek. Of course, Neal would do the same tired gala he'd been putting on for years. Why wouldn't he consider Northfield was changing, and that Theo was going to be left behind in the dust if he didn't capture more than the same old demographic of voters? She fumed and doodled notes in her notebook while she listened.

She had been doing a stellar job of not rocking the boat since her first disastrous meeting, in which she had the audacity to share her ideas and was set in her place, but the longer she listened, the more she thought back to what Theo had said in her bed yesterday. Theo genuinely cared about Northfield, not only because he had a legacy to uphold, but because he had a vision for the town's future.

No, she would keep her mouth shut like the good little assistant she was hired to be because she needed money more than she needed to be right.

But that wild streak that showed up at the most inopportune times in her life and got her in trouble had a mind of its own. She cleared her throat, and all the eyes in the room turned to her. She met Neal's gaze and pulled out her most dazzling, glittery smile. He looked startled for a second, before wariness settled on his pinched features.

"I have an idea," she started, her voice steadier than she felt. "Why not combine the two? Keep the traditional elegance of the gala but infuse it with the energy and fresh thinking that echo Theo's campaign promise?"

She had their attention now, and with the innate sense of a performer, she painted a picture. "You could have food stations with local restaurants that represent Northfield's diverse culinary history, and live music from local bands throughout the night." She was warming to the idea now, sitting on the edge of her seat. She shot a quick look at Edward and Cade, who looked interested, while Theo's eyes remained unreadable.

"Instead of speeches, you could have interactive displays where guests could engage with Theo's policies, and the whole thing could be livestreamed to share on social media for everyone, not just the people that can afford the price of a ticket. That way, it's not just a gala, it's a statement of who Northfield is and what you stand for."

The room was silent for a moment after she finished, and her stomach felt weightless. She didn't want to look at Theo and see dismissal or, worse, polite interest, especially after baring her soul to him the day before about her fear of success.

She'd taken a risk, and even if it didn't pay off, she knew it was a good idea. She knew it the way she knew color and patterns, deep in her soul. She sat back and waited with her heart in her throat.

Suddenly, Edward clapped loudly and enthusiastically in the silent room. "By God, I think that's brilliant! Think of the buzz that would create, and how many new people you could reach. Of course, it's up to you, Theo, but the Grand River Hotel would love to host an event like this."

"Exactly," Amber nodded, wilting a little in relief. "A gala like this would make it accessible to everyone."

"It's brilliant, Amber," Cade said, shooting her a warm smile. "Fresh and innovative."

Amber turned to Theo, already planning her next line of reasoning, only to find him grinning at her.

"That's quite a leap from tradition," Neal said sharply. "It sounds like a festival rather than a gala. Our core donors might not appreciate such radical changes."

"Our core donors are important, but so is broadening our appeal. Amber's ideas are exactly the kind of innovation that shows we're forward thinking, and that starts with how we engage our community," Theo said firmly. "Amber, will you take the lead on planning this?"

She nodded confidently. *Say yes first, panic later.*

"We'll get started with the planning on our end," Edward said. He stood up and pushed in his chair. "The Grand River Hotel has hosted countless galas but nothing quite like this. This is going to be a truly special night. I'll put you in touch with our event coordinator, Cheryl. Just tell her what your vision is, and she'll work with you to make it happen."

Amber shot a glance at Neal, who was packing up his folder. His face was set in stone. She had made an enemy out of him, but she was smart enough to know he would never have approved of her even if she had stayed silent.

Excitement coursed through her because, whether he was her enemy or not, she'd just had a taste of victory, and as with that first taste of anything sweet, she craved more.

As the room began to empty, Amber stood up with her notebook and pen.

"That was a brilliant idea," Cade said at her elbow.

"Thanks," she said, a little breathless at the admiration on his handsome face.

"Would you like to get dinner?" he asked. "I'm in town for one more night, and I'd love to eat somewhere other than the Grand."

Amber recognized the look on his face. Interest. Admiration. Attraction. She had dealt in those feelings like currency all her life. It was familiar and comforting, even, and she felt a little flutter of excitement.

But she wanted to savor her victory. Alone.

"No, thank you. I can't," she said.

Her gaze sought Theo's across the room, holding it for a second that seemed to stretch out before he finally turned and left the room.

She had the distinct, unsettling realization that there was one person she wouldn't mind sharing her victory with after all.

Chapter Seventeen

"Touch me, Theo. I've been waiting to feel you all over me."

His sexy assistant wound her arms around his neck and rose on her tiptoes, offering her full, pouty mouth for his kiss. He captured her lips and licked into her hot, sweet mouth. She tasted like cinnamon candy and sex, and he wanted to devour her whole.

Her fingers weaved through his hair, stroking lightly and making him shudder. Theo kissed the side of her neck, nipping the cord there until he felt her knees go weak, then licked and sucked lightly as her throat tipped back and she cried out, long and low.

"I want to feel you, Theo. Make me feel you so deep," she whispered. Theo's hand cupped the back of her neck and tilted her head back to see her eyes. They were half-closed with lust. Theo shuddered. She was his greatest fantasy come to life, and he couldn't get enough, fast enough, deep enough to satisfy him.

He lifted her off her feet and pressed her into the wall. Her legs in those fucking pink high heels spread wide, notching her heat perfectly into his erection before settling tightly around his waist. Her fingers trailed down to his chest and teased him there.

"Need you," she whispered in his ear. "Need to feel you inside me." Her hands were driving him crazy, leaving little trails of fire on his chest and stomach. Her mouth was open and so sweet, teasing him with her little gasps and moans. She was hot and hungry, exactly how he fantasized her to be.

She lifted her breasts and offered their heavy weight to him. Her sundress slipped to reveal the hint of her pink nipple over the top, and he went feral. He lowered his head and licked a hot line down the curve to her nipple, standing up so prettily for him to suck and play with.

Theo shifted her against the wall and thrust against her, while she arched greedily, her damp panties the only flimsy barrier between them.

"Yes, take it, Theo. Take what you need," she breathed and sucked his lower lip into her mouth.

Rooooroooooo.

Theo's eyes opened and instead of Amber's hot, wet, sucking tongue, Theo felt a swipe across his cheek. His hand came up. "What the..." He cracked one eye open and looked into the soulful eyes of his dog.

Rooorooooo. Puddin's head went back, and she howled in pure ecstasy—the way she greeted him every morning.

"Get off me," he said. She lapped his face again and panted her doggy breath at him lovingly. Theo reached down and adjusted his raging hard-on. His heart was still pounding, and he ached where he'd been pressed against Amber against the wall. *Fuck.* So much for that dream.

Pudding looked at him reproachfully and rolled over onto her back. She had never spent even a single night in the crate. That first night she had looked at him just as she was looking at him now, and Theo learned he was a pushover for soulful brown eyes.

"Come 'ere, girl," he sighed as he looked at the clock. Five forty-five a.m., an ungodly hour to be awake, but he had been a runner all his life. Running was one of the only things that allowed him to stop thinking and just use his body.

Puddin' moaned again, and he gave her what she wanted—the best belly scratch of her life—and thought about Amber at work yesterday. She had done something he'd thought impossible—change an event that had been the same since his grandfather was in office. And Theo was proud to admit, her ideas were good. Better than good.

Cade had thought so too. Theo had overheard him ask Amber to dinner. The relief he'd felt when she had refused had taken the wind out of him. He prided himself on his self-control and rationality, but the thought of Amber with Cade stirred unfamiliar feelings in him. Amber was free to spend her time with anyone she chose, of course, and Cade was a good guy, well-liked and successful. There was no need for him to feel the stab of jealousy about them together, yet Amber affected him differently than any other woman. She got under his skin and made him care about things he wouldn't normally.

It was ridiculous. He had no claim over her and no right to feel any kind of possessiveness.

After a quick shower, Theo packed the groceries he had shopped for the night before and hit the road. He had no idea what he was going to face at Amber's house, or if she'd even open the door, but he wasn't kidding when he said he would be there at six thirty a.m. to run.

The idea had come to him when he left her house after taking care of her when she was sick. She looked so despondent, telling him how she was afraid to take risks to go after what she really wanted. He was going to show her that she could do this one thing, even if he had to manhandle her into it.

It was going to be a challenge. He knew how stubborn she was, but when he put his mind to something, he always won. He took the stairs up to her apartment and knocked on the door. No answer. No surprise. He knocked again.

The apartment door across the hall opened, and Val, with her backpack on her shoulders, poked her dark head out and looked around suspiciously.

Theo had met the teen when she had stopped by Amber's apartment the morning Amber was sick. She had shown up looking like death to check on her friend, and when she found him, she'd panicked, thinking that Amber was going to get in trouble for not showing up for work and told him the whole story. Val was so sick she could barely stand up straight while they talked, so Theo had sent her back to bed with a promise that Amber's job was safe, but she had given him some very valuable insight into Amber first.

Val's version of Amber was one he was still coming to terms with. Instead of being frivolous with her time and money, she had been shouldering the weight of another family, paying bills that stretched her own already thin finances even more. And all in secret.

His perspective had been shifting ever since and, combined with Neal's shitty criticism, had morphed into a profound respect for her in stark contrast to the facade she painted for everyone else. With the exception of Johnny. He'd definitely noticed she was more herself with him than anyone else.

But he wasn't stupid. He knew Amber wouldn't appreciate him knowing about something she kept hidden, even from her family. She had too much pride for that. So he had taken the stack of bills she had hidden in her couch of all places and ordered her a new air conditioner and not said a word. It was the least he could do.

"Are you coming or going?" Val said, squinting at him.

He looked down at the groceries. "I'm here to pick Amber up for a run."

"Shoot. My bus is coming, or I would totally stick around to watch this disaster go down. Good luck," she called, running down the stairs.

Theo pounded again, and suddenly a very growly, very scary-looking Amber answered the door. Her hair was tangled around her shoulders, and she wore an oversized black KISS T-shirt that fell to the top of her thighs—no shorts in sight. Theo took a deep breath and steeled himself. He was here to prove something to her. He wasn't here to wonder what she wore to bed at night.

"What?" she said, rubbing her eyes sleepily, which was one of the most adorable things Theo had ever seen. But he knew better than to show a sign of weakness.

Brusquely, he pushed past her and walked to the kitchen with his groceries. "It's six thirty." He checked his watch. "You were supposed to be up and ready. We're running today."

"The hell we are," she said, yawning. "You can run. I'm going back to bed." She leaned against the door with her hands behind her back, looking deliciously rumpled and sleepy, as if she'd spent a long night being thoroughly fucked. An image from his X-rated dream flashed through his brain and Theo scowled.

"I told you I'd be here."

"And I told you, I'm not a runner. Pick another dare." She rolled her eyes. "Do you want me to streak across the village green? I've totally done that before, but I'll do it again. Do you want me to sing karaoke at the gala? I'll do that too," she offered smugly. "But I don't run."

"You're running," he said evenly. "I'll give you ten seconds to get into your bedroom and put on whatever you need to run in, or I'm going to help you."

Her chin lifted. "You wouldn't."

He gave her his best stare, the kind that could make a criminal tremble back in his prosecuting days. "Try me. Ten... nine..."

She straightened up slowly, thrusting out her breasts, a gleam of challenge in her eye.

"Eight... seven..." Theo slid a hot gaze up and down her barely covered body, and a flare of lust shot through him. He held her gaze with a silent dare.

Her hands went to her hips.

"Six... five... four..."

She smiled smugly. "I have a better idea," she said, tugging up the hem of the T-shirt so that it danced at the cleft of her thighs. Theo's mouth went dry. "Let's compromise. Come to my bedroom, and I'll show you something you've been thinking about since that night at the lake."

He shook his head. He wasn't unaffected. He just wanted her to prove to herself she could do something more.

Her eyes narrowed just as he said, "Three... two... one." She bolted from the door, but he rushed her in two long strides and tossed her over his shoulder. His palm landed on her bare ass, and he took a moment to learn its shape. Round, supple flesh. His question was answered: she didn't have anything on except for panties under the shirt.

"Now you're just copping a feel. Put me down!" she whined and pounded on his back with her fists. Theo grinned.

"Stop fighting or you won't like what I do," he said cheerfully. He headed toward her bedroom while her bare feet kicked in the air.

"Don't you threaten me." She wrapped her arms around his

waist, lifted his shirt, and nipped his back with her sharp little teeth.

"Ouch." He winced and gave in to the temptation, landing one hard slap on her ass on his way to the bedroom.

"No, you didn't," she gasped, arching back and trying to cover her ass with her hand.

"I did," he said, rubbing the spot lightly. Amber had the best ass he'd ever seen. Round and plump and perfect. "And I'll do it again. You're not going to get out of this. We're running."

"Put me down!" she squealed. He reached her bedroom and tossed her down on the bed, where she bounced up onto her elbows and stared him down. He read the desire in her eyes and the mischief, but he wasn't going to be derailed by any of her nonsense.

"I'm not a runner. I told you, but I know how to do other things well," she said, reaching for him. He stepped away from the bed.

"Then we'll walk until you become one," he said patiently.

"I don't like walking."

"Then you'll run." He opened her drawers and pulled out a pair of shorts.

"I'm not wearing that." She had dropped the femme fatale act and was pouting now. Theo sensed victory, but he kept his face impassive.

"You have another ten seconds to get dressed or—"

"Or you'll spank me again? Maybe I'll take all day." She leaned back on her elbows again and crossed her legs. He caught sight of purple panties.

"Or I will get you dressed. And Amber?" Her lips pouted in that way of hers that made him want to swoop down and cover her sweet little sex-kitten mouth with his, but he forced a scowl on his face. "You won't like what I pick out for you."

He could see her brilliant mind mulling it over.

"Fine," she said in disgust, "but this is going to be no fun for you because you're going to see how awful I am, and I'll just slow you down."

He stared her down.

Her hands went to the hem of her shirt, and she raised an eyebrow. "Usually, when I take my clothes off, the other person looks happier about it." She dragged the shirt up, and just as it hit the top of her ribs, Theo turned around quickly and left. He wasn't a saint; he was already trying his best to keep his hands off her luscious body, and he didn't know how much longer he could hold out.

Ten minutes later, Amber came back out into the living room, her face scrubbed and her hair in a ponytail.

"Here," he said, handing her a banana, "eat this before we go."

"I hate bananas." She wrinkled her nose but took a reluctant bite, and he shuffled her out of the apartment before she could give him any more stripteases.

"How far are we going?" she asked suspiciously as they stretched on the steps outside her building. "I have to work today, and my boss is a real asshole."

He shot her a look. "Very funny. We're running two miles today."

"Two miles?" Her mouth dropped open. "I don't think I could walk two miles. How about I ride my bike? You have to ease me into this deal. Nice and slow. But I bet you wouldn't know anything about that." She smirked.

"Aren't you the one that told me I excel in everything I do?"

She snapped her mouth shut.

They started off easy. The sun was rising, hazy and humid already. Theo did his best to keep his eyes straight ahead, instead of on the bouncing curves in Lycra next to him. He kept a steady pace until she had a hard time talking to him.

"I need a break. Let's sit down here on this bench," she gasped, pointing at the end of Main Street.

Theo looked at his watch. He had spent the night researching a popular 5K program, and he had all of his stops planned for her.

"A little bit farther," he coaxed.

She bent down with her hands on her knees, huffing and puffing, but she let him bully her into another respectable few yards.

They did an easy loop around the village, through the green where people were fishing in the canal and passed moms running with their kids in strollers. He was proud of Amber, although he wasn't ready to give her any praise. He knew she'd stop if he did, but she kept up and eventually stopped complaining. He had a feeling that had more to do with not having any breath to spare.

Back up in her apartment, she dragged herself to the shower with a limp wave of her hand. "Shower. Bye. See you. Later," she said, panting.

Theo grinned and made his way to the kitchen. He found the blender in the same spot he had left it, took out all the glass containers of lettuce, apples, celery, carrots, spinach, kale, and seeds he had brought over, and got to work.

Fifteen minutes later, Amber padded out of the bathroom in a short colorful kimono robe. "Oh," she said in surprise, "I thought you went home."

"Drink this," he said, handing her a tall glass of green juice.

She looked at it then at him, as if he had betrayed her. "You made me run, and you're making me drink that? What did I ever do to you?"

He laughed, something he realized he did often with her around. "This isn't part of our dare. It's just good for you. Drink this and I'll make you an omelet."

She looked like she was going to dig her heels in, but then a sly look crossed her face. "Fine," she said, "but I want you to do something for me."

"What?" he asked warily.

She marched over to her giant work bag and pulled out a file folder. "I'll drink this"—she held up the glass—"if you add these events to your calendar."

Theo took the file silently and read it over. It was a copy of his calendar for the next two months. All of his usual weekly meetings and events were on there, but she had shuffled a few evenings around to add in an outdoor movie night, the Northfield carnival, and the Fourth of July fireworks along with a few other local events. Aside from the carnival when he was a kid, he hadn't had the time for any of these events. There always seemed to be something else more pressing, or Neal had him scheduled to attend something that attracted an older demographic.

"What did you take off my calendar?" he asked.

"I didn't get rid of anything. I just managed your time more efficiently, which is what you hired me for, right? Come on. This is fair. If I'm going to train for a race, you have to agree to experience the magic of a small-town summer."

"Okay. I'll go," he said, surprising himself. He grinned. "That was a great tagline, by the way. 'Experience the magic of a small-town summer.' You sure you didn't major in marketing?"

"I majored in beer pong," she said with an eye roll. But then, "Really?" She asked, a pleased smile spreading across her face.

He pushed the glass toward her. "Yes. Now drink up, Red Hot," he said.

She put the straw in her mouth and sipped the green juice. She kept her eyes on his and sucked slowly. When she pulled the straw away, she licked her lips and grinned. "You just wait. I am going to make this your best summer ever."

Chapter Eighteen

"I THINK I PULLED A HAMMY," Amber said. She sat on the chair in front of Charlotte's desk, looking over her legs morosely. No pretty heels today. She had to wear her flats after Theo had tortured her with his running schedule. She hadn't really thought he meant *every* day, but the man was a sadist.

He had shown up at her door at six thirty on the dot every morning for the last week, looking disgustingly chipper and dragged her along with him on his torturous runs.

To add insult to injury, he bullied her into drinking his disgusting green juice and eating eggs when they were finished. She hadn't had sugar since last week, she thought balefully. It was true she didn't really crave it, but still. It was the principle.

Theo was out with Neal at a meeting, and she was in Charlotte's office nursing her sore feet. On top of her sore legs and lack of sleep, she was working harder than she ever had before on the gala planning. While Cheryl from the Grand River Hotel was the one executing the details, it was still more work than she had ever done before, and to make it even more stressful, if her idea flopped and no one came or they hated it, it was Theo who would suffer. She was so not cut out for this.

"I think you might be overreacting just a bit," Charlotte said. She leaned back in her seat, and Amber took a moment to admire her. Charlotte was killing it with the new look. Her fitted dove gray blazer with a blush-colored camisole made her skin look luminous, and she wasn't trying to blend into the wallpaper anymore. "You've survived Theo's boot camp for what, a week? I have a lot of money in the pot that you'll make it until the 5K, so you can't quit now."

Amber narrowed her eyes. "Todd, what did you bet?" she called down the hallway.

There was a beat of silence. "I'd rather not say."

"He bet two days," Diane said from the front desk. "He's already out," she added smugly. "I bet two weeks, so you better not quit yet."

"Thanks for the vote of confidence, you traitors," Amber said huffily.

"Don't be mad," Todd said. "After your car wouldn't start that last time, you Ubered the two blocks from your apartment to work. That didn't exactly scream 'athlete.'"

"I had four-inch heels on," Amber said indignantly. "Those are sitting-pretty shoes, not walking shoes."

Charlotte looked at her kindly. "We're all very impressed you're doing so well."

"Now I won't quit, just so you'll win the pot."

"Don't do it for me," Charlotte said. "You're doing this for you."

"I'd rather do it for you," Amber laughed. "I have less chance of failing."

"You're not going to fail. This is just going to require more effort than you're used to." She leaned back. "Haven't you ever wanted something so badly that it wasn't an option to quit?"

Amber picked at a nonexistent thread on her navy pencil skirt. "I don't think I've ever made it that far."

"What would that look like for you?" Charlotte probed gently. "What would it be? I don't think it's any job in this office, is it? Not that you're not doing a great job as Theo's assistant. I just get the feeling there's something else you'd rather be doing with all your creativity."

Amber shrugged self-consciously. "I guess I've always wanted to open a vintage clothing boutique... maybe with some of my own designs mixed in. But that's a long shot." She laughed lightly. "Can you imagine me owning a business? I'd have no idea where to start."

Charlotte smiled. "I do. I'd be happy to help you create a business plan to take to the bank."

Amber's chest squeezed for a moment with how much she wanted that, but then reality popped her bubble. "Maybe someday," she murmured instead. "How are things with you and Johnny? You two have been seeing quite a bit of each other, right?"

Charlotte toyed with her pen. "Yes, we have." The pink in her cheeks was a dead giveaway.

Amber rubbed her hands together, glad to be on more familiar ground. Matchmaking always made her feel better. She might not believe there was one right person for her, but she did enjoy living vicariously through her friends.

Charlotte hesitated. "Johnny told me you two were together briefly years ago."

Amber winced. She would never forgive herself if their stupid foray into being lovers ruined the good thing Charlotte and Johnny clearly had going. "It's true that at one point we gave it a go, but that's all it was. We quickly figured out we're much better off as friends."

"I know. He said as much," Charlotte said, nodding thoughtfully. "But lately, I've been wondering if he's sticking around for the right reasons. For me, not just this version of me, you know?" She gestured to her chic suit and new hair.

How well Amber knew that feeling. She'd rather not dwell on it, but oh, yes, she knew. She knew exactly what it was like to wonder about men and their reasons for wanting her. The men she had chosen over the years were much fewer than she let on for that reason. How could she know they were with her, or the version of herself she allowed them to see, when she kept the rest of herself so well hidden?

"I've known Johnny for years," Amber said. "He's genuinely one of the good ones. Have you talked to him about how you feel?"

"He's been wonderful, but it's me. There's this nagging doubt that I'm not enough for him, you know?"

"I do know, and the truth is, you just have to be yourself. If he's the man we want him to be, he'll want every version of you." Theo's words from the morning after he took care of Amber flashed in her head.

I like this version of you.

"He'll want every version of me," Charlotte repeated softly. "That's a lovely thought."

Yes, it really was.

Chapter Nineteen

"ARE YOU TIRED, girl? Why don't I just take you back to the house to get you some water? See? She's tired. She has short little legs like me." Amber blinked up at him, and Theo just shook his head.

It was Saturday morning, and Theo had shown up bright and early with Puddin' in tow because Amber had begged him to bring the dog to run with them. He frowned at her while she smiled angelically, her hazel eyes warm and pleading as she looked up at him.

The early morning light cast her face in a soft glow, highlighting the flush on her cheeks and the slight sheen of sweat that made her skin glisten. Strands from her ponytail had escaped and clung to her neck, tempting him to reach out and touch her throat.

He sighed, knowing the two of them had bested him this morning. "I'll finish the run. You bring her back to your apartment, and I'll meet you there." He ignored the relief on her face. They still had a month to train for the race, and he was going to make sure she ran it, even if he had to drag her the whole way.

Truthfully, she had done better over the last two weeks than he had ever expected. Despite her complaints and delaying tactics, she was just stubborn enough that if he teased her and made it into a challenge, she kept up for the most part.

"I knew you had a soft spot for us," Amber teased. She held his eyes, and the familiar rush of lust shot through him. He'd been doing an admirable job of training her without giving into the urge to touch that soft, sweet body again.

His hand ached with the desire to touch her, day in and day out at the office. It was a unique form of torture, one he was prolonging with these early morning runs, when she looked so soft and sleepy that he wanted to take her back to her bed and sink between her thighs and feel all that wildness moving beneath him.

There was nothing easy about her. She was like a hurricane in his life, disrupting even the most routine, mundane parts of his day with her laughter. He found himself looking forward to work for entirely different, much less noble reasons, than he'd had all his life. The tip-tap sound of her high heels when she inevitably came in late and tried to sneak into her office, the shape of her beautiful body standing in his doorway with a nonsense note and a teasing smile on her lips.

The desire to know her had taken him by surprise with its intensity. He had known many beautiful, more accomplished women in his life, but none had taken a hold of him so thoroughly.

Theo finished his run and was doubling back to pass the village green when he saw Amber with Puddin' in her arms, talking to a group of women holding yoga mats. He squinted, recognizing a few of the ladies as regular commenters from the town's Facebook page. Todd usually kept him informed of the chatter, but even Neal kept an eye on this particular group of women. They were in the coveted twenty-five-to-forty-year-old age range, consisting mostly of undecided voters. It drove Neal nuts that they hadn't managed to get through to that demographic while Beckerman seemed to have gained their support early on.

For an instant, unease gripped Theo. Lord only knew what Amber could be saying to them.

"Mr. Mayor!" Amber called, and he steeled himself for the worst before crossing the street.

Whatever it was, he would deal with it. She just didn't know the rules of politics. He could fix anything that she managed to fuck up for him, he told himself as he joined them.

"Hi, Mr. Mayor," Amber said as he approached. Theo studied her for signs of mischief, but she looked excited. "I was just chatting with my new friends about where they got their green juice, and wouldn't you know, it's right next to Lily's new studio."

He narrowed his eyes at her, wondering where she was taking this. "Is that right?" he said pleasantly enough. Puddin' howled, and he automatically reached out his arms to hold her. The old girl rubbed her face alongside his in ecstasy and swiped at his cheek with her tongue. Theo absently petted her. She didn't like to be ignored.

"We were just chatting about how much you enjoy green juice, too, and I thought how fun would it be to do a juice date with the mayor?" she said, her eyes twinkling. "That way you could hear about what matters to your constituents on a more casual, regular basis."

Theo saw where she was going, and he was impressed.

"Oh, yes, we love going to the juice bar, and I've been meaning to ask you about that petition we had going around to put a dog park next to the canal." A woman with a yoga mat strapped to her back nodded approvingly at him. "I can see you're a dog lover, too, Mr. Mayor."

"Yes, and we've been saying for years that Northfield needs

a Little League complex for our kids," another woman chimed in while her friends nodded. "We tried to get to a community meeting to talk about it, but evenings are hard for me to leave the house with the kids' sports and getting them to bed on time, you know?" Theo didn't, but he nodded, fascinated.

Amber smoothly made plans for a weekly juice date with anyone who wanted to come to talk with him informally. All the while, Theo was internally shaking his head. He had walked over thinking he was going to clean up a mess, and Amber had single-handedly created an authentic way to connect with a whole demographic he had never talked with before.

"Wait! Before you go, let's take a selfie for the mayor's new social media channels." Amber herded them all together, and Theo found himself grinning at the phone while Amber snapped away.

He shook his head silently as they walked away. A dog park? A baseball complex? How was this the first time he had heard of this?

Amber looked up from her phone. "There. Posted. You totally thought I was going to ruin things for you, didn't you?" she asked with a sly look on her face.

Theo smiled. "Race you back to the apartment."

"Nope," she said immediately. She stopped walking and crossed her arms. "I already did my two miles."

"You walked the second one." He held her elbow and herded her into a fast walk.

"I'm tired. It's the end of the week. Don't I get a rest day?" She sounded so woeful that Theo couldn't help but laugh.

"You get a rest day tomorrow. Come on. I'll make you carrot juice this time."

"Oh, goodie."

Chapter Twenty

"I'm not paying for all these vegetables, you know," Amber said as Theo added yet another bunch of greens into the canvas market bag. She waved to Sawyer Manning, who was lifting a crate of butter lettuce out from the back of his farm truck, displaying the bulging muscles his profession had given him. "No offense, Sawyer. You know I always buy your aunt's honey."

On their run the following Saturday, Amber had caught a whiff of corn dogs and dragged Theo to the farmers' market. Her idea backfired when Theo purchased two reusable bags and proceeded to fill them with enough fruits and vegetables to feed her entire building for the week.

"I didn't think you were," Theo said. He handed Sawyer cash and stuffed another bunch of kale in the bag.

"No offense taken," Sawyer replied, tipping his worn straw hat toward her with a roguish grin. They had gone to school together, and Sawyer had taken over his family farm a few years ago. Amber always made sure to stop by his stand to pick up his aunt's local honey and baked goods if he had them.

"Sawyer, have you met Mayor Clairmont?" Amber asked.

"Sawyer's a part of the Northfield Sustainable Agriculture Initiative," she mentioned.

"Can't say that I have," Sawyer admitted. He took a bandanna from his back pocket and wiped his hands off, offering one.

"Call me Theo, please," Theo said, shaking his hand.

"The initiative could really benefit from more community support, maybe even a partnership with the town," Amber said casually. "Sawyer, the mayor's been looking for ways to support local sustainability efforts."

Sawyer nodded. "Any help from the town would make a huge difference."

"I'd like to hear more about that," Theo said, nodding. "Maybe we can set up a meeting to see how the town can help."

As they headed toward the Amish farm stand, Amber couldn't help but smile.

"I'd tell you how good you are at this job, but I can tell you're already patting yourself on the back," Theo said dryly.

Hannah, the young girl behind the table, had an assortment of jams and fresh baked goods displayed. Amber's mouth watered. Theo put a glass jar of sauerkraut in the bag.

"I am, aren't I?" she said delightedly. She took the sauerkraut out and replaced it with a bag of to-die-for snickerdoodles.

Theo took them back out.

She stopped and glared. "Hannah, tell the mayor he does not want to mess with keeping these cookies away from me. It will get ugly."

Theo grinned, dimples and all, and she melted a little. "Compromise?" He held up a carton of peaches. "I'll make you a peach crumble with these."

Amber snatched it from him. "We'll take both," she said. "Hannah, have you met the mayor yet? And how are your parents? Are they here today?"

"They're around here somewhere. My mom said she missed seeing you at the Maple Street Center."

"Oh, really?" Amber shot a glance at Theo, but he was looking over the fruit. "Tell her I said 'hi,' please. Come on, Mr. Mayor. The kettle corn is over there." Amber hustled them on before Theo could ask any questions, stopping at every table to introduce him to everyone she knew.

Now, back at her apartment, freshly showered and wrapped in her silk kimono, Amber couldn't help but marvel at the sight of Theo putting away food in her kitchen as if he had been doing it for years. And here she was, absolutely killing it with his PR campaign. Was this a forever type of job? She wasn't sure, but for now it felt incredibly good to be acing something for a change.

A month ago, she had been living off bananas and ramen, with her bank account scraping the bottom and a constant stress headache hovering. Now, there was a sexy, buttoned-up mayor casually making himself at home in her kitchen, while she watched in just her robe. The contrast was stark. Overwhelming. Thrilling.

But what struck her the most was that more and more, she could be herself with Theo. There was no need to channel anyone else, even with all of her chaos and quirks on glaring display. He seemed to want to be around her, mess and all.

Life was wild.

"Drink this," Theo said, handing Amber a green concoction. Amber barely flinched; she was so used to them now.

She sipped and swung her bare legs from the counter where she sat and let herself preen a little. Just a bit. Because she was damn proud of herself for helping Theo.

"That was pretty good work with the yoga ladies last week, right? And the farmers would be so happy to have you supporting local agriculture. Oh, you're going to the outdoor movie night tomorrow, right? I'll be there with my family. It's always a fun night with all the kids, and there's snacks and a dance party..." she trailed off, realizing she had been close to rambling. She flashed him a quick, sheepish smile. "Sorry, I got a little excited."

It was just... she didn't feel like being very glamorous right now. She was freshly scrubbed, her hair was wet, and she felt a raw, unfiltered happiness bubbling inside her in a way that was unfamiliar but not unwelcome.

"It was brilliant work." Theo grinned at her and opened the fridge to put away the lettuce and kale. He even washed it before storing it, she noticed before getting distracted by the show. Theo's shorts clung to him, outlining powerful thighs and draping interestingly around other... parts.

From where she sat, she could see the high, taut curve of his ass and the black waistband of his underwear peeking out of the top. The sight sparked a warmth in her that had nothing to do with the heat outside and everything to do with the sexy man in front of her.

If she wasn't careful, she might just tug him by the waistband of his shorts into the V of her legs and wrap herself around that hard body. She wondered what he would do.

She knew he felt the attraction between them as much as she did, but she doubted he'd act on it. He'd probably never done an impulsive thing in his life, for one, but that whole boss-employee dynamic was another big red stop sign for him.

She picked up a peach from the basket on the counter and rolled it in her hand, a confusing mix of emotions swirling inside her. Theo had bought strawberries and cherries too. They were ripe and fragrant in her small kitchen, soft to the touch, and still warm from the sun. She narrowed her eyes.

"That's it. That's all I get? I just set you up with a direct line to your biggest variable in the election, and all you've got for me is 'good work'?" She mimicked his deep voice.

"I'll cut it for you." Theo took the peach and rinsed it then moved her ankle aside with one big hand to open the cabinet under her and pull out her cutting board. The feel of his hands sent a flood of warmth through her body. He peeled the ripe fruit deftly and sliced it then turned to the fridge again. Unaffected. It was like waving a red flag at her.

She picked up a slice of peach and bit into the juicy wedge. She picked up another and weighed it in her hands and, without thinking, let it fly toward Theo's back.

He turned around with such a look of shock on his face that she burst out laughing. "Oh, relax," she choked out. "Haven't you ever had a food fight?" His face was a glorious mixture of disbelief and horror, which made her giggle even harder. Mr. Straight-and-Narrow Theo Clairmont had just experienced his first, and probably only, food fight. "Your face," she got out. "You look so—"

Splat.

A peach slice landed on her neck and slid down into the deep cleavage of her robe while they both watched in shocked silence.

And then it was on. Amber grabbed another slice of peach and threw it at Theo, only when she turned around toward the counter, he was right behind her.

"Oh no, you don't," she said, snatching the entire pile of fruit slices into her hand before he could. He crowded her against the counter with his body, his arms caging her in on either side. For a second, she struggled, her instinct to fight kicking in, but when her bottom pushed back into him, she froze. Theo was achingly hard against her. The hum of the refrigerator and the ragged breaths she drew in echoed in the kitchen.

She leaned back, testing his strength. His heavy shoulders curled securely around her. His forearms with the sun-kissed hairs that so mesmerized her were on either side of her body until one of those big hands wound around hers and she let her fingers go limp around the peaches. Warm, sticky juice ran over her palm and between her fingers, but Theo didn't let go.

Instead, slowly, so slowly she wanted to scream for not knowing where and when, his hand grasped hers and brought it back to his mouth. He sucked the juice off her, running his sleek tongue around and between her fingers, letting her feel the sharp nip of his teeth in the fleshy part of her palm. The eroticism of his hot mouth on her made her moan, and she dropped her head back against his shoulder.

Her free hand lifted to tangle in his hair and pulled his head down closer. His lips were against her ear. She could feel the faint rasp of his beard against the sensitive skin of her cheeks and see the dark sweep of his lashes hiding his eyes. She tilted her head back farther, swaying her bottom back teasingly against him.

He pressed against her hard then, a sudden thrust that pushed her into the counter with a firmness that made her gasp. His cock was a hard ridge against her soft bottom, and she let out a little "oh" of sheer delight at the contrast before pressing back greedily. His other hand settled against her throat, thumb resting lightly on the pulse fluttering there.

"You love to tease." The sharp bite of the counter into her hips and the hot hardness of him behind her, trapping her body between them, made her dizzy with need. "Don't you?" He thrust again, a firm, controlled press that left her nearly breathless.

"Mmm," she moaned.

Theo laughed softly. "What's that, sweetheart? No mouthy little comments?"

She felt more than saw the white flash of his teeth. The hand against her throat dipped down into the front of her robe, where it closed over her bare breast underneath. Theo's thumb trailed over leisurely, pushing the silk open from each side. She looked down and caught her breath at the sight of his large tanned hand against the smooth white curves of her breasts. Delicately, he stroked the robe over the hard point of her nipple, brushing the silk back and forth. Goose bumps broke out on her skin. She felt the sharp points of his teeth grip the side of her neck, licking the sweet peach juice there, and her knees gave out.

The world seemed to narrow down until Amber could feel only the heat of their bodies and the rapid beat of his heart against her back while he tasted her.

"Amber, open up. My hands are full." Johnny's voice broke through their bubble.

Theo stiffened immediately, the warmth in his blue eyes gradually replaced by a guarded coolness as he lifted her gently off him. Amber stepped back, closing her robe and trying to smooth her hair to regain some semblance of normalcy.

"I'll get the door," Theo said.

Johnny appeared in the kitchen doorway, his eyes flicking between Theo and Amber, taking in the scene—the scattered fruit, Theo's stained shirt, Amber's flushed cheeks—with a frown.

"Am I interrupting something?" Johnny's voice was tight, the underlying tension palpable.

"No, just a... food fight. You know, as adults do." She tried for a laugh, but it fell flat in the charged atmosphere.

Theo remained silent; his gaze locked with Johnny's in a silent standoff.

After a moment that stretched too long, Theo cleared his

throat. "I was just leaving. Johnny, a word, please?" He nodded toward the door.

Johnny's eyebrows rose in surprise, and Amber's curiosity was piqued. What could Theo possibly need to discuss with Johnny? And why now, in the midst of their... whatever this was?

"Yeah, let's go out to my car for the rest of the bags. I brought stuff to make breakfast." Johnny said finally.

"Wait," Amber said to Theo as he turned to follow. "I..." For once, she didn't have a thing to say. Everything she felt was in her eyes, though.

Theo smiled faintly. "Drink your juice."

She stared at the door after it closed, the taste of peaches on her lips.

Chapter Twenty-One

"HEY, Mister. You got a dollar? Me and my friends are short for a bag of popcorn."

The boy looked up at Theo hopefully. He held a baseball glove in one hand, and his face was red and sweaty, covered in freckles and more than a little dirt, as if he had been playing hard in the sun all day.

He reminded Theo of summer nights playing baseball and capture the flag with Grant and Ford on these same fields when they were kids.

Theo fished around for his wallet and handed the kid a five. The boy's face lit up, and with a "thanks!" he took off running to the baseball field, where a crowd of kids waited.

Northfield's only school, a red brick building just outside the village, was packed with families for the outdoor movie night. The field was covered in blankets and lawn chairs set up in front of the portable movie screen blown up against the side of the building.

The town hosted several of these over the summer months, but this was the first time Theo had attended. It wasn't that he disliked movies, or even socializing on a warm summer evening with the community, but Theo had never considered his presence at these types of events as welcome.

He didn't have a family to bring, or a wife, or even a long-term girlfriend he would consider bringing to a family event like this, and he felt stiff and more than a little out of place. He had called Ford to see if he wanted to come and bring Landon, but they had plans to see a ball game already, although he was meeting him at the Pub for a drink later. Most of his other friends didn't have kids yet, but he had agreed to Amber's schedule changes, and he always kept his word.

And that was how he found himself surrounded by a mass of children hopped up on cotton candy and popcorn on this Sunday evening instead of reviewing the annual budget report with a cold beer and a ball game on TV. And Puddin'. She was particularly attached to his favorite chair, often snoring loudly while he worked until late at night.

Lately he had found himself looking forward to having another living, breathing thing in his house, even if it was a diva of a dog with an equally ridiculous name. His house was too quiet now, which he had never minded before. It was funny, but he found himself often listening for the tap-tap-tap of a sexy pair of heels.

As dry as his usual Sunday evenings could be, they were less intimidating than walking into the chaos in front of him. It wasn't a black-tie event with a seating chart, or a meeting he had an agenda for, and he didn't recognize as many faces in the crowd as he would at his usual community events.

Theo hadn't picked those events, either, but his father and grandfather had attended them religiously, and he had taken them over when he was elected. Golf charity events, black-tie dinners, art exhibits; he knew exactly how to navigate those. They were attended by people he knew because they all went to the same events, year after year.

But this was entirely different. He recognized a few people and stopped to exchange pleasantries, but everyone seemed to have their own groups of families and friends to enjoy the night with. Blankets as far as he could see were spread out in a patchwork of connected quilts and lawn chairs. Theo didn't have either.

He wandered toward the concession tables and bought a package of Red Hots. Talked with the organizers of the event. A little girl dropped her Popsicle and cried next to him, so he bought her a fresh one.

And he stood there, uncomfortably aware that he was out of his league.

He considered calling Amber to see if she was there already, but he didn't want to disturb her night off with her family. She had been so excited talking about it in her kitchen yesterday. Almost as excited as when he touched her breasts and bit her neck.

Theo forced those images out of his mind before he further embarrassed himself. The attraction between them had simmered on the edge of exploding for so long, he wasn't sure how much longer they could hold out. But it would change things between them.

Working with her already had. He was more aware than ever of how dull life had become lately. Work had taken over his life for so long, he didn't know how to enjoy a simple summer evening. Worse, he had no one to share it with. It was a sobering thought, but the part that made him deeply uncomfortable was the realization that perhaps all his ideas about the town had taken into consideration the wants and needs of only a small part of the community.

He had been so focused on continuing his family's legacy, the one his father and grandfather had shaped, that he was missing the chance to create his own legacy. His campaign promise had been to move forward, but it was becoming clear he was mired in the past.

Amber had known that instinctively. She had told them all of her first day working his office what he needed to do, and he hadn't listened. He wished now that he had.

The sunset had taken away some of the heat of the day. Crickets started singing from the trees around the field when the lights strung haphazardly around the blacktop lit up and music began to play from the speakers.

And then, from the middle of the makeshift dance floor, he heard her laughing. She was spinning two little curly-haired girls in a circle, all three laughing as they spun faster and faster. They all wore glow sticks around their necks, and the girls twirled around in princess dresses while Amber's white sundress swirled around them. As if she could feel his eyes on her, she turned around and smiled. Warm, genuine, delighted. Theo felt something shift in his chest.

"Look, girls, it's the mayor," Amber said, pointing. Two round, blond heads followed her finger.

And one of them charged.

"Oof." Theo swayed at the force of her little body launching into his legs. "Ah, you must be Savannah," he said.

The blond cherub shook her head.

Theo frowned. "Tessa?"

"Savvie," she said, eyeing him with what looked like extreme disappointment.

"My apologies," Theo said gravely. She patted his leg and smiled up at him. Warm, genuine, mischievous. Just like her aunt.

"Say 'hi' to the mayor, ladies," Amber said. She was slightly out of breath, her cheeks pink, her eyes bright with laughter.

Tessa waved shyly.

Savvie reached up her arms. "Up."

Theo's eyebrows shot up. He looked at Amber, who just shrugged and grinned.

"Up," Savvie demanded once again, and Theo picked her up gingerly. She was small and sticky and smelled faintly like sunblock and cotton candy.

The little girl held his face between her chubby hands and stared into his eyes. She leaned close until their noses were almost touching. Theo was conscious of Amber taking a photo, but he dared not look away from the three-foot force of nature holding his face.

"Savvie," Amber said warningly. "No biting."

Theo backed away instinctively, only to be drawn back. Clear blue eyes met his. "Canny."

Theo tried to turn his head to look at Amber, but the little wild one held onto his ears.

"Candy? The mayor doesn't have any candy, Savvie," Amber said. "Now let go of his ears. That's not polite."

Savvie grinned, tiny white teeth showing, and pointed at Theo's jeans pocket. "Canny."

"Oh," Theo said, handing her the Red Hot box in relief. "Here you go. Maybe ask your mom and dad before you eat—"

"They're spicy," Amber warned at the same time, but Savvie looked at them with scorn and popped two in her mouth. She chewed and swallowed and grinned at them.

"Down." She pointed. Theo set her gently on the ground next to her sister.

"You eat candy?" Amber asked, the surprise evident in her voice.

"They were for you," he said gruffly.

"Oh," she said. There was a wealth of feeling in that *oh*.

"I hope you're hungry," a short, dark-haired woman huffed as she walked up and thrust a wicker basket at him. "I brought leftovers."

Theo took the basket in bemused silence and peeked inside. Thick slices of lasagna were packed inside clear to-go containers, along with two bottles of wine. His nose twitched at the scent of basil and tomatoes.

"Aunt Rosa," Amber said, kissing the woman on the cheek and then doing the same to several more who had joined them. "Mom, Aunties, I think you know Mayor Theo Clairmont."

Theo watched as Amber greeted each of her relatives. He knew the Hart women by reputation and through various business councils they belonged to. They were considered pillars of the Northfield community, each running their businesses with professionalism and a savviness that he had always admired.

"This is my sister, Allie, and her husband, Davis," Amber said, introducing a good-looking couple. Savannah and Tessa were a perfect blend of the two, with their mother's delicate face and their father's eyes. "They have three others, Sammy, Ben, and Claire, who are all on the playground, and you know Lily and Evie from the ribbon-cutting ceremony."

"Hi, Mayor," Allie said, her eyes sparkling mischievously, much like Amber's. It seemed to be a trait all the Hart women shared.

"Call me Theo, please," he said. "You have a beautiful family."

"You're getting the whole family tonight, you lucky man," Allie said. "Davis can help run interference if you need it. He's used to dealing with us."

Davis nodded. "Just say yes when they try to feed you, or it gets ugly."

"I'll look forward to it," Theo said, hefting the basket. Aside from taking Georgie to the Maple and Main Street Diner once a week, he didn't often get to eat a meal he hadn't cooked himself. As the family teased and laughed with one another, Theo felt their warmth and humor and let himself enjoy the evening.

Soon, the opening score of the movie began playing, and the crowd settled onto blankets and chairs. Disappointment surged in him, but as he turned to make his exit and leave the family to enjoy the night together, he felt a tug on his jeans.

"Come sith." The little girl looked less energetic now that it was dark. She was rubbing her eye with one hand, and her other found his and tugged.

He looked at Amber, who shrugged. "Better do what she says." She followed him over with a sleepy-looking Tessa in her arms.

Savvie led them to a large red, white, and blue quilt and sat down in a puff of purple skirts and patted the space next to her.

"Off." She pointed at his shoes.

"Ah..." He looked at Amber, who smirked at him.

"She wants you to take your shoes off, boss."

Theo hesitated, but Savvie didn't. She took her purple sandals off and then pointed an imperious finger at Theo's shoes. He sat down and tugged them off, lining them neatly next to the blanket.

Savvie shook her head. "Sockth."

He knew when he was defeated. He peeled those off, too, and when Savvie scooted over and wiggled her chubby toes next to his in the cool grass, he even laughed. It felt slightly foolish, but it also reminded him of being a kid playing barefoot on these same fields.

Theo sat back and leaned his arms behind him, watching Amber settle her nieces on her lap when the movie started. She stroked the silky curls on the girls' heads, wearing a soft look he had never seen on her face before, and the squeeze in his chest clamped tighter. She looked happier than he had ever seen her, which was funny because she wasn't even smiling for once.

She said she could barely take care of herself, much less kids, pets, or even plants. But as Theo watched her with the little girls, he wondered what had given her that idea when it was obvious she had so much love to give. Who convinced her of that lie, or, he brooded, why had she convinced herself?

Gradually, the twins fell asleep. Davis came to scoop the girls up and back onto their blanket to cuddle as the evening lost the heat and humidity of the day. Theo found a blanket in a bag next to them and spread it over Amber, who murmured her thanks. He turned his head slowly and found her looking at him.

The light from the screen flickered on her unsmiling face, putting her features in shadow except for her bright eyes, and the soft flutter at the hollow of her neck. Her white sundress reflected the flickering light of the screen. The thin straps were tied into bows over her small shoulders. They seemed too small to him to carry any weight at all, much less the stress and worry over Val, Holly, and Sandy. Who worried about Amber?

He had the surreal feeling of standing on the edge of a precipice, wanting to see what was on the other side of a place he had never explored before, but caution and reserve, his old standbys, kept him tethered to firm ground.

They were leaning back, their arms behind them on the blanket, when her hand found his later. He looked over in surprise at the heat of it, a warm, firm press of her skin that sent a bolt of pure lust through him as physical as if she had reached over and squeezed his cock.

His breath caught and then held.

He should go home. He knew he should.

"Ford's meeting me for a drink at the pub later. Join us?" he murmured instead.

Chapter Twenty-Two

A WAVE of nostalgia hit Amber when she stepped into the pub. It was packed, along with the patio area, which Killian had strung with twinkling lights and speakers for the warm summer months. Eden's sultry voice filled the bar, singing Amy Winehouse with her customary blend of soul and sex. *Whew.* Amber paused to admire the delivery. It wasn't every day a small-town bar got to hear that much raw emotion.

It had been over a month since she'd stepped foot into the pub. Aside from her semesters away at college, that was the longest stretch she had gone since she had taken her first job as a hostess under the old owner. She missed the place. She missed Killian too. It had taken her a while to lick her wounds, but she was finally ready to see him. The familiar spicy scent of Miguel's famous Buffalo wings mingled with the laughter and chatter around her while she scanned the room for Theo. Cap was the first one to see her, and he made sure everyone else did too.

"Amber! There's our girl!" Cap's voice thundered across the room. He beckoned her over, arms wide open to give her a massive bear hug. The rookies were next, with Jake scooping her up until her feet were kicking the air, and Ethan with a kiss on her cheek and another hug that made her ribs creak. She greeted more of her regulars and some new faces, and soon she was back in the middle of the fray as if she had never left, teasing and flirting with the guys while they exaggerated about who missed her the most.

It was familiar and flattering, slipping back into her old role, charming and teasing anyone around her. She didn't have to rely on anything other than an easy smile here. Yet it occurred to her that she didn't actually miss bartending as much as she thought.

She preferred the freedom of flirting and teasing much more when it was on her own terms. The performance, the constant need to be "on" to make more tips when sometimes she'd rather just go home and sew whatever she was working on, or God forbid, not smile at all unless she felt like it. Funny how stepping back into her old world gave her an appreciation for the new one she was making. The thought made her feel even lighter.

"What's it like working for the mayor?" Jake asked. He threw a heavy arm over her shoulders and drew her closer to his barrel chest. "He better not be working you too hard."

"Yeah, how come you never come in to visit?" Ethan wanted to know. "You were the best bartender the pub ever had. Now we have Simone, and she can't do the cherry trick," he said sadly.

Cap cuffed the rookie. "Because she's married, you dumbass." He looked at Amber and grinned. "He's right. It's not the same without you here, but you do seem happier now."

Amber laughed lightly. "Flattery will get you everywhere, Cap."

"You get enough flattery," he said gruffly. "I'm just happy you landed on your feet again." His grizzled white cheeks were ruddy from the heat and the beer, making him look like Santa Claus.

Amber leaned up to kiss his cheek. "I'm so happy to see you," she said, meaning it. Cap was one of the very few men in her life, aside from Davis, whom she genuinely thought the world of. How lucky they were both part of her family now.

"Glad to see you back, Amber," Killian said from behind her. Amber turned around and looked up at her old friend. He held out his arms with a silent question, and she walked into them. Killian hugged her tight, all of the awkwardness melting in the face of their long friendship.

"Don't be mad at me anymore. I've missed you," he said before kissing the top of her head.

"I'm not mad. I brought that on myself." She smiled crookedly while he studied her. "I just needed time to figure some things out."

Finally, as if he was satisfied with what he saw, he nodded. "You'll always have a job here. I want you to know that."

"Thanks," she said, "but I think I'm actually doing okay."

"Are you happy?"

"Yes, I am happy, or I'm getting there, anyway." She let the words settle around her, wondering for a moment if she truly meant them, or if they were merely something Marilyn would say. It occurred to her that she hadn't been happy in any real sense of the word for so long that it was a foreign feeling. She had momentary happiness when she was with her family, or laughing with friends, but to feel content in her life, happy, as Killian asked, was a new and tender feeling.

Scary, really. As if at any moment the other shoe would drop. It was a sobering thought.

As if she had called his name, she looked up to find Theo watching her from across the bar. He was dressed casually in jeans and a dark button-down that fitted lovingly over his wide shoulders. The sleeves of his shirt were rolled up over his forearms, and the top two buttons undone, exposing the strong, tanned column of his throat.

Earlier, on her blanket, with his shoes off and his feet in the grass next to her, he had been so relaxed with her and her family. It was so easy to imagine other scenarios where he sat next to her, barefoot and smiling with two little girls next to them. The longing of it nearly made her breath skip.

Stop that. Those were dangerous feelings, and she was much more practical than that. Instead, she focused on the powerful lines of his body standing tall among the people surrounding him. He held a beer in his hand, talking to a group of people, but his eyes were on hers.

Direct. Heated. Waiting.

She knew hers were just as revealing. If she closed her eyes, she could still feel his rough palm cupping her breast in her kitchen. Could hear his ragged breath in her ear while they watched her silk robe stroke her nipple into a stiff, aching point while he ground his cock into her. A throb of longing in her belly pulsed lower, down to the insides of her thighs, and back up to spread between her legs. This feeling she knew exactly how to handle.

"Jesus, you're an open book." Johnny hooked an arm around her waist and pulled her into him, wrapping her in his arms when she tried to pull away.

"What do you mean?" She frowned at him. His wide shoulders blocked her view of Theo.

Johnny buried his head in her neck and whispered in her ear. "You're not thinking."

The rough scratch of his beard scraped her, and she tugged away in irritation. "What's that supposed to mean, and where's Charlotte?" She grabbed his ear and yanked like she used to when they were kids.

"Ow." Johnny stopped whatever he was doing to her neck.

"I'm saving you two from making fools of yourselves in front of everyone," he said grimly. "Come on, let's dance." He herded her out to the dance floor, keeping his big body between hers and Theo's.

"You're being annoying." She looked around him, but Theo was no longer there. Damn. "And where's Charlotte?" she asked again, angry all over again on behalf of her friend. "Weren't you supposed to go out tonight?"

"At bingo night with her mom," he smiled goofily. "She wouldn't let me go, but I'm meeting her later."

Amber softened at that smile. "You really like her, don't you?"

"I wouldn't go to bingo for just anyone." He spun her around and when she was back in his arms, he looked more serious. "Be careful, Amber."

And there it was, the nebulous feeling that she couldn't quite shake.

She searched his eyes. "What do you mean?"

"Everyone's watching what happens with you two. You're working for him, the morning runs, and now he's meeting your family. If things don't work out, it won't be the golden boy of Northfield who'll feel the damage. It'll be you. I don't want to see you hurt again." He searched her eyes, and Amber remembered Johnny as a fifteen-year-old kid fighting over her honor.

"It's fine. There's nothing going on between us," she lied. "I'm just trying to get him to loosen up a little, you know, be a man of the people and all before the big election."

Sure. If loosening up meant hot-as-sin food fights in her kitchen in which she ended up topless. That was definitely to benefit his political career. Very selfless of her, really.

She smiled, bright enough to block out any more of those sensible thoughts. Everything was fine. *Fine*. She had it all under control. She knew not to get attached. Please. She could write a book on not getting attached. "You don't have to worry about me, you know. I'm not a kid anymore."

He spun her out and back gracefully. "I'll always worry about you."

"Hey, what did Theo want to talk to you about yesterday?" she asked when they came back together.

"He wanted to know about us." He dipped her low, and she held onto his shoulders.

"What did you tell him?"

Johnny spun her again, and when she came back, he was grinning that bad-boy smile. "Not a goddamned thing."

"I KEEP TELLING people that happy hours are supposed to be happy." Ford slid onto the barstool next to Theo.

"It's not happy hour," Theo said. He watched Amber being touched by yet another man, this time the one she'd stuck her tongue out to the night she was fired. The kid bear-hugged her, and her little white sundress swung back and forth teasingly across the back of her thighs. He set her down, and she immediately settled under his arm, smiling up at him.

"It's always happy hour here," Killian said, sliding a beer in front of Theo. He followed Theo's gaze. "Ah, Amber's here," he said, shooting Theo a knowing look. "Is that what you're brooding about?"

"I'm not brooding," Theo said, brooding. Okay, he was. But the night had turned out to be vastly different than he had thought it would be, and he was allowed to brood a little.

"Rochester's Most Eligible Bachelor can't brood," Ford said. "What's the problem? Did your date leave you hanging again?"

"Fuck off," Theo said.

"Is that any way for the mayor to talk?" Ford grinned. "I'm

shocked." Killian opened another bottle of beer and set it in front of Ford, who used the tip of it to point at Amber. "Is that the problem?"

Johnny, the big bastard, was dancing with Amber now. She was tucked in against his chest close enough to make Theo's teeth grind.

Killian sighed. "That's definitely the problem," he said, giving Theo a look.

"There's no problem," Theo growled at his two closest friends. "Amber's my assistant. We met up at the movie night at school and walked over for a beer. That's all."

"That's all," Ford said thoughtfully. "Is that why you're glaring at John Rossi like that? Because I'm telling you, that's one guy I don't think either of us could take. He's a big son of a bitch."

"Why would I care who my employee spends time with?" Theo turned his back on the two of them, but the mirror behind the liquor on the back wall showed their reflection. Amber wasn't laughing like she usually was. There was no outrageously seductive smile for the man holding her in his arms. They were talking now, barely moving on the dance floor, and Theo was somehow even more pissed than he was when he watched her flirting.

And, yes, jealous too. The icy-hot burn of watching her be so intimate with someone else. She was so goddamn guarded, but he had caught fleeting glimpses of her under the dazzling smiles and outrageous things she said and did. Tonight, he thought he had sensed a shift between them, in which she had been willing to open up.

"Don't look at me." Killian shrugged. "I have a policy against dating employees for a reason. Nothing but trouble there."

That's the fucking truth.

An hour ago, he'd been next to Amber's warm, sweet body

on a blanket under the stars, and now he was watching her being mauled by the one man Amber smiled at like she smiled at him. Who else got to see that beautiful smile? Who else had known the feel of her sweet, lush body pressed against his? Who else had felt the weight of her breast and felt the flutter of her heartbeat underneath his hand? If he closed his eyes, he could still feel the curve of her lovely ass pressing against his cock in her kitchen.

Bitterness and jealousy swelled in him, and he was ashamed. He wasn't this kind of man. He had no right to feel this way. She hadn't promised him anything. He hadn't asked either.

But he wanted to. Sitting next to her tonight, he had wanted more. He had thought she wanted it too.

Talk about whiplash.

While he watched, Johnny spun her out and back, and she wound up in his arms again, laughing up at him.

Jealousy, ugly and vicious, swirled in him, and he felt small. Theo pushed back from the bar abruptly.

"You're leaving already?" Ford asked. "I just got here."

"Been a long day," Theo said. "Here, drinks are on me." Theo laid a few bills on the bar and turned to leave. He would go home and lose himself in work for a few hours. It was his go-to when he needed to find order and reason.

Halfway to the door, he heard his name.

"Hey, boss, where are you going?" Amber smiled up at him. Her eyes were golden brown in the dim light. Her skin under her white dress looked like satin. He wanted—that was all. He wanted.

Desperately. Hungrily. In the basest way, he wanted her lush body, and in an entirely unfamiliar way, he wanted the version of her he had glimpsed earlier. Softer, less guarded. Happier. Real.

"Headed home," Theo said, gently disengaging her arm. "Have a good night," he said politely. Tightly. As if he weren't hard as a rock and going to go home to jerk off to thoughts of untying the little ribbons on her shoulders and burying himself in the hot, wet center of her.

"So soon? It's still early, or is your warm milk waiting for you?" she taunted him. "Oh," she gasped, her eyes going wide in delight. The first chords of "Don't Stop Believing" thrummed from Eden's guitar, and the packed bar started cheering. "I love this song. Come sing it with me." She tugged his arm toward the stage. "Eden always calls me up for this one."

"I'm never getting on that stage," he said curtly.

"Come on." She leaned in closer. "This time won't end up in a tattoo, I promise." Her eyes sparkled at him teasingly. They were next to the long, dimly lit hallway where Killian's office and storeroom were when Theo stopped abruptly.

He pushed her into the first room and kicked the door shut with his foot, crowding her against the door in the dark room. The silver glint of kegs and CO_2 tanks along the walls made the room feel close and intimate.

"What are you doing?" she laughed, turning around. "Are you crazy? Someone could have seen us." She leaned back against the door.

"Isn't that what you like?" he asked her, knowing he was wrong, but frustration and desire drove him now. "Putting on a show?" He took a step closer, so close she had to lean her head back against the door. Eden's voice rose and fell from the barroom, but the sound of Amber's breathing filled his ears.

The air between them shifted instantly. Her laughter died away, replaced by a charged silence. She smiled slowly. "Oh, I see now," she said softly, shifting her hips against his swollen cock. "Is that what this is about? You want me, but you won't let yourself have me?" She drew her finger down his chest, leaving a burning trail in her wake. His stomach clenched. "Always the perfect gentleman."

His pulse raced. Slowly, his hands came to her shoulders and caught and lingered for a moment on the little bow, where he fingered the fabric. How easy it would be to tug the ribbon and see all that creamy skin. She wanted him as much as he wanted her, he was sure of it. He could see it in her sultry eyes and feel it in her ragged breathing.

He didn't miscalculate that emotion. It was the only one she didn't hide.

But he wanted more.

"Take what you want," she breathed. Her lips were pink, tilted up in that wickedly curving smile that made him so crazy.

He quickly gripped her wrist and brought it back to the door next to her head. Her breasts rose and fell steadily against her chest, so close he could feel the press of her nipples through his shirt.

She slid one arm around his neck and raised her lips. "Finish what you started in my kitchen." She rolled her hips against his, deliberately. Hard. Notching her softness perfectly against his hardness.

"Don't," he said harshly. "Just—" Now it was his breathing that echoed in the small room. Every muscle in his body was rigid with pent-up desire. He wanted to lift her up and feel her legs tighten around his waist, to untie her dress and see her beautiful bare breasts in his hands, and suck her nipples until she went wild. And most of all, finally, finally thrust into her wet, welcome heat while he fucked her against the door.

Jesus. This was insane. This wasn't him. They were in a supply closet, for fuck's sake. He ran a hand through his hair, frustrated beyond measure. "I have to go," he said very, very quietly.

"I thought..." she started then stopped abruptly.

"You thought what?"

"Never mind," she said, lifting that little determined chin. "It doesn't matter." She smiled ruefully. "It doesn't matter," she said, as if she needed to hear it again.

She turned to leave. Theo stepped up behind her, tight and close to her body, until she was pressed between him and the door. Her scent filled him, the soft curls of her hair brushed his face, and he let himself breathe her in.

It could, he wanted to say. *It could matter to us both.* But he didn't say that because she wasn't ready to hear it. She might never be, and he would just have to live with that.

He straightened up and opened the door for her.

Chapter Twenty-Three

AT SIX O'CLOCK ON Monday morning, her alarm went off. She struck a hand out blindly and turned it off, cracked one eye open, and groaned. The sheer curtain in her bedroom revealed a dark gray sky that looked ready to open up and pour at any minute.

She made up her mind. She wasn't running today.

Theo would be mad about it, but she wasn't feeling any sort of generosity for the man at the moment. His abrupt goodbye at the pub had left her feeling emotions she made it a habit never to feel.

She was so disappointed she had spent the rest of the night flirting with all the usual crew. It was a superficial attempt not to feel the emptiness that grew in her as she watched Theo walk out. That kind of high never lasted, but it was something when she felt abruptly like she had nothing.

Not even the ability to sleep in anymore.

She punched the pillow and got up. Theo had ruined her. Her body was so used to waking up early, she couldn't go back to sleep. Even her usual breakfasts of muffins and coffee made her stomach hurt now. She'd never admit it, but she craved green juice and eggs.

What had he done to her?

And why hadn't he stayed last night?

The answer to either of those questions was more than she wanted to think about before the sun was up.

But she was done running. She didn't care what other events he went to for the rest of the summer. It wasn't even in her job description to schedule them, and aside from a nice little bonus if he won reelection, it was no skin off her back if he never went to another community event.

Theo was a sadist, and she wasn't going to let him boss her around anymore.

Or hurt her by leaving.

She was the one who left.

That was why, when he knocked on the door promptly at six thirty, she was ready to pounce.

She swung it open even as his hand was still in the air.

"I'm not running today," she said, lifting her chin. "It's raining, and I'm tired, and I want a break," she said belligerently.

Theo looked her over, assessing her for injuries, she supposed. Out of habit, she had put on her hot pink bike shorts and a black sports bra. "I'll do yoga instead," she said grudgingly. It was a good compromise because she did actually like the way she felt after exercising, though she wasn't going to give him another point on his side of the scoreboard. "I'll see you at work." She turned around and shut the door, but Theo's hand shot out and grabbed it.

"You're running," he said grimly. "Get your sneakers."

"I'm not running. I quit." She crossed her arms and glared.

He stared at her, the disappointment written all over his face doing something awful to her insides. "The race is in two weeks."

He took a step toward her.

She backed up. "I'm not running."

"Oh, yes, you are," he said. Theo swooped down, grabbed her sneakers next to the door, and picked up her foot in one swift move. She wobbled on one foot and complained bitterly while he wrestled her sneakers on.

"I told you I can't do this. I'm tired, my legs hurt, and I can't do it." Her voice rose toward the end. She felt tender this morning and closer to tears than she had been in years. It made her want to start a fight. "You're always pushing. All you do is push, push, push, and I'm tired of it."

"Come on, Red Hot. The faster we get it done, the faster it'll be over."

He was merciless, prodding her down the stairs with a large hand clamped on her back.

Theo stopped at the stairs outside. "Stretch," he said curtly. "We'll take it easy today."

"You never take it easy." She put her foot on a stair and leaned forward, muttering to herself.

"Other leg." Theo was doing his own stretching, implacable as ever. The coil within her twisted.

"Did you eat?"

"I had a banana," she snarled. "Do you want to know why I'm so tired? Huh?"

"Run," he said, ignoring her. He set a slow, easy pace.

That pissed her off too. Of course he would humor her. She knew that was illogical, but she was spoiling for a fight now.

"I was up late... last night... using my... electronic boyfriend... and he ran out of batteries." She huffed along, pissed that her delivery was punctuated with her panting. Honestly, did running ever get any easier? She'd been at it for weeks, and it was still so damn hard. She wanted to quit at least every other day.

Theo's scowl deepened, and he picked up the pace. Purposely, she was certain. She was quiet for the first mile, mostly because she couldn't physically speak and run at that pace, but then her mind started to get in the way of her body. Her calves hurt; her thighs hurt. She hadn't eaten a proper breakfast like Theo was always harping on about.

The skies opened up in a deluge, pounding her face and her eyes, and her sneakers became a soggy mess. Her bike shorts and sports bra were soaked through, outlining her body, and all the while she seethed.

Theo's silence grated at her. He never argued. He was always cool and rational. Just once, she wanted to see him be a mere mortal and lose his temper.

They were running past the village green, almost to the gazebo that looked out onto the canal, when she'd had enough. She stopped abruptly, panting. "I'm not going any farther." Rain dripped down her face and into her mouth.

Theo stopped and turned around. He wasn't even breathing hard, the jerk. "We're more than halfway there."

"I'm done. I hate running." She swiped away the heavy, wet hair that had escaped her ponytail and was plastered in her face. "And I hate you!" The delivery was ruined with the panting, but she glared at him anyway.

Theo's jaw clenched. His T-shirt was plastered to his body, each of the blocks of muscle in his chest and stomach outlined clearly. For once, his neat hair was a mess, dripping down onto his face like hers.

She was so angry she wanted to cry. But she never did that. Fight it was.

"*Fuck*, Amber." Theo thrust his fingers through his wet hair and held them there on top of his head, pulling as if he wished it were her neck. "You push everyone around you—why won't you push yourself?"

"What?" she took a step back as if he had thrown a punch. "What are you talking about?"

"You say that I push you? You're the one who pushes." He stepped toward her, and she backed up again, feeling the gazebo at her back. "You push Val to go to college, and you pushed Charlotte out of her shell. You push my buttons every fucking day with that smart mouth of yours. Push yourself, Amber. For once in your life, just fucking do the work."

"I am doing the work!" she screamed, past all rationality. "I've worked harder in the last month than I have in my entire life, and you're telling me to push more? I don't have it in me. It's not there." She was panting and aware that the rain might've turned into tears on her face.

Suddenly, he gripped her shoulders hard, and crowded her back into the gazebo. His face was fierce as he glared at her. "Stop fucking doubting yourself and just do the goddamn thing," he shouted. He was so close she could see the little droplets of water on his eyelashes and dripping off his nose. His hands gripped her bare shoulders, hot where the rain had made her cold.

"I can't," she screamed in his stupid, horrible, beautiful face.

His grip tightened, pulling her up on her toes and into his body.

He kissed her.

For a moment, she was so shocked, she froze. The stroke of his tongue forced her out of her stupor. She wrapped her arms around him, tangled her fingers in his thick, dark hair hard enough that he grunted, and jerked him closer. It was a battle of lips and tongues and sharp teeth. Dimly, she was aware of the bite of the wood gazebo against her back and the contrast of cold rain and hot, hard man where his body pressed against hers. She clawed at him to get closer, devouring him, because it was never enough. His beautiful hair was slick and wet in her fingers. She held on tighter.

Theo's mouth slanted over hers, fitting their lips together. His tongue slid against hers, demanding and rough. She sucked it, thrilled to take a piece of him inside her. A furious burst of desire melted her insides, and she was suddenly trying to crawl up his body, just as fiercely demanding as he was.

More so.

He pulled her up tighter until her weight rested between him and the gazebo. They panted in between hot, wet, sucking kisses. His hands gripped her ass, holding her tighter, sliding down to her knee and bringing it around his waist, making her feel the long, thick burn of his cock through the thin material of her shorts. Her breathing stuttered and stopped, starting again with a gasp when one strong arm moved to her lower back and molded her even tighter to his hard body. He ground into her where she needed him the most. "You... make... me so... fucking... crazy."

"Shut up..." she panted, rubbing herself on him. "Shut up..." —she nipped and bit his lips—"...and kiss me."

Gradually, his kiss changed. His hands cupped her face, his fingers threading through the back of her hair to hold her while he kissed her softer still until she sagged against his hard chest. Only then did he let her mouth go reluctantly. He dropped his forehead against hers with a heavy groan. She couldn't seem to move her arms from around his neck. They stood there for a moment, each breathing heavily until he gave her knee one last squeeze and let it slide down his body.

She dropped her forehead against his chest.

"For a vanilla guy, you know how to use your mouth," she said.

"You have no idea what I can do with my mouth," he said

tiredly, giving her one more quick, burning hot press of it against hers. She shuddered.

She looked around in a daze. It was still raining but more of a sprinkle than a downpour, and the sun peeked out from behind the darker clouds. Soon the heat of the day would quickly dry the rain and people would be walking their dogs and running along the canal. Across from her, nailed into the telephone pole, Davis Beckerman's poster stared at her with a fake, smarmy white smile.

She pushed against his chest. "Back up before someone sees us."

He lifted an eyebrow, but he gave her space. "Would that be a problem for you?"

"For me? No. For you? Yes. Huge problem. The last thing you need is to be seen kissing your employee in the rain." She tried wringing out her sports bra, but it was no use. She'd have to walk back home waterlogged.

He gave her a look but didn't press her, and she was glad.

"Let's pick up the pace on the way back to make up for that last shitty mile," he said.

What?

Her lip trembled, and she looked up at him, searching his cool blue eyes. "When are you going to give me a break?"

"When you start believing in yourself," he said simply. He turned around and started running.

She took a few steps. Realized it would take her longer to get to where she wanted to go, steeled herself, and started to run at her own pace.

Chapter Twenty-Four

"YOU SIGNED ME UP FOR WHAT?" Theo's eyebrows rose nearly to his hairline.

"I signed you up for the dunk tank," Amber replied smugly. She tied the red bandanna in her hair a little tighter and tugged down her blue gingham sundress to a more appropriate length for a family carnival. "Consider it payback for making me run every day. You know that's not a fair dare. Just because you're going to these community events doesn't equal me training for a 5K."

Theo sighed deeply. "Now we're running four miles tomorrow."

"You're all talk, boss," Amber said. "Consider this another PR strategy. What better way for you to connect with the community than them seeing you half-naked?" She wiggled her eyebrows lasciviously. "This is going to win you major brownie points with the female voters."

They were standing at the entrance of the carnival, held every year on the Fourth of July in the parking lot of the Northfield Fire Department. Tents, carnival rides, and lights stretched out before them in a kaleidoscope of colors. It was one of

Amber's favorite town events of the entire year and not just because of the funnel cakes. Her entire family was somewhere in the crowd, including Val and Dylan. She had driven Val, who quickly ditched her as soon as they got there. Amber had to promise up and down to Val that she wouldn't "act weird" if they ran into them.

"Now put a smile on your face and get naked, big boy."

Theo's eyes narrowed. Honestly, he had no sense of humor. The memory of his face before he kissed her in the rain yesterday made her skin heat. He might not have a sense of humor, but the man could kiss. Good lord. The memory of that kiss in the rain singed through her body until the July sun wasn't the only thing making her sweat.

"Amber..." he said warningly.

"What's the use of having a body like that if you're not going to show it off?" Theo's expression grew even more flinty. "Fine. Here, I grabbed your swim trunks when I stopped by to let Puddin' out." Sadly, she tossed him the navy board shorts.

Theo started to respond, but one of the ladies from the juice crew waved at him and came over.

"Hi, Mr. Mayor. We had such a great time at our juice date," she said. "I got my whole neighborhood to sign the dog park petition like you suggested."

Amber held back a smile and stepped back, letting Theo do his mayor thing.

Soon, there was a crowd of people surrounding the dunk tank, more for the view than anything else, but hey, PR was all about how things looked. And her boss was an absolute stud of a man. She made sure to snap a bunch of pictures for his social media account with the hashtag #dunkthe-hunkmayor. Theo would probably be a sourpuss about it, but if there was one life lesson she had under her belt, it was that sex sold.

"Step right up!" she shouted. "Who wants to dunk the mayor?"

"Hi, Aunt Amber," Sammy said. He gave her a grin, wide and infectious in its enthusiasm. Holly and Ben joined him, and she gave them all a hug. Man, she loved these kids.

"Hey, kids. Want to dunk the mayor? He loves it." She nodded over to Theo who sat on the platform, dripping wet from the last dunk. "Right, Mayor Clairmont?"

"Can't think of anywhere else I'd rather be," he replied, sounding almost sincere.

"Thanks, but I spent all my money winning Holly a gold-fish," Sammy said. Pointing at the clear bag Holly held protectively, he turned bright red. They smiled shyly at each other while Ben made a gagging noise.

"I used all my money on Thor's hammer," Ben said. "Other-wise, I would. Sorry, Mr. Mayor."

"It's on me, kids." She pulled out a ten-dollar bill from her back pocket and handed it to them. "Go tell your friends there's more where that came from if they have a good arm."

"Sweet, thanks, Aunt Amber." Sammy missed all three throws. He shrugged good-naturedly while Theo settled back looking smug. "This is why I play guitar instead of baseball now. Ben, you're the pitcher. You try." He stepped back while Ben swung his arm to warm up.

Theo's smug grin was wiped off his face with Ben's first pitch. He took the dunking like a champ, exaggerating his fall and staying under long enough that she peeked over to make sure he was fine, even though the tank was only four feet deep. He came out of the water like the Loch Ness Monster, roaring with his arms up and water splashing everywhere, getting everyone around him wet, making the kids laugh and scream and run away.

"Looks like the mayor has a flair for the dramatic," Annette said, dabbing water off her Chanel bag from Theo's theatrics. Despite the heat, Annette was effortlessly chic in a pastel yellow summer dress that didn't have the audacity to wilt in the sun. Not many people had audacity around Annette. She merely had to look at people with her cool gray eyes to make others stumble to do her bidding. Amber had spent years trying to master that look with no luck.

Amber grinned at her mom. "Isn't it great?"

"It definitely shows something." Annette nodded, her eyes lit with sharp humor.

Theo joined them, rubbing his chest with a towel, and held out his hand to shake Annette's. "I aim to please, Ms. Hart." Even standing there dripping wet with his broad, sun-kissed chest bare and his hair slicked back by water, Theo's confidence rivaled Annette's formidable presence.

Each was the epitome of sophistication and poise—qualities Amber had tried to imitate over the years yet could never get just right. Instead, she stuck with a more literal, smack-you-in-the-face approach: blatant sex appeal. "But I have to admit, this one was all your daughter's idea."

"I have no doubt about that," Annette said. "My daughter has always had a talent for bringing out the best in people. I've noticed your campaign has gained momentum since she joined your team," she added pointedly.

"Mom," Amber hissed. How mortifying could she be?

Theo's smile broadened. "She's definitely got me stepping outside of my comfort zone. Can't say that I mind as much as I thought I would," he admitted, flashing his own thousand-dollar smile at Annette. "Especially in such good company."

Oh, stop it, Amber told herself. *He's just being charming.* But it still kindled something warm and lovely inside her.

Annette seemed to assess the dynamic between them before

nodding. "I can see that," she said, smiling faintly. "See that you don't take it for granted."

Phillip Beckerman sauntered up for his shift at the dunk tank, wearing a Hawaiian shirt and red sunglasses. He held her hand a little too long when Theo introduced them, while his smile managed to be overly bright and entirely insincere. He definitely practiced that in front of the mirror.

"Nice work on the socials, Theo." *Har har har*. Even his laugh grated on her. Too loud and too long to be for anything other than show. Major tool. "You finally decided to join the twenty-first century." *Har har har*.

They left quickly and wandered around the carnival, stopping frequently to chat with people. Theo chatted. Amber ate her way through the carnival.

With a frozen lemonade in one hand and fried dough in another, she looked up at Theo. "Want some?" she asked, her mouth full of cinnamon-sugar-fried dough going directly into her arteries, and she didn't even care.

He bent down and ate the piece she offered him straight from her hand.

"What are you doing?" she hissed. "Someone might see you."

Theo studied her then lifted a brow. "I thought you don't care what people think about you."

"I don't, but you need to. I thought you were trying to change your image?"

Theo frowned. "I don't owe anyone an explanation for my personal life. I'm committed to my work, but outside of that, my life isn't up for public debate."

"Well, we don't have to make it easy for gossip to start," she said, exasperated. "Hey, let's go on the Ferris wheel."

Theo looked a little sick. "Heights and spinning. Two things I don't love."

Amber's face fell. "All right." She looked around for something else that would give her the thrill she was chasing. The Tilt-A-Whirl? Lame.

"Wait," Theo said, grabbing her elbow and pulling her back around. "Let's give it a try," he said hesitantly.

She beamed at him. "Look at you, risk taker. Georgie would be so proud."

"She can tell me how proud she is if this thing doesn't fall apart while we're on it." Theo gingerly stepped onto the metal platform and closed the door of the cart that would take them one hundred feet into the air. "Are you sure this is safe?"

"Oh sure, permits, everything. It's completely aboveboard," she said breezily. Ferris wheels had always captivated her. She craved the exhilaration and the little twinge of fear because it made her feel alive like nothing else did. To be suspended there, high above the trees, made everything else in life seem small in comparison. There was nothing like it.

Theo looked pale across from her.

"Here," she said, handing him the lemonade. "I'll come sit on your side. It's a better view anyway."

"No, you stay over there." He looked alarmed. "We should keep the cart balanced." The cart rose higher and stopped, allowing more people to get on.

"Oh, stop," she laughed. "People have been necking on Ferris wheels for as long as they've been invented."

She settled down next to him. Theo's body was tense, and he held onto the bar next to him so hard his knuckles were white.

"How long is the ride?"

"This is one of the longest ones. That's why it's my favorite."

"Great," he said. With a creak, the Ferris wheel rose higher. Theo stared straight ahead. His jaw ticked.

"What can you see on your side?" She felt him breathe in

sharply against her. "Just look, Theo. You're going to waste your chance to see this beautiful view of our town. Let yourself enjoy it." She leaned next to him, watching the tops of the red-and-white-striped tents flutter in the evening breeze. The sweet scent of popcorn and caramel corn drifted up.

The string lights around the stage below made everything softly glow along with the neon lights from the rides. She spotted Sammy and Holly walking around, and she could've sworn she saw them holding hands. She smiled to herself. Young love. So cute.

He sat back, paler than before. He needed a distraction.

"So, about that kiss yesterday," she said casually. "That was in the top ten, for sure."

Theo's hands relaxed a little on the side of the cart. "It was better than top ten."

"Eh," she said flippantly. "I've had better." She hadn't.

Theo didn't look nervous at all now. He looked smug. "Top five, at least."

"You know how to use your tongue. I'll give you that," she added grudgingly. Credit where it was due and all. "Hey, I know what we can do up here. Let's play truth or dare."

The look on Theo's face turned wary.

"Just say 'truth.'" She rolled her eyes. "We both know you'll never pick dare."

"Baby steps. I'm on the wheel of death, aren't I? Truth," he said.

"What did you talk to Johnny about on Saturday morning?" she asked immediately. That conversation after the "hot peach" incident, as she had dubbed it in her mind, had nagged at her for a week.

Theo looked uncomfortable for a minute, as if he was still debating playing along.

"You have to answer. That's how you play the game."

Theo sighed. "It's not a secret. You're going to find out anyway."

"Find out what?"

Theo looked out over the tree line to the lake in the distance. "I asked Johnny to fix your car and to send me the bill."

"What?" she asked, unable to hide her astonishment. "Why did you do that?"

"I wanted to know you were safe," he said simply.

It hit her square in the chest, making her blink at the stab of unfamiliar emotion. "I'll pay you back," she blurted out. The scoreboard tipped even more in Theo's direction, and her breath got short and tight in her chest.

He shook his head slowly. "I don't want you to pay me back. You might as well know I took your credit card statements and the loan letter from the debt collection agency and paid them off too."

"What? I was going to pay them. You can take it out of my paycheck," she said almost desperately.

"I don't want to do that either. Consider it payment for the work you're doing with the gala if you need to. None of that work is in your job description. Or take it how I intended it, as a gift. You give gifts all the time. Please accept mine." The way he looked at her made her heart pound in her ears. A little sad. A little rueful. Raw.

"I'll pay you back so we're even," she whispered. It was too much money, too much emotion, too foreign to have someone look out for her like this.

The scoreboard had always been skewed in his favor, leaving her off balance. She had spent her entire adult life pretending that she had things under control, only to come to this moment and realize Theo saw right through her.

Theo shook his head slowly. "It was never a competition.

We've always been on the same team." There was no judgment there, only a soft understanding that made her feel suddenly dizzy, as if she had a fear of heights instead of him.

She had nothing under control at all. She handled the feelings welling up inside her like she always did. "My turn," she said, almost angrily. Defiantly. "I choose dare."

"Pick the truth," Theo countered. That cool, assessing look she remembered so well was back, along with the eyebrow. She bristled.

"Why? Eager to get at more of my deep dark secrets? I'm an open book."

"You're far from an open book," he said. "What is Johnny to you?" he asked abruptly.

The question caught her fully off guard, and she sat back as if he had shoved her off. "Does it matter?" she finally asked.

"It matters," Theo insisted. "You said you don't do relationships, but I can see there's something there, or there was. What is it?"

"That's too bad," she said flippantly. "I choose dare. So, what is it, Theo? What's your big bad dare?"

Theo didn't hesitate. "A swim in the lake."

She was almost disappointed. If you grew up in New York, swimming in one of the many lakes was a favorite summer pastime. "That's pretty tame, Mr. Mayor. Are you sure you can't think of something bigger?"

Theo smirked. "Naked. Right now. Let's go, Red Hot."

"HERE ARE THE RULES," Amber announced as soon as Theo's car rolled to a stop in a secluded corner of the beach parking lot. There were only a handful of cars parked along the far end.

Most of the town was still at the carnival, waiting for the fireworks to begin, but it was still a risk.

Theo hesitated and considered cautioning Amber or even taking back the silly dare, but Amber was almost humming with the energy of his challenge. She was already kicking off her sandals.

"There are no rules. This is my dare," Theo said. He leaned back in his seat and watched her with hooded eyes. Despite the dark interior of his car, her skin glowed in the lamplight. Her dress displayed the delicate lines of her collarbones and the top swells of her breasts. If he looked hard enough, he could imagine how fast the pulse in her neck was beating. It would match his.

"Of course there are. I'm an expert skinny-dipper, boss," she scoffed.

He didn't miss the emphasis she put on *boss*. She was putting distance between them. The irony of her taking her clothing off to put distance between them wasn't lost on him. But he was a patient man, and he knew what he wanted was worth the wait.

"Rule number one: you have to count to ten in the car to give me a head start." She paused, her eyes glittering with mischief. Her excitement was palpable in the small car.

"And rule two?"

"This one is the most important one." She leaned in close enough that Theo could smell her floral shampoo and a hint of the cinnamon candy she loved. "Number two: you can see me naked, but only if you catch me."

"That's not how you play..." he growled, but she put one long slender finger over his lips. She looked wild and carefree in the seat of his car in the moonlight. Theo felt his heart hammering in his chest and a slower, harder pounding beginning in his groin at the thought of finally seeing all of her beautiful body laid bare.

"Ready?" she asked, her hand on the doorknob.

"Set." She climbed out, one graceful leg poised to run, and turned to look at him with a smile. He thought he could never get tired of watching her.

"Go!" The door slammed behind her, and she took off like a nymph, heading straight to the woods that led to the beach.

Theo sat still for a moment. The logical, honorable part of him started to count. "One... two... Fuck it," he said viciously. He ran.

The parking lot was edged by a dense thicket of pine trees, with a winding path that led down to the public beach. Through the branches, Theo caught a glimpse of golden hair weaving along the tail. He quickened his pace, his heart hammering against his chest. Every cell in his body vibrated with life, the chase igniting a primal instinct in him to pursue until he was almost soundless in the dark woods.

Her laughter, light and teasing, floated back to him, punctuated by a startled "shit"—she probably stepped on something. Silly woman left her shoes in the car. He passed her red bandanna, flung to the side of the path. Anticipation spiked, and he lengthened his stride to put an end to the chase.

"Come and get me," she taunted, running faster to the dock. In one smooth move, she reached down for the hem of her dress, drew it off over her head, and tossed it just before she ran onto the wooden dock. She was close enough now that he could see the smooth globes of her ass in the moonlight.

A lacy purple bra hit him in the face. It slowed him down just long enough for her to get to the end of the dock, where she turned around, bare except for the thin blue lines of her underwear. She was magnificent. Her body curved like an instrument. Smooth, graceful lines dipping in and flaring out. He wanted her more than anything in his life. He stopped running and drank her in.

Slowly, she lifted her hands into her hair and pushed it back over her shoulders, revealing herself even more. The lake was calm, the soft lapping of the water against the dock and the faint hum of the carnival music across the lake the only sounds as she stared back at him boldly. Her breasts were full, with dark pink tips that tilted upward, her softly curved stomach leading to graceful thighs. Even her feet were a work of art. Pink-tipped and dainty. White hot lust ripped through him.

"Amber," he breathed.

"I took pity on you and slowed down, Mr. Mayor," she said teasingly. "I'm a runner now, you know."

"You cheated," he said.

She raised her eyebrows. "Are you not looking at me naked?"

"You're not naked," he said, his eyes dropping to her bikini bottoms.

A slow, flirty smile curved her lips. "Oh? Then take care of that."

Theo reached out, gripped the fragile strips of fabric, and yanked her forward. They came off in his grip, and he was left holding a scrap of nothing. Amber laughed and turned around, lifting her arms into a perfect swan dive off the dock.

He grew up swimming in this lake. His family owned a lake house on the other end, and he knew every dock and swim spot, but his heart hit his throat when he saw her graceful dive into the water and held until she popped back up.

"Was your naughty dare everything you thought it would be, Mr. Mayor?" she said, leaning back and backstroking. Her nipples broke the water, wet droplets beading her skin as the water rippled around her.

Theo undid the buttons on his shirt.

"I'm telling you, there's nothing you can do that would scare me. I've done it all," she said, lazily stroking parallel to the shore.

He shrugged his shirt off, followed by his belt and pants while he toed off his shoes.

At his silence, Amber stopped swimming and looked up. "Oh," she breathed, the sound full of surprise and appreciation. He stood on the edge of the dock, naked and proud, fearless, with his rock-hard cock pointing at her like a target.

She laughed softly. "I guess you did like it."

He dove into the cold, clear water. When he burst through the surface, laughter greeted him.

"I didn't think you had it in you," she said. Her eyes lit up with mischief. "Georgie would be proud." She splashed water at him.

He growled and stroked toward her in the water. He could touch the bottom where he was, but he didn't think she could.

"Don't talk about Georgie when I have a hard-on," he said, gripping her slippery waist.

"Is that what that was? I thought it was your *vast* competitive spirit." She floated out of his hands and dipped under the water.

He felt the water tremble just before she touched his leg. She wound a small hand around his calf, lightly tracing the contours of muscle and bone with a featherlight touch before letting the tips of her nails drag across his skin as she pulled away. Her head broke the surface, and she found his gaze. The world outside of the lake ceased to exist, leaving only the sensation of cool water and heated skin. She took a breath before diving below again.

He controlled his breathing and waited.

The next touch was a brush against his back, winding around his body to caress him in the most sensitive places. He closed his eyes and tried to identify the drag of her nipples across his back, the faint brush of her belly over his ass, two hands sliding up the front of his thighs while he stood still. It was erotic, mysterious, seductive. Slow, liquid fire burned in his veins.

Amber's head popped up through the water, her hair slicked back, a wicked grin still on her face. She disappeared before he could reach her. Suddenly, two hands gripped his cock, bold and firm, giving him a hard squeeze that made him groan. His breathing quickened, his chest rising and falling as if he were the one holding his breath under water. She circled her thumb around the round head of him, rubbing and stroking him with wicked hands. Theo felt her hand slide down and cup his balls, gently pulling and stroking them. "Fuck," he swore.

He reached for her, pulling her body up out of the water and flush against his, from breasts to hips. She wrapped her arms around his neck and fitted herself tightly against him, rubbing against him under the water. He could feel her tight nipples pressed against his chest and heard her breath hitch at the contact. His cock nudged insistently against her stomach, pressed tight between their bodies. He gripped her waist and lifted her up, lining himself perfectly into the even hotter cleft between her thighs, where she tightened her legs around him.

"That escalated quickly," she whispered. Her breath came in short, shallow pants in the silent lake.

He gripped her hips tighter and rocked firmly between her legs. Her head dropped back, exposing the tender skin of her throat. He bent his head and grazed her skin there with a possessive kiss. "You keep underestimating me," he murmured against her skin.

"I think we keep underestimating each other," she said. "I wonder why that is." She looked down at the water. "Do you think the worst of me?"

He tipped her chin up with a finger until he could see her eyes. She wasn't smiling now, and it was the hint of uncertainty that made his chest ache. "I think the best of you, and as soon as you stop underestimating yourself, the whole fucking world will too."

"Do you think I'm—" she stopped, and he could see the emotions play over her face. Hopeful, like she wanted to believe him. Scared that he could be wrong.

He waited for her to finish, willed her to fill in the blanks of her version of herself, but she stopped. Her chin rose out of his hands, almost like she was steeling herself. "Yes," he said, simply. Quietly. "Yes, to everything you're thinking. I think you're wickedly sharp and incredibly talented. Gifted. I think you know things about people they don't even know themselves, and you show them so they can shine right alongside you. You're funny as hell. Loyal. Hardworking. Gorgeous." *Mine.*

The sudden boom that echoed across the lake made her jump, and she bobbed up in the water against him. Above them, the first sunburst of brilliant blue splintered the sky, reflected on the water, and floated slowly down.

"The fireworks are starting," she said, turning away from him. Her eagerness for the distraction was palpable. He needed it too.

He turned her around in his arms, and they floated like that, looking up at the sky. While she watched the colors exploding in the sky, he watched her and wondered how this woman, this outrageous, bold, tender, and beautifully uncertain woman, had woven her way so deeply into his heart.

All too soon, the faint sound of "God Bless America" began, and Theo reluctantly let her go. The carnival would clear out now, and inevitably others someday be drawn to the lake on a hot summer night. Theo had come a long way in the risk department, but getting caught skinny dipping with his assistant wasn't something he could chance.

"We have to go."

"Val will be looking for me," she said regretfully.

"Come on. I'll take you back."

Chapter Twenty-Five

THE HEAT WAS GETTING to him.

Theo turned the cold water of the shower off and stood there, dripping wet and still boiling hot. His insides were hot, fiery hot with lust and desire, a pounding, physical need that pulsed in his veins all day long.

It was Amber. Even now, closing his eyes, he remembered the feel of her body in the water last night, the sensuous slip and slide of her body along parts of his, teasing, stroking, rubbing. Her body leaning back against his, weightless in his arms except for the heavy words he had spoken.

Mine. He had wanted to say it, but he knew she wasn't ready to hear it. He wasn't at first either. On paper, they didn't make sense, but that had ceased to matter.

And now they had crossed an invisible line.

He towel-dried his hair and shaved methodically, going through the motions, rationalizing each step of the way, like it was a puzzle he could solve if he fit the pieces together just right.

But there was only one solution.

He wanted her. There was no more playing or teasing.

They had teased each other long enough with their silly truth-or-dare games, and he felt with a deep certainty that something had to change. He couldn't continue like this, and they couldn't go back.

Not when he knew the shape of her body intimately.

Not when she had shown him what his life had been missing.

It was almost laughable to think he could resist her. He had met her on likely one of the most unpleasant nights of her life. Every protective instinct within him had surged at the sight of her walking down the road alone.

Even then, when she was seated in the back of Grant's cruiser, with her chin jutted out as if she would do battle with the world, he had admired her spirit. Here was this young woman, a kid really, with a sharp tongue and an even worse attitude, who took a bad situation and came out swinging.

He had Grant look up her address the next day and went back to check on her to make sure she was all right, but she sent her sister out to send him away. So he'd left. He knew her pride, more than anything, had been wounded, and he gave her space to heal in her own way.

Eventually, he went back to law school, and when they did finally cross paths, it was clear she had chosen to keep him at a distance with a version of herself meant to push him away. He had honored that and kept things cool between them, but that night had changed his life forever, even if she didn't want to acknowledge it.

Working with her every day, sharing the highs and lows of their runs, learning about her, smelling her, touching her body, taking care of her had only intensified his desire, and now he wanted all of her. It wasn't something he considered lightly.

Despite his casual relationships, Theo never entered something before he had studied all the angles and thought through each step like a high-stakes chess game.

He thought through the opinions and judgments of the town. Even Neal's perspective, which might have held more weight in different circumstances, was carefully considered and dismissed.

All the reservations and calculations fell away, and he knew what he wanted with an intensity that surpassed mere desire and went straight to the heart. He wanted her and it was time.

~

"HAVE you heard from the boss man today?" Amber asked nonchalantly as she sat on the edge of Charlotte's desk, swinging her hot pink heels to see the silly poof of fur wave. If someone asked her point-blank, she would not admit that she had dressed this morning not for herself but for someone else: Theo.

After last night at the lake, she had expected him at her door at six thirty a.m. for their usual morning run, but instead she woke up to a text telling her to sleep in, that he had something to do in the morning. It was almost crushing how disappointed she was.

Instead of turning off the alarm and going back to sleep, she got up and ran on her own. She had a streak going, after all, and the race was just a week away. Bitter disappointment was her company as she sweated out three miles on her own. She cheated only a little when her lungs felt like they might collapse, and she needed to sit for a bit. It was nice for once not to have Theo pushing her to get up and try harder and just do it.

But she missed him.

Charlotte's sky-blue chiffon blouse and cream suit had a Grace Kelly vibe today as she sat behind her computer. "Yes, he had a personal issue to take care of this morning," Charlotte said. "He said he'd be in a little while, but you just missed Johnny. He said your car's all set and he took back the loaner."

"Oh," Amber said, all the wind taken out of her sails. How could she be disappointed in Theo with that kind of generosity? She would pay him back. She had already started calling all of her credit card companies to get the final balances to keep track of what she owed. The heavy weight of her finances had been there for so long, she was barely able to imagine a life without it. Hope and a nebulous, deep-seated fear whirled in her confusingly.

"How are things coming with the gala planning?" Charlotte asked.

"Okay, I think," Amber nervously. She picked at a string on her sleeve.

"Just okay?"

Working on the gala had been surprisingly fun for Amber, giving her something to focus on other than lusting after her boss, but now that the day had almost arrived, nerves were starting to rear their ugly head. Who thought it would be a good idea to let her plan this? She couldn't even think about it without getting queasy.

There had been quite a few humiliations in her life already, but this event was important to Theo and therefore important to her. It had to be successful. She couldn't bear it if she failed him. "Have you seen how many tickets we've sold?" she asked Charlotte.

Charlotte looked at her computer and clicked around a few times. "We're almost sold out," she said, surprised, "and that's with the extended space at the Grand River Hotel."

Fresh nerves flooded Amber. She didn't want to put it into words, even to Charlotte, that despite never working on anything harder in her life, with the exception of running, she was terrified she was going to fail spectacularly and quite publicly.

In fact, in any of her previous efforts—schooling or jobs—this was the time when she would usually give up, afraid to continue, afraid of what failure would feel like. But now, despite all that fear still being there, compounded even more by how important the night was to Theo, Charlotte, Todd, and even Neal, she had to stick it out.

It was enough to send her back to her office to look for emergency sugar rations, but her drawers were empty.

She looked up a while later when she heard Theo come in, and her body unconsciously relaxed. He stopped by each of the offices, giving Diane her chocolate croissant and dropping off fresh-baked donuts for Charlotte and Todd, before stopping in her office.

"You better not be coming in here with green juice after giving them sugar," she said archly, leaning back so he could take full advantage of her wrap dress.

Theo flashed a grin, leaning against the doorframe. *Dimples showing before ten a.m. should be outlawed*, she thought crankily. His suit was crisp, beautifully tailored, and his pristine white shirt hugged his tall form perfectly.

He held up two hands, a paper bag in one and a to-go cup in the other. "How about both?" he asked.

She melted. "I suppose," she said. She reached for the sugar first, setting it next to her on the desk, trying not to stare and failing.

She let her gaze take a slow, delicious crawl up and down his body. She knew the shape of that body now, the feel of those powerful thighs between hers in the water, exactly how long and thick and hard he was, rubbing between her legs.

Desire so intense it made her catch her breath made her sit up and clench her thighs together against the ache there.

Only to find him staring at her with the same intensity.

The slow teasing between them had grown until the tiniest touch would make them explode. Her senses were in overdrive. She wanted to lick his neck and taste him. She saw his beautiful face and wanted to press hot kisses on that firm jaw and his smiling mouth. She wanted to trace his dimples with her tongue. She wanted to follow him into his office and get down on her knees and take him into her mouth and watch him fall apart.

She needed to get hold of herself.

Theo moved away from the doorframe and into her office, leaning over the desk with his arms stretched wide, pulling the fabric of his suit taut around his hard biceps.

Only his eyes offered a clue to the intensity behind the man in front of her, looking at her with raw need. The electric current between them hummed so loudly, she wondered how it wasn't heard throughout the entire office.

"Will you come to my house and let the dog out tonight?" His casual tone belied the intensity in his eyes. Anyone listening would think they were merely talking about Puddin', but she understood his request, and her answer was clear.

"Yes," she responded, her lips curving. "I'll be there." *Yes, yes, one thousand times yes.*

The intensity in his gaze burned brighter when his cool blue eyes dipped to her lips. "Good," he said swiftly. In a movement quicker than she could register, he bent down and ran his tongue across her bottom lip. Her breath hitched at the secret little invasion.

"I'll be in my office," he said with a grin.

Chapter Twenty-Six

THE SOFT BUBBLING of the hot tub in Theo's backyard should have been relaxing. Instead, the water reminded Amber of last night, when she had waited for Theo in the lake, and how this night wasn't going to end in frustration.

This time, she would know what it was like to feel Theo deep inside her body. She would learn what he sounded like when he came, what his hands felt like gripping her, and watch the satisfaction on his face while she screamed his name.

She was no longer under the assumption that the mayor was uptight.

A man with that much hunger in his eyes when he looked at her knew of things beyond roses and candlelight and missionary sex. Anticipation cast a buzz across her skin, along with the bubbles skimming over her bare body.

Theo's backyard was a good distance away from any curious neighbors, and the pergola that the hot tub sat under had lattice walls for privacy. She had fed and thrown the ball for Puddin' and put her on the couch in the sunroom to snooze. Then she poured a glass of Theo's excellent wine and slipped into the hot tub to wait.

"I like seeing you here." The low, husky drawl sent instant heat into her veins.

Theo leaned against the French doors, his hands in his pockets, his head tilted as he studied her.

He still wore his silver aviators, but he had shed his suit jacket somewhere in the house, leaving only the white button-down shirt that clung so lovingly to his beautiful hard shoulders and biceps. His red tie was still properly knotted, his trousers pressed, and his wingtips gleamed when he crossed one in front of the other.

All of this beautiful man was hers for the night. She sank lower into the water. He was going to have to work for it.

"Can't see much from over there," she said. "Come here." She patted the edge of the tub in invitation.

He made her wait.

"What do you have on under there?"

She imagined his eyes beneath the sunglasses flickering over her lower half, covered by the steady stream of bubbles, and something hot and deliciously womanly twisted her insides.

"Find out." She sipped the wine, noticing how her hand trembled on the stem.

Slowly, he straightened away from the doorframe, and walked toward her without taking off his glasses, as if he were the one in charge tonight. Little did he know, there were few places in this world she felt more confident than the bedroom.

Sex had always been a pleasurable escape for her, one she knew exactly how to make feel good. She might fail miserably at relationships, but she enjoyed sex for what it was: pure, unadulterated fun.

He sat on the edge of the tub near her shoulder. "This is good," she murmured, handing him the glass of wine. He took a sip and moved it out of the way. His silence heightened the anticipation in her. Her body was thrumming with need already. Slow, slick heat pulsed in her belly and between her thighs, turning her nipples into hard pebbles under the water. Still, he was silent.

He touched her face first.

A gentle brush of the back of his fingers against her cheek. Soft. He traced her eyebrows next, slid one long finger down the bridge of her nose, before resting just his thumb on her lips and tugging the bottom one down.

She parted her lips. He was salty and rough against her tongue when she licked him. She could feel the heat of his body radiating from him. His scent filled her along with the humid air. Clean, masculine, a faint hint of expensive cologne. She trembled.

She had a fierce desire to grab him by the tie and bring him down into the tub with her and make this first time quick and dirty. They had all night to explore each other. She wanted to feel the hard thrust of him when he first entered her. She wanted to run her fingers through his perfect hair and mess him up, hear what he sounded like when he moaned her name.

His finger led the way to her jaw, tracing the line there, then her throat. He paused like that, directly over her pulse, and smiled for the first time. She let out her breath and tilted her head back to rest against the tub, content to let him take the lead for now. She was surprised by her passivity.

In her experience, she was the one who took charge. It felt safer that way, leading where she wanted and pulling back when it dove into places she didn't. A trickle of uncertainty pulled at her. She felt in the dark without being able to see his eyes and test his emotions through their cool blue or the darker shade they turned when he was aroused beyond all measure.

"Truth or dare?" she whispered.

His fingers continued to move over her neck and the tops of

her shoulders, lightly skimming, teasing, but staying well above her breasts or anywhere else her skin ached to feel him.

"Truth," he said.

"What are you thinking?"

"I'm thinking this is a very bad idea," he murmured. He dropped his hand away from her collarbone. Instantly, a chill replaced it. Disappointment came crashing down, and she felt her face fall. He lifted a hand and took off his glasses.

Finally, she could see his eyes. Any lingering doubt or disappointment faded. They were dark, velvety blue, looking back at her with an intensity that made her breath skitter to a stop. "And we're going to do it anyway."

"I thought you were going to say you changed your mind," she said, her breath coming back in shallow pants. "Or you didn't want me."

He slid his palm around her neck and tilted her head back to meet his eyes. "I want you more than I want my next breath. I want to sink my teeth into you and taste you and leave my mark on your skin. I want to fuck you until you scream my name into my pillow, and then I want to fuck you again, so you feel me for days."

A flush rose up her chest to her neck and cheeks, and she felt dizzy with heat and need. "You want me to feel you for days?" she asked faintly.

"I want *you*," he corrected her. "Whatever way I can have you."

His words sent a shiver through her, whether from desire or fear at the intensity in his voice.

She sat up with an instinct to leave. For the first time, she felt real fear with him. Men like Theo were used to getting what they wanted.

She had watched him work ruthlessly for months now, sacrificing sleep and anything else that came between him and his goals. To be the object of that much intensity scared her.

When he looked at her like that, there was no flimsy bravado or persona she could hide behind. It was only her, in all her truest, messiest, most vulnerable self.

He must have read the fear on her face because he smiled knowingly, as if he saw right through every one of her pretenses.

"Your turn. Truth or dare?" he countered.

"Dare," she said. "Always."

"Show me what you have on under the water."

She took a deep breath, feeling the fear recede as she stepped back onto firmer ground. Amber looked down at the bubbles concealing her up to her throat. "What makes you think I have anything on?" she teased, raising an eyebrow.

She braced her arms and lifted herself onto the side edge of the tub. Water streamed down her naked body, dripping off her breasts, catching on her nipples to bead there, down her stomach, dripping between her thighs.

She leaned back on her arms and watched with pleasure as his eyes widened and his nostrils flared as his gaze roamed over her body. She'd never felt sexier in her life. The imbalance of it, with Theo fully dressed and her bare, shot through her like a drug, deliciously improper.

"Spread your legs."

"Is that another dare?" she asked. Slowly, she opened her legs, exposing herself fully to him.

She was bare and slippery with need. His jaw clenched, and he yanked his tie undone. He made quick work of his buttons while she watched.

Lazily, she touched herself, a teasing, light stroke of her fingers on her bare mound. She dipped her fingers between her slick folds, spreading moisture to her clit before circling lightly there. The little bud was hard and aching, almost too sensitive to touch or she'd come before even feeling his beautiful, hard body against hers. Lust, bold and heavy, consumed her.

He swore and tore the rest of his shirt off and then yanked his plain white cotton undershirt over his head with one hand, leaving his chest beautifully bare. Six squares of muscle lined his stomach. They were perfectly symmetrical, with two larger squares next to each other above, lightly covered in dark hair.

Theo's body was a lean, powerful, sculpted testament to good nutrition and regular exercise. Not something she ever aspired to herself, but she was thrilled to enjoy the benefits of all that hard muscle naked against her.

She wanted to feel him inside her.

"You'll have to wait for that, sweetheart." A slow, amused grin lifted his lips, and she realized she had said it out loud. He clamped down on her hips and turned her body to let her feet hang over the side of the tub. He was between her thighs now. She drew him closer with her wet legs wrapped around his hips.

He bent his head and kissed her, a lingering stroke of tongue and lips that teased what was to come. She caught his bottom lip between her teeth and tugged gently, trying to take control, but Theo unwrapped her arms and stepped back. "No, not yet," he said, low and commanding, giving her a hard look. "I want to taste you first."

He settled two hands on her thighs and bent his knees, eye level with her pussy. She wasn't a shy person by any means, but she suddenly felt exposed there in the openness of the backyard. She drew her legs together. Two large, warm hands on her thighs stopped her, spreading her legs farther apart with his shoulders.

She braced herself on her arms on the edge of the tub and tilted her head back, moving her hips involuntarily upward, seeking his mouth. "Do you need directions?" she teased.

"You can tell me the answer to that when I'm done," he

murmured, and then she felt his mouth, hot and wet, sucking kisses all around the soft, bare skin of her lips—everywhere but where she needed it most.

"Give me your mouth," she begged, running her fingers through his hair, messing it up, and gripping harder. She felt, more than heard, his dark laugh against her damp skin.

He yanked her closer to the edge of the tub, slid his arms underneath her thighs, and wrapped around her legs, using two hands to hold her open. "You have to learn patience," he said with a swipe of his tongue on the side of her clit. She gasped and jerked her hips forward. So close.

A soft stroke on the other side, teasing, teasing. He dipped his tongue lower, dangerously, thrillingly, lower, inside of her, fire-hot, and leaving her aching. She *was* impatient. She wanted to come. She wanted to feel him buried within her, but his implacable hands held her still for the onslaught of his mouth and teeth and tongue.

She edged closer to the tub until her tiptoes touched the ground to gain leverage against his mouth and press her wet, aching pussy where she needed the friction. He licked and nipped her lips, and she whimpered again, shocked that he had elicited such a weak sound from her. Only then was she rewarded with his tongue exactly where she wanted it.

"Oh, yes, there, right there," she whispered. Theo seemed to read her body better than even she did. He teased her with strokes and flicks and circles, finding out what made her gasp, what made her clench and moan. She would've said she liked it all if she could've taken a breath. Her first orgasm took her by surprise; in under sixty seconds, she was curled around him, thighs quivering, arms wrapped around his shoulders, holding him close while she gasped out a shuddering orgasm.

Theo stroked her hips and thighs, rubbed his face against her inner thighs, letting her catch her breath. When she wasn't seeing stars, she sat back and reached down for his belt. Theo stood up, the bulge in his suit trousers straining the fabric. Her mouth watered.

Just as she slid the belt through the loop, Theo picked her up, wrapped her legs around his waist, carried her over to one of the chaise lounges, and laid her damp body back on it. She stretched her arms above her head and her legs out, toes pointed. At once, she was relaxed from the intense orgasm and ready to play again.

"Your turn," she said, hooking a hand in his belt loop to tug him closer. Her fingers brushed against the short, coarse hair on his stomach that led like an arrow down into the band of his underwear.

Theo's stomach muscles clenched in resistance. Instead, he placed a large hand in the middle of her chest and gently pressed her back, settling between her legs at the end of the chaise. The way he handled her, so firm and proprietary, was a surprise. A delicious one.

"Not yet. Fuck," he murmured, gripping her thighs and looking her over. "You're beautiful."

She leaned up to kiss him, deep and wet, tasting herself on him. She took her time, licking delicately and thoroughly. "I want to see you, too," she said when she pulled away.

His hands on her thighs gripped her legs tighter, drawing them farther apart. "Later," she thought she heard him say, but he was already pressing hot, sucking kisses on her clit. Then a nip that had her arching her back and pushing herself into his dirty, delightful mouth.

"What—" she gasped. "What are you doing?"

"Can you give me another one?" he asked between hot kisses.

"Of course I can." She was still floating from the first one, but if he insisted...

He was more ruthless this time, having watched exactly what made her pant and cry out. This time, he added two fingers, slowly pushing into her and twisting while he sucked her clit. She was so wet she could hear the sounds of her arousal. It didn't matter.

She was lost to the sensations he effortlessly created within her. She tried to keep her eyes open to watch what he was doing, but the sight of his dark head bent over her, his beautiful hands and mouth and tongue giving her such exquisite pleasure, was too much.

She closed her eyes and came again, this one ripped from a place deep inside that left her panting and shaken. She floated back down to earth to the feel of Theo's hands on her breasts, idly stroking her nipples and the sensitive undersides before sliding lower.

Again, his fingers stroked her expertly, lightly rubbing either side of her clit when she flinched at the sensation on her swollen, tender flesh.

"Give me one more," he whispered against the fragile skin between her hips. He looked up, and she shivered at what she saw. His beautiful hair was mussed from her fingers and a flush of color on his cheekbones along with his eyes, hungry and watchful on her.

It was as if he was purposely unraveling her layers, physically and emotionally, and leaving her exposed and vulnerable. Maybe that was his intention all along. If so, he had succeeded. She had no shred of pretense left, and for once it didn't matter.

"I can't," she said shakily. "I can't take any more." Her body still quivered from coming so hard.

His lips pulled the tight red bud of her clit into his mouth and sucked gently.

"Oh... oh," she sighed. "If you insist."

He was gentle and slow this time, which was good because

she was sensitive and tender to the touch but a slave to that feeling that he coaxed out of her. He used his mouth and his tongue and fingers and licked her straight into a third orgasm that left her unable to form words as waves of pleasure rocked her.

When she opened her eyes, Theo was grinning down at her, dimples on full display. "Nothing to say out of that mouth of yours now, Red Hot?"

"I'm going to show you exactly what I can do with this mouth," she said. "Later. When I can feel my legs again."

"We're just getting started."

She closed her eyes and sank back into the chair. "I take it back. I take everything back. You're a sex god who hates missionary and is allergic to rose petals."

Her eyes flew open again when he scooped her into his arms. "Hold on tight."

She twined her arms around his neck and her legs around his waist and tucked her head under his chin, ready for whatever came next.

THEO TOSSED Amber onto his bed and took a moment to admire the sight.

As soon as she hit the bed, she bounced up, propped herself up on her elbows, and stared at him as boldly as he watched her. Her hair was still piled into a loose bun on top of her head, with damp pieces falling around her face. Her lips were swollen from kisses and her cheeks flushed with red. Her breasts were full, with pink tips that pouted up at him, begging for his mouth. The long line of her torso with its intriguing dips and valleys led down to her sweetly curved stomach and the paler skin of her mound. She was every fantasy he had come to life, lying in his bed with a witchy smile on her red lips.

He made quick work of his belt then pushed his trousers down, neatly taking his underwear with them, and toeing out of his shoes and socks all in one fell swoop. Quick. Efficient. Eyes locked on the woman in his bed.

"Lie back," he growled.

Her eyes glittered, but she leaned back, one knee drawn up to cover herself. He wanted more. He wanted it all. "Open your legs."

A shiver went through her at the rough command, and slowly, she inched her legs open to reveal the sweet, bare pussy he had devoured. He could still taste her. He was going to taste her again before the night was over. His cock jumped, and he palmed it while he watched her spread herself for him. Her eyes were half-closed with desire.

"My turn," he said. His heart pounded, hard and fast, inside his chest, but he forced himself to slow down. He had waited this long for her, and he wanted to wring every drop of pleasure from her body until she was limp and boneless, happily exhausted in his bed before he took care of his own pleasure.

He knew with the same certainty that he knew the sun rose in the east and set in the west that if he gave her a moment to think when they were finished with this, she would bolt. He craved the version of her that she hid from most people, and he had set to work on stripping her bare.

"I'm yours," she said simply, and something possessive and primal surged within him again at the word. *Mine.*

Theo moved between her thighs, holding them open and teasing her clit with his cock. He stopped just before entering her and asked with a wicked glint in his eye, "May I fuck you now, please, Ms. Hart?"

"So polite," she laughed huskily and reached out to stroke his cock. "You may indeed fuck me now, Mr. Mayor."

She held him with two hands stacked on top of each other and stroked him tight and hard. His head fell back, and he let out a "Jesus" when she let one hand cup his balls and stroke. "Condom," he gritted. He wasn't going to last much longer, and he wanted to come inside her this first time.

He was leaning over her, stretching in his bedside drawer for a condom when he felt her mouth.

The shock of her wet, velvety warmth wrapped around him made his eyes close briefly in pleasure. He looked down to see her looking up at him with that naughty twinkle in her eyes that made him crazy with lust. Her lips stretched around the head of him, sucking lightly. She lifted her head off the pillow to take him deeper, and his hips jerked involuntarily.

"Fuck," he whispered. "Your mouth. I love your beautiful fucking mouth."

She let him go with a soft pop and grinned up at him. This time, she took him deeper, tilting her head back and opening her mouth wide to give him access to her throat. He felt her hands grip his hips and guide him in. He knew she couldn't control how deep he was with her on her back, so he let her set the pace. She pulled him deeper, deeper, and deeper still. She moaned around him as if she loved the taste of him. He let himself enjoy it for a few more strokes before pulling away and moving back down her body.

"Later," he said, "I'll use that mouth of yours." He swooped in and kissed her softly, gently on the lips. "Now I'm going to fuck you." He gripped her ankles, placed them one by one on his shoulders, and snugged up close enough that the backs of her thighs rested on top of his. Her breathing grew shallow, and her hands reached out to his cock again. He let her tease him with soft, stroking fingers before brushing them aside to roll the condom on.

He was physically shaking from need. His cock throbbed so close to her hot cleft that he could push inside that warm slickness and lose himself in her. "You ready, sweetheart?"

"So ready." He looked up, caught her involuntary shiver, and grinned.

She stuck out her tongue in response. "Let's see what you've got, boss," she taunted, lifting her hips to rub herself against his shaft harder.

Theo bent down until his elbows were on either side of her face, threaded his fingers into her hair, and looked at her fiercely. "Say my name when I'm inside of you." With one slow, burning hot push, he was inside.

"Oh my—Theo," she gasped. Her hand clenched on the comforter as she arched up into his thrust.

Theo hissed and pulled back, thrusting another inch, working himself into her tightness. She was tight and hot, a perfect fit as he pushed in deeper and deeper until he was seated fully. Theo paused like that, forearms on either side of her head, eyes locked on each other while he throbbed inside her.

The time for teasing was gone. The look in her eyes was wild and dark and raw, as if he was finally seeing the real Amber. He wanted to beat his chest or howl or do some other insane thing in relief and happiness that she was finally, finally letting go. The reality of it took his breath away as he looked in her eyes.

She blinked and it was gone.

"Your turn," she whispered, a seductive smile taking over her face. He recognized that dazzling smile for what it was: her defense, and he let her have it.

He was shaken too.

She gently pushed him off her and turned around to face his headboard, thrusting her ass up and leaning over to hold the wooden slats of his bed. She looked over her shoulder coyly, spread her legs wider, and swayed. "I want it like this," she said, pushing herself back at his cock.

He rubbed her cleft slowly, up and down, with the head of his cock, feeling that slickness coat him until he pushed in. Her thighs quivered, and she let out a little moan at the invasion. He leaned down to her smooth back, nuzzling the satiny skin and enjoying the way his hand looked on her beautiful body.

She whimpered at the touch and thrust herself back harder on his cock. She was wild and hotter than fire, thrusting her plump ass back on him. He let her find her rhythm until he couldn't anymore. Threading one arm around her waist and the other gripping her shoulder, he took over the pace, firm and controlled, while she begged.

"Oh, please," she whispered, the words sounding like they were dragged from her throat. She reached back and gripped his thigh to pull him closer still. "Theo," she panted. "Oh, please, give it to me." Her hair had come undone, and little wisps of it clung to her face. She was a wild, wanton sight, begging him for her release.

He reached around her, slid his fingers into her slickness, and traced her spread lips around his cock, pressing the heel of his hand on her swollen clit with the firm strokes she liked. She was panting, little moans and growls coming from her as he set about taking her apart again.

The fourth time she came, she cried.

Theo held her tighter, feeling every pulse of her inner walls around him, chasing his own release. The pressure rose higher and hotter still until, with a hash cry, he came. She shuddered and dropped her head down, grinding her hips back on him like she couldn't get enough.

He would have smiled if he had any strength left. Instead, he pulled out with a hiss and tucked her into his side. They rested like that, spent and peaceful, until the sound of Puddin's unhappy yips filled the room.

"I'm just going to check on her," he said, getting up to let the mutt in. Puddin' took a flying leap and landed in the middle of the bed.

"Hey, baby," Amber murmured, not opening her eyes. She reached out blindly to pet her on the head. "What happened to her crate?"

"She cried when I put her in there," Theo said sheepishly. He pushed the dog gently to the end of the bed and settled against Amber again, ignoring Puddin's wounded look. "You okay?"

Her eyes were closed, and she was grinning. He reached over and gave her a quick, hard kiss on the lips. She looked tousled and sleepy and very well fucked. He wanted her all over again. He wanted *her*, in every way.

"Admit it, Puddin' was a good idea," she said after a while, petting the little dog's head. She had wormed her way up between them again and was splayed out on her back waiting for a belly rub. "You love her."

"She's grown on me," he admitted.

"You're a natural. Someday you'll make a wonderful father."

"I hope so," he murmured, feeling his eyes growing heavy. "I'd like a big family like your sister and Davis's. Do you want kids?" When he opened his eyes, she was lying quietly, watching Puddin'.

"I don't know," she finally said. "Maybe someday." By the tone of her voice, he could tell she was pulling away, putting up her defenses again, brick by brick. "I left my clothes downstairs," she said after a while, sitting up.

He knew of only one reliable way to get her to stay.

Theo wrapped an arm around her waist and hauled her back to bed.

"Woman, you damn near killed me. Let me rest and I'll make you food."

She paused. "What kind? I've seen your fridge," she said suspiciously.

"Pancakes." He cracked an eye and watched the debate play on her face—run or stay? He casually sweetened the deal. "With chocolate chips."

"Theo, you know you don't have any chocolate or butter here."

"Chocolate, butter, and syrup. Bought it just for you," he murmured sleepily, somewhat shocked that he was actually tired. He hadn't fallen asleep so easily in a year at least, but he couldn't keep his eyes open. "Come back to bed."

She finally settled back down with a huff. "Fine, but I'll only stay if we can do that again."

He pulled her tighter into the curve of his body, where she fit perfectly, her hips against his, her back to his front. "We can do that all night long."

He nuzzled his face into her sweet-smelling hair. Puddin' yawned loudly and let out one last disgusted yip about being relegated to the end of the bed. She did a few circles before plopping down on Theo's feet.

Theo smiled. He had both of his girls with him now.

Chapter Twenty-Seven

Amber slipped out from under Theo's heavy arm and paused for a moment, watching him sleep. He looked so peaceful next to her. She pressed a light kiss to his arm rather than his handsome face. She didn't want to wake him and have him watch her leave.

Something told her that Theo would want her to stay, and she couldn't do that.

They had dozed for an hour or so, then Theo got up and, true to his word, fed her chocolate chip pancakes with plenty of butter and syrup while they stood in the kitchen.

She had been amazed to see that Theo did indeed have all the ingredients to make her favorite pancakes and teased him mercilessly about how he should have a green juice instead to keep that amazing bod. He had ended that quickly by stripping her naked right there on the kitchen counter, pouring syrup over her breasts, and licking it off.

She took back everything she said about the mayor being vanilla.

She should have known that Theo was excellent at anything

he put his mind to, and her pleasure was number one on his list. Lucky, lucky her, the man was an animal in bed.

It was the look he gave her afterward—so full of tenderness and understanding—that had left her feeling exposed and filled her with the urge to run.

Theo wasn't interested in the *idea* of her. He wasn't satisfied with the version of her that everyone else was. Theo wanted to see the real, flawed, imperfect parts of her she had hidden so deeply under layers of self-preservation.

She didn't know if she could bear to see his disappointment at what he might find.

She had kissed Puddin' goodbye where she slept at the end of Theo's bed and crept out soundlessly to drive home at dawn. Theo would be up soon to run, and when he found her gone, he would come to her. She expected him, but she needed a moment to put herself back together from the inside out first. Last night had been intense. Incredible. Terrifying.

"Oh, hey, walk of shame," Val said, smirking at her from the top of the stairs of their building.

Amber froze in mid-step up the stairs. "Good morning," she said, trying to sound nonchalant. "You're up early."

Val snorted. "And you never went to bed, did you?"

Amber drew herself up to her full height. "I'm an adult," Amber said regally. "I don't have to explain that I was simply working late on gala stuff and decided to sleep at the office."

"Uh-huh. So, 'working late' is what we're calling a beard rash all over your neck?"

Amber fumbled around in her purse for her key. "What are you doing up so early, anyway?" She turned around and paused. Val's hood was up, and her black hair was pulled forward over her eyes.

"I'm taking the SAT test," Val said with a trace of nervousness. "My mom's outside waiting to drive me. She needs the car today."

Shock filled Amber, right before elation. She tried to keep her voice nonchalant so as not to spook her. "Right. Good luck. You'll do great."

Val hiked her backpack higher and kicked at the worn carpet on the landing outside their apartment doors. "Yeah, well, I decided last minute to apply for late admission to a few local colleges, like you said." She peeked up at Amber. "If you still think that's a good idea?"

Amber deliberately kept her face neutral. Her heart was near bursting. "Yeah, I think it's a great idea. Call me if you need a ride home."

She took a long, hot shower to clear her mind, but images from the night kept making her hot and bothered again, so she gave up and sat on the couch to watch TV.

Good lord, was the man good at *everything*? He had taken control the moment he got home and found her in the hot tub, and she hadn't minded one bit. It was so unlike her. Theo was bossy and dominant but also so incredibly sweet and tender with her. It hadn't even occurred to her to fight it. She went along for every bit of the wild ride.

She blushed and fanned herself with a magazine, just thinking about some of the things he had done to her that she had never let anyone else do.

At exactly six thirty, he knocked on the door. She knew he would. She would have been disappointed if he didn't.

She opened the door to let him in, not missing the way his eyes flared when he saw her in her short silk robe.

He strode in and kissed her. No hesitation, no asking permission. Theo kicked the door shut and pushed her up against it, kissing her like he was a sailor home on leave. He pushed his fingers into her hair and tilted her head back for his mouth. It was long and deep and delicious. She sighed happily.

When he pulled back, he didn't let go of her face. "Don't ever sneak out of my house again," he growled.

"I didn't want to wake you up, and I had to go," she whispered, her heart still hammering like crazy in her chest from that kiss.

"You were running." He said it so confidently, she wanted to kick him.

"Maybe I was done using your body," she said tartly. "Did you think of that, Mr. Mayor?"

He grinned, all white teeth and dimples. She felt it between her thighs. "I wasn't done with yours." Then he picked her up over his shoulder and headed toward her bedroom.

"Theo," she whisper-yelled in deference to her sleeping neighbors. "Put me down." She bucked against him.

"Quit moving." He spanked her then rubbed the offended spot so nicely that she wiggled again just to have another. "No panties, Ms. Hart?" he murmured, exploring her softness. His fingers lightly dipped between her cheeks, and she shot upright.

A shocking, intense heat surged through her at his bold touch, making her gasp. She didn't think she'd ever get over her uptight mayor's shockingly dirty bedroom side. He gave her another sharp slap on the fullest part of her ass that made her moan and wiggle some more.

He tossed her on the bed. "What was that for?" she asked breathlessly.

"That," he said, undoing his belt, "was for running scared this morning." Amber popped up to watch him unbutton his jeans and reach back to pull his T-shirt off.

He sat down on the edge of the bed and dragged her over his lap until she straddled him. She was wet and throbbing already. As soon as she settled over him, she rolled her hips over his thick shaft. Hot, hazy lust gripped her until she was frantic, aching to feel him filling her.

She couldn't get enough of his body, running her hands over the hard planes of his chest, tugging the hair there, and leaning forward to lick his nipples. She bit down lightly on the hard point, and he grunted.

He gripped her hips hard and lifted her above him. "This—" he said, "is for your smart mouth," and he pushed her down onto his rigid cock. Hard. Deep. So hot her hearing nearly went out and she saw stars. She was pleasantly sore from last night, but the burn from him inside her now edged a thin line between pleasure and pain.

She couldn't get enough. She rolled into him, feeling the burn and stretch as she took him deeper, and the wave of lust made her tip her head back to chase where it was going. "Oh my God," she gasped.

She had started to shake when suddenly he clamped his hands on her hips and jerked her up and off his cock. "Fuck," he swore viciously. "Condom," he gritted out.

"I'm good, and I'm on the pill," she gasped. She was poised above him. Her thighs trembled with the need to sink onto him and ride.

Theo closed his eyes briefly. "I'm clean too."

"Then we're good," Amber said, lowering herself delicately onto him. She took only the round head of him into her body and teased him, but Theo took control again and pushed her down farther onto him, stretching her and making her feel the delicious burn of his generous size. He pushed the robe off her shoulders roughly, his eyes hot as they moved over her naked body.

She braced herself with her arms on his knees behind her and lifted herself while they watched. She came down hard enough to make her breasts bounce. "Again," he demanded, watching her fuck him.

She grinned and slowed down to tease him, but Theo gripped her hair and tipped her head back, forcing her breasts up and out for his mouth. Licking and biting, and finally sucking her nipples one at a time deep into his mouth in a rhythm she felt echoed between her legs. His hands gripped her hips again, taking control back, and he pulled her tighter onto him in a fast, tight rhythm that was sending her spiraling quickly into a climax. He reached down between them, spread her, and pressed her hard on his pelvis so her clit rubbed him in the exact right spot on every downstroke.

She closed her eyes and felt the burning hot flames licking her from her insides, winding her tighter and faster toward coming. Theo bucked up against her, at the same time pulling her down and into his pelvis, and she lost all thought and reason, coming violently hard on him.

He let her go limp, playing with her breasts, stroking her back and hair gently while she floated. Eventually, reason came back to her, and she felt him deep and throbbing inside her still. She leaned forward and licked his neck.

He didn't waste a second. Swiftly, he turned her over to her back on the bed and thrust into her. She loved the way he handled her—no hesitation, just firm and knowing. There was a freedom to giving up control with Theo that terrified and excited her in equal measures.

She wrapped her arms around his shoulders and hung on until, with a final thrust, he came with his face buried in her neck.

A while later, Theo rolled to his side and looked at her. "I meant what I said, Amber. Don't sneak out like that. This isn't that."

"This isn't what?" she said carefully.

Theo looked irritated. "This wasn't just a one-night stand."

"Then what is it?" she asked carefully.

"We're not a secret, for one. I refuse to hide whatever this is between us."

Amber rolled over onto her back so she wouldn't have to see those beautiful blue eyes. He was making it difficult to remember all the reasons why she never did this exact thing they were doing now. "I don't think that's a good idea," she said calmly, despite the pressure in her chest. "Your campaign is doing so well, and—"

"Fuck the campaign." He rolled over to look at her. He was so beautiful, like a marble sculpture of an angry god. She wanted to soothe him as much as she wanted him to say, "Okay, no big deal. We'll just have sex, then," like all the other men in her past had when this conversation inevitably came up. Not Theo, though. He was too honorable for that.

"This is the morning after, for me. This is going to the farmers' market and making breakfast together. This is us spending the day together. It's real. I know that scares you, and that's why you took off, but that isn't what this is for me."

She stiffened, panic welling in her stomach. "Don't fall for me, Theo. I'm not made for that. I'm not good for you or your future. I told you I don't do relationships."

"Shh." He pushed her hair back behind her ear. "Stop looking at me like that. I'm asking you to trust me right now," he said. "Will you do that? Will you trust us?"

Could she? She didn't know, but she wanted to, and that had to matter. She nodded hesitantly.

"Thank you. That's all I'm asking for, and a promise that if you get scared, or angry with me, or need a break, you'll come to me to talk. No more running away. Things are going to happen between us. I'm going to do things that will piss you off, and you're going to do things that make me crazy, but you can't leave like that. That's not how this is going to work."

He was so earnest right now, telling her to take a chance on him when, in reality, he was the best man she had ever known. If it didn't work with someone as kind and filled with integrity as Theo Clairmont, she was destined to be alone.

The thought made her want to cry. Her stomach growled, and she seized the distraction like a lifeline. She grinned. "So, the farmers' market and breakfast? That sounds nice."

"Yeah, it does," Theo said, grinning back at her. "It sounds amazing."

Chapter Twenty-Eight

"WHAT ARE YOU GUYS DOING HERE?" Amber asked her sisters the next Saturday afternoon. "It's really not a good time," she said, trying to close the door.

Allie jammed her foot in while Lily and Evie pushed it open, and they came in anyway.

"Okay, then, come in," Amber muttered.

It wasn't that she was unexcited to see them, but she wasn't ready to show anyone how overwhelmed she was at the moment.

"We came to kidnap you for lunch, but it looks like you need more than that," Allie said, eyeing the organized chaos of Amber's living room. Spreadsheets and papers were stacked on her coffee table, gray fabric scraps she was sewing for decorations were scattered across the couch, and lists of attendees and menu options were taped to the walls.

"What is all this?" Lily asked, picking up a fabric swatch. She looked concerned.

Amber hesitated. She was torn between wanting to push her sisters away, to maintain the facade of having everything under control, or letting them in to share some of what had been weighing her down for weeks. Seeing their genuine concern cracked her resolve. "It's... for the gala. Did I not tell you guys I took over the planning and organizing for it?" *Ha ha ha. No big deal. Just six hundred people poised to watch me fail spectacularly and lose crucial funding for Theo's campaign. Ha ha ha.*

She felt sick.

"No, you didn't tell me," Allie said. "Did she mention it to you?" she asked Lily and Evie. They both shook their heads. "This seems like kind of a big deal not to mention to your family." She fixed Amber with a stare.

"It's not a big deal. I just sort of had this idea for making the Hope Gala an even better, bigger event for Theo's campaign, but his campaign manager doesn't think I can pull it off, and it's just..." Her voice broke off. "I'm trying to get everything perfect, and... it's a lot." Amber sat on the couch heavily.

Allie moved closer, her tone softening. "This would be a lot more feasible if you weren't trying to do the work of ten people. Why haven't you asked us for help?" It was her sister's expression that made her crumble. Allie was one of those deeply caring people who would give you the shirt off her back if you needed it.

"I know you all have things going on too," Amber admitted. "I was doing fine until I suddenly wasn't. The event coordinator at the Grand River Hotel has been taking care of everything, but I got this last-minute idea to change the decorations, and it snowballed to another little thing I thought I could make better, and now I'm not sure I can finish everything on time. I've got this charity race tomorrow, and the gala the weekend after that, and I'm just a little stressed right now is all." Her voice wobbled. "Nothing a little sugar and caffeine fix can't cure." She tried to smile because her sisters' faces were so concerned, but all she could manage was a sigh. "I can handle it."

Lily set down the fabric swatch and sat on the couch next to her. She took Amber's hand. "It's okay to ask for help." Her soft green eyes were sympathetic. "We're your family. I could totally help with the decorations. I've got a glue gun, and I'm itching to use it."

Evie pushed her glasses, purple with rhinestones today, up her nose and peeked at the guest list on the table. She whistled. "This is a lot of people. I can help. I make spreadsheets all day long at the library. I'll organize everything into a list for you. Would that help?"

"I don't know. I just feel like I need to prove I can handle this." She hesitated, not sure how much to share with something so new and fragile still. "I'm terrified of messing it up," Amber confessed. "It's not just my reputation on the line. It's Theo's future too. This event is a huge deal for his reelection. And I don't want to be the reason he fails. I don't want to let him down."

Her sisters were a lot of things. Slow on the draw was not one of them. Amber watched them engage in a whole conversation without using words. "Is this about more than just the campaign? Is there something going on between you two?" Evie asked carefully.

"No. Maybe. No," Amber stammered. Then she groaned with frustration. She took a deep, steadying breath and faced the mix of fear and exhilaration that she had been avoiding. "Honestly, I have no idea. I have zero experience with this."

The looks again. Amber ignored the three of them eyeballing one another. "I know what you're thinking, and it's not that." It wasn't *that*. It couldn't be because *that*—falling for Theo—was the worst idea she'd ever had. She had done plenty of ill-thought-out things in her life, like dancing on a bar, or wearing four-inch stilettos to walk the dog, but she could handle those consequences. Falling in love had the potential to shatter her.

The thought alone made her feel like getting up and leaving her own apartment.

"Sometimes it sneaks up on you whether you want it or not," Allie said dryly. "I wasn't looking for a relationship when I moved back here with Sammy, but I fell in love with Davis when we got to know each other. It was how he took care of me and how he listened to me and believed in me when I didn't yet." She blushed. "And we had this chemistry from the second we met that I knew wasn't a fluke."

"Oh please, it's not nice to brag," Evie said, fanning herself. "Your chemistry's so hot, it almost makes me pregnant."

Amber laughed at Allie's red cheeks. "How about you, Lils? How did you know you loved Tucker?"

Lily twirled a fabric flower petal between her fingers. "I don't know if there was a specific moment," she said. "We've been together since ninth grade." She shrugged half-heartedly. "It was just easy, I guess."

She looked so sad for a second that Amber squeezed her knee. "Just because things started one way doesn't mean they have to stay like that forever," Amber said gently. Lily nodded but didn't say anything. It was always tricky to talk to Lily about Tucker. She wanted to tell her to ditch him and start over with someone who treated her like she deserved... like how Theo treated her.

She swallowed hard. "I don't know what I feel," Amber confessed, the words feeling both terrifying and liberating. "But I'm scared to death I'll mess up the best thing I've ever had." Falling in love with your boss never worked out. They would inevitably break up, and then what? She'd be out of a job and a relationship. Everyone knew it was the saddest cliché in the world. Johnny's warning flashed in her head.

If things don't work out, it won't be the golden boy of Northfield who'll feel the damage. It'll be you.

Saying the words out loud was foreign. She didn't even recognize herself. The vulnerability. The fear. It was everything she had avoided all her adult life, and yet here she was. It was enough to make her hyperventilate.

"Being scared just means you're human," Allie said. "Fear's part of the package. But you can't let fear make your decisions for you. We're in this with you, every step. Maybe it's time to open up to Theo too. Let him see the real you." Allie nudged her shoulder. "Besides, what if your kind of chaos is exactly what the mayor needs?"

"No one needs my kind of chaos, including me," she muttered.

Chapter Twenty-Nine

"I'm gonna throw up." Amber groaned. She paced back and forth in front of the clock tower on Main Street, trying to keep her eggs and green juice down—the breakfast Theo had made her when they woke up together this morning at his house, where she had woken up every morning of the last week.

"You're not going to throw up. You've been training hard and working for this," Theo said patiently.

He had been talking her off the proverbial ledge for the last half hour. He must be getting used to her theatrics, seeing as they hadn't spent a single night apart since that first night she did the walk of shame in the early hours of the morning only to have him come after her.

Theo wasn't kidding. When he made up his mind, he didn't waste any time. She didn't know the endgame of their relationship, but he had spent the last week showing her exactly how good it could be between them.

Last night, they had been lying in bed after he had just convinced her to do something very naughty even for her that was probably still illegal in some states, when he threw her for a loop.

"Next year for the gala, you should hire someone to help you." His hair was messy from her fingers, and there was a bite mark on his collarbone from when she'd gotten too excited. "You're working too hard for what I'm paying you," he said, cupping her bottom.

She lifted her head from his chest and stared. "Next year?" Her voice was faint. For some reason, she hadn't ever thought of her job in Theo's office as permanent. Maybe because she never stayed at one job long enough to make plans, but what really surprised her was her answer. "I won't be here next year."

"Where will you be?" His roaming fingers stopped at the crease of her thigh.

"I'm going to open my own clothing boutique." She didn't know where the words came from. She certainly hadn't made any plans, but once they were out, they felt right. She could ask Charlotte to help her create a business plan, and Lily just opened her own studio. She could help her open a little shop in the village. Why couldn't she take a shot at her dream too?

The enormousness of it made the room spin. She stiffened, ready to defend her brash decision, but Theo let out a whoop and rolled her under him.

"Yeah?" Theo grinned down at her happily. "You're going to be a kickass business owner."

That was it. No belief that she would fail. No hesitation. He just assumed she would be successful. He probably had no idea what that did for her heart. It actually trembled. He kissed her long and deep then, and he distracted her with his tongue and fingers until she couldn't think straight, much less panic.

That seemed to be his strategy. All week long, the man kept her in a steady supply of food and orgasms, and just as he sensed her anxiety rearing its ugly head, he made her run off the excess energy, and they started the process all over again.

The Dash for a Difference 5K had seemed so far away

when Theo said that he signed them up, but today was the day
for Amber to make a fool out of herself in front of the entire
town.

Theo had insisted that they run a few laps up and down
Main Street to get warmed up, but it hadn't helped her anxiety
to see all the people lined up to wait for the race to begin. Her
entire family was there, including Cap, Sandy, Val, and Holly,
not to mention all her regulars were either running or watching
the race from the sidewalk on Main Street too.

Her stomach roiled again. "I don't know why I let you
convince me to do this. I'm not a runner."

"Pull it together, Hart," Theo said, giving her shoulders a
brisk rubdown. "You're gonna kick ass and get a medal."

"A medal? I've never won anything in my life," she scoffed.
"What if I trip and fall in front of everyone?"

"You'll get back up again and finish the race." Theo's face
was implacable. His aviators glinted in the sun, concealing his
eyes but not his dimples.

"What if I throw up?" It was a distinct possibility.

"I'll make sure not to step in it."

"What if I have to pee?"

"It's three miles, Amber. You can hold it." He was trying
hard not to smile now, and it made her even more mad.

"What if I just spent all these weeks training and I can't
even finish it?" She finally hissed what was actually making her
sick to her stomach.

"You will," he said firmly. "This was your goal, and you're
going to make it happen." Theo's confidence gave her a little
boost. She bounced a little like Rocky, trying to pump
herself up.

"Promise?" she asked.

"It's you that has to promise yourself."

"It's so much easier when it's for you," she muttered.

"Stretch your sore calf, so you don't get a cramp. Here," he said, tossing her a T-shirt. "Take this to pin your race bib on."

"I don't need to stretch," she said absently. "What's this?" She held up the T-shirt. Theo's name under the sponsors caught her attention first. Then she read the title of the race: The Maple Street Center Dash for a Difference.

"This is what we're running for," he said simply. He smiled softly, nodding at what he saw on her face.

Her heart surged in her chest, clogging her throat, and she just stared because he knew. He knew what it meant to her.

"Amber! Amber!" Someone shouted, and she turned around before she could say anything. Allie and Davis with Sammy, Ben, Claire, Savvie, and Tessa all stood on the sidelines, waiting for her to run. Lily stood next to Evie. Annette and the aunts were there. Amber wanted to find a rock to crawl under.

"Oh great, my whole family is here to watch me fail."

"Racers, take your places," the runners heard over the intercom.

Theo led Amber over to the other racers and gave her arm a reassuring squeeze. He looked entirely too fit and calm this morning in his gray shorts and snug T-shirt. His legs were hard with muscle, and his golden tan reminded her that he was a real runner while she was only pretending.

Theo seemed to sense her spiraling as usual because he looped his arms around her and settled her into his big body. It felt so good, Amber didn't care if anyone thought the mayor hugging his assistant was strange. She settled her hips against his and breathed in—warm skin and clean soap, a purely masculine combination that worked on her like a grounding force.

"Remember, it's just me and you running like we always do," he murmured in her ear.

That made her feel marginally better. She adjusted her racing bib one last time.

Suddenly, she grabbed Theo's arm. "If I don't finish, don't be mad, okay?"

Theo bent his knees to look in her eyes. "You're going to run this race, and then we're going to have a drink at the pub. And you're going to feel amazing."

"Get set," the announcer bellowed.

"If you say so," she muttered.

He grabbed her hand. She pulled away, conscious of the people around them. She didn't care about anyone's opinion, but she didn't want anyone to gossip about Theo. He gripped her hand tighter.

"Go."

If Theo hadn't been holding her hand, Amber would've stood stock-still and let all the other runners trample her, but he dragged her along with him. He must have known she needed that extra push.

The first mile was nice and easy. Theo had it all calculated out, so all she had to do was get into the right headspace and put one foot in front of another. Eventually he let go of her hand, and when she looked up, he smiled.

She was feeling pretty good now. The loop was a nice, scenic route along the Erie Canal, the weather was warm but not boiling, and it was good to feel alive and healthy in the middle of a crowd of people with a common goal.

She could totally do this.

She *had* been training for over a month.

She was strong and healthy.

She kept a steady stream of positive self-talk and focused on her breathing like the badass runner she was.

Theo ran easily next to her. His long legs could easily outrun her, but he kept near and chatted easily with the people running around him. Once, she looked over and caught him grinning at her. She gave him a cheeky thumbs-up.

"You're doing great," he said, not even breathing heavily.

The second mile, things fell apart. The cramp in her calf that Theo had warned about hit her full force until she had to slow down to a stop. She was surprised by how crushed she felt.

"You go ahead. My stupid calf. Don't you say I told you so," she muttered as people passed them.

"Stop for a minute and stretch, and then we'll keep going." They were in a residential neighborhood now that was lined with maple trees. Theo helped her limp to the shady curb.

"I don't think I can do it. It hurts."

Theo stooped down to brace her foot up on his knee and started rubbing the knotted muscles there firmly with his thumbs until she felt it ease up. "Just take it easy. It will go away."

"I knew I wouldn't finish it," she said sadly.

Theo crouched down in front of her. "Quitting isn't an option, Hart. You're crossing that finish line if I have to carry you over." He had his stern all-business mayor look on his face, and that eyebrow spiked up.

She gave in to the impulse and reached up to kiss it. His skin was so warm and inviting, she did it again, on his cheek this time.

Theo sat back with a smile. "I can't run with a hard-on, honey. How do you want to finish this?"

She tested her leg. "It doesn't hurt anymore. I want to try running again."

"That's my girl," he said with a grin, those sexy dimples creasing both of his cheeks.

She had to slow her pace down after that, and it had shaken her confidence, but the cramp held off. It was getting hotter, and her breathing felt tight and constricted in the humid air, while Theo didn't even look winded by the end of the second mile marker.

One by one, the doubts in her head came back, and no amount of positive self-talk could beat them out. She stopped abruptly and blurted out, "I don't think I can do it."

"Come on, Hart, push!" Theo turned back, grabbed her hand again, and tugged, but she dug her heels in.

She was panicking now. "I can't do it after all. I'll just cut across the green and meet you at the finish line."

"We're not doing that." He half pulled, half dragged her along for a half a mile, prodding her and teasing her the whole way until she was forced to follow or be dragged. "I didn't fall in love with a quitter," he said so casually she almost missed it.

She stopped moving. "What did you just say?"

Theo grinned at her. "You heard me, Red Hot. I'm in love with the woman who's going to finish this race."

He loves me.

"Stop panicking and run," he said. "Look how close you are."

They were so close to the finish line now. She could see the balloon arch waving in the wind and hear Puddin's excited yips as the dog waited for them. The sight energized her, and with a renewed bust of confidence, she started to move again.

She smiled up at Theo. "We're almost there," she said, laughing with the sheer joy of seeing the end in sight.

She found herself grinning as she ran.

Fifty yards from the finish line. Forty yards. She had her groove back now. The warm breeze didn't feel suffocating now, and she could appreciate the run for what it was. Mental stamina as much as physical. Maybe her legs were made for more than sashaying after all.

She was so going to finish this race.

Theo let go of her hand and dropped back.

"What are you doing?" She whipped her head back in confusion.

"Go on," Theo said from behind her. "Run," he yelled. He had dropped back even farther.

She started to panic. "I want to do this with you," she said.

He shook his head, still smiling. Those fucking dimples. Her heart quivered. "Do it for yourself, Amber."

She looked back at the arch, where her family was screaming her name, and oh good lord, they were holding cardboard cutouts of her head.

She looked back at Theo and felt a surge of something so deep, so vast, it scared her. He had dragged her, pushed her beyond what she thought she could do, and now he was letting her go to take the last steps to finish on her own. He must have seen the emotions on her face because he nodded and gave her one last push. "Go get that medal."

She took a deep breath, lifted her chin, and ran through the ribbon.

Annette reached her first and hugged her fiercely. "I knew you could do it."

Amber half cried and half laughed. "You did?" she asked, dazed. "I didn't even know if I could. How did you know?"

"Because you're my daughter," Annette said simply. She dabbed at her eyes with an Hermès handkerchief. "It was you who had to believe it." And then her sisters were hugging her and making jokes about how she was only second to last after Mrs. Ludlowe, number 105, who strolled across the finish line while gabbing on her weekly phone call to her sister.

Amber looked for Theo in the crowd. He was standing off to the side, chatting with the organizers. He looked up as if he felt her searching for him.

"Thank you," she mouthed at him.

He just nodded, but she saw the pride on his face. It gave her that scary good feeling again. Oh God. She really was falling for him.

Later, after she collected her medal for finishing number 104, she hung it around her neck and caught up to him where he was petting Puddin'. Ford and Landon, his tow-headed son, each gave her a high-five.

"You crushed it," Ford said. "I didn't know you were a runner."

"Yeah, me either," she said. "104. Not bad, huh?" She held up the medal proudly.

"You were amazing. Number one in my book," Theo said.

"Even with my wonky finish?"

"Especially with your wonky finish. Ready for that drink now?" Theo slung an arm around her neck and pulled her closer.

She didn't even bother to see if anyone was watching. She simply didn't care.

Chapter Thirty

THEO LOOSENED his tie and ran a hand through his hair, exasperated after spending the last half hour on the phone listening to detailed last-minute updates about the gala tomorrow night.

"This all sounds great, Cheryl," he said, impatiently checking his watch. It was after five already, and, aside from the occasional tapping of Amber's heels, he knew everyone had already left for the night. "Yes, I know Amber's done a wonderful job. I'll be sure to tell her."

He looked up from his computer when a yellow Post-it note landed on his desk. He read it.

Golden Ticket

He read it twice and blinked. Amber stood next to his desk, watching him read it. The tight-fitting royal blue wrap dress she wore with his favorite pink heels outlined her beautiful shape, a shape he had spent hours exploring, teasing, pleasuring over the last two weeks.

He knew her favorite way to sleep was on top of him, leaving him no choice but to sleep deeply for the first time in years, with the smell of her hair in his nose and her hand tucked into his.

She hated watching TV, and she read romance books before bed.

She hid chocolate in her freezer for emergencies.

She closed her eyes when he made her come so he wouldn't see the emotion she could no longer hide.

She still hadn't said she loved him.

Loving Amber was a study of patience, but he was in this for the long haul. She kept herself well protected, shielding her vulnerability skillfully with dazzling smiles and teasing. He wanted to protect her and reassure her he would wait as long as she needed to realize that he was here to stay.

"Cheryl, I have the utmost trust in you. Looking forward to tomorrow." He put the phone back in its cradle and leaned back. "What's this?" He held up the yellow note.

"That, Mr. Mayor," Amber said, propping her delicious ass on the edge of his desk, "is your golden ticket."

Theo raised an eyebrow. "Care to explain?"

"You told me once about a fantasy of yours. I believe you said it involved this desk." She rubbed her hand slowly along the heavy mahogany wood. Theo's heart started a slow, sweet pounding in his chest as he remembered that conversation.

What is the most scandalous place you fantasize about having sex?

My desk. After hours in my office, against it, bent over it, or on your knees under it.

"Did I?" he murmured.

She bent forward, a sexy little smile on her face, and put her lips to his ear. "I'm going to make it come true."

The top of her dress offered him a teasing glimpse of lush, creamy skin when she leaned down. She caught his look and laughed, low and husky.

The room was quiet and dark, with the wooden slats of the shades tipped to keep the bright sun of the day out. Theo inhaled, catching a familiar hint of her spicy perfume and arousal.

He knew her. She was a deeply sensual woman. She knew how to savor pleasure, how to give it generously, and how to pretend that was all there was between them.

He planned to be here when she realized every fragment of herself she had shared with him over the last few months hadn't left her exposed and vulnerable like she feared but seamlessly woven together to build her whole.

"Is everyone gone?" he asked. He touched the back of her thigh, just under her skirt, trailing his fingers up and down the silky skin there. He paused when he felt the band of a stocking around her thigh. "What's this?" he murmured, surprise in his voice.

He traced the line between the lacy edge of her stocking and the bottom of her panties and controlled his breathing. He could lay her down right now on his desk and push into her warm, wet heat, and his fantasy would be complete, but the sexy little half smile she wore told him she had more in store for him.

"Everyone's gone. It's just you and me, boss."

He caught her chin in his hand. "Say my name," he growled.

She slipped her hands into the top of her dress and pushed it down to her waist. White lace cups held her breasts, so sheer her nipples showed. They were hard already. *Jesus.*

"Anything you want, Theo," she said, sliding down to her knees gracefully in between his thighs and reaching for his belt.

Theo watched her clever little fingers unbuckle his belt and unbutton his trousers. Her hair fell loose and sexy around her shoulders, and her eyes glinted like she had a naughty secret. She was breathtaking on her knees for him.

"Anything?"

She looked up from where she was drawing his zipper down. "Anything."

Her lips parted with a question when he reached down to help her to her feet. He could feel the shiver that ran through her at his touch, and he held back a smile. He knew she would be slick and wet for him, ready.

But he wanted something else first. He guided her to the space in front of his chair, between his thighs, and he leaned back again to watch her.

"Take your dress off."

She didn't hesitate. The tie at her waist fell loose with one tug, and her blue dress cascaded down her body like a waterfall to pool around her high heels. She stepped delicately around it.

"Turn around."

She was flushed, the creamy skin of her cheeks a rosy color that spread down her chest, to the top of her breasts. She glanced over her shoulder, an unspoken question in her eyes, when he put a hand in the middle of her back and firmly guided her down to lean on her arms.

Theo took a moment to drink in the sight in front of him. She was a vision of contrasts. Innocent white bra, the delicate strap crossing her rib cage. The scrap of white lace panties barely covering her full, round ass. The nude silk stockings that left a tempting strip of her thighs bare. And those fucking heels. The diamond on her ankle sparkled playfully at him.

"Theo," she whimpered. "Touch me. Please." She spread her thighs wider and swayed her hips in front of him.

He touched her there first. A handful of flesh on either side of her thighs, watching his hands sink into her and enjoying the mark on her otherwise perfect skin. He traced the garters up, over the round curve of her ass, over her hips to her waist, and pulled her back to drape over his lap, another contrast his eyes drank in.

His navy suit, professional, custom made, against her nearly naked body. His thumb found the flutter in her throat. He pressed a kiss to the warm, secret spot under her ear he knew drove her crazy. Her breathing grew faster.

"I thought this was your fantasy," she choked out.

"This is my fantasy. Watch." He slid his hand from her throat to her shoulder, taking down the strap of her bra, first one side, then the other until her breasts spilled out from the cups. They were too tempting to leave. He pinched her nipples, rolling and stroking, slapping the side to watch them jiggle until she was grinding back on his rigid cock and moaning.

Her stomach was concave where she draped over him. He followed the outline of her ribs down past the line of her garter to slide under her panties, where she was slick. "Jesus, you're fucking perfect."

He didn't make her wait. Hitching one of her thighs over the arm of his chair, he spread her wide and dipped two fingers into her swollen pussy, dragging the moisture over her clit and rubbing light circles. "You are my fantasy, Amber. Just like this, coming all over my hand. Will you do that for me before you get on your knees and suck me?"

"Yes, please," she whispered. "Kiss me." She reached up and tugged him down to meet her lips. He kissed her hard and desperate, matching the thrust of his fingers and the hard press of his palm against her clit until she started to shake. She clamped her legs around his hand and rolled her face into his neck while she came.

"I love that your fantasies include me having an orgasm," she finally said, sighing. She turned around on his lap and draped her arms around his neck, kissing him gently before sliding to her knees in front of him.

She unbuttoned his shirt while he pulled his tie over his head. When she rested her hand on his bare chest, spreading her hands wide to touch his nipples, he inhaled sharply. She tipped forward and licked the little brown disk then bit it delicately.

He leaned his head back to watch.

Her busy little fingers didn't stop for long. She worked on his belt and trousers next until she held his heavy cock in her hands. He was fully erect, so rock hard, he flinched when she touched him. She rested her face against the side of his shaft and looked up at him with heavy-lidded eyes.

"You look beautiful on your knees for me," he said, propping his chin between his thumb and forefinger.

She bent forward, looked him in the eye, and delicately licked the bead of moisture on the tip. He couldn't hold back his groan then. Slowly, she dragged her hands up and down the muscles in his thighs, letting him feel the light scratch of her nails before touching him with her mouth.

When she took him into her mouth again, she licked him up and down slowly, making him slick. He ran his fingers through her hair, gathering the loose waves in his hand to watch.

"I've been waiting for you to show me what you can do with that mouth," he murmured. With one hand on his cock and one in her hair, he parted her lips again with the head. "Suck."

She parted her lips and took just the tip of him into the heat of her mouth. He felt like he'd been branded by fire. She sucked lightly then more deeply, as he grew wetter from her tongue until he was fully in her mouth. She added her hands, rubbing the base of him with one hand, and his own fell away. With her other, she cupped his balls, using her mouth and her lips and her tongue to take him apart, the little witch.

He sucked in a breath. "Yes, *fuck*. Just like that."

He had to remember to breathe. Her breasts spilled over the cups of her bra, so pretty against the leather of his chair. He teased her nipples while she took him into her mouth deeper and stroked him tighter and faster until he finally stopped her with a hiss. She pulled back, and the sight of her swollen, glistening lips was enough to make him come. "I'm close." He should warn her, in case she didn't want him like that.

She grinned. "I know," she said before closing her mouth around him tightly. The effect was immediate.

Theo squeezed his eyes shut and let go, letting the fire consume him fully. Dimly, he was aware of her hand threading through his, a connection like a lifeline while he shook from the aftereffects.

When he opened his eyes, she was smiling up at him. He kissed her lips gently and helped her into his lap again. "Thank you."

She settled against him, nuzzling against his chest. "It was my pleasure," she sighed. "Next time, we play out my fantasy."

He stroked her back lazily. "Anything you want."

Chapter Thirty-One

"Not too much. I don't want to look like I'm trying too hard," Val said.

"Got it." Amber dabbed a little more of the soft pink shimmer onto Val's eyelid with precision. She took a step back, surveying her handiwork with a critical eye.

It was just the two of them getting ready tonight—Sandy had taken the night off, but someone had called in and she was forced to stay to work a double, and Holly was at Allie's. Amber had splurged on manicures and pedicures for both of them earlier. Now, back at her apartment, they were putting the finishing touches on their hair and makeup.

"There." Amber looked at Val's reflection in the mirror, and a knot tightened in her throat. "You look beautiful, honey." Val's hair was pulled back into a chic knot, leaving only tendrils framing her face instead of the usual heavy hank of hair she hid behind. She looked softer, younger. Happy.

Val studied herself, an uncharacteristic look of worry making her forehead furrow. "Do you really think so? I know everyone else will wear ball gowns, but this feels much more me, you know?" Val smoothed down the full skirt of the black dress.

It fit her like a dream after Amber took in the bodice. Val had paired it with her black high-top Converse, a little touch of her mixed with the retro dress.

"Vintage is always in style. You look gorgeous and confident," Amber said, holding her eyes in the mirror. She tried not to get too mushy, but she really was so proud of Val.

It had been a big summer for both of them. Val's letter of acceptance to the State University of Geneseo had come last week. Amber hadn't even tried to hide her excitement when Val opened the letter. Neither of them had. They had screamed and hugged, and Amber had taken Val, Sandy, and Holly out for ice cream. Val was going to commute in the fall and work part-time waiting tables at the pub. Big changes were ahead for both of them.

"Hey now, it's not like I'm moving. I'll be next door," Val said.

"Stealing my food and lounging on my couch, I hope."

"Hello, of course. I'm going to be a broke college student. I'll be over every night for dinner with Holly."

Amber took a chance and gave her a quick hug. "I hope so," she whispered.

Val squeezed her back. "Okay, okay, enough of the sappy stuff or you'll ruin this perfect eye makeup." Val cleared her throat and stepped back from the mirror. "Let's talk about your dress. You outdid yourself on this one."

"I should hope so. It took me weeks of sewing to get these beads on." Amber's dress was the simplest creation she ever made but also the most stunning. It had neither of her go-tos: there was no bold color choice or outrageous amount of skin drawing attention to herself. At first glance, it was a simple gold sheath dress that fit like a second skin, with a scoop neckline and thin straps.

It was up close that the dress went from merely chic to spectacular. Amber had spent weeks sewing tiny glass beads in intricate patterns all over the dress, making it sparkle wherever light reflected off it. In the soft glow of the Grand River Hotel's ballroom lights, the dress would shimmer and make all the evenings she had worked on it worth it.

But she couldn't think about the gala right now, or about everything she had riding on it being a success for Theo, or she might pass out.

"Come here," Amber said. "Let's get a selfie in the mirror to send to your mom. I know she really wished she could be here to see you all dolled up." She snapped a few pictures and sent them to Sandy and thought about Annette.

How many of these moments had Annette missed when she was trying to put herself through school and working nights when Amber and her sisters were little? Most of them. A wave of gratitude swept through her for her mother. Both women were doing what they had to do for their families.

"I feel so naked without my hoodie on," Val said, smoothing down her skirt. "How do you dress like this every day?"

As Amber studied them critically in her smudged mirror, an epiphany struck her. "I suppose both of our wardrobes serve the same purpose."

"What's that supposed to mean?"

"They both keep people out. You wear yours like armor, and well"—she smiled ruefully—"sometimes I take mine off for the same reason."

Val tipped her head. "Maybe it's about finding a balance between the two."

"Or figuring out who's worth taking it off for," Amber added. She grinned. "We are so deep."

They both turned at the tentative knock on the apartment door. "That would be Dylan."

Amber greeted him and stood back to watch when Dylan,

looking dapper in his tux, handed Val a corsage. He was tall and a little gangly still, but the way he looked at Val adoringly convinced Amber that Val's night would end differently than her own ball.

Val was strong and smart, and she had Amber watching out for her if she needed anything. She deserved her own chance to make memories tonight.

"Hi, Ms. Hart," Dylan greeted her next, looking a little more nervous. "You look very nice too." But so charming.

They made a beautiful couple. She couldn't have been prouder if she were Val's mom. She snapped a few more pictures for Sandy and sent them off.

Time to get them out of here before she started sobbing.

"Okay, kids. Have fun." She looked at Dylan sternly. Whether he was a charmer or not, she had to say it. "Listen. I work for the mayor, and I will make your life hell if I find out you were drinking and driving."

"No, ma'am. I won't." Dylan looked solemn.

Ouch. He ma'am-ed her. She really was getting old.

"Remember, I'm only a phone call away. I'll have my phone on me all night. Call me if you need anything at all."

"Relax, Mom," Val said. "I'll be fine." But she leaned over and kissed Amber's cheek. "Thank you for everything," she whispered softly.

Amber squeezed one last time before letting go.

THE GRAND RIVER HOTEL was lit from within, reflecting the polished brass and crystal chandeliers hanging in the ballroom when Amber walked in. She had always loved the elegance of the hotel.

When the girls were little and Annette was working downtown as a waitress and the tips were good, Annette would some-times let them dress up and bring them to the Grand River for a fancy cup of tea. Amber had loved watching the elegant people coming and going from up and down the grand staircase and imagining herself doing the same thing one day.

Edward Sterling had spared no expense tonight for the Hope Gala. Her eyes were immediately drawn to the ceiling, where hundreds of delicate faux doves had been suspended, the soft ambient light catching their silky wings and making them glow.

All the nights this past week sewing each one individually had been worth it when she saw the whimsical effect.

There was still a half hour until the event started. The room was full of servers and florists putting the last-minute touches on the tables. Towering glass vases held arrangements from Aunt Sophia and Aunt Giulia's florist shop: white lilies and roses with greenery, tiny shimmery lights, and miniature silver doves. The entire effect was breathtaking.

The ballroom buzzed with that excited energy that built before a party. Amber felt the anticipation, too, only hers was a tad more nervous than excited. Theo had assured her for weeks that the night was going to be a wild success, but she didn't have his same confidence.

Truthfully, she was kind of in awe that she had even a little part in something this beautiful.

She stopped to chat with several vendors she knew before making her way to the elevator. Cheryl's office was on the second floor, and she wanted to check in before the party started.

"Don't you look stunning?" Cheryl said when she saw her in the doorway. "Is that designer?" she asked with an admiring eye.

Amber smoothed her hand down the slinky fabric. "No, I made it," she said, looking down at the beaded dress.

"You are so talented," Cheryl said. "The doves were a fantastic idea too. I think they add the perfect touch to the night."

They talked about a few last-minute details, and when Amber turned toward the elevator to leave, Cheryl tucked her hand into Amber's elbow and led her to the ornate staircase leading down to the ballroom. "Everyone should walk down these stairs in a fabulous dress at least once in their life," she said, patting Amber's hand and leaving her at the top of the staircase.

The ballroom was full now. Music and laughter floated up from the ballroom below, and she scanned the floor, looking for a tall, darkly handsome man in a tux.

Aunt Sophia, with Captain by her side, stood chatting with Annette, who was elegant as always in a black Hervé Léger. Amber spotted Charlotte in a stunning green ball gown with Johnny next to her in his Northfield Fire Department dress blues.

Todd, with his date, Anthony from the Red Lounge, stood by the bar, chatting. She had fixed them up recently and was still patting herself on the back for another successful match.

Neal lingered next to the bar, making good use of the open bar, if his flushed cheeks and unsteady movements were any sign. Throughout the guests, news crews and photographers blended unobtrusively into the crowd to share the event with the public.

Pippa Shelton was there, in a striking red mermaid dress that did wonderful things for her coloring. A photographer stood next to her, snapping photos of the guests. Amber's stomach tightened with nerves, but she was a performer, if nothing else.

She took a deep breath and stepped down to the first stair. As if they were connected with a wire, she found Theo watching her with appreciation and something darker in his eyes.

She breathed easier seeing him and took another step down. The feel of his eyes on her, so appreciative and warm, soothed the rest of her nerves, and she smiled softly at him. Almost shyly. Other people were noticing the look on his face as she walked down the stairs, turning to watch them.

She made her way down, eyes locked on Theo's, and when she reached the last stair, he met her, held her hand, and brought it to his lips.

"You are stunning," he murmured.

She saw the flashbulbs from the corner of her eye, but when Theo looked at her like that, it was hard to care about anything at all.

As if on cue, the music started, and Theo held out his arm. "Care to dance?"

"Yes," she breathed. His tuxedo was silky smooth under her hand, the arm under it taut with muscle when she placed it on top and followed him to the dance floor. She couldn't have said what the song was or if they did more than sway from side to side like a pair of teenagers in a high school gym dance.

His hand where he held it against his chest was warm and protective, and his arm around her back was a solid wall. His eyes, his beautiful blue eyes, looked at her with all the emotion she couldn't say. But she felt it.

"Have I told you how beautiful you are?"

She laughed. "I believe you did this morning. And then again after breakfast and before lunch."

His white teeth flashed. "Not nearly enough, then. Did you make this dress?"

"Yes. Do you like it?" she asked. "It's not something I'd usually wear, but it felt right."

"I love it. You've never looked more like yourself," he said.

A warmth began in her chest, spreading dangerously close to her heart and filling her with an emotion she almost didn't dare name. She looked past his broad, silk-covered shoulder. "Everything is so magical tonight. I remember coming here as a little girl with my mom and imagining what kind of world the people who came here lived in. It always felt like I was stepping into an alternate universe."

He spun her in a circle. "I think you've always been in your own world," he murmured, "and everyone else is orbiting around you."

"It's the dress," she said, suddenly shy. She looked away. "It's just another version of me."

His arm tightened around her waist, and she looked up again. "Every version of you is my favorite version."

If she was floating at the end of the dance, she didn't care because the night was a dream she didn't want to end.

Johnny and Charlotte danced by them, in their own world, as much as Amber imagined she and Theo were. Theo crooked an eyebrow. "When were you going to tell me they were a couple?" he asked.

"You figured that out?"

He nodded ruefully. "I think I was the last one. I was too jealous to see it."

"I know," Amber said. "I liked it."

"I think after the election, we should go away for a long vacation together. Have you ever been to Paris?"

She laughed. "Paris? The farthest I've been to is Niagara Falls."

"We're going to fix that."

Amber would've laughed, but suddenly it wasn't funny. Suddenly, she could see that future—traveling together, Theo being reelected, her opening her own boutique, and maybe someday starting a family together. She *wanted* that future, and it didn't seem silly at all. It was exactly what she wanted.

She floated for the rest of the evening, talking to the different vendors Cheryl had arranged to represent the best of Northfield, trying a sampling of the delicious foods, and drinking too much champagne because it tasted good, and she felt even better.

They sat for dinner with Georgie, Theo's tiny, adorable grandma. She had her nurse with her and was in a wheelchair, but when Georgie saw Amber, her whole face lit up.

They chatted throughout dinner about all the wonderful memories she had of Theo as a little boy and how proud she was of the man he had become. Before she left, she patted Amber's hand. "I knew my Theodore would fall in love with a firecracker. Give him hell for me," she said, winking.

And there was that feeling again, that breathless, bottomless exhilaration. Was this love? Should it feel this terrifying?

Theo's hand settled, warm and solid, on her thigh, as if he could feel her panicked thoughts. He rubbed softly while he talked with Neal next to him, and she breathed in the moment, anchored by him.

After dinner they danced again, and this time, she didn't look away from Theo's eyes. The flash of cameras barely registered. It was the two of them in the middle of hundreds of pairs of curious eyes, but only one pair of cool blue ones mattered to her.

"Thank you for making tonight such a success," Theo said, reminding her of something that had been nagging her.

"What made you choose the Maple Street Center?" she asked.

Theo looked at her steadily. "Because that night Grant and I picked you up changed everything for me. Just like it probably did for you."

Amber stumbled, but Theo's firm arm guided her. "What do you mean?"

"It was the first time in my life I faced a situation where I couldn't right a wrong, no matter how much I wanted to. I knew that someone had let you down, even if you wouldn't admit it or let me help. Being on the board of Maple Street is a way for me to help."

"You did help me that night. I would have had to walk home in heels with a ripped dress," she said lightly. Her stomach was still fluttering.

"I would have done more," he said, looking at her directly.

And, oh. *Oh.* Now she knew for sure what that emotion was swelling her heart and making it hard for her to swallow around the lump in her throat. It wasn't terrifying after all. It was beautiful and soft. Tender. She knew this because it was reflected in his eyes, directed back at her. *I love him.*

She smiled then, just for him. Not for the benefit of the cameras or the surrounding people watching them. It was for Theo because she loved him.

His eyes went dark and so utterly warm and dipped to her mouth. Then he kissed her.

In full view of her family and reporters and photographers, he kissed her. Thoroughly. Possessively.

She closed her eyes and soaked it in, Theo's soft lips and his cologne that made her want to lick him all over, the way his arms held her close to his body, and his hands cradling her face. It was a lingering, bold kiss that sent a message to everyone in the room.

Amber leaned in and enjoyed every second of it.

Chapter Thirty-Two

AMBER HUMMED on the way to the bathroom. The two glasses of champagne were making her feel bubbly and light, like she was still kissing Theo in the ballroom.

That kiss would be all over the town's Facebook page for sure tomorrow, but she couldn't bring herself to care. It had felt so right, like a declaration and a promise of what the night would bring her later. She couldn't wait for later. Theo in a tux was giving her all sorts of dirty fantasies. He did like when she brought them to life.

She thought about the Post-it she had given him with his golden ticket on it. If she lived to be one hundred, she would never forget last night in Theo's office. She laughed softly then looked around to make sure no one caught her silliness.

"You should be laughing," Neal said. He was in the doorway of the hotel's lounge room, leaning slightly on the frame. Even the dim lighting couldn't hide his red-rimmed eyes. His bow tie was loosened, and his short, fine gray hair looked damp around the edges.

"Hello, Neal. Are you all right?" She didn't really care, but he was a friend of Theo's family, and she didn't want him to ruin Theo's night.

Amber looked around for someone to help her if he passed out. She had been around enough inebriated people in her life to know the look. "Come in here. Let's sit on the couch for a minute." She led him over to a couch next to the fireplace and sat down next to him to think through her options. Theo had her phone in his pocket, so she couldn't call him.

"Let's just sit here for a few minutes until you're steadier on your feet. I think you've had too much to drink," she said. The alcohol on his breath was enough to knock her over. She tried to keep the distaste off her face, but it was difficult.

"Here I was thinking we should toast," he said. He wasn't slurring, but his eyes had that unfocused look that Amber recognized as well on his way to a bender. He pulled out a silver flask and took a swig.

"What do you mean?" she asked, edging away from him. Maybe she could just leave him here and bring Theo to Neal. It would be less embarrassing for him in the long run.

"I mean, you won. You got everything you wanted. You got Theo panting after you. How does that feel, by the way, to know that he's going to lose this election? Will you still want him then?" He gripped her elbow tightly enough to leave a bruise.

"Now I know you've had too much to drink. Take your hands off me, and we'll go back out into the other room." She sat up stiffly on the couch. Neal's grip on her arm tightened painfully.

"You're always trying to call the shots," he muttered, his eyes dropping to her chest. A shiver of revulsion took her. "You think you can do that with Theo because he's fucking you, but you're not putting out for me."

A wave of exhaustion overwhelmed her, and suddenly she was so very tired of everything. The rumors she could never escape, that she had made part of her identity in order to control them, the men in her past who had looked at her the exact way Neal was looking at her now.

It was all so fucking exhausting, and she was done.

"That is old and tired, Neal. I don't care what you think or what anybody else thinks. Theo is a grown man. He can make his own decisions." She tried to stand, but Neal leaned in, making her back farther into the couch. This close, she could see the little broken red blood vessels around his nose and cheeks.

"Sure, he can," Neal said, his lips twisting. "But when you're sucking his dick in his office, it makes it a hell of a lot easier to say yes."

Amber felt the blood rush from her head. Had he... seen them? Her horror must have played out on her face because he laughed nastily.

"Yes, I saw you on your knees for him last night when I went back to the office. But you've always been a little slut, haven't you?"

"What?" Amber froze. Until that moment, Neal's words were merely disgusting, but at his last sentence, she went still. "What did you say?"

Neal's lips stretched into a parody of a smile. "Theo told me about that night with Grant when they got the call to pick you up. How your boyfriend left you for being a dirty slut with all his friends."

"I don't know what you're talking about." Her lips felt numb. Theo had told him? Uncertainty and a dull, throbbing hurt filled her.

Neal's moist hand slithered over her breast. She caught it, but his other hand was there to take its place immediately. He squeezed her breast, leaning over her until he was nearly on top of her. "Always with your tits out like a little whore," he muttered, squeezing hard. "How about you show me these big fucking tits of yours?"

"Get off me," she hissed, shoving him back. He wasn't nearly as solid as Theo, but he was larger than her, and he didn't move. How dare he? How *dare* he touch her, question her, throw that night in her face? Anger surged, nearly choking her with its bitterness. "Get your hands off me."

His hand tightened, painfully twisting her breast in one hand while the other went for her hair, pushing her farther back into the couch. She drew her knee up to kick him, but he was on top of her now, panting and grappling with her dress. He was heavy and panting in her face, and all she could do was push, push, push, and it wasn't enough.

Rage, white-hot and immediate, filled her when she felt his lips at her neck. She shoved him hard, anywhere she could land between his ear and his neck. He was relentless, pressing wet kisses to her throat and the tops of her breasts.

Suddenly, his weight was gone, leaving her startled as she looked up. Theo had Neal pinned to the wall by his lapels; a crimson river of blood flowed from Neal's nose. "What the fuck, Neal?" He shoved him harder. Neal's head knocked into the wall behind him with a sickening thud. "What the *fuck*?"

"Look what she's done to you," Neal sneered, blood staining his teeth. He pointed a shaking hand at Amber. "You're going to throw everything away for this slut?"

"How could you do this?" Theo's breathing was ragged. Raw with pain.

And, oh, did that cut deeply. Not Neal, not his hands on her body, twisting her flesh painfully, but Theo's voice. The hurt and anger, the betrayal—it twisted her heart even as her own hurt threatened to spill over.

She sat up. The music from the ballroom filled the room along with the harsh breaths of the two men in front of her. The door to the lounge was still open. Anyone could walk by and see them.

She got to her feet and put a hand on Theo's back. "Let him go, Theo." His body was taut with surpassed anger. She pulled his arm away from Neal's tux. "He's not worth it."

"Did he hurt you?" Theo glanced at her, and she nearly took a step back at the rage in his eyes.

"No, he didn't," she said. He couldn't. He'd barely chinked the surface of her. "He's not worth it. Let him go."

Theo dropped his hands and stepped back from Neal, his movements sharp with barely contained fury. "I never want to see you again," Theo said, cold fury in the bite of his voice. "And if I ever see you around Amber again, I will forget you ever meant anything to me."

Neal laughed bitterly. "You're really going to throw everything away for her, aren't you?"

"What I do with my life is no longer your concern. You're fired, effective immediately."

A sudden flash startled them as a camera went off in the room. Pippa stood in the doorway with her photographer by her side.

"Are we interrupting something?" she asked, looking around the room with sharp eyes: Neal's bloody face, Theo's scraped knuckles.

Amber froze, horrific images of that photo being published and the stories that could swirl. Panic rose in her throat, but Theo stepped toward Pippa.

"Nothing at all." Theo's voice was dangerously soft. "Neal's had too much to drink. He was just leaving." He fixed Pippa with a look.

Pippa looked like she had more to say, but she nodded and left, with Neal behind her, and then it was just Theo and Amber.

The hardness on his face disappeared. He crossed the room and held her hands gently. "Are you all right?"

She nodded numbly. "I told you not to tell anyone."

"Tell anyone what?" Theo was chafing her hands between his. She realized they were frozen with cold.

She cleared her throat. "That night when you and Grant picked me up in his squad car. You told me you would never tell anyone, but Neal knew."

"I swear to God, I didn't tell him. I don't know how he knows. Maybe Grant mentioned it to him, or Neal asked about the calls we went on, but it wasn't me, Amber. I wouldn't lie to you."

She pulled her hands away just as Val's ringtone went off— "Smells Like Teen Spirit." Theo pulled her phone out of his pocket.

"That's Val." She grabbed the phone from his hands. "Hello? Val? Is everything okay?" She heard the crackling of a poor connection and Val's voice. "Amber," came in and out. "Help," and then the line went dead.

Panic, lightning fast, flooded her. "I have to go. Val needs me," she said, running out the door.

"I'm coming with you." She felt Theo at her heels, but she only had the same chant in her head. *Val Val Val.*

Outside the hotel, a sea of cars and valets waited. Her car was buried in there somewhere. She looked around frantically.

Theo strode to a bored-looking valet. "I need the key to the first car there." He pointed at a BMW with its top down.

"Is that your car, sir?" The valet couldn't have been more than twenty. He looked between them nervously.

"Yes," Theo lied. "Give me the keys." He slapped a handful of bills into the kid's hand.

The valet's eyes widened. "Whoa. Here you go." He tossed the keys to Theo and started counting.

Theo turned back to her. "Let's go."

"WE'RE ONLY a few minutes away. She'll be okay," Theo said, grinding the gears as he accelerated.

Amber twisted her hands and looked out the window. Every horrific scenario she had ever seen on the news flashed before her eyes as they drove. She concentrated on the rhythmic thud of her heartbeat, trying to anchor her swirling thoughts.

Dylan's car was parked on the side of the road about a mile down from the venue. Amber's heart leaped to her throat, and she jumped out of the car before it fully stopped. She could only see the skirt of Val's dress and her black Converse. Dylan stood in front of her.

"Val!" she choked out, her heart thundering in her chest.

"Oh, hey, Amber." Val peeked around Dylan, and she looked... fine.

Amber's breath rattled back in her lungs in great shudders, as if she were Lily trying to breathe in the middle of an asthma attack.

"Hey, Theo. Thanks for coming," Val added.

Amber stopped. "Are you... okay?" she asked. She felt disoriented, like she was living halfway between the present and the past.

"Dylan's car got a flat. We don't have AAA, so we called you for help. Do you think you could give us a ride?"

It took a minute for Amber to bring herself solidly back to the present. Theo was faster than she was, but then, he didn't carry the weight of another night on his shoulders.

"Yes, of course we can. Why don't you guys get in the car, and I'll call my service?" He was amazingly unruffled, in full authoritative mayor mode, taking control and fixing things while Amber felt... fragile. The shock of adrenaline made her feel sick.

When Val walked by, she looked at Amber closely. "Is everything okay?" she asked uncertainly. "I hope I didn't ruin your night." Her makeup was still perfect. Not even a trace of a wayward tear to mar it. Relief welled in her, enough to make her eyes prick with tears. She had wanted Val to have a perfect night so badly.

"No, no, everything's fine." She cleared her throat and pulled herself together. "I'm just glad you're okay. How was the ball?"

"Eh." Val shrugged. "The music sucked, and they didn't have any vegetarian options, but other than that, it was fine." She grinned. "Just kidding. It was a great night."

The ride back to Amber and Val's was quiet, aside from Dylan and Val talking softly in the backseat. Even in the dark, as the streetlights passed, she could see the muscles in Theo's jaw ticking as they drove.

When they pulled into the Phoenix's parking lot, Val and Dylan hopped out. "Dylan's going to come up with me for a while. Thanks again, guys." She slammed the door closed.

The car was silent. Amber put a hand on the door handle, every instinct in her clawing at her to get out and run away.

"No more running, remember?" Theo pinned her with his gaze. He got out of the car and came around to her side of the car to help her out.

In her apartment, she kicked her heels off and sat on the couch, where she drew her knees up to her chest. The air-conditioning pumping from the windows was the only sensation in her body. Everything else felt numb. Cold and numb, including her heart. She stared straight ahead. "I can't do this," she said quietly, forcing the words through her stiff lips.

The soft, so goddamn vulnerable, parts of her back behind a wall of armor, fortified once more.

"That's not talking. That's giving up." Theo sat down on the couch next to her. She flinched at what she saw on his face. "I never said a word about that night," he swore. "I don't know how he found out, but I didn't tell him."

"I believe you," she said, because she did. It didn't matter anymore, anyway. That night had ceased to hurt her a long time ago, she realized. The lingering burn of the whispers no longer scorched her memories or held any power over her.

"Then why are you running?"

"I'm sorry," she whispered. "I thought I could, but I just... can't." She couldn't look at him anymore. She could bear her own heartbreak a million times over, but to see Theo's was unbearable. This feeling, the hard knot in her throat and the ache in her chest, was why she never let herself fall in love.

Theo had broken through all the barriers she had carefully constructed over the years with his lovely caretaking and his insatiable need to show her how much more she was than she ever gave herself credit for.

But she didn't want to see it. He never understood that. How could she not see it with such strong women in her life? She knew it, and she still couldn't make herself choose to love.

Theo's hands clenched. The first spark of anger she had seen in him. Aside from his hands on Neal. That sight was etched in her mind forever.

"You can't do this? Bullshit," he said sharply. "You're scared. You're so damn afraid you won't let yourself love anybody else. But I'm not anybody. I'm telling you that I love you, and I will never hurt you. I love you, Amber," he repeated, and she flinched at the calm steadiness of his voice.

Of course, it was easy for him.

He wasn't utterly terrified of losing himself in someone else.

"So what if I am?" she said fiercely. The prick of anger was familiar and welcome. She leaned into it. She could control that emotion. "You've always pushed me, but I can't go any further, Theo. I don't want to."

"Don't do that," he said softly.

"It was never going to last," she continued as if he hadn't spoken. "We're too different. And what if Pippa publishes that photo? The news will have a field day with that. I can see it now, 'Local bartender involved in a love triangle with mayor and staff.' That would ruin your chance for reelection." She looked at him, pleading. "This would never have worked in the long run. You know it's true."

Bitterness nearly closed off her throat, but she forced the words out. "It's better for both of us to end it now, before it gets any harder." She tried hard to keep her voice unemotional, but the tremble betrayed her.

Theo shook his head, his eyes so steady on hers she had to look away. He always saw through her. No one else had ever tried to, really. They had been satisfied with the version of her she let them see—but not Theo.

"That's bullshit. You know I don't care about any of that. I love you. I've never wanted this job if it meant losing you," he said roughly, spearing her heart effectively in half.

"Well, maybe you should," she cried. "You're meant to lead, Theo. Northfield or somewhere bigger down the road. Don't throw it all away for... this. It never lasts with me." She waved her hand between them. "I told you not to fall in love with me. I told you." To her horror, tears dripped from her eyes.

"Coward," he said, softly. Knowingly. It was almost her undoing. She turned her head, but he cupped her chin and turned her head to see her eyes. He leaned in and pressed a tender kiss to her lips. "I told you to trust me." Light as a breeze, he kissed her, first one corner then the other, sending shivery hot sparks of desire through her.

She closed her eyes and let the desire wash over her. This she knew.

She turned her body toward him and opened her mouth, capturing his fiercely. Suddenly, she was starving for the taste of him. She bit his lower lip and sucked it, tasting the wine he'd had earlier. It made her wild. She moved closer, trying to feel instead of think.

She pushed the beautiful tuxedo off his shoulders and got to her knees on the couch, but her dress was too tight for her to straddle him. She made a frustrated sound only to trail off on a moan when Theo pushed it up over her hips and lifted her over and onto his lap, flush against his swollen erection. Her fingers went to his belt frantically. It was clumsy hands and sharp elbows and hot desire. Fast. Fast. Fast before she had to feel the hurt again.

And then he was inside her.

It hurt with no foreplay, but she welcomed the stretch and burn of her body. Anything was better than the pain in her heart.

It was fast and fierce, almost painful in its intensity. She clung to his shoulders and tried to control it, but he wouldn't let her. His hands gripped her hips, and he bucked up into her deeper, holding her still for his thrusts, as if he knew he couldn't hold on to her any other way.

"Oh, Christ," he rasped against her throat, delicately biting the sensitive curve where her shoulder met her neck, making pleasure spike along her entire body until she nearly screamed.

"Yes," she gasped. "Please... please... I need..." She caught her breath on a sob and threw back her head, squeezing her eyes closed at the shocking intensity.

She tried to hold out. She bowed her body and hid her face

in his neck and let out a sob, but he wouldn't let her hide that from him either. His hand cradled her head in one hand, forcing her to look at him, while the other forced her up and down, hard, on him until it became too much, and she closed her eyes to escape with a scream of pure pleasure.

The intensity caught her off guard, and her vision blurred around the edges until she collapsed on him, holding on to his neck. He bucked up into her once more before holding her tightly to him while he came.

Their ragged breathing echoed in the otherwise silent apartment. She rested her forehead against the strong column of his throat, watching the muscles working there, feeling his chest rise and fall with the emotion he was so obviously trying to control. She wanted to stay like this forever, held and cherished, in their own cocoon.

The fabric of his zipper pinched her inner thigh, and she lifted her head reluctantly. His eyes were dark velvet again. Looking at her with so much emotion, she ached.

"Truth or dare?" he asked.

"What?" She looked at him blankly. "This isn't... I don't... I don't want to play that," she stammered.

She had nowhere to look except for his eyes. How she had ever thought they were cool was beyond her. Theo's eyes burned into hers now, seeing straight through to her weakness and exposing pieces of her she had buried a long time ago. Shame burned her now because she knew what she had to do.

"Fine," she said. "You want to play this game? Dare." She held his eyes in a silent challenge. She knew what he was doing. He never let her hide herself from him. Even the parts of her she didn't like, he forced her to face them head-on.

"I dare you to give us a chance," he said evenly.

She could still feel him pulsing inside her. God, she would miss this. She would miss *him*.

She blinked the wetness from her eyes and lifted her chin. "I pick the truth, then."

"Do you love me?" His voice was quiet now.

She couldn't lie. "I don't want to play this game. You win." She saw the devastation on his face, and it was too much. "I quit." She lifted herself off him and stood.

"Amber," he said. "Don't do this."

"Goodbye, Theo." She got up and went to her bedroom, closed the door, lay on her bed in her new dress, and stared up at the ceiling.

Her head ached where Neal had pulled it. Her body was tender where Theo had been inside her. It was merely a nuisance in the face of the crushing pain in her chest.

How funny that just hours earlier, she had started the night with yet another version of herself, a stripped-down, authentic version that needed no pretense or bravado.

And now, alone in her bedroom, she wanted to pull every flimsy scrap of fabric from her closet and pile it on herself as if they were bandages she could wrap the broken pieces of her heart in.

Relationships, pets, and kids. How silly she must be to think this time would be any different when the only thing that had changed was her wardrobe.

Tears filled her eyes. She tried to keep them open as long as she could so they wouldn't spill over, but eventually, when she heard the door close, her body betrayed her.

Chapter Thirty-Three

THEO SAT in the chair opposite his grandmother, Georgie, in her formal living room. The slurp of the straw in her strawberry milkshake broke the silence.

"Rummy!" Georgie slapped down her cards for him to inspect.

"Well done." He scooped the cards up to shuffle. "Up for another round?" He shuffled the cards deftly. It was Sunday morning, a week after the gala. Theo had spent a sleepless week working until his eyes burned and running for miles until his body was sore and exhausted. Still, he heard her words, over and over again.

I quit.

Even louder, he heard what she didn't say. No "I love you" from Amber.

He concentrated on shaping the cards into submission.

"No," Georgie said. Theo looked up. Georgie hadn't been up for meeting him out at their usual breakfast spot when he called. Theo had picked up takeout and come to her instead. She looked ever tinier than usual across from him. "It's no fun to beat you when you look like a wounded puppy. What happened? Everything was so lovely when I left you two last week, and then everything imploded."

"Imploded" was a good word for what happened this week.

The morning after the gala, Pippa released the photo of Amber, Neal, and Theo, along with a headline: "Campaign Chaos: Mayor Theo Clairmont's Alleged Love Triangle Shocks Northfield." When word got out that Neal had been fired for his inappropriate conduct toward Amber, his fall was steep and swift. Professional contacts, family, and friends distanced themselves until he fled the state in disgrace.

The rumor mill continued speculating, and more articles hit the news cycle. Someone—Theo was almost certain it was Addison—came forward with a "tell-all" about Theo's dating life. It was mostly nothing, but the town Facebook page had been buzzing about it nonstop.

To round out the shitstorm, Puddin's owner came forward to lodge a complaint that Theo had stolen his dog. He didn't actually want Puddin' back, Theo was darkly amused to learn, but he "wanted it known what kind of man the mayor was."

The campaign's trajectory had taken a nosedive ever since. Charlotte and Todd were working overtime to manage the PR crisis, but Beckerman's polling numbers had skyrocketed while Theo's were solidly in the toilet.

It was everything Amber had feared happening, yet Theo found himself indifferent to the chaos.

Georgie walked to the piano and began to play. The music filled the room, and he drifted in the notes for a while.

"I'm sorry, Georgie," he said after a while. "I might have ruined my chance at being reelected."

Georgie's fingers stilled. "Oh, Theodore," she said tenderly. "Don't you know that doesn't matter in the long run? All we've ever wanted was for you to be happy. That's your legacy more than anything else."

Theo nodded. He knew that. He supposed he always did. Falling in love with Amber had been the easiest decision he'd ever made. And the most fulfilling.

He had never been happier in his life than in the months since she came to work for him. He could see their future so clearly, and whether or not that included being the mayor, Amber was there next to him. But he had done what he could to show her, and he failed.

"I lost her." Theo blinked. He didn't intend to burden George with anything more than lifting her fork to her mouth, but never in his life had he wanted anything more than Amber. Not his job. Not the respect of the town. He loved her so much it hurt to breathe.

Georgie continued to play. "Do you love her?" she asked quietly.

"Yes."

"Does she love you?"

Theo didn't hesitate. "Yes." He knew it, even if she had never said it. The look on her face, the joy that lit her up from the inside out whenever he told her he loved her, hadn't lied. She loved him. "But she's scared."

"Fear is a powerful thing. Sometimes love needs space to breathe and grow," Georgie said gently. "Continue being the man she fell in love with and let her find her way back to you when she's ready."

Theo went home, threw the ball for Puddin', gave her belly scratches, and an extra treat. He answered more emails from his largest donors about his next steps, assuring them of his commitment and strategy moving forward despite the recent setbacks.

He thought about every run he and Amber had taken, every

time she didn't believe in herself, and how he had believed enough for both of them. She needed to believe in herself now.

He made dinner, gave Puddin' her bone, and stood on the back patio and watched the sunset.

He picked up his phone and sent a message.

THEO

I love you. P.S. Eat a vegetable.

She didn't even recognize herself.

Amber lengthened her stride when she hit Main Street and concentrated on her breathing. Running for the hell of it. Who would have thought? But every day for the last three weeks, she had woken up, put her sneakers on, and dragged herself outside to run, knowing that if she stopped, it would be so much harder to start again.

She was so tired of starting over.

In the weeks after she left Theo, she had looked for something, anything, to distract her. She went back to the pub and picked up some shifts to pay the bills, even though Theo paid her a bonus in her final check that made her gasp. She wasn't going to be eating ramen and bananas for dinner for a long time.

She considered calling Lucy about a dozen times to experiment with a new color for her hair. She went out with Johnny and Charlotte a few times, but being around their new love was more painful than she could handle.

She looked for anything to distract her, but in the end, she found herself lacing up her sneakers instead.

God, running still sucked. But Theo had been on to something. Sometimes you just had to suck it up and push through.

Tears pricked her eyes at the thought of Theo, but she'd had enough crying in the last three days to last a lifetime. While she ran, she thought about patterns. Hers.

How many times had she been on the cusp of something good in her life only to sabotage herself? For so long, she had thought it was just her thing. She was just flighty and irresponsible, despite being surrounded by successful women. She was the odd man out.

But every time her sneakers hit the pavement, her thoughts became clearer.

Flightiness wasn't a personality trait. It was a defense mechanism she had perfected. She wasn't the flawed one in her family. She was afraid. Afraid of failure, yes. But she was even more terrified of success. Every time she got a hint of it, she did something to ruin her chance of happiness. Her lungs burned, and sweat dripped into her eyes. It stung, but she welcomed the discomfort.

The runs were never easy. Maybe they never would be, even after training consistently, but she wasn't afraid of the work anymore. Today, her lungs were tight. The band of her sports bra dug into her shoulder painfully. She welcomed the physical pain. Used it to push farther.

Main Street was waking up when she ran down the sidewalk. She waved to several people but didn't stop to talk. Theo's office light was on. She didn't look to see if he was inside. But she wondered what suit he was wearing today. Did he sleep last night, or had he lain awake until the early hours like she had? She missed Puddin's kisses. She even missed Theo's green juices. She missed him.

THEO

I love you. P.S. Eat a vegetable.

She didn't respond, but she looked at the text a million times a day. And she thought about patterns.

She ran past the newspaper stand, barely glancing at the headlines. Theo's name was still plastered on the front page, just as she feared.

She didn't spare a single thought for Neal's scandal. She chose not to press charges when she found out he was leaving town. He had brought that on himself and was paying the price, but Theo's years of hard work and dedication had been reduced to tabloid fodder, undermining everything he had worked for. It was everything she had feared would happen, and she didn't know how to fix it.

Annette's interior design studio lights were on when she ran past. Impulsively, she jogged up the stairs and found her mother in the back office, looking at her computer screen with her glasses perched on the end of her nose.

"Hey, what are you doing here? Don't you have to work—?" Annette started, but when she looked up, she stopped and half stood. "Oh, honey. What's wrong?"

Amber collapsed in the chair across from her mother's desk. "I'm fine," she said automatically. Smiled, even though her breath came in fast pants, making little puffing noises like she couldn't get air deep enough in her lungs. Theo would tell her to slow down, control her breathing. She panted harder.

"Here," Annette said, walking around her desk with a bottle of water. "Drink this. What's going on? And stop smiling, for the love. It's just me."

The smile dropped from her face. "I don't know," Amber said. "I just... I feel... God, I'm so tired." She bent her head and rubbed her eyes.

Annette sat on the chair next to her. "What are you tired of?" Annette asked gently. Knowingly. She rubbed Amber's back in light, soothing circles like when Amber had a nightmare as a little girl.

Amber was quiet for a long time. "Everything," she finally

said. "I'm scared to chase my dream because I might succeed." She paused. "I'm afraid to love because I might fail. I'm so tired of being stuck."

Annette sighed. "I know, honey. I see so much of myself in you."

"You do?" Amber looked at her disbelievingly. "But you've never run away from anything in your life."

"Oh, I have. When your father left, the fear was paralyzing. Alone with four girls depending on me and no job, no money, no education. Those were the scariest years of my life. I didn't know which direction to go in or which career to go back to school for, but I didn't have any other choice except to move forward."

Amber listened quietly, shocked to her core to hear her mother had felt exactly like she did. All her life, Annette was an indomitable force of nature, almost superhuman in her strength. She felt like Dorothy seeing the Wizard of Oz behind the curtain now.

"I had no idea," Amber finally said.

"I made sure you didn't. I wanted you to see me as strong enough to take care of you girls and not need to rely on anyone." She paused. "But maybe, in teaching you to be independent, I inadvertently taught you not to let anybody else in."

Amber dropped her gaze. Talking about Theo was still too painful.

"But we can change that, hmm?" Annette said. She reached over to squeeze Amber's hand. "Like Allie and Davis? You're allowed to choose happiness too."

"Do you ever see that for yourself?"

Annette looked out through the window behind her desk. "I think I'm too set in my ways now to make room for anyone else." She shrugged ruefully. "But a mother always wants better for her children, and I think there's something better out there for you."

Amber lifted her head and stared at Annette, her smart, talented mother, while something solidified within her. The parallels between her and her mother's approaches to life and love were stark and suddenly undeniable. "I wouldn't know where to start."

Annette smiled. "Start with yourself, of course."

Chapter Thirty-Four

THE STEPS of the juice bar were already packed with the residents and business owners, along with reporters and news crews waiting for the press conference when she got there.

Theo stood in front of a podium with Charlotte and Todd flanking him. Amber took him in eagerly. His dark suit was perfectly pressed, his white shirt and red tie crisp in the midday heat. So achingly handsome.

Her heartbeat slowed down before speeding up again, so fast she put the heel of her hand to her chest because, oh, it was so good to see him.

She studied him eagerly, noticing that the tiny lines around his eyes were more pronounced and the corners of his beautiful mouth pinched. She wondered if he had been sleeping.

She had spent the last few weeks planning and working to make her dream into something tangible with Charlotte's help. Charlotte had listened to her ideas about the boutique and had helped her write a solid business plan. She even went with Amber to the bank to apply for a loan. They were still waiting for an answer, but Charlotte said she had a good feeling.

Start with yourself, her mother had said.

Nothing was signed yet, but it felt good to finally stop wishing and start actively working for something she wanted. There was just one more thing...

Amber wove closer through the throng of people, waving hello to Allie and Davis, who stood next to Lily and Evie. Annette and the aunts all stood nearby, listening. Everyone was waiting to hear what the mayor had to say about his campaign. She found a spot next to her family where she could see him.

"Are you okay?" Annette asked her quietly.

Her hands started to shake. She fingered the little yellow square of paper she held nervously. "Yeah." She smiled shakily. "I think I will be."

"Hello, everyone." Theo's voice rose over the murmuring of the crowd. Calm. Assertive. "Thank you for coming today, and thank you to the Juice Express for inviting me here to clear the air." Theo glanced at the women in yoga outfits who circled him like protective hens, and he smiled. "First, I want to address the recent departure of Neal Barclay from our campaign team. His actions and behavior are entirely his own and do not reflect the values and hard work of my team. Charlotte Thornton and Todd Myers have dedicated countless hours to serving our town with integrity and compassion. Their efforts shouldn't be over-shadowed by the actions of one individual.

"Over the last few weeks, several claims have been made against me regarding my dog, Puddin'."

At her name, Puddin' lifted her head from Charlotte's chest and let out an indignant howl. Someone chuckled in the crowd.

"I did not steal her; however, I did rescue her, and I would do so again. My actions were in line with my lifelong commitment to stand up for those that can't stand up for themselves, including our four-legged friends. I will never apologize for protecting the vulnerable in our community.

"Finally, I'd like to address the claims about my personal

life." He paused and looked out at the crowd. "My personal life has been exactly that—personal. But I believe in transparency and honesty, especially with you, the people who trust me to lead. I want to be clear: I have only ever loved one woman," he said quietly. "I'm here today because I believe in Northfield and in making a difference in our future. If there are any questions, I'm here to answer them."

In the hush that followed, Amber took a step forward and raised her hand. "I have a question, Mr. Mayor." Her voice was clear and purposeful, if a little wobbly. Heads whipped around to stare, but she was all in now. She kept her eyes locked on the only person who mattered.

Theo's eyes widened at the sound of her voice. He cleared his throat. "Please ask, Ms. Hart." His voice, so calm and confident before, was gruff now.

The crowd was silent in anticipation, adding to her nerves. But she knew exactly what to do.

Amber walked to the podium and handed him the Post-it note. It was limp from her sweaty hands, but the words were clear and bold on the yellow paper. She watched Theo's lips move as he read the words.

"Truth or dare?" He looked at her, and she felt her heart twist at the look on his face.

"Yes." She cleared her throat. "Pick one. Please," she added nervously.

The silence was absolute. A camera crew jostled through the crowd and stopped next to her.

"I choose dare." He looked at her with that one eyebrow arched. She wanted to trace the familiar curve with her lips.

She smiled then.

"I dare you to ask me again."

"Truth or dare, Ms. Hart."

"I choose the truth." Her voice was clear and proud.

Ask me how much I've missed you. Ask me if I've been running or if I've been eating something besides sugar. Ask me how your love has made me strong enough to believe in myself. Ask me if I love you again, Theo. Please.

Understanding dawned on his face, along with a slow, sexy smile. "Do you love me?" he asked.

"I love you, Theo Clairmont," she said, her voice wavering with emotion. "I love your honorable heart and your sense of right and wrong. I love how hard you work to take care of the things you love." Her voice broke, but she forced the words in her heart through the knot in her throat, encouraged by the warmth in Theo's eyes. "I love how gentle you are and how you make me laugh. You're truly noble and wonderfully humble and so deeply kind, and I love you so mu—"

Before she could finish, Theo closed the distance between them, lifted her against his chest until her feet left the sidewalk, and kissed her swiftly on the lips. She smelled his warm, familiar cologne, and tears welled in her eyes from the sheer relief and joy of being in his arms again.

She twined her arms around his neck and laid one on him to the roar of the crowd.

Pippa shoved a mic toward them. Her sisters got out the tissues. Annette sniffed, but Amber ignored it all and kissed the man she loved.

When she finally came up for air, she leaned back to see him grinning down at her, dimples and all. "I'm sorry I pushed you away," she whispered. "I was so afraid of being hurt that I hurt you first. I love you so much," she whispered.

He kissed her again, softly this time. "It's about damn time."

And then he grinned, dimples and all.

Epilogue

Theo stood inside Second Chance Chic, Amber's new boutique, on grand opening night and listened to the buzz of excitement and laughter around him with a proud grin on his face. Amber's family had pitched in over the last month to turn the little shop on the corner of Main Street into a vibrant, boho explosion of colors.

The front display window held fairy lights and mannequins in flowing, vintage maxi dresses hand-embroidered by Amber herself. Theo knew because he had helped her steam and press each one in preparation for tonight. Each corner of Second Chance Chic was artfully arranged with scarves and handbags, jewelry, and clothing sourced from local designers as well as her own designs.

Amber had cut the ribbon earlier in the night, and the party was in full swing now. Music and champagne flowed while they celebrated Amber's success with their loved ones.

Her entire family, plus Ford and Georgie, Cap, Johnny, Charlotte, Diane, and Todd. Val sat with Holly and Sandy. She had declared college "overrated," but Theo knew she loved it.

She had shown him her dean's-list letter with a proud smile on her face, and she was considering applying to study abroad now that Sandy had regular work hours and a hefty raise as Theo's new assistant.

Amber had asked him to consider hiring Sandy to replace her, giving her more time home with the girls. Sandy was ruthlessly efficient and organized and had quickly fit right in with Diane to run the office.

Theo sat next to Georgie on the plush vintage couch in the corner and took in Amber's vision. He was so damn proud of her. She flitted around, greeting her family and friends, practically glowing and so thoroughly in her element.

Their relationship had only grown stronger since she moved into his house shortly after that press conference when she told everyone she loved him. The memory still made him smile.

In the days following, the surrounding buzz in town and on social media grew, but it turned out people enjoyed seeing a love story unfold right in front of their eyes with a little help from a PR queen. Amber had taken over with her photos and stories on social media about Theo's lifelong dedication to Northfield, and he had won the election in November by a landslide.

Now, as he watched Amber mingle with her guests, he thought about their future. He had a ring picked out and airplane tickets for Paris at home, waiting for them later. But tonight was for Amber. He wanted her to shine all on her own.

Not that she needed any help from him in that department. She had gone old Hollywood tonight with a slim-fitting, wine-colored dress and, Theo noted with interest, her black ankle strap heels. He had big plans for those heels later too.

"Sthmile," the curly-haired princess in his arms demanded. Savvie's dress sported permanent marker and what looked to be pink frosting, but she was as unaffected as ever. Theo grinned and kissed the top of her sticky hair. The little hellion and her sweet sister had him wrapped around their fingers but good, and they knew it. He didn't mind.

Maybe someday they would have kids of their own, but he was perfectly content to watch Amber make her dreams come true now. They had all the time in the world.

He didn't think he'd ever get tired of watching her passion and creativity flourish as she pursued what she loved most.

Amber caught his gaze from across the room, and she smiled, so soft and joy-filled and confident, that he was nearly taken down to his knees. He would happily spend the rest of his life looking for opportunities to make her smile like that.

The mic in the corner that Amber had set up for announcements gave feedback that made the crowd cover their ears, laughing as Sammy and Ben sang obnoxiously loudly. The kids were all taking turns singing, much to the crowd's amusement.

Theo glanced at the mic, and an idea sparked.

He set Savvie down gently next to Davis.

"You okay, man?" Davis asked. "You look a little pale." Over the last year, Theo had become good friends with Davis and Allie both. Davis was a straight shooter, a family man, and someone Theo respected.

Theo took a deep breath and felt slightly sick. "I'm about to do something I said I would never do again."

Davis broke into a grin. "It's the Hart women. They have a way of making you dive off into the deep end." He clapped him on the back. "It's a hell of a ride."

Theo gulped and made his way over to the kids. "Sammy, can I have a word?" He talked to Sammy for a minute, who did an admirable job of not laughing at his idea before grabbing the mic.

Theo's collar felt too tight, and he was suddenly light-headed, but when he looked up, Amber was smiling at him from across the room, and everything was Technicolor again.

Theo cleared his throat and tapped the mic. "Hello, every-one." He was surprised by how steady his voice was. "I hope you're all enjoying the grand opening of Second Chance Chic."

The sea of faces broke out into clapping and cheers. "Tonight, we celebrate the newest business in Northfield and also the hard work, the dreams, and the dedication of an incred-ible woman—Amber Hart." He held her gaze during more applause and cheers.

And arched his eyebrow. *Dare me?*

Her smile stretched wider, mischievously wider, and she nodded faintly. *Dare you.*

"I'm not much of a singer, but someone once told me that life is more fun with risks." Georgie blew him a kiss from the couch. "Please bear with me because this is for you, Amber."

As Sammy strummed the opening chords of the Proclaimers' "I'm Gonna Be (500 Miles)," the room erupted into cheers, Amber's loudest of all. Theo found her across the crowd and grinned, holding her gaze, his heart squeezing with the love and laughter he saw reflected there.

And then he got into it, because never let it be said that Theo Clairmont didn't know how to have fun.

THE END

~

IF YOU ENJOYED THIS BOOK, please consider leaving a review to help other readers find it. Thank you!

~

WANT MORE of Amber and Theo? Would you like to read about Theo's proposal that didn't quite go as planned?

Subscribe to my newsletter by tapping the link or use the QR code below to read the MAYBE SOMEDAY WITH YOU bonus scene!

Already subscribed? Keep an eye out for the playlist inspired by this book and nab Northfield's most infamous recipes right in your inbox! Norah xx

Continue the Series

Don't miss Lily Hart's story next in *If You Were Mine*.

When Lily Hart's perfect life crumbles at the altar, she hikes up her wedding dress and hitches a ride with the brooding, mysterious sheriff, Rush Callahan.

Rush's vacation plans for a solitary week at a remote log cabin get a lot more interesting with a feisty redhead along for the ride... and only one bed.

Preorder *If You Were Mine*.

Continue the Series...

Don't miss Lily's story next in *If You Were Mine*.

When Lily Hart's perfect life crumbles at the altar, she hikes up her wedding dress and hitches a ride with the brooding, mysterious sheriff, Rush Callahan.

Rush's vacation plans for a solitary week at a remote log cabin get a lot more interesting with a feisty redhead along for the ride... and only one bed.

Preorder *If You Were Mine* now!

Connect with Norah

Northfield Bonus Materials

Want to read bonus scenes, listen to the playlists inspired by this series, and nab Northfield's most infamous recipes?

Subscribe to my newsletter for all the bonus content.

Join our Facebook reader group for bonus content, sneak peeks, sales, and book news.

Follow me on Amazon for preorder and new release alerts.

For book sales and news, follow me on BookBub.

Or tap the QR code for all the links!

Acknowledgments

If you're reading this right now—thank you!

Without readers, I'd still be making up elaborate stories in my head while pretending to watch TV with my husband at night. Thank you for loving Northfield as much as I do.

As always, thank you to Tom and our three kids. I'm so lucky to call you my people. I love you so much.

To Julie Days, fellow romance author, incredible critique partner, and kindred spirit. You're next, babe! Got my pompoms and champagne ready!

To my beta readers and friends, Jessica Romito, Ali Curtis, Mari Luis, Amanda Knipfing, and Melissa Brown. Thank you for reading the early draft of *Maybe Someday With You* and giving thoughtful feedback and encouragement. This book is better because of you.

Thank you to my wonderful ARC team and all the creative and inspiring book reviewers who take a chance on my books and share them with friends, on your socials, and from the rooftops. You're vital to us indies and so, so appreciated!

Thank you to Echo Grace for another set of beautiful covers.

And thank you to Nancy Smay at Evident Ink. Thank goodness Theo made Amber run the 5K instead of a marathon!

About the Author

Norah Pritchard has been reading romance novels since middle school when she found her mother's gold mine of mass-market paperbacks, and she hasn't looked back since.

She teaches in higher education by day, and by night, you can find her writing about swoony, sexy heroes and sassy, independent ladies who aren't afraid to ask for what they want. She lives in New York with her husband and three children. .

Find her at norahpritchard.com.